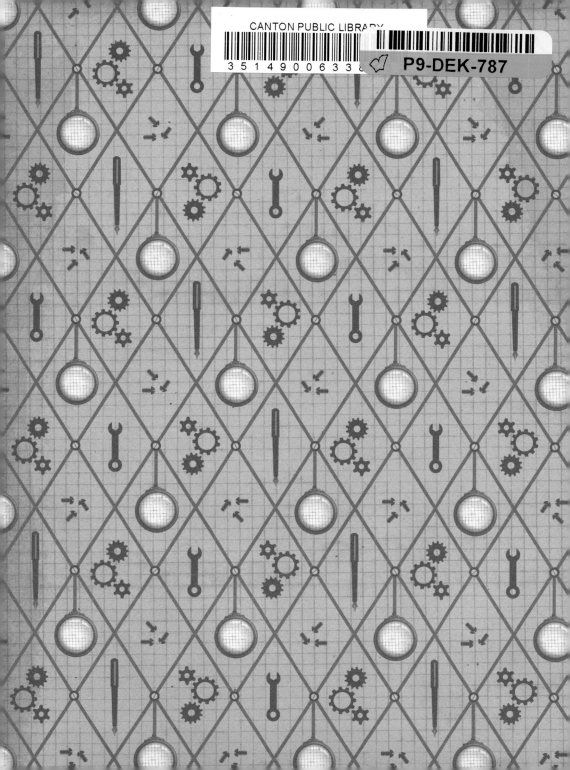

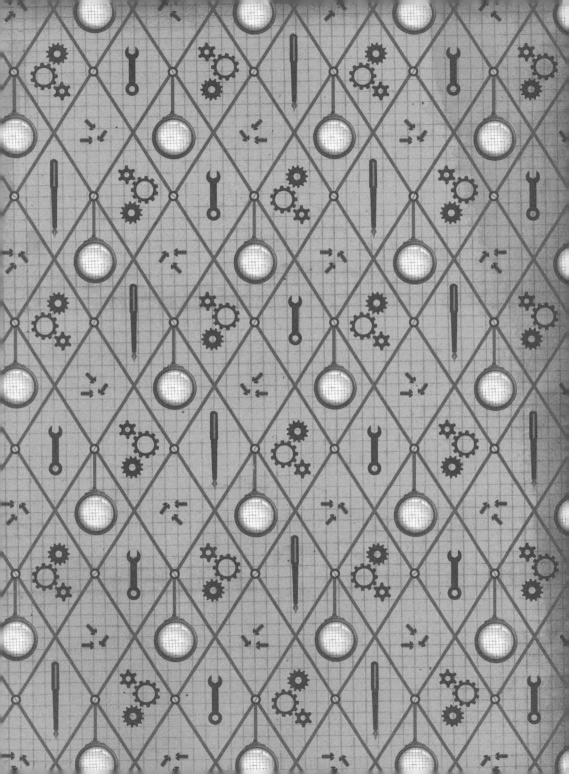

TO MR. LEMONY SNICKET, ASSUMING HE IS A HE —ELLIS WEINER

TO MEGAN, PAXTON, AND CHARLIE —JEREMY HOLMES

Library of Congress Cataloging-in-Publication Data available.
ISBN 978-1-4521-1184-1

Manufactured in China.

FSC
www.fsc.org

MIX
Paper from
responsible sources
FSC® C012521

Design by Sara Gillingham Studio.
Typeset in Parcel, Chronicle Text, and Chevin.
The illustrations in this book were rendered digitally.

10 9 8 7 6 5 4 3 2 1

Chronicle Books LLC
680 Second Street, San Francisco, California 94107

Chronicle Books—we see things differently.
Become part of our community at www.chroniclekids.com.

# THE TEMPLETON TWINS

## TWINS

## MAKE A SCENE

WRITTEN BY
**ELLIS WEINER**

ILLUSTRATED BY
**JEREMY HOLMES**

BOOK **2**

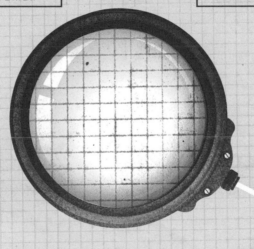

*chronicle books · san francisco*

Dear Reader:

Please accept my heartfelt
apolog

THE

TEMPLETON
TWINS

HAVE AN IDEA

ABIGAIL

JOHN

BOOK

WRITTEN BY
ELLIS WEINER

ILLUSTRATED BY
JEREMY HOLMES

# A NOTE TO THE READER
# ABOUT THE NOTE OF APOLOGY

Dear Reader:

I was going to start this book with a note of apology, written with my own hand. I was going to say how sorry I was if, while you are reading this book, you find yourself dismayed at having NOT read the book that comes before it, which is called *The Templeton Twins Have an Idea*. (And which for my convenience shall, from now on, be referred to as *TTTHAI*.)

However, I have decided not to apologize to you. In fact, I have decided that it is *you* who should apologize to *me*. My work in narrating this book would be much easier if I could be sure that you had read the first book.

If you had, you would know who (almost) everyone is. You would know what Professor Elton Templeton does. You would know in what ways Cassie, the Templetons' dog, is ridiculous. And you would of course know what an excellent narrator I am, and thus be prepared to enjoy still more excellence in narration.

But since some of you haven't read *TTTHAI*, I shall have to introduce all these things to you. I suggest, therefore, that those of you who haven't read the first book write me an apology. You may use the following as a model, or use your own wording, so long as it is deeply apologetic.

Dear Narrator:

Please accept my (most humble apology/ heartfelt expression of remorse/deepest sentiments of sorrow) for not having (read with uncontainable glee/thoroughly enjoyed at least twice/devoured in a single sitting) your previous narrative, THE TEMPLETON TWINS HAVE AN IDEA (TTTHAI).

I (have no one to blame but myself/know full well the disgraceful nature of my neglect/ solemnly promise never to allow such an oversight to happen again).

Yours truly in true apology,
The Reader

Do I accept your apology? I think we can all agree that I cannot. The damage (to my feelings) is done. Let's move on.

# INTRODUCTION

Allow me to introduce myself. I am—as you already know—the Narrator. And allow me to introduce you. You are—as *I* already know—the Reader. I knew I would see you again, although of course I may never have seen you before and, whoever you are, I can't actually see you.

This book is Number 2 in a series of books about the Templeton twins. If you have read book Number 1, then you already know two important things: a) that I was forced to write the first book against my will; b) that I am, similarly, being forced to write this one even though I don't particularly feel like it; and c) that there is no "c)" because I said two things.

In the pages to follow you will encounter:

1. ABIGAIL AND JOHN TEMPLETON— A.k.a. (which means "also known as") the Templeton twins. They are thirteen years old. They are not identical twins (who look very, very much alike, but are always of the same gender), but fraternal twins. They look like brother and sister, which is an excellent thing, because that is what they are.

2. PROFESSOR ELTON TEMPLETON— He is the twins' father as well as a world-famous inventor of clever and occasionally useful devices.

3. CASSIE THE RIDICULOUS DOG— Cassie is a smooth-haired fox terrier, all white except for bits of black and brown here and there. She has little triangular ears and a tail that is the size and shape, *but not the color*, of a carrot. She is, like most fox terriers, insane.

4. DEAN D. DEAN AND DAN D. DEAN— These brothers, as it happens, *are* identical twins. They are about thirty-three years old. Dean D. Dean is extremely handsome and wears elegant clothing. Dan is not quite as

handsome—"identical," when used to describe twins, means very similar, but not *exact copies of each other*. Unlike his brother, Dan dresses normally, whatever that means. Dean—as you will soon see—is the more "dynamic" of the two, which is a polite way of saying that he is the bossier one.

Readers of the first book will be deliriously happy to encounter these people again in this book. However, if they hoped (because they loved the first book so very much) that the entire *story* of this book would be the same as the story in the first, they will be disappointed.

They're not the only ones. I'm disappointed, too. I would much rather copy, word for word, the first book, than have to think of *an entirely new series of words* for the second book. But, sadly, I have no choice. I hope you appreciate all the trouble I'm going to, thinking up and writing down all these new words. But I doubt that you do.

This, then, completes the Introduction. I hope you enjoyed it. (Although do I? Really? Probably not.) The important thing is, you will by now have noticed what is *not* here.

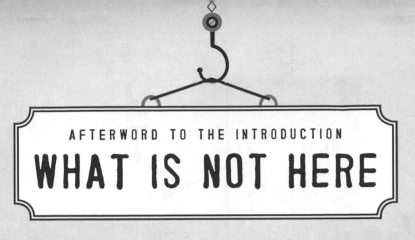

# WHAT IS NOT HERE

W hat is not here is a summary of the things that happened in *TTTHAI*. If you have not read the first book, or if you have read it but forgotten what was in it, then you do not know:

1. Why Dean D. Dean hates Professor Templeton.
2. How the twins acquired Cassie, the Ridiculous Dog.
3. What the specific hobbies of the twins are.
4. The details concerning the Professor's Personal One-Man Helicopter (POMH).
5. All the brilliantly clever ways Abigail and John thwarted (yes, "thwarted." This is an excellent word and you should make use of it in your daily life, as I do.) Dean D. Dean and Dan D. Dean.
6. Who did what and said what to whom, when, why, and how.

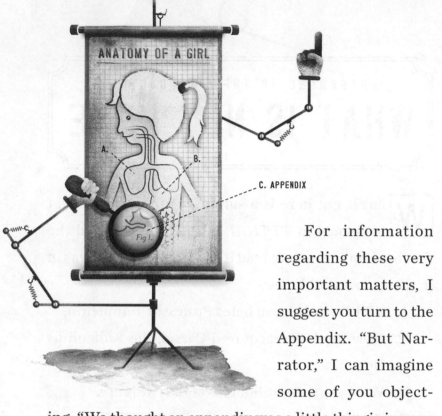

ANATOMY OF A GIRL

A.

B.

C. APPENDIX

Fig 1.

For information regarding these very important matters, I suggest you turn to the Appendix. "But Narrator," I can imagine some of you objecting. "We thought an appendix was a little thingie in your body that sometimes has to be removed. A book can't have an appendix! Does it, like, have, like, a kidney, too?"

Please. I am not impressed by your sarcasm. It is true that there is such a thing, in the human body, as an "appendix." It is a small organ near the . . . well, near the other, more important organs. Whereas an appendix in a book is a section at the end of the book that provides some useful background information. In fact, a book can have more than one appendix. These are two ways in which the book-appendix is different from the human-body-appendix. Isn't that interesting? Just take my word for it. It is. Now let us begin the second book itself.[1]

FOR FURTHER STUDY

1. Where is your appendix?

2. Are you sure? Are you sure you didn't leave it in your "good" jeans?

3. Yes or Yes: The Narrator, to no one's surprise, is off to a fine—no, an *excellent*—start.　　Y　　Y

---

1. But first: I assume that there will be readers who are too lazy, impatient, or rude to read the various Introductions. They will, therefore, not have read this footnote, which you—because you are an excellent and thorough reader—*are reading at this very moment*. As a reward, I am going to share with you the following important information: The first two paragraphs of Chapter 1 describe incidents that did not, in fact, take place.

Won't it be fun to see the faces of those who could not be bothered to read the Introductions when they find out how they have been fooled? (Actually, I have no idea whether it will be fun or not. I won't be there to see their faces when they read—and believe—those first two paragraphs of Chapter 1. If you are there, and it *is* fun, let me know.)

# THE ACTUAL START OF THE ACTUAL STORY STARTS

O|h, no, John!" cried Abigail Templeton to her brother. "Six dancing dinosaurs have kidnapped our dog, Cassie, and taken her to Paris, France!"

"We must thwart them at once, Abby!" replied John. "But first I must have my appendix removed!"[2]

The Templeton twins had been living in their new house for about a week, doing all the things they usually did—going to school and coming home, completing their homework, pursuing their hobbies, caring for Cassie (their ridiculous dog), and making meals—before Saturday finally came, and their father, the famous Professor Elton Templeton, was able to give them a tour of the college where he had recently started working.

So, after a breakfast of waffles and bananas, the twins climbed into the car, along with their (still-ridiculous) dog, and their father drove them to the campus.

Now, if I know you, you are wondering: "What took the Professor so long to show the twins around?" I'll tell you, because you deserve to know. Well, wait. I'm not so

---

2. If you have read the Introductions, you know just how seriously to take this explosive, thrilling, thought-provoking news. If you haven't, then you don't. Let's move on.

sure you do deserve to know. But I will tell you anyway, as a favor. Then you'll owe *me* a favor.[3]

The Professor had been unable to give the twins a tour of the new college right away because it was very important that he get to work immediately. Over the past few years, the college had not had enough students, and so was in danger of going out of business. The college had hired Professor Templeton and given him an urgent, vital assignment: to create an invention that would be so wonderful and remarkable and splendid that colleges and universities all over the world would want to buy one for themselves. Money from those sales would make it possible for the Professor's college to remain in business.

And so, for the first week, the Professor did nothing but attend meetings and think of ideas and work calculations and sketch out basic designs for a new invention.

The name of the college was the Thespian Academy of the Performing Arts and Sciences. People called it TAPAS, for short. Now, I happen to be one of the few

---

3. Please remember this, because it is quite possible that I will ask you for a favor later on *in this very book*.

people who know that the word "tapas" is a Spanish word for a series of appetizerlike snacks served in small portions on small plates at bars and restaurants—very often, in world-famous Spain itself.

In this case, however, the name TAPAS is what we call an "acronym," which is a made-up word formed by the first letters of a chain of words or names. For example, FAQ is an acronym for Frequently Asked Question.[4] Similarly, TAPAS is an acronym for the Thespian Academy of the Performing Arts and Sciences.

Yes, I know: The first letters of "of" and "the" and "and" do not appear in TAPAS. That is often the case:

---

4. Frequently Asked Questions, as you may know, are questions that are asked frequently. I have my own list of Frequently Asked Questions (FAQs). Here it is:

**The Narrator's FAQs (Frequently Asked Questions)**

1. Huh?
2. Are you serious?
3. How come?
4. Wait—what?
5. Really?
6. What time is it?
7. But why?
8. Do we have to?
9. How should I know?
10. What do you mean?

The first letters of unimportant or inessential words often do not appear in acronyms. This is perfectly normal and nothing to be upset about.

This college was devoted to teaching acting, singing, dancing (or "dance," as people who dance refer to dancing), and the many other important crafts and technical skills related to performances of all kinds.

Each building resembled an object or a symbol that was in some way connected with that department's art or craft or skill. For example, the Department of Acting occupied two buildings that were shaped like the famous dual—one might even say "twin"—masks of Comedy and Tragedy that are commonly used to symbolize Drama. The Department of Script Writing was in the form of an immense typewriter. The Department of Wardrobe was shaped like a gigantic armoire.[5] And so on.

"Look at these statues," said Abigail Templeton as she, her brother, their father, and their notably silly dog strolled around campus. "They look kind of . . . tired."

---

5. "Armoire" is a French word. You pronounce it "arm-WHAH." It means— I think—"a place to keep your arms." Or maybe not. Look, never mind what it means.

It was true. The central quad ("quad" is what colleges insist on calling their big, grassy yards) and many of the spaces between the buildings were decorated with statues of actors, singers, dancers, directors, playwrights, gaffers, grips, d-girls, and best boys.[6] But all the statues were chipped, or rusted, or had pieces missing.

The Professor nodded. He said,

> **THIS PLACE IS IN TROUBLE. THAT'S WHY WE'RE HERE.**

It was while the Templetons had paused near a statue of William Shakespeare that a man wearing sunglasses and a bushy beard suddenly encountered the family. He carried a single folded sheet of yellow lined paper. He stopped for a moment and seemed startled. Then he quickly looked away and, with a busy air, marched off.

John watched the man stride across the quad. "That guy looks familiar," he said.

"You know," the Professor said. "A lot of actors teach here. You may have seen him in a movie or on TV. Anyway, my workshop is just over there. In the Department of Lighting."

---

6. I have no idea what those last four jobs involve. Do you? Oh, please. You do not.

The Professor led the twins and their always-thrilled-with-everything dog in the direction that the mysterious man had gone. As they walked, Cassie wagged her tail like crazy and panted and looked around as though walking past a building was the most exciting event of her life, and the Professor explained his latest invention.

"What is the difference," he began, "between a play—or a musical, or an opera—and a movie or a television show?"

Abigail said, "A play is live."

"Television shows can be live," John said. "News is live. So are sports."

"You're both right," the Professor said. "But even live television shows use something that plays can't use."

The twins traded a look that said, wordlessly, "Wait. We know the answer to this."

"Cameras," they both said at the same time.

"Excellent," the Professor said. "And what do cameras permit us to do that we simply cannot do in a live performance onstage?"

The twins thought about that. So let's all think about that as well, by which I mean, let's *you* think about it.

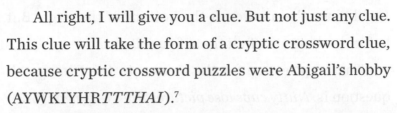

Waiting for you to think about it . . .

Come on, we don't have all day.

All right, I will give you a clue. But not just any clue. This clue will take the form of a cryptic crossword clue, because cryptic crossword puzzles were Abigail's hobby (AYWKIYHR*TTTHAI*).[7]

Cryptics (as they are called) are different than regular crossword puzzles. The clues themselves are little puzzles. There are certain rules that *most* cryptic clues follow, one of which is that the definition of the word (or phrase) is either at the beginning or the end of the clue. The rest of the clue is the puzzle you have to solve. (Cryptic clues also tell you how many letters are in the word, or words, which make up the answer.)

Thus, a cryptic clue might be "Hateful dance? It's only a game (8)." You would know, from this, that the answer is one word, with eight letters, which literally means either "hateful dance" (whatever that can possibly mean), or "It's only a game."

I shall place the solution to this clue in a footnote.[8]

---

7. As You Would Know If You Had Read *The Templeton Twins Have an Idea*.
8. See footnote on the next page.

By this, I do not mean that I will come to your house and attach a note with the answer on it to your foot. I mean I will place the answer at the bottom of the page. But before looking at it, first try to figure it out.[9]

The cryptic clue for the answer to the Professor's question is: *Nutty cups lose pictures from very near* (5-3)

Words like "nutty" or "crazy" signal you to recombine the letters of the words before or after. The numbers tell you that the answer consists of a five-letter word and a three-letter word joined by a hyphen.

If you can't figure out the answer (or if you can't be bothered to try), you may look at the bottom of the page if you wish.[10]

Where were we? Ah, yes: The twins were trying to tell their father what it is that cameras allow us to do that we can't do in a live performance.

Without much confidence, Abigail guessed, "The camera can record it so that people can watch it later?"

---

9. Oh, please. Did you even *try* to figure it out? Very well: The answer is BASE-BALL. "Base" means, among other things, "bad, hateful, vile, detestable," and so on. Perhaps you didn't know that, *but now you do.* A "ball" is a kind of dance. Baseball itself is, of course, a game. Isn't that clever?

10. As you can see, it isn't here. You will have to keep on reading.

"Or," John added, "show it in black and white, if you want to, instead of color?"

"Those are good ideas," the Professor said. "But that's not what I'm getting at. I'll give you a hint. This is something so obvious that it might be very hard to see."

Does that hint shock and surprise you, reader? Oh, I think it does. Because how can something be so obvious that you can't see it? "Obvious" *means* "easy to see." But sometimes, especially when we're looking for something that we think is tricky, we may see the obvious things, but we skip over them. We think to ourselves, "I know that what I'm looking for is tricky and hard to see. So this obvious thing can't be it."

Except sometimes it is.

"The answer," the Professor said, "is that cameras let us use close-ups. The camera lets us move in close to an actor's face, or hand, or foot, or an object—whatever we want the audience to be sure to see. We can fill the whole screen with it. You can't do that on a stage."

Thus, if you get "nutty" with (i.e. rearrange the letters in) "cups lose," you will find that the answer is:

# CLOSE UPS

The Professor paused and then said, somewhat dramatically, "And that is what this college wants me to do. To create a way to show close-ups onstage."

Now, if the Professor had said this to you, or even to me, we would have stopped dead in our tracks, and stared back at him with wild, bulging eyeballs, and trembled in terror, and clutched our hair and pulled it out in fistfuls, and cried, "BUT SUCH A THING IS IMPOSSIBLE! HOW WILL YOU EVER SUCCEED AT MEETING SO OVERWHELMING A CHALLENGE?" All right, perhaps I am exaggerating slightly. I myself would not behave in this way. But I'm sure you would have.

But neither you nor I are the Templeton twins, who were long used to hearing about their father tackling this or that impossible-seeming task.

That is why, instead of screaming in horror or fainting dead away, Abigail said, "That's interesting, Papa," and John said, "Neat. With some kind of lens?" and the Professor said, "Yes! Good thinking, John.

Come on, I'll show you." And all of them, including Cassie the You-Know-What dog, marched into the building of the Department of Lighting and Allied Illuminatory Sciences, which was shaped like a gigantic stage light.

Inside, the twins meandered around the Professor's workroom, admiring the long workbench and its clutter of equipment, wires, tools, and sheets of transparent plastic. They glanced at the whiteboard on one wall, with its calculations and rough, squiggly diagrams. They examined the surprisingly large array of batteries lined up on another table.

Then they heard the Professor mutter, "Hmm. What's this?" Looking up, they saw him standing beside his desk, holding a long sheet of lined yellow paper on which they could see a handwritten message.

"Someone left this for me," he said, and handed it to John.

"'Professor,'" John read. "'Dropped by to see you but you weren't here. Steve Stevenson.'" He looked up. "Who's Steve Stevenson?"

"I have no idea," the Professor said.

"That man we passed in the quad was carrying a piece of paper like this," Abigail said. "Maybe that was Steve Stevenson."

"Why didn't he say anything?" John asked.

His sister shrugged. "Maybe he didn't know who we were."

"But why doesn't this note include a way to contact him?" the Professor asked.

All three Templetons would have fallen silent and pondered this thought-provoking question, had not they all suddenly jumped with fright when they heard a loud, somewhat musical voice trill,

HEH-LOOO! PROFESSOR ELTON TEM-PLETON!

## FOR FURTHER STUDY

1. If you store your arms in an armoire, in what do you store your legs?

   a. A legoire.
   b. A leg storage facility.
   c. That is a very silly question and I refuse to answer it. The "arm" in armoire refers to the armor and weapons a knight in the Middle Ages used.

2. What is the opposite of "obvious"? Write your answer in the form of a recipe for chocolate pudding.

3. What is a hyphen? Of course I know. I want to see if you know.

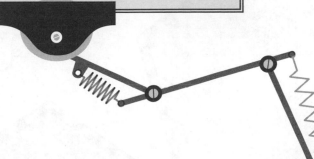

# CHAPTER 2

# A FLAMBOYANT LADY ARRIVES AND IS

SPLENDID(E)

S tanding in the doorway, resplendent in a flowing green and purple scarf and a deep-red blouse and a shimmering turquoise skirt, was a woman. She had fabulous jet-black hair fashioned into an elaborate "do," and wore numerous sparkling jewels on her wrist and around her neck.

"De-LIGHT-ed to meet you at last," she sighed. "They *told* me you were here, and I said, NO, no, I CAN'T be that lucky. But lo and behold: Here. You. Are." She extended her hand to be shaken, kissed, or admired. "Gwendolyn Splendide. Dean of TAPAS."

I shall assume you know how to pronounce the name "Gwendolyn." As for this lady's last name, it is pronounced "splen-DEED."

"How . . . I mean . . . that is . . . how do you do?" the Professor said. But it wasn't easy for him to say this, and you will need me to tell you why.

To Abigail and John, Gwendolyn Splendide was simply a rather flamboyant lady around their father's age. (If you don't know what "flamboyant" means, look it up. Not *now*, we don't have time.[11]) But to Professor

---

11. I will tell you—as, once again, I do your job for you out of the goodness of my heart—that it means something like "colorful, showy, outsized, or ostentatious in manner of appearance and/or demeanor."

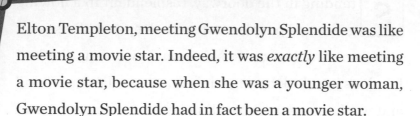

Elton Templeton, meeting Gwendolyn Splendide was like meeting a movie star. Indeed, it was *exactly* like meeting a movie star, because when she was a younger woman, Gwendolyn Splendide had in fact been a movie star.

The Professor had seen her in many films. She had always played beautiful, smart, ruthless women who committed crimes and manipulated people and who, in the end, either did or didn't get away with it. And, while the Professor had known that she was the dean of the Thespian Academy of the Performing Arts and Sciences, it had never occurred to him that he would actually meet her. And yet here she was—an older version of her movie-star self, but still quite spectacular. He was dazzled, and for this reason it was slightly difficult for the Professor to speak.

"Miss Splendide," he began, "allow—"

"Oh, please. DEAR Elton. Call me Gwendolyn."

"Really? Well. Um . . . Gwendolyn, allow me to introduce my children. This is John—"

Gwendolyn Splendide turned to John, held out her hand in order to grasp his, and cried, "And YOU must be John! So handsome!"

Before John could say anything, Gwendolyn Splendide wheeled on Abigail, then put her palm to her cheek in rapt contemplation, and said, "And this, surely, is Ardith."

**"ABIGAIL,"** Abigail said.

"Amaryllis."

**"ABIGAIL."**

"Agatha."

**"THIS IS ABIGAIL,"** the Professor said.

"Of COURSE it is," Gwendolyn Splendide said. "How strikingly similar to your brother you are."

"We're twins," Abigail said.

"You MUST be twins," the lady said. "Oh, I think we're going to be VERY good friends, don't you?"

Abigail shrugged.

"I just know it. And when Gwendolyn Splendide KNOWS something, she knows it."

Abigail indicated the dog. "And this is Cassie."

Gwendolyn Splendide bent down slightly toward Cassie and murmured, *"Enchantée."*[12] She turned to

---

12. "Enchantée" is a French word and is pronounced "awnh-shawn-TAY." I know it is very difficult for you to enunciate the sound "awnh," but you're simply going to have to try. It means "enchanted" or "charmed," and you generally say it to someone when you are not particularly enchanted to meet them but you want them to think you are.

the Professor and started to say, "Now. Elton. *Darling*. What—" She stopped. She thought a moment. Then her face lit up with an expression meant to convey "I am thinking and I have just thought of something." Then she said, "I have a brilliant idea. *Brilliant*. Tell me, Elton.

## DO THESE UTTERLY PERFECT CHILDREN REQUIRE SOME SORT OF CHILD CARE?

"No!" cried John and Abigail at the same time.

But the Professor nodded and replied, "Well, I *was* thinking about hiring some sort of nanny. Just to be in the house when they get home from school."

"This is PERFECTION ITSELF," Gwendolyn Splendide cried. "I have *just* the person for the position you are advertising."

"We're not advertising," Abigail said.

"SUCH a literal girl," Gwendolyn Splendide said. "What is more charming than that? In any case, I shall bring him to your home—shall we say tomorrow?"

"How about twelve o'clock?" the Professor said.

"Will noon suit you?"

"Twelve o'clock *is* noon," John said.

"How very right you are, Jason," Gwendolyn Splendide said. "Twelve o'clock is noon. Isn't it *wonderful*?" She leaned toward the Professor and pretended to kiss him on both cheeks by kissing the air on either side of his face. "Until then, all!" And with that, in a whirl of silk and a clatter of jewelry, she turned and left the workshop.

The twins turned to each other and exchanged a look that said, wordlessly, "ICK!"

Then Abigail began to say, "Oh, Papa, do we really have to have a nanny?" But before she could finish, she stopped, because she noticed that the Professor was staring at the doorway as if in a trance.

"I can't believe it," he said quietly. "I was just kissed by Gwendolyn Splendide."

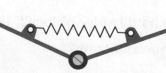

## FOR FURTHER STUDY

1. Have you ever met a movie star? Did he or she mention my name?

2. Gwendolyn Splendide referred to John and Abigail as "perfect children." Are you a perfect child? What proof do you have to support your answer?

3. Write an essay on the topic "It is probably not a good idea to speak French to dogs." It should be exactly three words long.

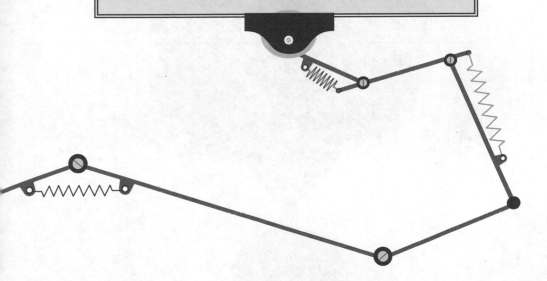

CHAPTER 3

# AN AUNTIE'S PLAN
# FOR MANNY MANN

T he next day the Templeton twins were upstairs while their father was downstairs, listening to a recording of classical music, when the doorbell rang. This, of course, brought Cassie charging energetically down from Abigail's room, barking and wagging her tail in an especially ridiculous manner. Professor Templeton paused the music and answered the door.

"Elton!" a by-now-familiar voice cried. "ISN'T it the most MAGNIFICENT day?"

Upstairs, John opened his bedroom door just as Abigail opened hers. They looked at each other. She rolled her eyes. He shrugged. They went downstairs. As they did so, they were joined by the barking, wagging, leaping, being-ridiculous Cassie.

Standing in the doorway was—as you no doubt have already guessed—Gwendolyn Splendide. She wore a sort of beige-colored jacket and beige-colored slacks ending in beige-colored shoes. That sounds like a lot of beige, but she also wore a deep-red blouse under the jacket, and a dark-purple scarf at her throat. Her makeup was perfect. She looked like (because, as you already know, she had been) a movie star.

Standing beside her was a young man of college age. He wore a white T-shirt with a big yellow smiley face, black jeans, and black sneakers.

"THIS," Gwendolyn Splendide said once Cassie had been quieted, "is my nephew. His name is Emmanuel Mann, although..." (here she leaned toward the Professor and spoke in a quiet voice, as though confiding a shameful secret) "he insists on being addressed as 'Manny.'"

The Professor held out his hand. "Pleased to meet you, Manny. Come in."

Manny Mann gave the Professor's hand a merry shake. He and Gwendolyn Splendide entered as the twins arrived. "And *these*," Gwendolyn Splendide sighed, "are the twins. Emmanuel, meet Jack and Adelaide."

"John and Abigail," Abigail said.

"Of course," agreed Gwendolyn Splendide.

The twins said hello to the young man, Cassie was quieted down *again*, and everyone moved to the living room, which was a pleasant, sunny space with a sofa, a coffee table, several comfy chairs, and many, many shelves completely filled with books.

Gwendolyn Splendide gestured and said, "Just LOOK at all these books. DON'T tell me you've written them all, you brilliant man."

"I haven't, actually," the Professor said. "Although I have read many of them. And so have the twins."

"Isn't that the most wonderful thing you've ever heard?" Gwendolyn Splendide said to no one in particular. Then she said, "Emmanuel, you should read more books, darling. But then, I should, too, shouldn't I? It's true. Gwendolyn Splendide should read more. Because shouldn't we all? Oh, but who has TIME?" Before anyone could reply, she said, "Let's get down to business. I understand that you are looking to employ a nanny. I should like to recommend my nephew for the job. He is excellent with children."

"Is that so?" the Professor asked politely.

"You bet!" Manny Mann said, perhaps louder than was necessary. "I think kids are great!"

Now, both John and Abigail were a bit put off by the young man yelling about how great kids are. And they could tell from their father's guarded responses ("Really? Oh, well, my goodness . . . ") that the Professor was wondering whether Manny was just saying that to make a good impression. But the twins could also tell that, to the Professor, Gwendolyn Splendide was simply too wonderful and dazzling in her radiant beauty for him to say anything but "Is that so?" Besides, the twins had some vague understanding that this lady was their father's boss. So they kept their objections to themselves.

The matter was settled. Manny was hired as the Templeton twins' new nanny. It was in this manner that he became—there is no other way to put it—Nanny Manny Mann.

After Gwendolyn Splendide and Manny Mann left, the twins took Cassie for a walk around the block and discussed this latest development. Abigail pointed out that, while it was probably a good thing for a nanny to be perky and upbeat, Manny looked like he might be *too* perky and upbeat.

Still, John pointed out, since they really didn't want a nanny to begin with, at least they could be glad that they had one who was happy to be there. Abigail agreed that it was certainly better than having a bossy, tyrannical nanny, like the one they had had previously.[13]

By the time the twins had walked Cassie around the block, they had decided to stop being cranky and to give Nanny Manny Mann a chance. Then they removed Cassie's collar and went up to their rooms to catch up on their hobbies.

You are, no doubt, wondering how the Templeton twins were proceeding with their hobbies. I will be happy to tell you—well, that's putting it too strongly. I'm not "happy" to be writing any of this, as you know. But I am *willing* to tell you.

First, John. John's hobby is playing the drums. The last time we looked, John's drum set consisted of a big bass drum with a pedal, a snare drum on a stand, a tom-tom mounted on the bass drum, and a floor tom-tom standing on legs. He had a hi-hat (two small cymbals on a pedal-operated stand that came together in a nice *chik*

---

13. (Note: We may as well all admit that when I say things like "previously" or "earlier" or "once before," I will be referring to things that happened in the first book. You may think, "That's not fair! What if I haven't read the first book?" But whose fault is that? Hint: It's your fault.)

sound) and two regular cymbals: a heavy one (a "ride") for keeping time, which stood on a stand to his right; and a lighter one (a "crash") for making big, loud, splashy noises, which was mounted on a stand to his left.

Well, the news regarding John is that now he had a third cymbal, given to him for his birthday by his father. (John's birthday is also someone else's birthday. I will give you three guesses as to who that is.) John's present was a kind of crash cymbal called a "China-type" that, instead of making a bright, shiny noise when you hit it hard, made a rough, raspy noise. The sound it made was only slightly better and more musical than the sound you'd get by taking a hammer and hitting a metal trash-can lid, or a big metal sheet for baking cookies. He loved it.

Of course, as you know if you've ever acquired something new (for your birthday, Christmas, Chanukah, Arbor Day, or National Fig Week), the new thing makes certain demands of you. You have to do the "work" of learning how to use the new thing in order to obtain the benefit (and the fun) of it.

So John took up his seat at the drums and, as he had been doing for the past month or so, practiced in a slightly new way. Instead of doing what he had traditionally done—reaching to his left to make a big, crashy sound—he taught himself to reach just a little bit to his right (where the new cymbal was) to make a different big, crashy sound.

And in doing that, he noticed something.

In order to make good use of the new cymbal, he had to pay special attention to it. And so he worried about the old cymbals less. He just *played* them. This meant, to John's surprise, that he played the whole drum set better.

You are no doubt wondering, "Why is the Narrator taking valuable time out of his day to tell me all this?" The answer is: Because it will have very important consequences later on. For now, let's just say that John was playing and practicing and having a wonderful time, so he didn't hear the phone ring.

Meanwhile, Abigail was in her room, being irritated at her latest cryptic crossword puzzle. Why "irritated"?

To answer that, we should pause here to remind ourselves that puzzles, like stories, articles, and everything

A.

B.

C.

else on the printed page (including books about the Templeton twins) are written by people. Although, actually, puzzles are not "written." The correct term for creating a crossword puzzle is "setting." You don't write a puzzle. You *set* it. (Do not ask me why. I find this fact as tedious as you do, believe me.) And among the books Abigail was given for *her* birthday was a book by a puzzle setter who ignored all the rules.

Here is the clue she was pondering:

*D (6)*

Yes, a six-letter word with only a single letter for a clue! There was no definition, no wordplay, no hints or hidden answers or real words to unscramble. Abigail stared at this and thought about it for half an hour (during which the phone rang downstairs, but she was so deep in concentration that she ignored it) before giving up and looking in the back of the book, where all the solutions were.[14]

---

14. I will save us all some time and put the answer here. The answer was DALLAS. It is a city in Texas. Now, before you throw this book across the room and declare that this is an outrage and an insult to cryptics, here is the explanation of the clue: It is a capital (and not a lowercase) D. It is, therefore, a big D. And "Big D" is a somewhat well-known nickname for Dallas. Of course, Abigail had never heard Dallas referred to as "Big D" before. No wonder she was cranky. You are probably cranky, too. Well, I'm sorry (to an extent).

She hated doing that. Having to look up an answer in the back of the book felt like losing the game. Then she came to the next impossible clue:

*No small bargain (3,4).*

The answer to this cryptic clue, then, called for one word of three letters and one word of four. Abigail realized that the words "no small" had a total of seven letters, as did the answer. Surely this could not be a coincidence. So she spent fifteen minutes recombining the letters in "no small" into three- and four-letter words. But none of the results (LAM SLON; SAM NOLL; LAS MOLN; etc.) made sense. So she did something she never did.

She gave up. She put the puzzle away and read a book.

In doing so, she made use of one of her father's inventions: the Leg-Mounted Centrally Hinged Book Holder with Gooseneck Light Source (or, as the Professor sometimes called it, the LMCHBHWGLS). This device was intended to solve one of the problems encountered when reading in bed—namely, when holding a book with two hands, it is difficult (if not impossible) to make use of either hand for such desirable activities as manipulating a cup of hot chocolate, twirling your hair, scratching your dog or cat, etc.

The LMCHBHWGLS solved this problem in an
ingenious fashion. Abigail sat on her bed with her back
against the headboard and her legs out straight, as one
does when reading in bed. Then she attached the two leg
clamps of the device onto her legs. Connected to them
were two arms that reached up to her book and held it in

her lap with two rubber-tipped graspers. Also attached to the leg pieces was a reading lamp affixed ("affixed" means the same thing as "attached." Don't ask me why.) to a long, flexible neck that she could bend in any direction.

Thus—and you cannot but be impressed by this fact—Abigail was able to read in bed while, *at the same time*, eating chips and dip with one hand and sipping from a cup of terrible limeade with the other, pausing in these activities only to turn a page.

About two hours later, Abigail and John came downstairs for dinner and beheld their father standing in the hallway, holding the telephone and frowning.

"That's odd," he said. "The phone rang about two hours ago, but when I answered a strange voice said, 'Professor Elton Templeton?' I said, 'Yes,' and they said, 'Please hold for an important message.' So I held, but I heard nothing. There was no music, no recording—it was just silence. Finally I hung up. Now I just discovered that there's a message on voicemail. And that message was left at exactly the same time I was waiting on the phone and hearing nothing."

Abigail shrugged. "It must be a coincidence. Both calls came at exactly the same time."

"What was the message?" John said.

"Well, that's another odd thing," their father said. "Listen." He called the voicemail number and switched the phone to its speaker. A prerecorded voice said, "-essage received . . . unday . . . at four-erty-seven pee em." Then a man's voice said, very quickly, "Professor! Steve Stevenson. I have some thoughts about the spotlight problem." There was the loud *click* sound of a caller hanging up.

"Huh," John said. "Him again."

"Yes," the Professor said. "And once again he doesn't leave any number where I can call him back. And there *is* no spotlight problem." He went on to explain that he assumed the caller was talking about the close-up device the Professor was developing. In his earlier notes to himself, the Professor had indeed written about possible problems that would arise if the performer in the close-up were being lit by a normal spotlight. "But I solved that," he said. "It hasn't been a problem for weeks."

"Well," John said, "when it was a problem, who did you discuss it with?"

Abigail added, "That person might have told Steve Stevenson about it, and he doesn't know you've solved it."

**BUT THAT'S THE MYSTERY,** the Professor said. "I have never discussed it with anyone. It wasn't ever that big a problem to begin with."

All three Templetons stood there silently, looking down at the telephone as though waiting for it to take the hint and explain to them what this all meant. It failed to do so. Eventually the Professor sighed, shook his head, and walked off toward the kitchen to make dinner.

John and Abigail looked at each other.

"I don't like this," Abigail said.

"Something's not right," John agreed.

This, in effect, was Templeton Twin-ese for "Let's keep an eye on this and, when the time comes, figure it out."

Abigail went back to her room and decided to give the cryptic one more try. She read the clue again ("No small bargain [3,4]"), looked at the grid , and *immediately* knew the answer.[15]

"HA!" she cried.

---

15. It had nothing to do with the number of letters in "no small." Rather, the first word had three letters. What three-letter word meant "no small"? BIG. What is a four-letter word for "bargain"? DEAL. The answer was BIG DEAL.

By walking away and coming back later, she was able to approach the problem from a different angle. Otherwise, she just would have been stuck with ALL SNOM and SON MALL and MNS LOLA forever.

This, too, will have important consequences as our story progresses.

## FOR FURTHER STUDY

1. When the Narrator describes a certain cymbal as making "a big, crashy sound," do you feel he is talking to you as if you were a big baby?

2. Write and perform a one-act play titled *The Narrator Is Right to Treat Us as Though We Were a Bunch of Big Babies, Because That Is What We Are.*

3. Solve this cryptic:

   *Grant, she ate our raisin! (Crazy! But a true statement about an important person.) (3,8,2,1,6)\**

\* Rearrange the letters in "Grant, she ate our raisin!" The answer is THE NARRATOR IS A GENIUS, which is, of course, a true statement about an important person.

CHAPTER 4

# IN WHICH FUN IS ATTEMPTED TO BE HAD

On the following afternoon the twins arrived home from school about ten minutes before Manny Mann was due to arrive. After quieting and calming the deliriously barking and wagging and being-ridiculous Cassie, they began discussing something that people their age—and possibly your age, too—seem to think is terribly, terribly important: what snack to make. Just as they had decided, and were going into the kitchen to begin assembling it, the doorbell rang, and there stood Manny Mann.

He was wearing a yellow T-shirt with the words ARE WE HAVING FUN YET?, black jeans, and black socks and shoes. The first thing he said, after John and Abigail had quieted Cassie (who had been barking in a loud and unhelpful manner), was, "Hey! Are you guys ready to have fun?"

"Um, I don't know," John said. "We have homework to do. But we're going to have a snack first."

"Would you like some?" Abigail asked.

"Sure!" the young man said. "Snacks are fun!"

The twins led him into the kitchen, where he immediately noticed an unusual device lying on a plate, surrounded by the ingredients for a peanut butter and jelly sandwich. "Hey! Whoa! Hold everything!" Manny Mann said. "What's *that*?"

It was the Professor's Point-Hinged Twin-Bladed Condiment Spreader—a.k.a. the PHTBCS. (You pronounce this—if you must pronounce it at all—as "FIT-BIKS.")

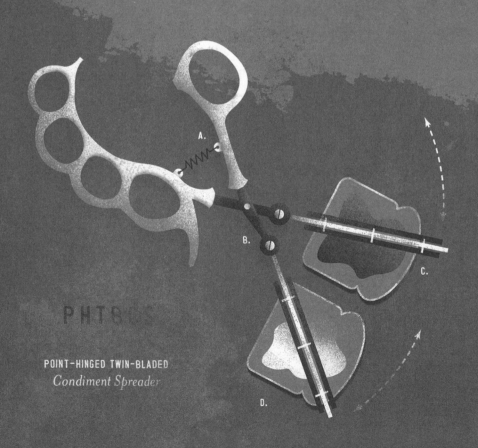

POINT-HINGED TWIN-BLADED
*Condiment Spreader*

This item resembled a big pair of scissors. But instead of sharp, cutting metal blades, it used two soft, flexible rubbery blades, like a pair of wide windshield wipers. These were mounted on handles. You placed two slices of bread side by side. Then you dipped one blade of the PHTBCS in the peanut butter, and the other in the jelly. You placed the peanut-butter-laden blade on one piece of bread and the jelly-laden blade on the other and closed your hand as though cutting something with the "scissors." The result: You spread both preparations on both pieces of bread in a single motion.

Manny Mann watched in delighted amazement as Abigail expertly manipulated the PHTBCS.

"Our father invented it," John said.

"THIS IS THE GREATEST THING THAT WAS EVER INVENTED!" Manny Mann proclaimed.

"He's invented better things than this," Abigail said. "But thank you."

John poured three glasses of lemonade (I know. It sounds repulsive. With such a snack I would drink milk. But what do you expect? They're *children*.), and the three of them sat around the kitchen table, eating their perfectly sensible snack and drinking their terribly inappropriate lemonade. Cassie, as usual, sat at Abigail's feet and stared with unblinking intensity at whatever Abigail put into her mouth.

Suddenly Manny Mann said, "Hey! I have a great idea! Let's open a lemonade stand and sell each glass for a bagful of gold! Won't that be fun?"

John said, "I don't think anyone would buy a glass of lemonade for a bagful of gold."

"But what if it's really *good*?" Manny said.

"Still," Abigail said. "That's too much. Besides, we have homework to do."

Manny looked disappointed and said, "Oh, all right." He grew silent again for about fifteen seconds. Suddenly he said, "Hey, I have a better idea. Let's go bowling and wear funny hats!"

"We can't," John said. "We really have to do our homework."

"But it'll be *fun*! Don't kids like to have fun?" Manny looked frustrated and frowned. He thought hard for a few seconds. All at once a look of great wisdom and intelligence took over his face. "Okay. Seriously. Here it is. Are you ready?" He paused dramatically. "We build a model of the Eiffel Tower out of jelly beans."

"Manny," Abigail said. "These are all great ideas—"

"I know! They're fun!"

"—but we have to do our homework."

"But that's not fun," Manny protested. "Look, what's more fun—having fun, or not having fun?"

Abigail said, "We'll have fun later." She stood up. "If you want to help, you can wash the dishes."

"I'll do the dishes," John said, also rising and collecting the plates.

"Okay, fine," the nanny said in a grousing manner, and slumped back in his chair and sulked.

"Well, okay, here's one fun thing," Abigail said. "We taught Cassie a new trick. Come on, John, let's show him."

John put the plates down and stood behind Abigail. All at once she backed into him so that his arms were sticking out on either side of her, as though he were taking her captive. She said in an exaggerated, fake-distressed voice, "Help! Cassie! He's got me prisoner! I can't get away!"

Cassie immediately went into a crouch and stared at John with squinty eyes. She started growling. Abigail then said, "Good girl!" and moved away from John, grabbed a little dog biscuit from a bowl, and gave it to the delighted animal.

"Isn't that neat?" John said.

"It's okay," Manny shrugged. "But it's not really *fun*. I had no idea you guys were so serious."

And he left the twins alone for the rest of the afternoon.

The next day Manny was right on time. But when the twins opened the door to his knock, they were astonished to see that his entire style of dress was different: He was wearing a crisp, unwrinkled pair of tan slacks, a white dress shirt, a navy-blue blazer, and a dark-red tie. As he entered the house he said, "I'm here to be serious. First, I think we should start off by ironing our socks."

Abigail—quite reasonably—said, "Huh?"

"No, wait," Manny said. "I can think of something more serious than that."

"Ironing your shoes?" John said.

"Don't be silly," Manny said. "Vacuuming the walls. Let's do that. Let's vacuum the walls and make this house really clean."

"That's not serious," Abigail said. "That's just . . . weird."

"Okay," Manny shrugged. "I have plenty more ideas." The nanny thought for a second, then said, "Hmmm . . . what's a serious food? Broccoli! No, it's green, and green is a fun color. Cauliflower! It's white, which is really serious. Okay. Let's—"

"Manny—"

"—open up a cauliflower stand, and sell bunches of cauliflower for a bagful of gold."

The twins took Manny into the kitchen, where they had made pretend pizzas from English muffins, spaghetti sauce, and cheese. They all sat down and started eating this adorable snack along with glasses of some hideous bright-red fruit punch that practically glowed in the dark. Finally Abigail said, "Manny, you're a student here at the Academy, right?"

"Yeah," Manny said. "I just started."

"Then don't you have homework to do? Books to read and assignments to write and projects and stuff?"

"I guess . . ."

"Then how come you don't do them?"

Manny hesitated. Then, from an inside pocket of his jacket, he produced a big plastic eyeglass case. He opened it and took out the biggest pair of glasses the Templeton twins had ever seen. They were big, not because the frames were oversized and comically enormous like a clown would wear, but because their lenses were so thick. He put them on. The lenses magnified his eyes and made them look like the oversized eyes of an owl in a cartoon.

"Watch," he said. Manny looked down at his snack plate. Immediately the glasses slid off his face and fell with a clatter onto the plate.

"Can you make the frames squeeze your head tighter?" John asked. "Or keep them in place with one of those straps around the back of your head, like athletes have?"

"I tried that," Manny said. He put the glasses back on. "But the frames can't get any tighter, and the straps dig into my head and pinch my hair. So I've sort of stopped reading. And doing homework." He trailed off and screwed up his face and suddenly and explosively sneezed. The glasses shot off his nose, bounced off his hands, and landed on the floor. "Plus, they come off when I sneeze." He bent down, picked them up, and put them back in their case. "Anyway, don't worry about it." From his inner pocket he pulled out a sheet of paper. "I wrote down a ton of serious ideas last night. It's kind of messy, though, because I wasn't wearing my glasses—"

"I have an idea," Abigail said. "You give us the list. We'll talk about it tonight, and tomorrow we'll tell you which of the things we want to do."

"Great!" Manny looked hopeful and pleased. "But what should I do the rest of today?"

"Hold your glasses on, and read," suggested John. "Or listen to music. Or take a nap."

Manny said, "Hey, I know! I'll write down some new ideas."

That night the Templeton twins held an emergency conference in Abigail's room. They began by agreeing that something had to be done. Unless they found some activity to occupy Nanny Manny while he was in their house, he would interrupt and distract and bother the twins every day with suggestions of "fun" things that they didn't have time to do, or "serious" things that were out of the question.

"We have to fix his glasses," John said.

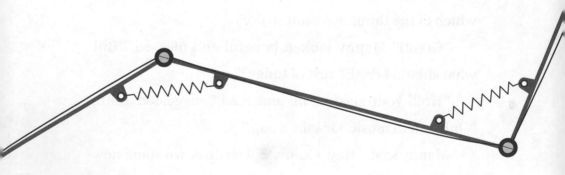

## FOR FURTHER STUDY

1. Fill in the blanks:

   The only occasion on which I would pay a bagful of gold for a glass of lemonade is if I were lucky enough to have the opportunity to buy it for the N_ _ _ _ _ _ _.

2. Write an award-winning screenplay for a blockbuster motion picture on the topic *Cauliflower: King of the Serious Vegetables.*

3. Answer Yes, No, or Please Repeat the Question:

   Is the horrible bright-red drink the twins had with their snack called "fruit punch" because a lot of innocent fruits were punched in order to make it?

   Y        N        PRTQ

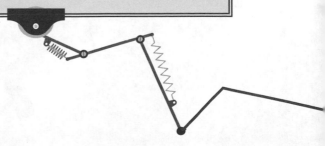

CHAPTER 5

# THE TEMPLETON TWINS CREATE A CREATION!

J ohn grabbed a long yellow pad of paper and Abigail grabbed a couple of pencils. (You will not be surprised to learn that she kept a large number of pencils in her room.) John started sketching a crude figure of a person, consisting of his head, neck, and shoulders. Around the figure's head John drew something that looked like a little cage, held up by little legs that rested on the figure's shoulders. Attached to the cage he drew a pair of glasses.

Abigail studied John's work over his shoulder. She murmured, "I like it." Then she thought for a minute. "But when he turns his head, the glasses will stay where they are and won't be in front of his eyes anymore. Can you make it so the glasses turn with him?"

John stared at the drawing. Then he smiled. "Oh! Sure!" He added four little zigzaggy vertical lines at the places where the cage part connected to the shoulder mounts. "Springs. The whole thing sits on little springs, which would let him turn his head."

"But that means it has to be attached to his head."

John drew a round piece like a sweatband. It circled the figure's forehead and connected it to the cage part.

"There. Now when he turns his head, the whole thing will turn with him."

Abigail's eyes grew wide. "I think this will work."

And John said the thing he always said when he had an idea and wanted to try it out. "Let's do it and view it!"[16]

I know you are very busy and have many important things to think about—or at least *you* think they're important—so I won't bother you with a description of how John and Abigail ran down into the basement, where their father's invention workshop was waiting to be unpacked and set up. I won't attempt to take up valuable space in your thoughts with an account of how they opened various boxes and crates, and acquired a collection of strips and rods and bands of metal, and the nuts and bolts needed to connect them, and an array of various springs. If they cleverly decided to cement lengths of foam rubber to the underside of the shoulder

---

16. This, as certain people who have read a certain book already know, was John's favorite catchphrase. It so happens that I have my own catchphrase. My catchphrase is, "Oh, really? Well, isn't it interesting that you think that? Although as a matter of fact, I happen to know that you are wrong and I am right." I say this all the time. People have told me that, as a catchphrase, it is not as short and punchy as it might be. In response, I merely repeat my catchphrase to them.

pieces (for comfort), and so had to find the rubber and the glue, you won't hear it from me. Of the tools they would need to assemble these pieces (screwdrivers, pliers, clamps, clips, etc.), I will say nothing.

You may be wondering why the twins didn't consult with their father about this invention. The reason is that the twins wanted to do it themselves. They didn't want to tell anyone about it until it was complete and Manny had accepted it with expressions of happiness and thanks and delight. We have all had this feeling. When we think we can do something, we don't want to ask our parents for help unless we feel we have no choice.

Of course, when I say "we," I really mean you. *You* don't ask for help unless you absolutely have to, because you are a child. I am different. I am a grown-up. So I have no problem asking my parents for help, *even when it comes to doing things I know I am perfectly capable of doing myself.*

Just last week I called up my mother and said, "Can you please pick me up a quart of milk at the Googly Woogly?" (The Googly Woogly is our local supermarket.)

"I'm busy," she said. "Why can't you do it yourself?"

"Oh, I assure you I *can* do it myself," I said confidently. "I just don't feel like it."

Then she said something like, "Tough. You do it or it won't get done," and hung up.

Of course, in the end I did it myself. But that is not the point. The point is, the twins wanted to do it themselves.

"You know," Abigail said, studying the eyeglass holder. "What if it did other things, too? Like, what if it had a cup holder?"

"And a reading light!" John said.

"And a pen holder for taking notes!"

"And a tissue holder, for when you sneeze!"

The twins thought these were excellent ideas, and set about adding various clips and clamps and holders to the frame. By the time they were done—which was, alas, somewhat past their bedtime—they had transformed the eyeglass holder into a many-functioned "reading module." It not only held the reader's eyeglasses in position, but it included a special mount for a plastic cup (and a long flexible straw), a small lamp to be aimed at the material being read, a pen attached by a cord for taking notes, and a holder for a pocket-sized pack of tissues mounted at exactly where the reader's nose would end up in the course of a moderately vigorous sneeze.

They tested it on John's head, and were delighted with how well it worked. And so, as the twins went to bed that night, each of them enjoyed that wonderful sense of accomplishment one feels upon completing a challenging but worthwhile task. It is a feeling with which I myself am quite familiar, as I know you know.

When Nanny Manny arrived the next day after school, he was back to wearing his usual clothes—in this case, a green T-shirt with a picture of a giant monster with the caption, I'M KIND OF A BIG DEAL, plus black jeans and black sneakers. He carried a little knapsack, out of which he pulled a piece of paper.

"I have a million new serious ideas," he said excitedly.

"Before we get to those," Abigail said, "we have a fun idea we want to try."

"Cool!"

They led Manny into the kitchen, where they had put a chair in the middle of the floor. Abigail took his knapsack and John had him sit. Abigail said, "You have to close your eyes until we say open them."

Manny shut his eyes and asked, "How does this game work?"

Now, in order to understand what Manny experienced next, it might be helpful if you closed your eyes. So, if you would be so kind, do that. Close your eyes.

WAIT! DO NOT CLOSE YOUR EYES. It occurs to me that, if you close your eyes, *and you are reading this book to yourself,* you won't be able to read when I tell you to open them. This could be a disaster. You would sit wherever you are right now, with your eyes closed, waiting for me to tell you to open them but unable to receive that very message. You would therefore just sit there, *forever,* eyes closed, until someone else—your brother, sister, financial adviser, or personal trainer—came into the room and asked what you were doing.

"I'm waiting for the Narrator to tell me to open my eyes," you would say. "I don't know what's taking him so long."

So, whatever you do while reading this, *keep your eyes open!*

Now, where were we? Ah, yes: Manny, on a chair

in the kitchen, his eyes closed, asking, "How does this game work?"

"We're going to put something on your head," John said. "And then you'll see what happens next."

"Like a hat?"

"Sort of."

"You're not going to crack an egg on my head, are you?"

Abigail laughed. "No. Although that *would* be fun."

While Manny sat there, John went into the laundry room and came back with the eyeglass apparatus and a small hand mirror. The twins gently lowered the device over and around the nanny's head. It fit pretty well.

Abigail dug around in Manny's knapsack until she found his glasses. She gave them to John, who clipped them onto the apparatus and adjusted the whole assembly so the glass lenses were properly positioned in front of Manny's eyes.

Abigail said, "Okay, Manny. Here we go." As John knelt in front of the nanny and held up the hand mirror in front of him, Abigail said, "Open your eyes."

How did Nanny Manny Mann react? That is an excellent question. I think I can best answer it by asking you a different, equally excellent question: How would you react if a friend came up to you and, without saying "Hello" or "How are you" or "Hey, watch this," just suddenly slapped you across the face with a dead fish?

I think we can all agree that you would react with absolute shock and confusion. And that is how Nanny Manny Mann reacted when he saw, in the little mirror, the image of himself wearing the eyeglass module that the Templeton twins had so cleverly and tirelessly worked to create for him.

"Whoa," he said. "What IS this thing?"

"It's a frame for holding your glasses!" John said with enthusiasm and excitement and other upbeat, happy words starting with the letter "e" (such as exuberance and effusiveness).

"Isn't it great?" Abigail said. "You can have a drink and read a book and sneeze and take notes all at the same time!"

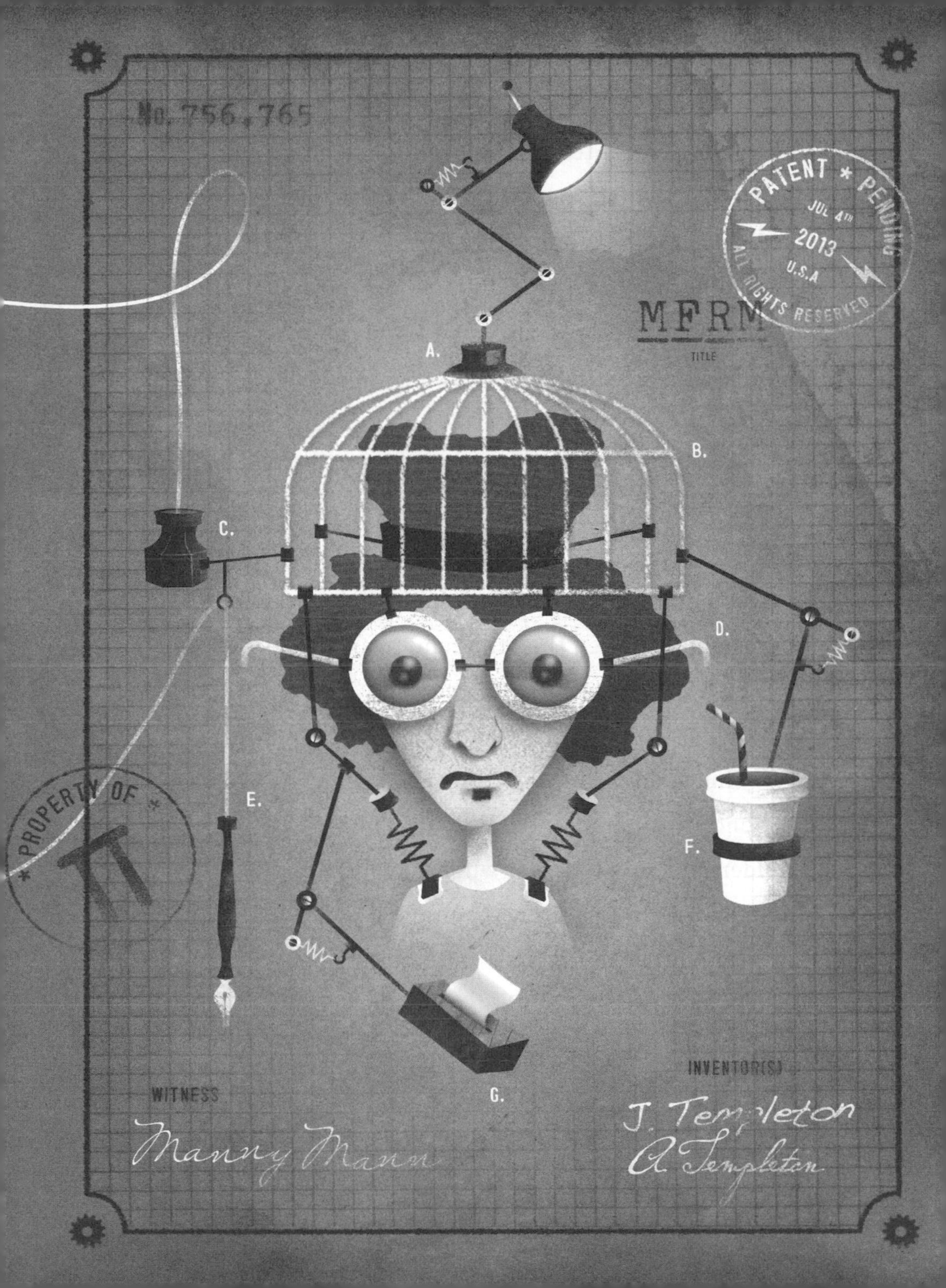

No. 756,765
PATENT * PENDING
JUL 4TH
2013
U.S.A
ALL RIGHTS RESERVED
MFRM
TITLE
A.
B.
C.
D.
E.
F.
G.
PROPERTY OF
WITNESS
Manny Mann
INVENTOR(S)
J. Templeton
A. Templeton

Manny squinted, and moved his head around, and looked to the left and to the right. The glasses moved with him, but not completely. The more he tried to position himself to see through them, the more they shifted away from him. The device wobbled around on his shoulders, and his face took on a pained grimace of dismay.

Abigail, sensing that the user of the twins' device was not as delighted as he might be, said, "Wait. You have to see everything it can do." She took the cup to the sink and filled it with water, then came back and inserted it into the cup holder. She inserted the flexible straw into the cup and positioned the other end near Manny's mouth. He took a sip and nodded and said, "Hmm." Then he turned to say something to John.

This sudden movement caused the water to slosh around in the cup, making it tip over, out of the cup holder, and onto the floor while, of course, first dumping all the water onto Manny's pants.

John lifted the device from Manny's head. "It might need some work," he said.

"Forget it!" the nanny said. "Can I just have my glasses, please?"

John removed the glasses from the device and handed them over. "I'll just wear them like this," Manny said. He put them on. He stood up. They fell off. He said, "Argh!" and picked them up and walked out of the kitchen.

That night Abigail and John did what they had not wanted to do: They explained to their father Manny's problems with his glasses, and then revealed the eyeglass invention to him while admitting that its intended user had been less than thrilled with it.

The Professor listened carefully and examined the reading module. Then he thought for a minute and said, "You created this to avoid the problem with the straps?" The twins nodded. The Professor said, "Mmm . . . " Then he said, "What you two have done is very resourceful and clever. But I think you've misinterpreted the problem. I do it all the time. You think the problem is one thing, and you solve it, but it turns out that that wasn't really the problem. In this case, you worked so hard to avoid straps that you came up with this very elaborate device. But the problem really isn't the straps. It's the *kind* of straps."

"So what's the solution?" the Templeton twins asked at exactly the same time.

"Oh, I'm not going to tell you," their father said. "That would take all the fun out of it. Just ask yourselves, 'What *is* a strap?'"

And so, after they had eaten dinner and finished their homework, the twins had another design meeting. For a fresh perspective on things, they held it in John's room. Abigail sat on his bed and John sat at his desk. His deep-red drums and the gleaming, brassy cymbals stood in the middle of the floor like an interesting sculpture.

"Okay," Abigail said. "What is a strap?"

Her brother shrugged. "It's a strip of some material that holds stuff together."

Abigail was about to nod when suddenly she stopped and said, "No, it isn't. I mean yes, it's a strip that holds something. But it doesn't have to hold stuff *together*. It can just hold something in place."

And in about thirty seconds they had figured it out. All they needed was a length of ribbon. At the last minute Abigail had another idea, so they added one more element to the design.

The next day, after a snack of big salty pretzels and horrible iced tea that any nonchild would think was too sweet, the twins announced to Manny that they had solved his eyeglass problem. Promising they were not going to put any big metal contraption on his head (nor were they going to crack an egg on him), they had him sit on the chair in the middle of the kitchen one more time.

Abigail found Manny's glasses and handed them to John. John performed a little manipulation with the glasses and the ribbon. Once again, Abigail asked Manny to shut his eyes. He did so. She lowered the eyeglass arrangement onto his head while John positioned himself in front of Manny and held up, not a mirror, but an open book.

"Okay," Abigail said. "Here we go. Open your eyes."

He did. He stared. "Cool!" he said. "What's that?"

"A book," Abigail said.

"*Obviously*. Which one?"

"*Alice in Wonderland*," John said.

"I can see it great!" the nanny said happily. "What did you do?"

Abigail stepped in front of him and held out the mirror. "Look." As Manny examined himself in the mirror, she said, "We attached a ribbon to the two earpieces of your glasses, and laid it down across *the top* of your head, instead of the back."

Manny jerked his head forward experimentally. The glasses stayed on. "Hey," he said. "It works." Then he added, "Although it looks kind of stupid, with that ribbon across my head."

"No problem," Abigail said, and she held up the final piece of the invention: a baseball cap. She placed it on Manny's head.

"This is fantastic!" the nanny said. He reached out and John handed him the book. "You know, I've never actually read this . . . "

Suddenly there was a brief clattering sound at the front of the house. The twins and their nanny hurried to the door and opened it. No one was there. The three of them stepped out onto the little front porch and looked up and down the street, but all they saw was a car driving off a bit faster than necessary.

"What's this?" John said, pulling an envelope out of the mailbox. On the front was written "Prof. Elton Templeton" and nothing else. "That's strange. It's not mail. It doesn't have a stamp or even our address. Someone just left it here."

"Maybe we should open it," Abigail said. "If it's something important, we should call Papa at the Academy and tell him."

Inside the unsealed envelope was a single sheet of notepaper. John read it and said, "Huh." He handed it to his sister. "'Professor,'" she read. "'I'm getting a catalogue of lenses from Claire Light and I'll leave it in your office. Steve Stevenson.'"

The twins decided that the message wasn't urgent enough to bother their father while he was at work, so they told Manny they were going to do their homework. Manny announced that he was going to get started on his own homework—as soon as he had read a few chapters of *Alice in Wonderland*.

As the twins headed upstairs to their rooms, Abigail said to her brother, "That Steve Stevenson is really strange. He didn't leave a phone number or anything."

It would have been nice if, at that moment, the twins had exchanged a look charged with tension and excitement and a hidden orchestra had played a dramatic "sting," a short, exciting burst of music along the lines of *DUN-dun-DUNNNNNNNNNNN* . . . But all that happened was that John said, "Yeah," and Cassie squirmed past both of them to run into Abigail's room and jump onto her bed.

## FOR FURTHER STUDY

1. If you closed your eyes when I originally told you to, how is it that you are able to read this question?

   a. I don't know.
   b. Someone else told me to open them.
   c. I disobeyed the Narrator and opened my eyes, and now I feel just terrible about the whole thing.

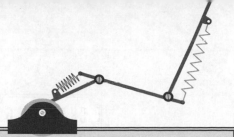

2. Circle one answer: I have revealed that "the Googly Woogly" is the name of our local supermarket. Will you use this new knowledge for Good, or for Evil?

For Good        For Evil

3. What kind of musical group would you want to accompany you everywhere you go, to play dramatic musical "stings" whenever something important happened?

a. A 72-piece symphony orchestra.
b. A bossa nova quartet with a saxophone player who can double on flute.
c. A ten-piece power ensemble playing the greatest hits of the '70s, the '80s, the '90s, and today.
d. All of the above.

CHAPTER 6

# THE RETURN OF SOMEONE NO ONE WANTED TO RETURN

O ver the next week the Professor had his hands full with finishing the close-up device. He spent much of his time in his workshop at the Academy refining his design, or onstage at the main auditorium trying out one version of the device after another. (When he received Steve Stevenson's latest note, he threw it away and muttered something about Steve Stevenson introducing himself in person "like a normal human being.")

At last the Professor assembled a prototype of the close-up device. (If you do not know what a prototype is, I suggest you look it up in a dictionary—or, read [or re-read], in its entirety, *TTTHAI*.) On the day that the prototype was to be installed at the Academy's main theater, the twins prevailed on Manny Mann to drive them to pay a surprise visit to their father. They brought along a thermos of tea and a vanilla-coconut cupcake (the Professor's favorite). They entered through the main audience entrance at the rear of the hall. Manny said, "Let me know when you're ready to go," then fell into a seat, put on his glasses (and his cap), pulled a book from his back pocket, and started to read.

John and Abigail looked down the aisle toward the stage. The curtain was open and the chilly white fluorescent work lights were on. Amid a swarming bustle of young men and women, the twins could see their father. The sleeves on his blousy white shirt were rolled back, and he was holding a big diagram and pointing something out to a tall, younger man beside him.

Behind the two men, and the center of everyone's attention, was a long bar that seemed to hover about ten feet above the stage and extended across its entire width. It was, the twins saw, held up by several cables distributed across its length and rising up toward the ceiling and out of sight. Designed to roll along the top of it was a wheel about a foot in diameter from which hung what looked like a gigantic, upside-down lollipop.

This, the twins knew, was the Live Performance Horizontal-Tracking Individual Close-Up Lens—a name that, I think you'll agree, is second-to-none in terribleness. So let us therefore refer to it as the LPHTICUL, which (for those of you reading out loud, either to yourself or others) we will pronounce "LIFF-tih-cool" which, in my opinion, is actually not a bad name for such a

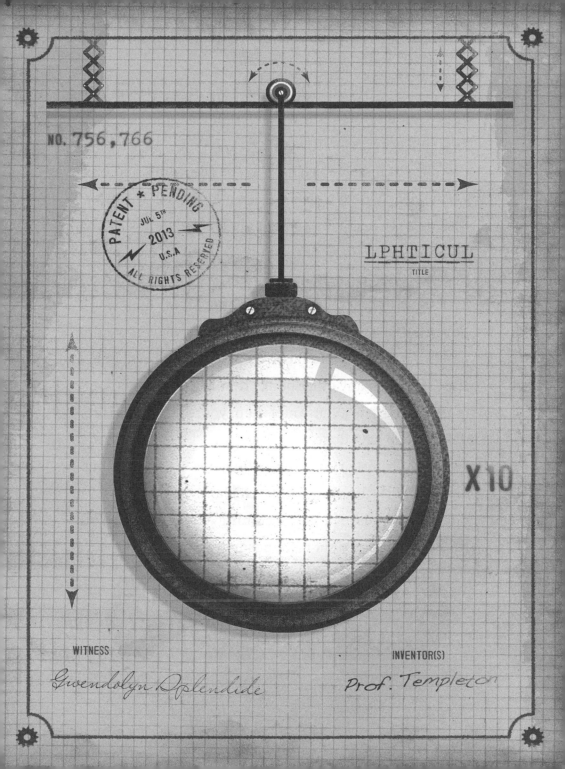

NO. 756,766

LPHTICUL
TITLE

X10

WITNESS

Gwendolyn Splendide

INVENTOR(S)

Prof. Templeton

device. The lens "lifts" the actor's face in a close-up, and "-icul" reminds us of the words "monocle" and "binocu-lars" and other references *to lenses*.

The Professor was happy to see the twins, and was extremely pleased by the cupcake and the tea. He intro-duced the twins to the young men and women working all around the stage. Some were students studying set design or theatrical lighting; some were on the staff of TAPAS as instructors or technicians. All of them were delighted to meet the Templeton twins, as you would be, too, if you were to meet them. Indeed, by reading this book (and any other books that feature them—*hint hint*), you have in a sense met them yourself, and you are delighted to have done so.

The Professor and his colleagues were chatting amiably with the twins about this and that when sud-denly they heard a voice coming from the rear of the auditorium cry out in a singsongy tone

## PRO-FESS-OR! YOU HAVE A VIZZ-I-TOR!

THE TEMPLETON TWINS MAKE A SCENE

Everyone looked up and beheld Gwendolyn Splendide marching dramatically down the aisle.

She was wearing bright-pink trousers and a matching bright-pink jacket over a deep-purple blouse, and she clattered and tinkled with an array of bracelets, earrings, and necklaces. Behind her, strolling smoothly along in an elegant suit of light, light gray, was a man. He was very handsome and he walked with the bouncy, confident air of a person who hadn't a care in the world.

The Templeton twins took one look at the man and their stomachs started to churn. The Professor, who until that moment had been twinkling and smiling about absolutely everything, saw the man and immediately grew grim.

"Well, who is THIS?" the man cried, as he and Gwendolyn Splendide mounted the short flight of steps leading onto the stage. "My partner AND his delightful children!"

The faces of Abigail and John were like masks of stone. "How did you find us?" John said.

"You have a lot of nerve, showing up here," Abigail said.

At this the TAPAS students and staff looked baffled and a little embarrassed, but Gwendolyn Splendide quickly explained, "Of course the CHILDREN know Mister Dean. He and their father are partners, you see."

"We know him," Abigail said. "We know—"

"Excuse me." The Professor said this quite softly—and, as is often the case, the very softness of his voice commanded everyone's attention. "Did you say 'partner'?"

"I certainly did!" cried Gwendolyn Splendide. Then she burbled a little laugh and announced, "Why, I AM being rude. And Gwendolyn Splendide is many things, but she is not rude. Everyone!

## THIS IS MISTER DEAN D. DEAN— THE PROFESSOR'S BUSINESS PARTNER!

As the men and women standing around the stage exchanged puzzled looks with one another and Dean D. Dean gave a merry wave to one and all, the twins went up to their father. They started to say something, but he held up his hand to quiet them.

"I'll deal with this, children," the Professor said. He stepped toward Gwendolyn Splendide and said, "Miss Splendide. I am well acquainted with this person. He has

attempted to obtain credit and money from my work in the past—to which he has absolutely no claim whatsoever. I assure you, he is no partner of mine."

"Plus he kidnapped us!" Abigail said.

"And he held us prisoner with a gun!" John added.

There was a moment of stunned silence. Then, led by the jovially twinkling Dean D. Dean, everyone (except the Templetons) broke into loud laughter.

"There you go again," Dean D. Dean said to the Professor. He pointed to the LPHTICUL. "Pretending I'm not your partner, when you KNOW I've been helping you all along with this wonderful invention."

"You have most certainly *not* been helping," the Professor said. "You have had nothing to do with it."

"Oh, really?" Dean D. Dean said. "Is that the case? Is that so? Is that a fact? Well then, answer me this . . . "

Addressing the rest of the onlookers, he said, "If I had nothing to do with this device, how is it that I know about the spotlight problem? And the lens fabrication difficulties? And the track electrification issues? And the RT rotational solutions?" He looked directly at the Professor and added, "These are real concerns, aren't they?"

Everyone seemed to hold their breath and look at the Professor. He frowned. "Yes," he said finally. "Yes, they are."

"And how would I know about them?"

"You read about them in an article!" John said.

"Oh, did I? Well, young man, it so happens that I did read about the Professor in an article. It was in the *New Engineering Weekly Snapshot* from some weeks ago, and it said how the Professor and his delightful twin children were moving to this Academy so he could work on this device. But that's all it said. It didn't have any details about any problems."

"He's right, John," the Professor said. "I haven't discussed the problems with the device in *any* article."

"Take that!" Dean D. Dean cried. "He hasn't discussed them in *any* article!"

"You've been spying on us," Abigail said.

"Oh, please," Dean D. Dean scoffed. "Oh, piffle. Oh, hogwash. Ask any of these people—" He turned to the onlookers and said, "Have any of you seen me around here before?" Everyone shook their heads no. Dean D. Dean turned back to Abigail. "You see?" He rolled his eyes. "'Spying.' Absurd." He looked sadly at Gwendolyn Splendide. "One would be vastly amused if one were not so cruelly insulted."

"Ha!" Abigail said. "If you're our father's partner, and you've been working on this project with him, then why *haven't* you been around here before?"

"Be-*cause* . . . " Dean D. Dean said in the kind of voice you would use to explain something to a toddler, "I have been working on the device at my *workshop*, little girl.

"And now," the handsome man continued, directing a very sad and disappointed look toward the Professor, "as usual, you want to take all the credit for it. Well, that's just wrong." He turned to Gwendolyn Splendide. "Don't you think so, Madame Dean of the Academy?"

"Why, I must say I do," the lady said. "Gwendolyn Splendide firmly believes that what's fair is fair."

"Dean D. Dean is delighted to hear it," Dean D. Dean said, smiling handsomely at her. "He is thrilled to meet Gwendolyn Splendide and to hear her excellent policy on fairness."

Gwendolyn Splendide smiled as she replied, "Oh, Mister Dean, Gwendolyn Splendide is equally thrilled."

Dean D. Dean suddenly appeared exhausted. "Then let us leave it at that." He pulled from the breast pocket of his jacket a sumptuous white handkerchief and mopped his forehead with it. "This has been such an ordeal. Will you—CAN you—all excuse me?"

And with that he turned away from everyone, as though overcome by his deep emotions. He held out a hand as though to say, "No, no, there is no need to help me. I'll manage," and, with a sad sigh indicating his disappointment with the human race but his brave determination to put up with it, he walked down the steps, up the aisle, and out of the building.

"Such an elegant and charming man," Gwendolyn Splendide murmured. Then she looked at the Professor. "I trust, Professor, that you will take this exchange under advisement, and give credit where credit is due."

The twins could tell that their father wanted to say something sharp and angry in reply. But they also saw him glance around at all the people waiting to get back to work, and at the LPHTICUL itself, and decide not to. Instead he replied, "I will indeed give this matter the attention it deserves."

"Lovely," the lady beamed. "Oh, *isn't* this fun? You technical people are so fascinating." She flung a hand at the ceiling, trilled, "*Au revoir, tutti!*"[17] and swept down the little stairway, up the aisle, and away.

The Professor called out, "Shall we get back to work?" and that, for the time being, was that.

That evening the twins made dinner while the Professor brooded in his office at home. Abigail made beef tacos,[18] while John made rice and guacamole.[19]

---

17. "Au revoir" is pronounced "aw-riv-WHAH," and is French for "good-bye." "Tutti" is Italian. It is pronounced "TOOT-ee" and means "everyone." I urge you to do this yourself. The next time you have to leave a group of people, instead of saying "Bye," cry out "*Au revoir, tutti!*" and see how everyone reacts.

18. These are actually extremely easy to make, especially if you buy an envelope of taco spices, which is what the twins did.

19. This is also fairly easy to make, and I will be happy to explain how on the next page.

# THE NARRATOR'S GUACAMOLE

First, however, there are probably readers who are wondering, "What on earth is guacamole, and how do you pronounce it?" It is pronounced "gwah-kah-MOW-lee" and it is a Mexican dish. In fact guacamole is a puree. Well, actually, it is a kind of salad. Although it is not actually a salad. I suppose it is more a kind of vegetable dip—although it is made from avocados, which are not vegetables. The avocado is a fruit, I think. (It grows on a tree and has a big seed in the middle of it. This, I think, is the definition of a fruit. Although strawberries don't grow on trees, and they have their seeds on the outside, and we all know—we think—that the strawberry is a fruit, so never mind.) You mash up the avocado, like a potato, except you don't cook the avocado, so it isn't really like a potato.

This whole topic is becoming somewhat annoying. I've decided I don't want to talk about guacamole. It upsets me. Instead, I'm going to tell you how to make coleslaw. We will use a recipe I call . . .

# THE NARRATOR'S ~~GUACAMOLE~~ COLESLAW

## You will need:

1 grown-up or responsible teenager

1 head of green cabbage

1 head of red (which is actually purple) cabbage

1 handful of flat-leaf (Italian) parsley

1 carrot

$^1/_2$ cup (120 milliliters) mayonnaise

$^1/_4$ cup (60 milliliters) plain (NOT VANILLA) yogurt

1 tablespoon vinegar

Pinch of cayenne

1 teaspoon celery seeds

$^1/_2$ teaspoon black pepper

$^1/_2$ teaspoon paprika

$^1/_4$ teaspoon garlic powder

$^1/_4$ teaspoon onion powder

$^1/_4$ teaspoon dried thyme

$^1/_4$ teaspoon dried oregano

Salt

Special equipment: box grater (This is not all that "special." Almost every kitchen has one. It's a silver, metal, boxy-shaped thing with different sized holes on its sides, used for grating hard food into shreds.)

# You Should Do This:

1. Ask—politely—your grown-up or teenager to cut the green cabbage in half and remove the core. Cut that half-piece into three or four parts. Peel off and discard the rough, dirty outer leaf. If you want, rinse the hunks briefly in cold water. Then rub each hunk against the biggest, longest holes on the side of the box grater. The cabbage will miraculously become shredded INSIDE THE BOX ITSELF. Repeat with all three or four hunks. Put the shreds into a big measuring cup until you have about 3 to 4 cups (240 to 320 grams).

2. Do a similar, but smaller, thing with the red-actually-purple cabbage. Cut off a hunk, peel off the outer layer, rinse, and shred, until you get about 1 cup (80 grams) of shreds. Put all cabbage shreds into a big bowl. Not a "sort-of biggish" bowl. A BIG bowl.

3. Have your older helper cut off the stems of the parsley, then rinse the leaves. If you want, drop the parsley onto a piece of paper towel and wrap it up, so the towel dries off the leaves. Then ask your helper to finely chop them until you have about ½ cup (30 grams), or even more. Dump the leaves into the bowl with the cabbage. Do not dump the paper towel into the bowl. Perhaps you eat paper towels with your coleslaw, but I assure you I do not.

4. Have your helper cut off the tip and bottom of the carrot. Using a vegetable peeler, peel the carrot and rinse it off.

Then, rub the carrot (end first; not the long way) against the second-largest holes in the grater, on one of its bigger faces. The carrot will, as if by magic, grow shorter and shorter as the holes grate it into shreds. Be VERY CAREFUL not to touch the grater with your knuckles. Stop grating before this happens, and either eat the little stump of carrot that remains or give it to a dog. Dump the carrot shreds into the bowl.

5. WITH YOUR BARE HANDS, WHICH YOU HAVE WASHED THOROUGHLY, toss the cabbage-parsley-carrot mixture until it is well blended. Take a moment to appreciate the beautiful four-color (light-green, purple, dark-green, orange) mixture you have created. Say to your helper, "Isn't that the most beautiful thing you have ever seen?" and dare them to say "no."

6. Spoon the mayonnaise into a medium bowl or a big measuring cup. Stir the yogurt so it smoothes out and spoon it into the mayonnaise. Stir these two ingredients together until they're smooth and blended. Add the vinegar and quickly stir it in, so that it thins out the mixture. Use any kind of vinegar you want. No. I take that back. Only use white or rice vinegar. No. I take *that* back. Use apple cider vinegar.

7. Add the rest of the ingredients to the mayo-yogurt mixture except the salt. Don't worry if the amounts aren't precise. WARNING: IT SAYS "PINCH OF CAYENNE," BUT DO NOT TAKE THIS LITERALLY. Meaning, do not

use your fingers to take a pinch, because cayenne is stupendously hot. USE A SPOON. If you use your fingers, and touch your fingers to your eye, YOU WILL REGRET IT FOR THE NEXT FOUR HOURS. Or, if this entire topic upsets you or your parents or guardians or attorneys too much, just skip the cayenne. WHATEVER YOU DO, do not skip the celery seeds, since that is what provides maximum slawness.

8. Stir the dressing until all the spices are combined. (You can add other things if you want: lemon juice, basil, dill, etc.) Then dump it all into the cabbage mixture. Using two big spoons, gently toss and stir everything until the dressing is distributed throughout.

9. Taste and see whether it needs salt. It probably does. But the mayonnaise you used already has salt, so we're waiting until this final phase before adding it. Go easy with the salt.

10. You can—and you will want to—eat it right away. But it gets better if it sits for a couple hours in the fridge. So cover it with plastic wrap and let it chill. Before serving, toss again, because some liquid will have fallen out onto the bottom of the bowl. Just stir it back in.

Although this slaw is not "Mexican," it would go great with Abigail's beef tacos. It also goes great with the Narrator's Meatloaf (the recipe for which is in the you-know-what book), and all sandwiches, hamburgers, etc., etc.

Over dinner, the Templeton twins and their father discussed the reappearance of Dean D. Dean. John started by asking why they couldn't just call the police and tell them that Dean D. Dean had done various bad—and probably illegal—things the last time the Templetons had encountered him.

But the Professor replied that those things had happened some months ago, and that the Templetons had no actual proof that Dean D. Dean (and his [twin] brother, Dan D. Dean) had done them. "The police can't arrest somebody, or give them a warning, just because you ask them to," the Professor explained. "They have to have some indication that the person is breaking the law."

"So what are we supposed to do?" Abigail asked. "Just wait around for them to do their next sneaky thing?"

"I'm afraid so, dear," the Professor said.

"Well, we won't have to wait long," John said. "He's already started lying to that Gwendolyn lady."

"One thing I don't understand," the Professor mused. "How did Dean D. Dean know about those problems I've been having with the device?"

"Maybe he asked people who are working with you," John said.

"I don't think so," Abigail said. "They all said they'd never seen him before."

"He must be spying on us in some way," the Professor said. "I just wish I knew how."

The twins traded a look that said, wordlessly, "I can't believe we have to deal with Dean D. Dean again! What an undesirable and vexing state of affairs!"

## FOR FURTHER STUDY

1. Select the correct answer:

   The Narrator continues to do:

   a. an excellent job.
   b. a superb job.
   c. a magnificent job.
   d. just a really great, great job.

2. Write an essay of 1,000 words on the importance of coleslaw in your daily life.

3. Write a letter to the editor of your local newspaper, describing how sorry you felt for me when I became upset at the topic of guacamole.

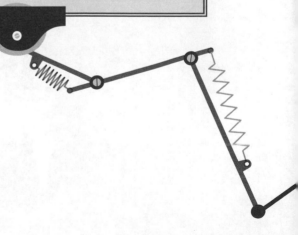

# CHAPTER 7

# SOMETHING IS UNEXPECTEDLY FROZEN!

T he public was scheduled to get its first official look at the Live Performance Horizontal-Tracking Individual Close-Up Lens (LPHTICUL) on a Saturday night at the opening of a new musical written by some of the students and faculty of TAPAS. The show was called *Let's Live Life!* and was about a group of students studying acting, singing, and dancing.

It was to open with an overture[20] (some introductory music), and then some dialogue between the main characters that would lead into the first song. This would be sung by the character of a young man studying acting at a college much like TAPAS, who was to be played by an actor who, in fact, *was* a young man studying acting at TAPAS.

One week before this opening performance, the Professor announced that the LPHTICUL was ready. A technical rehearsal was scheduled for two days later. (A technical rehearsal—you will be impressed that I know this—is a rehearsal mainly for the benefit of the lighting, scenery, sound, and costume people.) The rehearsal was

---

20. I am not in the mood to explain that the word "overture" is a French word. I may do so later in the text.

to begin at five o'clock that Monday afternoon, which meant that John and Abigail would be able to attend it after school.

They couldn't wait.

After school on Monday, the twins ran into the house and had a quick snack. Manny Mann arrived a few minutes later and, while he finished the rest of the vanilla fudge ice cream and snooped around in search of cookies, the twins did their homework. By ten to five they had (they *claimed*) completed their work, and Manny drove them to the auditorium. He planted himself in the last row with a new book, explaining, "I finished *Alice in Wonderland*. You know, you guys were right. It was fun *and* serious."

The twins moved toward the stage and sat in the front. The theater was empty except for the cast and crew, whose coats and books and backpacks were scattered on seats throughout the auditorium. The lights over the audience seats were low. The curtain was closed but lit up by the bright, spectacular stage lights. In front of it, the Professor conferred with Roger Prince, the director, and Claire Light, the lighting designer.[21] When the Professor noticed the twins, he excused himself, came down the little stairs from the stage, and joined them.

"We're not quite ready to start," he said after greeting each of them with a hug. "We're reviewing the cues for the sound effects. Come on, I'll show you."

The Professor led the twins toward the rear of the theater. In the center of the very last row, taking up the width of seven seats, was a console and a control panel with many switches and sliding controls and lights. Seated at it was a young woman wearing a pair of headphones. She took them off as the Templetons arrived.

"I was explaining the sound cues to them," the Professor said. "How many do we have in the show?"

"Forty-three," the young woman said. To the twins she added, proudly, "That's a lot. I pulled them from about six hundred we have in the booth upstairs. Look." She showed them a rack of about fifty cassettes, each with a tiny label describing the sound recording it contained.

---

21. Yes, the lighting designer's last name was Light. Do not be amazed at this. It happens all the time. I once knew a man who ran a construction crew whose name was David Powerdrill Steamshovel. All right, that is not true. But it does happen all the time.

A.

CRICKETS
TICK TOCK
TRAFFIC, HONKING
GIRL BURP
SNEEZE
THUNDER, QUIET
THUNDER, LOUD
FIRE CRACKER

COP SIREN TOWARD
COP SIREN RECEDE
COP SIREN ARRIVE
TREE FALLING

GUN SHOT, INDOORS
PIN DROP
GOOSE FART
RAIN

B.

C.

D.

"Today we'll practice turning them on and off at the right times in the show," she explained.

E.

She pulled a cassette from the rack, slid it into a slot, and pressed a button. Over the speakers placed all around the auditorium, the twins heard the sound of rain and a distant rumble of thunder.

John was about to say something like "This is so NEAT" when two figures appeared at one of the entrances off the lobby and swept down the aisle toward the stage. "Ah!" one said. "We're right on time. Gwendolyn Splendide is nothing if not punctual."

"As is Dean D. Dean," said the other.

The twins looked warily at each other and then at their father. He did not return their look. He was following the progress of Gwendolyn Splendide and Dean D. Dean and—you could tell from his expression— fearing the worst.

"Wait here," the Professor said quietly to the twins. He slowly walked down the aisle toward the stage, where Gwendolyn Splendide and Dean D. Dean were greeting other members of the staff and crew.

John looked at Abigail. "No wonder Gwendolyn likes Dean D. Dean so much," he said. "They both dress up like this *every day*."

"Come on," Abigail said.

The twins followed their father down the aisle toward the stage.

It is true that both Gwendolyn Splendide and Dean D. Dean were "dressed up," as they always were. She wore a deep-yellow pair of silky trousers and matching jacket, a white blouse, and a set of silver-and-ruby brooches and glinting gold necklaces and tinkling silver bracelets. He wore a dark-blue suit; a white, white shirt; and an orange tie with little dark-green dots. Everyone else in the entire building wore jeans and T-shirts and sweatshirts.

Gwendolyn Splendide spied the Professor and announced, "Professor. I was just telling Mister Dean here that I was sure you had thought about our previous discussion and had decided to share owner-ship and credit for your wonderful device, as is only right and proper."

"I have thought about it," the Professor said. He climbed the short stairway and joined them on the stage. "Now, if we can all focus on the task at hand—"

"The task at hand is for you to sign this," Dean D. Dean interrupted. He produced a sheaf of papers from inside his jacket and held them out to the Professor.

"Thank you," the Professor said. He took the document and, in a single smooth motion, tore it in half.

People audibly gasped. ("Audibly" means that you could hear it. You could actually hear them gasp with your ears, which is the best way to hear things.)

"Professor Templeton! I am appalled!" Gwendolyn Splendide exclaimed, drawing herself up in a demonstration of immense indignation. "That is a *legal document*!"

"It isn't legal until I sign it," Professor Templeton said. "Which I have no intention of doing." He handed the two halves of the document back to Dean D. Dean, then looked at the others and said, "Now. Shall we proceed?"

"Mister Dean, I am quite speechless," the lady said. "And when Gwendolyn Splendide is speechless she doesn't know *what* to say."

"Think nothing of it, Madame Dean of the Academy and Boss of Professor Elton Templeton," Dean D. Dean said, taking the torn document and stuffing it with his right hand into the left-side inner pocket of his jacket. "I foresaw this eventuality." With his left hand, he reached into the right side of the jacket. "Which is why I smartly brought two copies." He produced another sheaf of stapled papers. To the Professor he said, "You're not going to tear this one up, are you?"

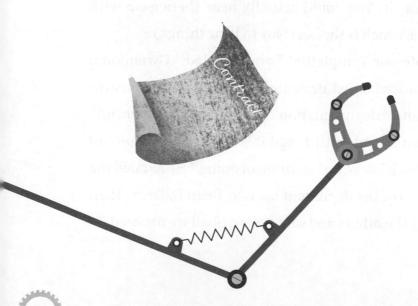

"I certainly am," the Professor said.

"Professor," Gwendolyn Splendide said. "I must tell you that Mister Dean's role as your partner is well known. Why, Steve Stevenson himself left a memo for me in my office today. He informed me of a number of issues and concerns regarding the device. He made it clear that the only reason he knew of them was thanks to a series of regular briefings he has had with Mister Dean here."

The twins, standing at the foot of the stage, looked at each other. Abigail spread her hands as though to ask, "How is that possible?" John met her glance and shrugged.

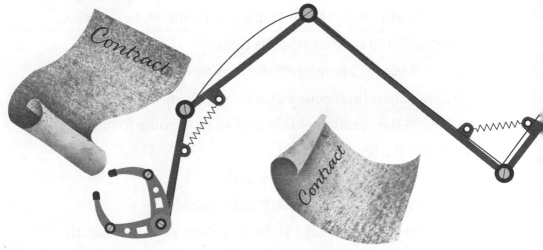

"It is therefore quite obvious to me," Gwendolyn Splendide continued, "that Mister Dean deserves to share in the success of this invention." She added, with great dignity, "What's right is right." Then she went on, in a more conversational tone, "Besides, if Mister Dean is denied his proper share of this creation, he would be entitled to sue the Academy—"

"Miss Splendide . . . Gwendolyn . . . I assure you," Dean D. Dean said in his most elegant and graceful manner. "I would never stoop to something so greedy and mean—"

"—and we might end up having to pay him a great deal of money."

"—although," Dean D. Dean continued, "as you so astutely put it, what's right is right."

"Indeed. Therefore," she resumed. "Until the Professor signs this document acknowledging Mister Dean's role in the creation of this device, I am going to have to freeze the production."

"WHAT?" Dean D. Dean barked.

"What does that mean?" John asked.

"It means that the show is hereby postponed until further notice," the lady said.

Dean D. Dean glared at the Professor, and then turned to the others and cried, "Do you see what he's doing? He's ruining it for everyone!"

The Professor stared back at him. "I'm not the one causing the trouble," he said. "As you well know."

Rather sternly Gwendolyn Splendide said, "Professor, I suggest you show your attorney this document so we can move things along as quickly as possible."

"Oh, that won't be necessary," the Professor said. He held out his hand toward Dean D. Dean, who placed the new document in it. The Professor immediately tore that one in half, too, and handed the pieces back to Dean D. Dean, who reached into the other side of his jacket and pulled out a third copy. He said nothing but simply smiled.

The Professor said, "John? Abby? Let's go," and marched off the stage and up the aisle with the Templeton

twins scrambling after him. Manny Mann looked up from his book and then got up and followed.

Outside, Manny said good-night and left the Templetons to themselves. At first no one spoke. Then the Professor said, somewhat cheerily, "Well, I'm starving. Let's go home and make dinner."

They drove in silence past the statues of actors and writers and directors, which had begun to look a little creepy and ominous in the late afternoon light. The twins looked out the windows and mulled over the situation. Finally John asked, "Papa, why is this so important? I mean, the device is neat. But how come everyone is fighting over it?"

"Because it could be worth a lot of money," the Professor said. "If it works—"

"Which it WILL," Abigail said. "I mean, it already does, right?"

"Well, yes, but anyway: It would be like inventing a new kind of spotlight or microphone. Every theater in every city would want one. Every theater department in every college. Hundreds of high schools will want one. And not just in this country. In every country, all over the world, wherever there are theaters. Every dance company. Every opera company. Rock bands will want one." He laughed. "Rock bands will want *four*. Even symphony orchestras might want one, for when musicians play solos. And every time someone bought one of these devices, the people who invented it would get a certain amount of money."

"You mean the PERSON who invented it," John said.

"Well, yes. Plus the Academy, which has paid for me to develop it. But if Dean D. Dean were legally named as someone who helped invent it—whether he really did or not—he would get money, too. And that's what he wants."

When the Templetons arrived home, Abigail made turkey burgers and John made slaw (!!!!!). There is, of course, no need for me to tell you how he made it (or how extremely delicious it was).

The family spent the rest of the night trying to do homework, trying to read, and trying to stop worrying. But no one could. Everyone's feelings had been somewhat bruised by the events at the theater, and it was difficult for any Templeton to fall asleep—except for Cassie, of course, who had no trouble whatsoever.

1. In the text, it says that "audible" means "able to be heard with your ears." And yet snakes do not have ears. Isn't that interesting? Yes, it is. Discuss.

2. I have just learned that the term "coleslaw" is an English version of "koolsla," which is a shorter version of "koolsalade," which is a Dutch term for "cabbage salad." Isn't that both slightly intriguing and yet also somewhat disappointing?

3. Explain, briefly, what Gwendolyn Splendide meant when she said that Dean D. Dean might "sue the Academy." Do so in the form of a traditional Hawaiian hula dance. If you do not know what that means, ask your parent, orthodontist, or teacher to explain it. They will tell you for free. Do not ask your attorney to explain it.

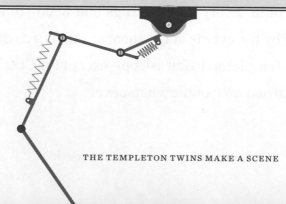

CHAPTER 8

# A SAD CHAPTER THAT WILL LEAD TO SOMETHING EXCITING

I must now inform you that, in their excitement to attend the technical rehearsal on Monday after school, it was possible that the twins did not do *quite* all their homework. One finds oneself harboring such suspicions because, on Tuesday, Abigail and John had a bit more homework than usual, suggesting that they had undone work still remaining from the day before. I frown on this, and I know you do, too. Still, we must remember that the Templeton twins are not perfect. Indeed, with the exception of myself, no one is.

That is why, the next day after school, the twins had no time for anything more than a quick snack (apples, cut up and dipped in honey, and—I am relieved to be able to say—a glass of milk), before going to their rooms and getting down to their homework.

Nanny Manny was not pleased with this. He wanted the twins to do their homework, yes. But ever since they had presented him with an easy, comfortable, lightweight means of keeping his glasses on—which, had the Professor invented it, would probably have been named something like the Trans-Cranial Fabric-Strip Eyeglass-Securing Device with Optional Concealing Headwear (or TCFSESDWOCH)—he had been reading up a storm and, to his surprise and delight, having even *more* ideas for "fun" and "serious" activities.

And so while Abigail pondered math problems and John tried to think of something to write about the Civil War, Manny could not resist the temptation to stick his head in their rooms and pelt them with ideas.

"Got a fun idea," Manny said, barging into Abigail's room. "Tell me what you think: We paint the whole outside of the house silver."

"Manny—"

"Okay, gold. Or both!"

"Let's discuss this later. I'm busy."

"Sure. I'll be back."

Shutting the door to Abigail's room, Manny walked briskly to John's room. He opened the door and was greeted with the barking of Cassie, who was lying on John's bed. "John. Serious idea. We shave off all your hair—"

"Manny—"

"—paint 'Save the Earth. Recycle' on the top of your head. See, that way—"

Cassie suddenly sat up alertly, perked her little triangular ears, barked once, and then leaped off the bed and hurried out of the room. John heard the front door close. He and Nanny Manny traded a look and went to investigate.

Downstairs they beheld an unusual sight: Professor Templeton, home early. He looked weary and worried. "It's me, John," he said absently. "Hello, Manny."

"Papa!" John said as Abigail joined them. "Are you okay?"

"Oh, I'm fine. Just very tired." He put his briefcase down slowly and scratched Cassie's head. "Now that Gwendolyn has frozen the production, a lot of people want me to change my mind about refusing to allow Dean D. Dean to share in my close-up device."

"Who wants you to change your mind?" Abigail asked.

"Everybody. Porter Shorter. Roger Prince. Claire Light. Four actors, three musicians, the orchestra conductor, and the person in charge of writing and printing the program. Plus others I can't even remember."

"They should mind their own business," Abigail said.

The Professor gave a little smile and made his way into the living room. "Well, it is their business, dear," he said, falling into a chair with a sigh. "A lot of people have worked hard on the show, and they want it to go on. But this isn't just about the show. It's about the ability of the Academy to stay open. They've paid me to develop the device, and they want to see if it works. If it does, it will make money, and the Academy needs the money if it's going to stay open."

"They can't really believe that Dean D. Dean helped you invent the close-up device," John said. "Because that's ridiculous."

"I don't know what they believe," his father said. "They may not really care. They just want to get the show going again. Although . . . " Here he paused and frowned. "Gwendolyn certainly seems to believe it. And that's what's important."

Now, I admit that this quiet, sad little exchange is not as much fun to read as when Manny bursts into someone's bedroom and says, "Hey, this'll be fun—let's cover your dad's car with melted chocolate!" or "Okay, let's be serious. Let's wash all the windows in the house.

With toothbrushes," or something of that nature. But this exchange is about to produce an exciting, dramatic development. So just be patient, if that's not asking too terribly much of you.

The Professor sent Manny home early. Because the twins had not had time to prepare dinner, the Templetons went out for pizza. Then they all came home. The Professor read, the twins finished their homework, and everybody went to bed.

Isn't that fascinating? No, it isn't. It's quite normal and routine. However, before they said good-night to each other, John and Abigail conferred in her room, and things became much more interesting and fascinating and so forth.

The twins talked a little about how terrible a person Dean D. Dean was, and how unfair it was that he was making their father so sad. And then suddenly Abigail paused, as though something had just occurred to her (which, in fact, it had).

"Remember when we thought the problem with Manny's glasses was the straps, but it really wasn't?" she said.

John nodded. "It was the *kind* of straps."

"What if that's what's going on here? What if Dean D. Dean isn't the real problem?"

"WHAT A THRILLINGLY INSIGHTFUL AND ASTUTE POINT YOU HAVE JUST MADE, MY BRILLIANT SISTER," John did not say. Instead he said basically that, but in a much more efficient way, by muttering, "Huh," followed by, "Because—" (He began to see what she was getting at.) "Because we've been thinking that the problem is Dean D. Dean," he said. "But really the problem is that people believe a story that isn't true."

"And even more important than *that*," Abigail said excitedly, "is that *Gwendolyn Splendide* believes a story that isn't true. And she's the boss."

"So *that's* the problem."

And with that, the twins commenced a brainstorming session. By this, I do not mean that they somehow caused thunder and lightning and rain to occur inside their heads. "A brainstorming session" is a get-together where people meet and try to come up with ideas for solving a particular problem.

The twins talked about Gwendolyn Splendide and how she was probably dazzled by Dean D. Dean's elegant clothes, because she herself was a wearer of and an admirer of elegant clothes. She also, they decided, must be impressed with Dean D. Dean's overall handsomeness and suave manners.[22]

They talked about Dean D. Dean, and the absurdity of supposing that he was capable of helping a genius like Professor Elton Templeton create anything. John said, "Dean D. Dean can't invent anything. He probably wouldn't even know how to turn Papa's lens device *on*."

And then—can you see what's coming? Because I must admit that I did not—Abigail had an idea so stupendous, so perfect, yet also so obvious, that John could only shake his head and say, "*That* . . . is genius."

That evening they told their father, and the twins burst into gigantic smiles when he said, "My goodness, I think that will work." The Professor grabbed the phone and made several calls.

---

22. Are you familiar with the word "suave"? Obviously, I am. It means smooth or relaxed, and it is, as so many words are, French. It is pronounced "SWAHV" and rhymes with BLAHV.*

* BLAHV is not a word.

## FOR FURTHER STUDY

1. Why is it that some ideas are only obvious once someone has thought of them? NOTE: If you can truly answer this, then you are even smarter than I am, so never mind.

2. True or False or Don't Be Silly: A brainstorm is a hurricane in one's head.

   T        F          DBS

3. How true is the following statement:

   "It will not surprise me to learn that the Narrator looks stylish, attractive, and 'smart' whether he is wearing normal clothes or fancy clothes."

   a. Entirely true.
   b. Pretty much completely true.
   c. True beyond question.
   d. As true as true can be.
   e. All of the above, plus "Totally true."

CHAPTER 9

# DEAN D. DEAN DEMONSTRATES HIS SMARTNESS

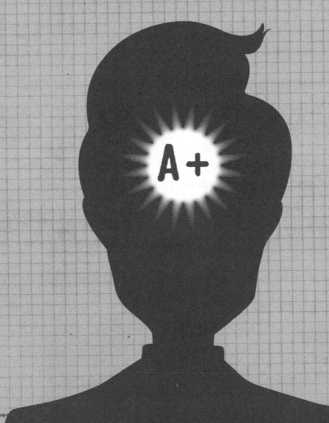

The Templeton twins were now called upon to face one of the most daunting challenges of their young, daunting-challenge-facing lives. But before we discuss that, I am going to assume that your next question is, "What does 'daunting' mean?"

I'm glad you asked it, to the extent that you really did ask it. "Daunting" means frightening or intimidating. It is one of those words you almost always see in just one or two forms. You either see "daunting" (as in "The Templeton twins now faced a daunting challenge") or you see "undaunted" (as in "No matter how daunting the challenge they faced, the Templeton twins remained undaunted"). What you never see is anything like "I would love to go skydiving but am daunted by it" or "I have no current plans to see the movie *The Screaming Undead Prowl Our Grocer's Frozen Food Aisle,* because I don't care for daunty movies."

Where were we? Oh, yes: the daunting challenge. The Templeton twins had to undauntedly face the dauntiness of the following challenge: to get through an entire day of school—to pay attention and answer questions and take out a piece of paper and a pen for a pop quiz, and form two lines for layups in gym, and "hang out" at lunch, and everything—when all they wanted to do was daydream about what would take place later that afternoon and cackle with satisfaction.

Finally the school day ended and the twins went home. As soon as Manny arrived they told him the plan, and he expressed his deep admiration for it by uttering, in a low tone of wonder, "Whoa. Serious *and* fun!"

He then drove the twins to the Academy, dropped them off at the Professor's workshop, and went on by himself to the theater. As he walked briskly down the aisle toward the stage he saw that the entire production team for *Let's Live Life!* was present, as was Gwendolyn Splendide. And standing beside her was Dean D. Dean. He was immaculately clad (clad is a slightly fancy way of saying "dressed") in a suit of light gray with a thin white pinstripe, plus a pale-yellow shirt and a deep-blue tie.

"Thanks for coming, everyone," Manny announced. "Professor Templeton is running just a little late but he'll be here any second now."

"I should hope so," Dean D. Dean said. "We are all very busy people." He gracefully waved an open hand toward Gwendolyn Splendide. "Especially Miss Splendide here—who, as you know, is Dean of the Academy and, therefore, the boss of everybody except me."

"Oh, Mister Dean," Gwendolyn Splendide said playfully. "The Professor told me he had an announcement to make. If it's what I suspect it is, I think you'll find this meeting quite—"

"Sorry we're late!"

It was Abigail, staggering down the aisle, her arms laden with a huge stack of drawings and typed papers. Behind her came John, lugging big cartons full of sketches, plans, and diagrams. Finally there came Professor Templeton, carrying a stuffed, bulging briefcase in each hand. The twins and the Professor labored to climb the little stairway that led from the auditorium floor to the stage, shuffled across to the middle as everyone moved aside to give them room, and dropped their various papers and boxes and briefcases onto the stage with little explosions of slaps and bumps.

"There," the Professor said, catching his breath. "Thank you all for coming."

Dean D. Dean stepped forward and eyed the pile of papers suspiciously.

**WHAT ARE YOU UP TO, PROFESSOR?**

he asked sharply. "Because I warn you: I will not be toyed with." Before the Professor could reply, he added, "And neither will Miss Splendide. Isn't that right, Madame President of Everything?"

"Why, yes, it *is*," Gwendolyn Splendide said.

"Of course," the Professor said. "That is why I owe you an apology, Mister Dean."

"How dare y—" Dean D. Dean started in surprise. "What? You owe me an apology?"

"Yes," the Professor said. "You said you've been working very closely with me on the development of the close-up lens, didn't you?"

Warily, Dean D. Dean said, "Yes . . . "

"And Miss Splendide, you believe that Mister Dean should be allowed to share in ownership of the device based on how much he has worked on it?"

"Based on his obvious familiarity with the project, yes, Professor," she said.

"I couldn't agree more," the Professor said. "Mister Dean, I trust you have another copy of that agreement I so rudely tore up the other day?"

Dean D. Dean pulled a document from his inside jacket pocket and handed it to the Professor. "Don't get clever. I have five more."

"Believe me, Mister Dean, I couldn't get clever if I tried." The Professor plucked out a pen from his own pocket, clicked it, and turned to the document's last page. He was just about to sign it when he gave a little smile, looked up, and said, "Oh. One thing. Before I forget . . . " He put the document and the pen down on the stage and picked up the first few pages from the stack that Abigail had carried in. Holding them up before Dean D. Dean's face, he said, "Look at this. The graph of magnification as a function of light intensity." He pointed to the paper and continued, "This little blip here—any idea where it came from?"

"Eh?" Dean D. Dean stared at the page and muttered, "Uh . . ."

"Because look at the value at thirty thousand lumens. What do you see?"

Dean D. Dean studied the graph but seemed not to know where exactly to focus on it. Finally he said, "I don't see anything unusual."

"Except for the fact that it's almost asymptotic!" the Professor said with excitement. "And then it straightens out again! Have you ever seen such a thing?"

"I, uh, no. Never have."

"And then, compare that—" The Professor, moving with unusual quickness, put those papers down and grabbed a drawing from the box John had carried in. "—to the results we obtained here." He pointed to a diagram. "And it makes no sense! At least to me. Perhaps you can explain it."

"Well . . . perhaps . . . " Dean D. Dean said, but then said nothing more.

"Remind me: Were we measuring incident intensity, or reflected intensity?"

"I . . . I don't—"

"Because, as I know you recall, we worked on this for a *week*," the Professor said, shaking his head at the memory of it. "Remember how it drove me crazy?"

"No. I mean yes. I mean I wasn't there."

The Professor snapped his fingers. "That's right! You were working on the reflector form, weren't you?"

"I—kind of, yes, in a sense . . . "

"And you did it brilliantly." The Professor turned to the crowd of onlookers, who were watching this exchange in fascination. "I kept saying to him, 'Parabola, parabola, parabola.'" He turned back to Dean D. Dean and asked, "And what did you say?"

"I don't remember." Dean D. Dean bent over and grabbed the document and the pen and held them out to the Professor. "Just sign this and we'll discuss it later."

"Of course." The Professor took the papers and the pen and was about to sign the last page, when he again put them down, opened one of his briefcases while murmuring, "Just one more thing . . . " and, with a look of perplexity, pulled out a table of numbers and waved it at Dean D. Dean. "Can you please explain these values to me? Because if they're accurate, I think you really may be on to something."

"Later!" Dean D. Dean snapped. He snatched up the document and the pen and stood up and held them out. "Just sign!"

The Professor shrugged. "Certainly." He took the pen, turned to the last page, and signed. He held on to the document.

"FINALLY," Dean D. Dean laughed. "All right. No, I cannot explain those values to you. I didn't work on that part of it. I worked on some other part."

"Ah! Of course." The Professor rolled up the document and shoved it into the pocket of his big blousy white shirt, then dug through one of the briefcases as he said, "You worked on the voltage problem." He laughed as he pulled out a diagram and handed it to Dean D. Dean. "Show them the mistake I made."

Dean D. Dean scanned the drawing frantically and said, "There's nothing wrong with this. It's fine."

The Professor stood next to Dean D. Dean and frowned at the drawing. "Oh. Sorry." He gently took it and turned it around. "You're looking at it upside down."

"I knew that! I meant it looked normal for upside down!"

"Did you work on the bulb specs?"

"I—Yes! I said it needs a bulb!"

"How many?"

"One! But a really good one!"

"Actually, it uses ten bulbs."

"Look, it doesn't matter!" Dean D. Dean held out his hand. "Just give me the document and we'll all get back to work."

"I think it *does* matter, Mister Dean."

Everyone—well, almost everyone—gasped. Because this last sentence was said, not by Professor Templeton, but by Gwendolyn Splendide. She was staring evenly and without warmth at Dean D. Dean. "I, for one, would like to know exactly which parts of this creation you *are* responsible for."

"Who cares!" Dean D. Dean cried. He reached out and snatched the signed document from the Professor's pocket and waved it around. "He admits I worked on it! He signed this!"

"No, he didn't," John said.

Dean D. Dean gave a gasping laugh of disbelief. "What? He did *so*! YOU ALL SAW IT! HE SIGNED IT RIGHT HERE! LOOK!"

He held out the signed page toward the twins. Abigail peered at it and read the signature.

X _General George Washington_

Then she said, sweetly—or, rather, fake-sweetly—"That's not your name, Papa."

"Mister Dean," Gwendolyn Splendide said sternly. "It is becoming obvious to me that you had nothing to do with Professor Templeton's invention."

"But—"

"You have deceived me. And when Gwendolyn Splendide is deceived, she feels like a fool." She directed a sad, sorrowful look at the Professor and said, "Professor, I owe you an apology. This creation is yours and yours alone." She addressed the others. "Everyone, the production is hereby unfrozen." All the production people were about to cry "YAY!" and applaud and give each other high fives, when they saw Gwendolyn Splendide wheel on Dean D. Dean and continue coolly, "Mister Dean, you may leave the building and I will thank you never to return."

142

THE TEMPLETON TWINS MAKE A SCENE

Dean D. Dean grit his teeth in fury as he glared, first at the Professor, and then at the twins. He drew himself up into a straight, dignified posture; adjusted the knot of his deep-blue tie; pulled sharply on the sleeves of his light-gray jacket; bowed toward Gwendolyn Splendide; and murmured, "As you wish." He turned away lightly, then looked back at everyone with an expression that said, "I am not embarrassed, and you will all rue the day you crossed me." He nodded and, with a single graceful step off the stage, plummeted into the orchestra pit, where he landed with a horrible clatter among the chairs and music stands and yelled, "OW!"

When Dean D. Dean climbed out of the pit, it was obvious he had injured his left foot or his leg. He looked up and saw that everyone was staring at him. "My role in these proceedings is not yet over," he said calmly. Then, limping, he lurched his way up the aisle and out the door.

Everyone was too stunned to speak. Finally Gwendolyn Splendide cleared her throat.

"Ladies and gentlemen," she announced. "I apologize for the unnecessary inconvenience I've imposed on you. Let us contact the cast and the orchestra and meet back here in twenty-four hours, at which time we will run through an excellent dress rehearsal and prepare for the opening, on schedule, of *Let's Live Life!*"

At that everyone finally *did* cheer and clap and start talking at once. Finally Roger Prince signaled for quiet. "The Dance Department has the stage all day tomorrow until around four-thirty," he said. "So let's say we'll start at five o'clock. Break at seven for dinner, back at eight, and we'll go however long we need."

As the excited group resumed chattering, John turned to his sister and said, "Dean D. Dean won't just say, 'As you wish,' and go away and never come back."

Abigail nodded. "Remember what he said last time?"

John nodded. The two of them said, at exactly the same time,

## 'THIS ISN'T OVER.'

## FOR FURTHER STUDY

1. Do you know what "asymptotic" means?

   a. No, but for some reason I believe that the
      Narrator knows what it means.
   b. No, but I have no doubt that the Narrator
      does, and that is what is important.
   c. No, but I am absolutely certain that the
      Narrator does, for he is indeed smarter than
      I am, as he has always maintained.

2. A train is moving westward from Istanbul (in
   Turkey) to Paris (France) with 100 people on
   board. Do any of them know what "lumens"
   are? If so, what are their names?

3. Show, in the form of a line graph or a pie chart,
   why you think this chapter was particularly
   well narrated.

CHAPTER 10

# A MYSTERY IS SOLVED AND THEN IS MYSTERIOUS AGAIN

T he twins got home from school at around 3:30 the next day. They went inside and dropped their book-laden knapsacks in the front hallway. And then, as though in response to a secret signal, they stopped and looked at each other. The house was silent.

"That's weird," John said.

Abigail nodded.

Can you guess what John thought was "weird" and why Abigail agreed with him? Oh, please. To figure out the answer to this question, I suggest—in fact I insist—that you think the following things, in exactly these words, in your own personal head:

1. Nothing happened to John or Abigail when they entered the house. Therefore the thing that is "weird" must be something they saw, something they smelled, or something they heard.

2. The Narrator has not mentioned anything that the twins saw or did not see, or smelled or did not smell. But he did say that "the house was silent." Thus, what is important is the fact that the twins *did not hear anything*. How could that be "weird"?

3. Silence is only weird if you expect to hear something. What might the twins have expected to hear?

I will now reveal the exciting answer to that question. If you guessed it correctly, please accept my heartiest congratulations. Well, wait. No, not my heartiest. I think I will reserve my heartiest congratulations for *myself*, for something wonderful that I will do. But I will offer you my acknowledgment that, by following the above (intelligent and perfectly worded) instructions, you were able to divine (which in this case means "guess") the answer.

*What was weird was the fact that Cassie did not come barking and leaping and wagging and being ridiculous to the door to greet them, as she always did.*

"Maybe she's sleeping," Abigail said, but in a voice that suggested she didn't really believe it. The twins went into the living room.

"Cassie?" John called. They paused and heard nothing. "I'll check upstairs," he said. "You look in the kitchen."

John ran up the steps, skipping every other one. Abigail hurried into the kitchen. "She's not here!" she called to her brother.

After a minute he came down, looking grim. "She's not upstairs, either."

At that precise second they heard a sharp knock on the front door. It made them both jump. They ran to open it and beheld Nanny Manny Mann. He was smiling. He said, "Big dress rehearsal today, right?" but, when he saw how worried the twins looked, he stopped. "What's up?"

"We don't know where Cassie is," John said.

"It's Dean D. Dean!" Abigail said. "He took her!"

"We don't know that—" Manny began.

"Who else could it be?!"

"Guys?" Manny said. "Before we freak out, let's make sure."

They looked everywhere: under every bed, in every closet and bathroom, and in the basement. But when they met back in the kitchen, all three of them had the same report: The dog was nowhere to be found. Then Manny turned toward the back door, which led out of the kitchen into the backyard. "Look. Somebody broke in!"

The twins joined him at the door. It was true: Someone had slammed something—a rock, say, or a hammer—into the mechanism that held the door shut, and shattered it.

"Okay," Manny said. "If Dean D. Dean took her, he'll call and tell us what he wants. But what if it was some burglar, and Cassie just ran out the door? That means she might be running around the neighborhood."

For the next hour John remained home in case a phone call came, while Abigail and Manny drove around, calling for Cassie and peering at every yard, porch, and garden they could. But they couldn't find her, and when they got back to the house John had to report that no call had come, either.

Then, to everyone's surprise, the doorbell rang. Imagine their utter amazement when they opened the door and saw . . .

But first, guess who they saw when they opened the door. And don't say "Cassie," because smooth-haired fox terriers aren't big enough to ring doorbells. I'll wait while you guess.

Still waiting.

You'll never get it. Indeed, *I* would never get it, and— as you know—I happen to be a nonpareil guesser.[23] But just guess anyway and then I'll tell you.

---

23. "Nonpareil" is, as I'm sure you suspected, French. It is pronounced "Nahn-pah-RELL" and means "excellent" or "great." It is also the name of a chocolate candy covered with millions of little white dots of sugar, which sounds delightful but which, frankly, I can't stand.

That's your guess? Well, you're wrong. Unless, that is, you said:

Dean D. Dean, holding a leash, at the end of which was a bright-eyed, ecstatic-to-be-alive Cassie.

"Hello, children," he said pleasantly, or at least in a manner he thought was "pleasant." He wore a sport jacket of tiny light-blue and gray checks, a pink shirt with no tie, and charcoal-gray slacks. He also had a big black bootlike cast on his left foot, and held a cane in his right hand. "I was passing by and saw this delightful doggie wandering around, so I thought I'd return him to you. Say hi, Cookie!"

Abigail was too amazed to speak. John, meanwhile, stepped forward and said, "It's 'Cassie.' And he's a she. Thank you." He held out his hand and Dean D. Dean gave him the leash.

Indicating the leash, Abigail said, "This isn't ours." She took the collar off Cassie and handed it, with the attached leash, back to Dean D. Dean. Cassie trotted into the house as though nothing at all was amazing or astounding or weird.

Abigail turned to Dean D. Dean and said, "You're up to something."

Dean D. Dean took a step away from her, opened his eyes wide in a protest of innocence, and said to no one in particular, "Well, I like that, I must say. I return this girl's dog to her, and this is the thanks I get. Yes, young lady, I am planning something. I'm planning to go back to my home, which—for your information—is at 2430 Golden Apple Road."

He turned and strode off—well, actually, he hobbled, using the cane to take the weight off his left leg—down the walk toward his car. But before getting in, he turned back to the twins and said, "That's right. I said 2430 Golden Apple Road, which is the address of the location of my residence. Where I live. You're welcome."

In the kitchen, while Cassie slurped up water from a dish on the floor and Abigail knelt beside her, stroking her back, John said, "This doesn't make sense. If he took her, why did he bring her back? You'd expect him to keep her to force us to do something."

"Maybe he thinks your dad will share that invention with him if he's nice," Manny said.

Abigail gave a little laugh. "Forget it. Dean D. Dean doesn't know how to be nice." She shook her head. "Also, why did he keep telling us 2430 Golden Apple Road?" Suddenly her eyes grew wide and she stared at John and Manny. "The rehearsal! Let's go!"

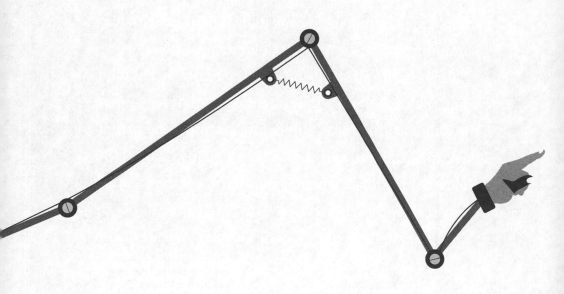

## FOR FURTHER STUDY

1. Which answer best describes the list of thoughts
   the Narrator provided to help you figure out
   what the twins thought was "weird"?

   a. Clear, well-organized, and logical.
   b. Kind, generous, and sensitive.
   c. Dashing, clever, witty, droll, deft, astute,
      and wise.
   d. All of the above, plus brilliant.

2. True or False or Believable? A Lie, Obviously,
   Narrator (Everyone: Yes?):

   Dean D. Dean's explanation of how he found
   Cassie is believable and persuasive.

   T       F       BALONEY

3. Keeping in mind the three principal causes of the
   War of 1812, when Dean D. Dean appeared at
   the door with Cassie, wasn't it amazing?

CHAPTER 11

# BAD DRESS

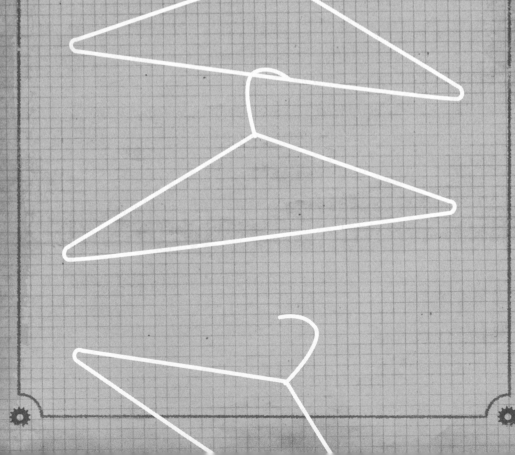

I f you have taken part in the production of a big musical, you will be familiar with what I am about to describe. If you haven't (because you think you are somehow above such activities, or you "don't have time," or you "don't like having fun," or whatever your supposed excuse is), then you are missing out on one of the most exhilarating experiences a person can have. And you likely have no idea what a "dress rehearsal" is.

One thing it is *not* is an occasion in which women's garments practice how to be women's garments. That is to say, it is not a "rehearsal" for "dresses." Rather, a dress rehearsal—of a play or musical or an opera—is a rehearsal in which everything is done exactly as it will be in the actual public performance. The actors wear their actual costumes and makeup. The actual scenery and props are used. If there is a band or an orchestra, the musicians play their actual parts. The actual light and sound cues are executed. Everybody *really means* it.

The atmosphere of a dress rehearsal consists of a combination of joyous celebration and nerve-wracking tension. Everyone is thrilled that the "big night" is almost here. But everyone is even more anxious over the fact that, from now on, it is too late for major changes.

Can you imagine such a thing? No, you cannot. That is why I insist you take part in a musical at your school, church or synagogue, army base, summer camp, community college, or astronaut training academy.

How, you are no doubt wondering, did this night's hastily assembled dress rehearsal for *Let's Live Life!*, with its full-scale, real-time debut of the Live Performance Horizontal-Tracking Individual Close-Up Lens (LPHTICUL) turn out?

Thank you for asking. It was a disaster.

Here is what happened: The twins and Nanny Manny Mann arrived at the theater to find a scene of enormous activity and excitement. It seemed that everyone was moving here and there and everyone was talking (or shouting) at the same time.

Abigail found all this tumult a little unsettling. We are not surprised at this. She was a brainy, writerly type, who enjoyed quietly figuring things out in her head. Whereas John—who, as a drummer, was used to being calm in the center of a lot of noise and hectic activity—found the hustle and bustle of this dress rehearsal interesting. Manny Mann started out thinking that the general excitement and high spirits of the event were a lot of fun, and then soon found himself even more interested by the sight of several very pretty actresses.

When the twins wandered onstage and inquired as to where their father was, someone pointed up toward the ceiling. The Professor was up on a catwalk, giving the LPHTICUL a last-minute inspection.

This does not mean that he examined the device while taking a cat for a walk. A "catwalk" is a narrow walkway built above the floor in theaters (and factories) that enables workers to examine machinery and equipment up near the ceiling. The Professor had climbed up a tall ladder and walked calmly out onto the catwalk high above the set and out of sight of the audience. The twins watched as he examined the device. He seemed perfectly pleased with what he saw.

Suddenly a burst of voices came from further "upstage" (away from the audience), where the twins could see various grown-ups standing around a young man. They heard people crying "What?!" and "You can't be serious" and "Oh, come ON . . . "

Porter Shorter, the stage manager, detached himself from this group and called up into the catwalk area, "Professor! Need you here. We have a situation."

The twins watched as the Professor crossed back to the ladder and climbed down. He joined Porter Shorter, who was standing with Claire Light, the lighting director; Roger Prince, the director; and a young student. Porter nodded to the student and said, "Tell the Professor what you just told us."

"I was crossing the quad, like, five minutes ago," the student said. "And this guy comes up to me and says, 'Tell everyone in the theater that Steve Stevenson wants them to know that somebody has sabotaged[24] the close-up lens and they should check it out.'"

---

24. Do you know what "sabotaged" means? And even if you do (which I doubt), do you know how to pronounce it? It goes without saying that I know both of these things. It is pronounced "SA-bo-tahzh," with the final syllable enunciated in the same way as the last syllable in "garage." Both of these words are French, and the "ahzh" sound is a very common sound in French words. You may also have heard that sound in the (French) word "decoupage," which is a craft technique for covering a surface in pictures. "Sabotage" means to tamper with or damage (which is pronounced "DAM-idge," not "dah-MAZH") something so that it won't work. A nice sentence full of French words, then, would be, "Hey, I have a good idea! Let's go out to the garage and sabotage the decoupage." I urge you to say this to someone the next time you go to France.

"What did he look like?" Roger Prince asked.

The student shrugged. "Just some guy. He had a beard and was wearing sunglasses."

Then everyone (except the Professor and the twins) started talking at once. Finally the Professor signaled for quiet and, when the tumult had died down, said, "I was just examining the device. And it looks fine. I wonder if this could be a prank."

Porter Shorter snorted. "Only one way to find out."

Everyone agreed that they couldn't lower the device, take it off its track, and inspect it in a workshop. That would take too long and tie up the stage, making it impossible to rehearse the show. Instead, Claire Light and the Professor agreed to go back up to the catwalk and inspect it there while the rehearsal got under way.

That is why, when the twins sat in the audience with a few dozen people from the Theater department, thrilling to the overture and waiting excitedly for the moment in the opening song when the LPHTICUL would descend and demonstrate what it could do, they were bitterly disappointed. Because it did not descend. The show just went on without it.

1

MISSED
STEP

2

MISSED
LINE

3

MISSED
NOTE

DRESS REHEARSAL

4

5

JUST
MISSED

THAT'S A
WRAP

They weren't the only ones disappointed. *Everyone* was. The actors and the dancers were disappointed. The crew and the orchestra were disappointed. And, perhaps because of that, many little things started to go wrong. Dancers slipped. Actors forgot their lines. Musicians hit wrong notes. A piece of scenery fell over. A lighting fixture burned out.

There is a saying in the theater that goes, "Bad dress, good show." It means: If you have a bad dress rehearsal, you'll have a good opening night. I don't know whether it's true, but that night, at the main theater at the Thespian Academy of the Performing Arts and Sciences, everyone *hoped* it was true, because this was one of the worst dress rehearsals in the Academy's history.

And, of course, there was the matter of the LPHTICUL itself. What if it didn't work? Then the future and the fate of TAPAS itself would be in doubt.

The only good news came during the intermission. The twins ran backstage to check in with their father, and arrived in time to hear the Professor telling Porter Shorter that he and Claire Light had indeed found an act of sabotage against the LPHTICUL.

"That Stevenson guy was right," Claire Light said. "The sabotage was in the lighting booth. Someone had thrown the breaker *and* rerouted the instrument into a bogus dimmer."

What does this mean? I do, of course, know. I wonder if I should tell you. Very well: A "breaker" is an important switch that automatically switches itself off in an emergency. It "breaks" the circuit, which cuts all electricity to the light in question, so that the light doesn't burn out or get damaged. When the breaker is thrown, the light doesn't go on—and it can't go on until the breaker is switched back on, or "reset." It is very possible that you yourself have breakers in your house or apartment. Ask your chief financial officer, great-aunt, or staff electrician to show you.

In this situation, just before a dress rehearsal, there would be no normal reason for anyone to throw the breaker, so everyone knew this was not only unusual, but possibly sinister.

What does it mean that someone "rerouted the instrument into a bogus dimmer"? I'll tell you, but first: Isn't that a wonderful sentence?

It means, basically, that someone had unplugged the LPHTICUL from its proper control and plugged it into some other one, so that, even if the breaker had been reset, the device still wouldn't work.

These two facts could only mean one thing: Someone had tried to interfere with the Professor's invention.

"What are we going to do?" Porter Shorter asked.

"Well, we fixed the problems in the booth," Claire Light said. "But we haven't had time to really check everything out. I think we shouldn't use it tonight. After the rehearsal, we'll go over it top to bottom."

"That will mean that the first time we actually use it will be during the opening tomorrow night," Roger Prince said.

She shrugged. "I know. But we have no choice."

"We don't want to risk anyone getting hurt," the Professor agreed. "But it's odd. This was a very minor bit of mischief. It was easy for us to discover and easy to fix. It's not exactly what I would call 'sabotage.'"

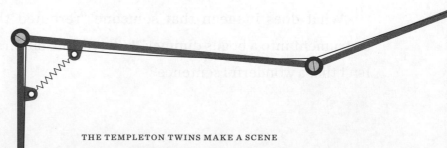

Everyone acknowledged the strangeness of this, but there was no time to discuss it. They all dispersed to get ready for the second act, which went just as badly as the first.

## FOR FURTHER STUDY

1. Using hand gestures, explain why you think the Narrator would be excellent in a lead role in a big musical.

2. If a dimmer dims a light and a breaker breaks a circuit, what does a cruller do?

3. Have you ever sabotaged a theatrical performance? If so, create a beautiful ballet explaining the name of the production you sabotaged, the date, the location, and the reason for the sabotage.

# CHAPTER 12

# THRILLING THINGS BEGIN TO HAPPEN IN AN EXCITING MANNER

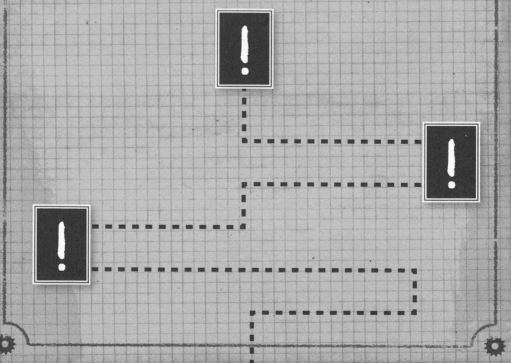

I t was Saturday. There was no school. The Templeton twins spent a pleasant morning neither playing the drums nor working on cryptic crossword puzzles, but running around, yelling and kicking and shouting. Can you guess what they were doing? Oh, please, you can so.

The Templeton twins spent the morning playing soccer. You will, or will not, be surprised to learn that Abigail's favorite position on a soccer team was as a forward, while John preferred to play defense. These positions have an interesting connection to the twins' hobbies, and it is unfortunate that we have no time to discuss that at the present moment.

Let us simply note that, for Abigail, the strategy and clever figuring-things-out required to get the soccer ball through the defense, past the goalie, and into the goal appealed to the part of her mind that unlocked puzzles. For John, the basic mechanical demands of blocking the other team's advance, getting the ball, and transferring it to other players on his team was as satisfying as playing a section of good, accurate timekeeping and then pulling off an interesting little transitional move on the drums.

I see that I have done what I said I would not do—I have discussed how the twins' preferred soccer positions were in some way related to their hobbies. You have very cleverly manipulated me into doing that, by not saying anything and just letting me blab on and on. Well, fine. I'm sure you're very pleased with yourself, but I can assure you it won't happen again.

After lunch, the Professor was catching up on his mail and the twins were arguing over whose turn it was to wash the dishes, when the phone rang. The Professor was needed at the theater to deal with certain technical matters. Rather than take the twins with him to "hang around" the theater for six hours, he decided to let them stay in the house, *alone and unsupervised*, until around five o'clock, when he would return and bring them to the theater for the grand official opening of *Let's Live Life!*—and, of course, for the first-ever public display of the Live Performance Horizontal-Tracking Individual Close-Up Lens.

And so it was—isn't that a splendid phrase?—that, sometime in the middle of the afternoon, the Templeton twins were alone at home when the doorbell rang. When the twins (and Cassie, barking in a particularly ridiculous manner) answered the door, they beheld a United Express Delivery person holding a large package.

The package looked heavy but turned out to be very light. "Templetons? Need a signature." He held out a clipboard and Abigail signed her name as John and Cassie watched from the open door. The delivery person left.

Suddenly, at the end of the walk, there was Dean D. Dean. He was still wearing the black, bootlike cast on his left foot. In his left hand, along with his cane, he held the collar and leash he had used when returning Cassie the day before. He waved a gigantic dog biscuit and called out, "Cassie! Here, girl!" And before John could stop her, Cassie dashed out the door, past Abigail, and right on up to Dean D. Dean! Can you imagine?

He gave her the biscuit and, as she gnawed on it, clipped the collar around her neck and started pulling her toward a black SUV that was parked right in front of the Templetons' house. Dean D. Dean looked up and called, "There's a beach ball in that box. Get your nanny to drive you to the park and throw it around. Meanwhile, we'll be at my house at 2430 Golden Apple Road."

He opened the passenger door and Cassie jumped in. He hobbled quickly around to the driver's side door, got in, revved up the car, and drove off. There was someone in the backseat, but the twins couldn't see who it was.

"We have to call the police," Abigail said.

"Wait." John looked not only vexed, but *extremely* vexed. "How did he know there's a beach ball in the package?" Suddenly he looked at his sister. "He sent it! He sent it so he could be waiting there when the guy delivered it, so he could lure Cassie out!"

Abigail impatiently pushed the box aside. "John, come on! I'm serious! We have to call the police."

The phone rang. Abigail went to the little table in the hallway and answered. Immediately a familiar voice said, "And no police."

She motioned John over and switched the phone to its speaker. She said, "Listen, Dean—"

"I said, do *not* call the police. Or we kill the dog."

Another voice could be heard in the background, saying, "What? No. Forget it."

"Dan—"

"I'm not killing anyone's dog!"

Dean D. Dean said to Abigail, "I'll call you back," and hung up.

As Abigail hung up, John said, "I don't think the police will do anything, anyway."

"Why not?" his sister protested. "They stole our dog!"

The phone rang again. John answered. "And no police," the voice said. "Or we will *sell* the dog."

The background voice said, "Dean, how? Once the police get here we won't have *time* to sell the dog!"

The voice sighed and said to John, "Or we will LET THE DOG RUN AWAY. Okay? Everybody got that?" And he hung up.

"We have to go get Cassie," Abigail said. "Right now."

"How?" John said. He snapped his fingers. "He told us how." John hurried into the kitchen, where a phone number had been attached to the refrigerator door with a magnet. He brought the number and Abigail dialed.

The person answering the phone barely had time to say hello before Abigail said, "Manny? It's us.

Dean D. Dean just stole Cassie. We need you to drive us to go get her."

Manny immediately said, "I'll be right over."

While the Templeton twins anxiously waited for Manny Mann to arrive, several things happened. Abigail began to fear the worst and started to get weepy. John had to calm her down. Then John thought about what had just happened and started to get weepy. Abigail had to calm him down. Then they had an urgent discussion about how they would go about rescuing Cassie . . .

And it is here that the latest lesson John learned from his hobby paid off.

You will recall that incorporating the use of his new cymbal into his practice routine had the effect of making his other cymbals seem a little less important. He *worried* about them less. And because of this he was actually able to do more.

The same thing happened now. "It's not enough just to rescue Cassie," he said. "We have to do *more* than that."

"You're right," Abigail said. "Which means . . . " She thought for a second. "What we need is a way to get

Cassie back *and* make the Deans go away. I mean, make them leave town."

"Okay, but why would they leave?"

"They'd leave if they thought they were going to get caught. That's why they said no police."

John nodded. "But if we tell the police, either they won't listen to us because we're a couple of kids, or they'll show up in their police car and Dean will let Cassie run away."

Abigail scrunched her face up in concentration. "So we need a way to get the police to show up *after* we have Cassie safe with us. Then the Deans will run away."

John began, "But we can't just . . . " Then he got that faraway, distracted look on his face, the one that signaled that a) he sensed that he had just had a great idea, but b) he had to wait until it traveled from the idea-having part of his brain to the idea-knowing part of his brain. Once it got there, he explained the idea to Abigail, who suggested some improvements. Then John dashed into the kitchen and down the steps into the basement.

He came back up carrying several things, including several lengths of thin rope, Abigail's knapsack, and his own cassette-playing "boom box" (as I believe it's called). At that moment Manny Mann arrived. Abigail grabbed Cassie's collar and leash, and she and John piled into Manny's car, and they all drove to—

Can you guess where? I know you think you can, but I have my doubts. Please. Take a guess.

"That's easy, Narrator," I can all but hear you say. "You think we're not paying attention, but we are! We happen to know with great confidence that they're going to 2430 Golden Apple Road. So ha ha HA, and so forth."

Good for you, for taking a (somewhat obvious) guess. And good for me, for knowing you would be wrong. Their first stop was the campus of the Thespian Academy of the Performing Arts and Sciences, where they parked near the main theater. Manny waited in the car while the twins went inside.

Things were unexpectedly calm. Neither the cast nor the orchestra had arrived yet. The curtain was drawn, but you could hear people calling out and laughing behind it. John pointed to something and Abigail nodded. He dashed over to where he'd pointed, obtained a certain object, and hustled back to his sister. They looked around, saw no one, shrugged, and hurried out to the car.

"Got it," Abigail said.

"Let's go," John said.

They—

But wait. It will have occurred to you that we have just read a description of John—with Abigail's help—taking something that does not belong to him. There is a word for this—"stealing"—and it is my duty to inform you that stealing is wrong, and one ought not to do it. I know you know this and, more important, I know

I know it. But I think we should forgive the twins on this occasion, for two reasons.

One is, they were only borrowing the object and intended to return it once they had used it. The other is that the object was an essential component of the twins' plan to retrieve Cassie and to thwart Dean D. Dean. The Dean brothers already had a long history of doing bad things to the Templeton twins, their father, and even their dog. Who among us can forget the time Dean D. Dean pointed a gun at Cassie and pulled the trigger? (Answer: Those who haven't read the first book YET.) The twins were willing to commit this little "crime" in order to correct a much larger crime that the Dean brothers had committed.

So, with your agreement that we will forgive the Templeton twins for having borrowed something without asking on this one special occasion, let's move on.

Manny got a little lost once, but the twins knew they had the right address when they saw the black SUV parked in front of 2430 Golden Apple Road. Then the three sprang into action. By this, I do not mean they started jumping up and down and bouncing all over the street and the front yard. I mean that they began to set in motion their Plan. They did the following:

- The twins got out as Manny Mann remained in the car.
- John took the boom box and the object he had obtained and cautiously made his way into the shrubbery alongside the little porch in front of the Deans' house. He hid the machine, *and himself,* in the bushes.
- Abigail put Cassie's collar and leash in her backpack and then—I can scarcely type this, my hands are shaking with such excitement—she walked right up to the front door of the house *and rang the doorbell.*

I know. Isn't that amazing? It's *amazing.* She just walked right up to the door and rang the bell. It seems so brave. You will notice that I have put a double space up there, before this paragraph. I felt I had to, in order to calm myself down before describing what happened next. There. I think I'm ready to proceed.

No, not yet.

Almost calm enough.

There. I have managed to calm myself down suffi-
ciently to describe what happened next.

The door opened. Standing there was Dean D. Dean.
He was dressed in a lovely tan suit, with a crisp white
shirt and a red-and-gold-striped tie. But so what? Just
because he was wearing nice clothes doesn't mean he
was a nice person. I urge you to remember that for
the rest of your life.

"I think you have my dog in there," Abigail said.

"Where is your brother?"

"At a drum lesson," she said. (You will, of course, realize that this was a lie. Like stealing, lying is wrong, and
one should not do it. But, as we discussed with regard to
the stealing (or borrowing) of the object earlier, I think
we may forgive Abigail for doing something one ought
not do. Abigail—who never lied—felt that Dean D. Dean
did not deserve to be treated the way one would normally
treat a friend, relative, colleague, acquaintance, or even
a total stranger. She felt it was permitted to lie to Dean
D. Dean this one time, in order to rescue Cassie. Some

people will not agree with her. But I do, and I expect that you do, too.)

"Oh, really?" Dean D. Dean said. He looked past her toward the street. "And how did you get here?"

"Our nanny drove me," she said.

Dean D. Dean's attention fixed on Manny Mann's car. He nodded grimly and limped past Abigail, down the steps, and over to Manny's car. He tapped on the window. Manny Mann lowered it. Dean D. Dean leaned in and said, "Abigail is going to visit with me for a little while. You can leave, and I'll bring her home later."

Manny Mann shrugged and said, "Okay." He started the car and slowly drove away.[25]

Dean D. Dean returned to the porch, opened the door wide, and said to Abigail,

**WON'T YOU COME IN?**[26]

---

25. Can you believe it!?

26. And she went in! Can you believe that? Frankly, I can't believe any of this, but it really happened!

# FOR FURTHER STUDY

1. It seems almost mean to interrupt the thrilling flow of the story with some silly questions, doesn't it?

   a. Yes, which is why I refuse to answer them.
   b. No, because I know the Narrator only asks these questions to advance my education and improve my reading experience.
   c. Yes, but now it's too late. You've tricked me into reading all the way down to answer "c."

2. When Abigail lied about John's "drum lesson," did you throw the book across the room and cry, "That is disgraceful! I refuse to read another word about such wicked children!"?

3. If you answered "yes" to question 2, how are you able to read this question?

CHAPTER 13

# THE TEMPLETON TWINS DO A VERY CLEVER THING *AGAIN*

T he inside of the Dean brothers' house reminded Abigail of some other place, and in a moment she realized what it was: the inside of their *other* house, the one the Templeton twins had been in the last time they had had to deal with Dean D. and Dan D. Dean. In other words, it was a poorly furnished mess.

Abigail walked down a little entrance hallway past a living room that contained just an old sofa and a big television. On the other side of the hallway was a dining room that contained nothing at all—no dining table, no chairs. The kitchen was straight ahead. Someone was standing in its doorway. He was wearing tan pants and a light-green shirt and was not nearly as beautifully dressed as his brother. As usual.

"Hi, Dan," Abigail said.

Dan D. Dean glanced nervously at his brother, who was just behind Abigail, and said, "Look, just get your father to sign over some share of this lens thing, and we'll let the dog go and that'll be that."

Abigail said, "How do I know you even have our dog?"

Dean D. Dean bent toward her with a big, fake, phony smile and said, "Why don't you call her?"

Abigail yelled, "CASSIE!" From a space beyond the kitchen, and below everyone—in other words, from the basement—came the barking of the agitated, ridiculous, smooth-haired fox terrier.

**BARKETY BARK BARK BARK BARK BARK BARK BARK BARK BARK BARK BARK BARK BARK**

"I want to see her," Abigail said.

"And so you shall!" Dean D. Dean said. "Go look in the basement."

"Dean—" Dan D. Dean said in a worried tone. "I'm not so sure that's a good idea—"

"Why, it's an excellent idea, Dan," Dean D. Dean said. "How else is this young lady going to make sure it's the right dog?" He took hold of Abigail's elbow and began to steer her into the kitchen, toward the basement door.

She stopped. "How do I know you won't shut the door and lock me in the basement?"

"Bwa-HA-ha-ha." Dean D. Dean gave a fake laugh. "Why would we do a silly thing like that?"

"You did it last time."

"That was different. Last time we kidn—I mean, we *visited* with you and your brother. This time we're visiting with your *dog*. The two visits are obviously not the same thing."

"Still," Abigail said. "You need to come down there with me."

Dean D. Dean's eyes widened as though he had just heard an excellent idea. "Why, that's an excellent idea!" he said. "Don't you think so, Dan?"

"I don't know, Dean—"

"Of course you do!" Dean D. Dean held out his hand to Abigail. "I will go downstairs with this lovely young lady, while you go on your errand."

"Oh, that's right," Dan said abruptly. "I have to go somewhere because, uh, of an errand I have to go run and, um, do something somewhere . . ."

"No," Abigail said, refusing to move. "Both of you have to come with me."

"I can't!" Dan said. "I have to run an errand!"

"Then I'm not going down there," Abigail said.

"As you wish," Dean D. Dean said. "You heard her, Dan. Both of us have to go down. You'll just have to run your errand afterwards."

"But what if there isn't time?"

"Dan, there will be plenty of time."

Dan D. Dean sighed and shook his head as his brother ushered him and Abigail through the kitchen toward the door to the basement. Dean D. Dean unlatched the hook that locked the door and put his hand on the doorknob, but then stopped. He turned to Abigail and said, "Of course, I don't want to let the dog out. So when I open it, be sure to hurry through."

He opened the door and stepped aside to allow Abigail to go first. Then the following things happened with unbelievable speed and breathtaking excitement:

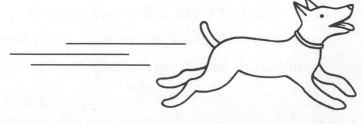

THE TEMPLETON TWINS MAKE A SCENE

Abigail sidestepped away from Dean D. Dean and *shoved him through the door,* down the basement steps!

Dan D. Dean cried,

**HEY!**

and grabbed her!

JOHN TEMPLETON CAME OUT OF NOWHERE (Well, not actually "nowhere." He had sneaked out of the bushes and into the house through the front door when no one was looking) and pulled his sister away from Dan D. Dean and shoved *him* through the door! And down the steps!

Cassie came charging and skittering and bounding up the basement steps and out into the kitchen, her usually bright white fur rendered somewhat icky with spiderwebs and dirt, her eyes mad with happiness and relief and smooth-fox-terrier ecstatic deliriousness!

The twins slammed the basement door shut and locked it with the latch.

Abigail took off her backpack and dug around inside it until she found Cassie's leash. She gave it to John, who called, "Cassie! Sit!"

Cassie saw the leash, heard the name tag and the license tag jingling on it, and began to leap into the air over and over and over and over and over and over and over (etc.) until John finally said, "Oh, for goodness' sake!" and grabbed her and clipped on the leash. MEANWHILE—

Abigail had taken two lengths of rope out of her backpack. She gave one to John and, with the other, STARTED TO WRAP IT AROUND HERSELF!

Let me repeat that. Abigail had taken two lengths of rope out of her backpack. She gave one to John and, with the other, STARTED TO WRAP IT AROUND HERSELF!

Once Cassie was on the leash, John began to wrap himself in his piece of rope, too!

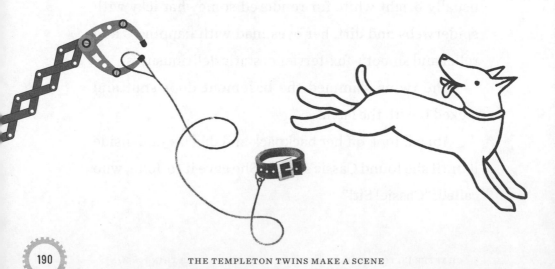

You are wondering: What could possibly be going on? Who wraps themselves with rope—especially in a strange house, with two grown-up (and angry) twin brothers desperate to get at them?

If you will kindly stop interrupting, you will see that certain things are happening in a certain manner. Your questions, and other thrilling questions, will be answered as you read the following:

One—or both—of the Deans began pounding on the basement door. "Very funny, little girl," Dean D. Dean said. He was not laughing and, indeed, gave no indication that he thought anything was in fact very funny. "Now let us out and you won't be hurt."

"We don't believe you," Abigail said, winding the rope around herself tightly enough so that it didn't fall to the floor, but loosely enough so that it wasn't uncomfortable.

"Who's 'we'?"

Dan D. Dean said, "I think the brother is there, too."

"YOU 'THINK'?"

"It happened so fast—"

"Shut up, Dan." Dean D. Dean moved closer to the door. "All right, look, you two. Let us out, and we'll let you go."

"Do you promise?" Abigail called back.

"Oh, yes, we promise."

"Well . . . " Abigail looked at John. He had finished wrapping rope around himself. He gave her the thumbs-up sign and, with Cassie on her leash, moved quickly—well, as quickly as the ropes around him allowed—out of the kitchen to the front door and then outside. Abigail put on her backpack, made sure *her* rope was properly adjusted, then called toward the Dean brothers, "Well, okay. If you promise. I'm going to unlock the latch. But you have to give me one minute to get out of the house."

"Deal!" Dean D. Dean said. "Splendid! Hurry up!"

Abigail called, "Okay, here I go," and then gave the latch a quick little flick with her finger. Immediately the Dean brothers, believing the door to be unlocked, slammed into it, expecting it to fly open. But it did not fly open. Abigail had not actually unlocked the door but had left it latched. The door shuddered but remained closed.

"OW!" someone called.

"You didn't unlock it!" Dean D. Dean yelled. "That's not funny!"

"You were supposed to give me a minute!" Abigail called. "Now step back." She paused. "I said step back!"

"We're stepping back," Dean D. Dean said.

"No, you're not. You're right next to the door."

"OH, ALL RIGHT. HERE." Dean D. Dean's voice receded a bit as he and Dan D. Dean backed down the basement steps. "All right? Happy now?"

Abigail quietly unlatched the door and then immediately shuffled as fast as she could out of the kitchen and through the front door.

John was waiting for her on the porch. Cassie was sitting excitedly nearby, her leash looped around a post on the porch railing. Quickly, Abigail put her hands behind her back and John coiled a smaller length of rope around them. Then he put his hands behind his back and, as best she could as they stood back to back, she wrapped a small length of rope around *them*. It was then time for the Dean brothers to appear—which they did, banging out the front door in wild desperation, and then stopping abruptly when they saw the Templeton twins.

Dean D. Dean gestured toward all the rope and said, "What . . . what . . . what . . ."

"I don't like this, Dean," Dan D. Dean said.

"What . . . what . . . "

"You kidnapped us, and then you tied us up," John said.

"WHAT?"

"I mean, look at us," Abigail said. "We're all tied up."

"WE didn't do that! YOU did!"

"*Oh, really?*" John said with unusual emphasis. "Is that going to be *your story*?"

"What—It's no story! We didn't touch you! Wh—"

"Dean!" Dan said, holding up his hand. "Listen."

Everybody listened. From somewhere in the distance, the sound of an approaching police car siren could be heard.

"Oh. Right. We called the cops," Abigail said. "I may have forgotten to mention it."

"THEY CALLED THE COPS!" Dan D. Dean said.

"So what?" Dean D. Dean said. "We haven't done anything. We borrowed their dog. Big deal. We'll deny it and it will be our word against theirs."

"You tied us up," John said.

"We did no such thing!"

"That's not what the police will think."

"Don't be ridic—"

Dean D. Dean suddenly stopped speaking. His eyes shifted from the twins (and their rope) to his brother. The siren grew louder. Dan D. Dean clutched his brother's arm and said, "We have to get out of here."

"All right, Dan. Now don't panic. I know it looks bad. The police—"

"The police aren't going to believe us!" Dan D. Dean's voice got more frightened with every word. "They're going to believe two children. What are we going to say— that they tied *themselves* up? No one will believe that!"

"But it's true!" Dean D. Dean barked.

He made a move toward Abigail, but immediately the Templeton twins dodged and weaved and dashed over to the far side of the porch. The siren grew louder.

"You can stay if you want," Dan D. Dean said, slapping himself all over until he found what he was looking for: the keys to the black SUV, in his pants pocket. "I'm leaving."

"But we didn't DO anything!" Dean D. Dean protested. "Except, okay, we *borrowed* the dog—"

"Dean! We have to go."

"NO." Dean D. Dean glared at his brother and said, "It can still work. Where is the, uh, costume?"

"In the house."

"Get it!"

The siren was getting louder. As Dan hurried into the house, Dean D. Dean sneered at the Templeton twins,

## YOU THINK YOU'VE WON. BUT YOU HAVEN'T.

Dan emerged carrying a paper bag. He offered a hand to help his brother hobble down the porch steps, but Dean swatted it away and said, "Start the car." Dan ran to the black SUV, threw the paper bag in the backseat, got in the driver's seat, and started the engine. Dean limped as quickly as he could to the car, flung himself into the passenger seat and, with an angry look at the Templeton twins, slammed the door shut. The black SUV drove off with a squeal and a roar.

As the twins wriggled and prodded their way out of the ropes, John called, "Okay, Manny!"

Out of the bushes on the side of the house, Manny Mann appeared, carrying the boom box. He was beaming. "That was the *coolest thing* I have *ever done*," the nanny said. "We are *finished* with those guys."

The boys traded a high five. But then John noticed that Abigail looked . . . vexed. Do you know what "vexed" means? It means "troubled" or "bothered." It so happens that I know what it means without having to look it up. Aren't you impressed? Oh, please, you are so.

"I don't think we are finished," she said. "You heard Dean. He said, 'It can still work.' They're going to do something terrible.

**I HAVE KIND OF A SENSE OF FOREBODING.**

Manny Mann said, "Huh?" But John, who was used to Abigail having an excellent vocabulary and had learned many words from her, knew that "a sense of foreboding" meant a feeling that something bad was going to happen.

I think this is a fine place to end this chapter. With a sense of foreboding.

## FOR FURTHER STUDY

1. Match the topic in column A with the correct description in column B.

| A | B |
|---|---|
| This chapter | Very exciting |
| The present chapter | Very *exciting* |
| Chapter Thirteen | *Very* exciting |
| The current chapter | Very exciting! |

2. True, False, or Hey, Wait a Minute: John was very clever in figuring out how to hide an entire police car in the bushes.

T    F     HWAM

3. Without looking at it in this sentence, spell "foreboding."

CHAPTER 14

# A TIMELY TEETER-TOTTER TALK

A s the twins and their nanny walked toward Manny's car (which he had simply driven around the block and parked up the street, before replacing John in the bushes), John reached toward the boom box and pushed a button. The little door swung open and John popped out the cassette (with POLICE CAR WITH SIREN APPROACHING written on it). "We'd better get this back to the sound control board at the theater before anyone notices it's missing," he said.

"We have time," Abigail said. "Let's drop Cassie off at home first."

Everyone agreed that was a good idea. Do I need to inform you that, as they drove, Cassie immediately leaped onto Manny's lap and sat between him and the steering wheel, and availed herself of the opportunity to paint unusual patterns with her nose on the driver's window as she excitedly looked outside? I decline to do so.

Abigail, meanwhile, brooded in the backseat. Finally she announced, "None of this makes sense."

"None of what?" Manny asked.

"None of anything! Look, we're pretty sure it was Dean D. Dean who broke into our back door and stole

Cassie, right?" John nodded. Abigail continued, "So why did he bring her back? Plus, who is Steve Stevenson? How come he told that student about the sabotage, but didn't come in and tell everyone else? And why was the sabotage so easy to find and easy to fix?"

John added, "Also, why did Dean D. Dean seem to know so much about Papa's invention, but when he was asked specific questions he obviously didn't know *anything* about it? If Dean D. Dean wanted to kidnap us, why didn't he and Dan just do it? Why did he send us that beach ball and keep telling us his address?"

They were driving past a park. Abigail asked Manny to pull over and suggested that they walk Cassie while they pondered these mysteries. And so Manny parked the car in a little lot near a small playground. The twins and their nanny got out. Abigail clipped the leash on Cassie and, lost in thought, slapped it into John's hand. "Let's split this up," she said. "I'll think about what we don't know." And she wandered off toward the playground.

"And I'll think about what we *do* know," John said. He handed the leash to Manny and he, too, started walking and thinking.

About a minute later the twins converged on the seesaw in the playground. It was as though they had planned to all along—which, of course they had not. Without saying a word the twins each took a seat and began seesawing up and down. Had you been there, all you would have heard for about five minutes was the repetitive squeak of the seesaw (which sounded roughly like "EEEK-ee . . . *EH*! EEEK-ee . . . *EH*!"), and the slight breeze in the trees. Even Manny and Cassie were silent as they meandered around in, respectively, a brooding and ridiculous manner.

Finally Abigail stopped the seesaw's motion and said, "The real mystery is Steve Stevenson. We've never met him. And we've never met anyone *else* who's met him, except for that student."

John nodded. "The only person who has met Steve Stevenson is someone who doesn't work on the show. That's just weird."

"Plus, Dean D. Dean didn't really kidnap Cassie yesterday. He just wanted us to think she was missing, and then he brought her back."

"On the same day that the lens was sabotaged."

"And then today, he really *did* kidnap her, but he kept telling us where she was. He didn't call Papa or the Academy and say, 'Give me what I want or we'll do something to this dog.' It was just *us* he was interested in. Why?"

John shrugged. "Something makes us special to Dean D. Dean. Maybe we have something he wants. Maybe he thinks we know something that nobody else knows."

"But what?" Abigail said. "We're hardly ever at the theater! Dean D. Dean has probably been there more times than we have." She paused and added, "Although we've never seen Dan there, have we?" She suddenly looked away. "Wait a minute . . . "

John's eyes went wide. "Abby! I know what *we* know that no one else knows!"

Abigail looked up at him and said, "So do I!"

The Templeton twins said at exactly the same time, *"We know who Dan is!"*

"No one's ever seen Dan at the Academy," John said. "Just Dean. Those people probably don't even know that Dean *has* a twin. But we do!"

"Okay, that's true," Abigail said. "But why does that matter? What does Dan have to do with anything?"

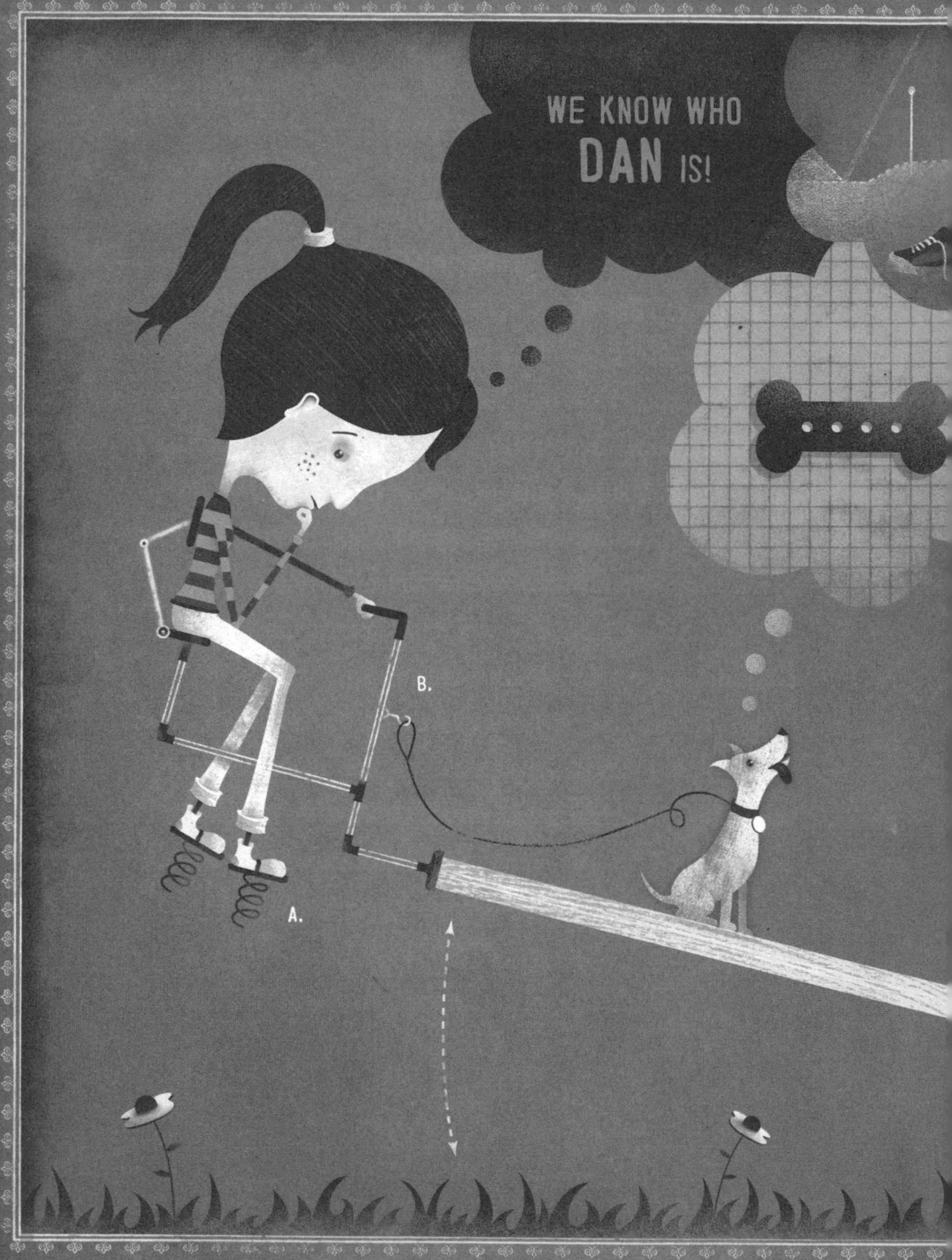
WE KNOW WHO
DAN IS!
B.
A.

WE KNOW WHO
DAN IS!

"Well . . . when Dean took Cassie yesterday, he knew that when we saw she was missing, we would worry. And call Papa or the police."

"*Or* stay home and wait for some phone call from whoever took her. Or drive around looking for her."

"Yeah, but . . . so what?" John frowned. "Why does it help them if we're stuck at home or driving around? Because—"

"Because then we couldn't go to the theater!" Abigail interrupted—somewhat rudely, in my opinion, but I suppose we should forgive her, considering the excitement of the moment. "We would have wanted to go right after school to watch them get ready for the dress rehearsal."

"So we wouldn't be there, and maybe recognize *Dan* if he was sneaking around!"

Abigail's expression was one of amazement and wonder. "*Dan* did the sabotage in the lighting booth."

"But wait." John frowned. "Why wouldn't they just have Dan do the sabotage during the day? While we're at school? Dean and Dan would know that we'd be at school from eight in the morning until three. That's plenty of time for Dan to do whatever he wanted."

Abigail looked stymied for a second, and then all at once grew animated. "Because! Remember what Roger Prince said when they scheduled the dress rehearsal? The Dance Department had the stage all day yesterday until four-thirty. The Deans probably figured it was too risky to try anything with all the dance people there. They probably waited until four-thirty, when the Dance people left and the musical people took over and things got confused for a while."

"YES! Dean kidnapped Cassie to keep us away from the theater until Dan sabotaged the stuff in the lighting booth. Then, once he was done, Dean brought Cassie back."

The twins got off the seesaw at exactly the same moment and commenced to walk around again. Abigail said, "Okay, but why did he bring her back? Why didn't Dean just keep Cassie? Especially since he was going to kidnap her again today."

"Well . . . if he had kept Cassie," John said, in an I'm-figuring-something-out-as-1-go tone of voice, "we would have spent all day yesterday, and all last night, and all this morning and this afternoon trying to get her back.

We would have brought Papa and other grown-ups—and even the police. He didn't want that. So he kept telling us where she was, over and over. He knew we would go to his house, but he didn't want us to go there *until this afternoon*. It's like he was waiting for something . . . "

"I've got it!" Abigail cried. They stopped walking. "Dan did the silly sabotage yesterday. And he made the sabotage easy to find, and easy to fix, *on purpose*. So everyone would think, 'Okay, we found the sabotage and we fixed it.' And it worked! They've all stopped looking for problems."

"But then today," John said, "they took Cassie, got us to their house, and were going to keep us in the basement—for the same reason. So we couldn't be at the theater—"

"—while he went there again."

Abigail squinted, remembering something. "Dan kept saying, 'I have an errand to run.' He was waiting until we were trapped in the house, and then he was going to go to the theater to—"

They looked at each other. And at exactly the same time they both said, "To steal the lens."

"That's what Dean D. Dean meant when he said, 'It can still work,'" Abigail said. "We don't have time to take Cassie home. We have to get to the theater right now!"

The twins ran after Manny, and then everyone, including Cassie the you-know-what dog, piled into the car and set off for the TAPAS campus and the theater.

I think we can all agree that we have reached an extremely exciting moment in this story. But if you found yourself thinking, "Um, excuse me. The Dean brothers can't just breeze into the theater and steal this big piece of equipment, while the stage is swarming with cast and crew getting ready for Opening Night, and while Dean D. Dean has a bad foot and can barely walk," then you are as—well, *almost* as—intelligent as I.

Because, in fact, the twins' theory was wrong. The Deans were not planning on stealing the device.

What they were planning was much worse.

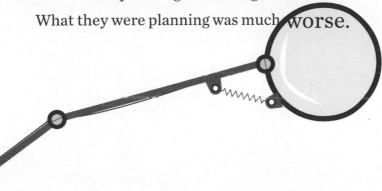

## FOR FURTHER STUDY

1. Weren't you impressed with how the Narrator described the sound of the seesaw?

2. Which do you prefer to think about—things you know, or things you don't know? Present your answer in the form of a short skit about Christopher Columbus.

3. What did Abigail mean when she said, "What?"

THE TEMPLETON TWINS MAKE A SCENE

# CHAPTER 15

# THE TEMPLETON TWINS REALLY DO MAKE A SCENE

A t the twins' urging, Manny drove about as fast as a person could drive through a quiet neighborhood and with a dog in his lap. They reached their destination about an hour before the show was to start. People were already milling about out front of the theater, buying tickets or enjoying the early evening before going in. The twins were about to get out of the car when John said, "Wait. We can't leave Cassie in here."

"I'll take her," Manny said. "You guys go."

The twins maneuvered their way through the crowds outside and milling around in the lobby. No one had been admitted to the theater itself, but the ushers at the doors recognized the twins and let them in.

The first thing the twins did upon entering the empty auditorium was to see if the young woman in charge of the sound was at the control board in the last row. To their disappointment, she was. So after the twins greeted her, Abigail motioned for her to join her in the aisle and said, "Can you explain something to me?"

"Sure," the young woman said, and left the console to stand beside Abigail, who pointed at the big loudspeakers mounted high on the walls on either side of the stage and asked, "Do those ever fall off?" While she spoke, John tiptoed over to the sound console and silently replaced the police siren tape in its storage slot. By the time he rejoined his sister, the sound director had laughed and said, "I hope not! No, they're bolted into the wall."

Abigail thanked her and the twins hurried down the aisle, up onto the stage, and into the wings area behind the curtain. "We have to find Papa now," John said.

"Wait," Abigail said. "Steve Stevenson knew what Dan was planning to do yesterday. Maybe he knows something about what Dan is planning to do today. Let's see if we can find him."

In the wings, Porter Shorter, the stage manager, was consulting papers on a clipboard, wearing a headset and talking into a microphone and seeming to do five different things at once. As the twins arrived, Claire Light hurried up to him. "Porter," she said. "I have a question for your guy. Steve Stevenson. Where is he?"

Porter Shorter covered the mouthpiece and said to the lighting director, "What are you talking about?"

"Steve Stevenson. Your assistant. Where is he?"

"He is *not* my assistant. I don't *have* an assistant."

Claire Light looked puzzled. "I heard Steve Steven-son was with you."

"No, I think he's with Ron," Porter said. (The twins knew that "Ron" was Ron Carpenter, the head set designer and chief of the construction crew.)

John looked at Abigail. She was nodding intently. "Come on," she said.

The twins made their way out of the stage area to the work areas in the back and ended up in the big, warehouselike space where the sets for Act II were kept. Several students were there, giving last-minute touch-ups of paint to the scenery. John asked one of them if Ron Carpenter was around and was directed to a tall man across the floor. The twins went up to Ron Carpenter, who was speaking to an assistant.

"Excuse me," Abigail said.

The tall man scowled. "Who are you? What are you doing back here?"

"They're Templeton's kids," someone said.

"Oh. Okay." He smiled at the twins and said, "What's up? Make it fast."

"Do you know Steve Stevenson?" Abigail asked.

Ron Carpenter shook his head. "Who *is* that guy?" he laughed. "No. I've never met him."

Abigail asked, "He's not your assistant?"

"I wish. I think he's Claire's assistant."

"Thanks!" Abigail said.

She led John back to the wardrobe room, where Emily Garment, a plump, brisk woman who was head of the wardrobe department, was pinning up a costume on one of the actresses. Abigail said, "Excuse me—"

The woman, whose mouth held a line of tiny straight pins between tightly shut lips, shook her head and made a noise that even the twins knew meant, "Not now. I'm busy."

"I just have to ask you one question. Do you know Steve Stevenson?"

The woman rolled her eyes and grunted, "Mm! Mm mm-mm mm-mm MM mm."

Abigail turned to John and said, "I think what she means is, 'No, but everybody ELSE does.'"

The woman nodded her head "yes."

The twins walked quickly away. Out in the hallway, surrounded by people dashing here and there, John was suddenly aware of a new sound: a faint sort of whispery, rumbly murmur, way off in the distance. And in a second he realized what it was. It was the audience, starting to file into the theater, settling in, greeting each other, and building up their excitement for what was about to come.

Abigail said, "That's everybody. In all the departments—costumes, and sets, and lighting, and sound. Nobody has ever met Steve Stevenson, but everybody thinks everybody *else* has met him."

John said—somewhat impatiently, if you must know—"Come on, we have to find Papa."

The twins set off to find their father. The Professor was in the stage manager's office, surrounded by reporters, giving an interview. Photographers lurked around, their cameras chattering and snapping photos. And presiding over everything was Gwendolyn Splendide. She was stunning in a black silk suit over a vivid pink blouse, and absolutely glittering and jingling with jewelry.

"Papa!" Abigail whispered.

The Professor, acutely aware of the fact that he was being watched by reporters and cameras, smiled and said, "Not now, dear. It's almost curtain time!"

"It's an emergency!" John whispered more loudly.

"Oh, the delightful TEMPLETON twins," Gwendolyn Splendide sang. "*Aren't* they superb? James and Ahndrea, DO join us."

John looked at Abigail. Abigail looked at John. They turned and marched out, back into the auditorium (which was by now about three-quarters full, and buzzing), down a side aisle, up onto the stage, and into the wings.

"*We* have to do it," John said. He noticed his sister's attention was fixed on something high above him. He turned and looked. It was the LPHTICUL, hanging in place.

"They don't plan to steal it," Abigail said. "They *really* sabotaged it."

John nodded. "Come on."

They dashed over to the ladder that led up to the catwalk on which their father had examined the LPHTICUL. Abigail went first. She had just managed to climb the first three rungs, with John immediately behind her, when the twins heard a sharp, "Hey! You two! Get down NOW."

It was Porter Shorter. He was furious. "What do you think this is?"

"There's a problem with the lens," John began.

"We caught it last night and checked it again this morning. There is no problem." A young woman from the stage crew, in black pants and a black shirt, was hurrying past. Porter Shorter all but grabbed her arm and said, "Watch these two for me until intermission."

"But—"

"Just make sure they stay out of trouble." He walked off, muttering.

The young woman scowled. "Fine." She looked at the twins, who were fidgeting with nervousness. She made a sour, put-upon face and said, "Come on."

She led them to a small room. Inside were several chairs, a small couch, and a table laden with bottled water, cans of soda, and a big plate of cookies. Abigail saw them, caught John's eye, and said, "Hey, can we have a cookie?"

It is here that I must tell you that the Abigail who asked this (perfectly reasonable) question was unlike the Abigail we have grown to know and admire. Because she did not ask it in her normal, intelligent, sensible-person voice. She asked it in the voice of a silly little girl. This, of course, immediately got John's attention.

The young woman, who did not know how unusual this tone was for Abigail, threw herself into a chair and waved her hand. "Sure. Whatever."

The twins went up to the table and Abigail said as softly as she could, "We have to get out of here. Let's be brats."

John nodded and reached for a cookie. Abigail then reached for the same one. "Hey!" John said in as childish—and loud—a manner as he could. "You can't have that one! It's mine!"

"I saw it first!" Abigail whined.

"You're such a *liar*, Abigail," John said. "You did *not*."

"You're the liar, John!" she replied. "Plus you're a poopyhead!"

"Shhh!" the young woman said sharply. "People can hear you!"

"Tell John to stop being a poopyhead!"

"I am NOT a poopyhead!"

"Are too! Are too! Are too!" Abigail reached out and— and believe me, I am as appalled by this as you are—began to grab for as many cookies as she could.

"STOP it!" John said, and grabbed her hand. "Put them DOWN."

"John, quit it!"

"SHUT UP!" the young woman said, half commanding and half pleading.

"Abby, let them GO!" John swatted his hand down onto the edge of the plate, which flipped it up into the air and sent the cookies flying all over the room. The plate landed on the floor with a clatter.[27]

John pointed and said, "See what you made me do, Abby!"

"Oh, you are in TROUBLE, John," Abigail said, her eyes wide with (fake) horror, while trying not to laugh.

"Guys, look," the young woman said, trying to be calm. "Now let's just clean all this up—"

"You can't boss us around," Abigail sneered.

---

27. This—what the twins just did—is called "making a scene." It's an old-fashioned term for behaving in an emotional manner in public and embarrassing innocent bystanders. It is not to be confused with "doing a scene," which means to perform a part of a play or a movie, or "making the scene," which is another old-fashioned term meaning, to arrive at or take part in an event.

"Yeah, only our father can tell us what to do," John also sneered.

"WELL, WHERE IS HE?"

"In Porter Shorter's office," Abigail said sweetly.

"Fine. STAY HERE." The young woman ran out of the room.

And, after a second, so—of course—did the twins.

## FOR FURTHER STUDY

1. "Brat" is a nickname for "bratwurst," which is a kind of German sausage. When Abigail said, "Let's be brats," did she mean, "Let's be a couple of German sausages"? Why or why not?

2. Emily Garment, the wardrobe mistress, had straight pins in her mouth because she was pinning up a dress and needed a number of them close by, in a hurry. You do know never to put pins in your mouth, don't you? Or don't you?

3. Are you a poopyhead? How can you be sure?

THE TEMPLETON TWINS MAKE A SCENE

# A BRAVE AND DARING FEAT OF COURAGE AND FEARLESSNESS!

Even though the backstage area was swarming with people, the twins reached the foot of the ladder to the catwalk without being challenged. Why? Because the show was about *ten minutes* from starting, and everyone was frantic and absorbed in their own tasks, with some final little emergency to tend to. After a quick glance revealed that no one was watching them, the Templeton twins started to climb the ladder.

Abigail went first. In th—

I suggest that you sit down before you read what follows. If you are already sitting down, I suggest that you stand up, pull yourself together, and sit down again. I also recommend that you have available a glass of water, a fan, some smelling salts,[28] and a tank of oxygen, in case you are overcome—as you almost certainly will be—by the astounding events I am about to narrate and the expert manner in which I am about to narrate them.

Abigail went first. In the beginning it was easy, but by about ten rungs up she started to get anxious. There was

---

28. I am quite sure you don't know what "smelling salts" are. They are *not* little shakers of salt that can smell. That would be absurd, because if we know nothing else, we know that salt shakers do not have noses. Smelling salts are certain chemicals that, in the olden days before you and even I were born, people used to hold under the noses of persons who had fainted, to revive them.

simply no room for error. One false step or missed grab and she could fall a great distance to the stage.

Then there were six rungs to go. The air started to feel thick and stifling. Five rungs, and she was distressed to note that her hands were getting sweaty and slippery. Four rungs—it was actually becoming hard to breathe. Three rungs—she heard John say, "You okay?" and gasped, "Fine." Two rungs—her foot slipped off a rung. But her other foot held and she tightened her grip. One more rung—and she pushed off hard with her feet and pulled herself up onto the catwalk. John, whose arms were stronger from playing drums, looked not quite as frazzled as he came up behind her.

The catwalk was basically a long, narrow bridge, lined on either side with a metal banister that ran at the height of the twins' shoulders. About a foot above the catwalk and extending alongside was the single track that the device rolled along. It was about at the level of the twins' knees. Abigail and John made their way down the catwalk until they came to the LPIITICUL.

What they beheld was a single metal wheel, about the size of a Frisbee, fitted to the track. Hanging from it was

CHAPTER 16: A BRAVE AND DARING FEAT OF COURAGE AND FEARLESSNESS!

225

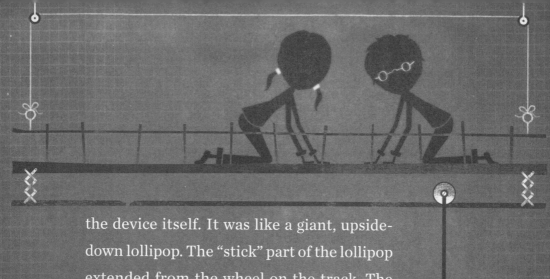

the device itself. It was like a giant, upside-down lollipop. The "stick" part of the lollipop extended from the wheel on the track. The "candy" part of the lollipop was the close-up lens itself, a round piece of glass about the size of a knight's shield.

Mounted near the top of the stick was a box of controls. It was screwed shut. John fished his Swiss Army knife out of his jeans pocket, extended a screwdriver blade, and managed to extract one of the two screws holding the cover plate shut.

A sudden swelling, rainlike noise arose from below. It was the audience, applauding. "Hurry up, John!" Abigail whispered. John grimly nodded and started in on the second screw.

The orchestra started playing the overture,[29] a collection of little samples of the music from the entire show, strung together in a sort of musical introduction. The twins knew that when it was over, the full stage lights would come up, the curtain would rise, and the show would begin. They had no idea how much time they had before it would be time for the device to be lowered for the first close-up.

John pulled out the second screw and opened the cover plate. Inside the box was a tangle of wires in red, blue, yellow, green, and black, like a thousand sleeping worms.

"John?"

"Wait—" He peered at the wiring, looking for something that had been pulled loose or cut.

"*John.*"

"WAIT."

"Look."

John looked. Abigail was pointing, not at something inside the control box, but below it: The upright piece

---

29. "Overture," as I explained earlier—look, never mind. It doesn't matter at the moment. Things are too exciting. Other similar French words, if you must know, are "furniture," and two more that just now I cannot be bothered to think of.

of the assembly—the stick of the lollipop—was hanging off the wheel by a single, loose screw. The other screws that would have mounted it securely were gone. One jolt, and the only screw holding the entire device in place would pop out. The whole invention would go plunging down to the stage, perhaps hurting, or even killing—yes, killing—someone standing directly under it.

Abigail dropped onto her stomach, reached as far down as she could, and grabbed the upright piece. "You have to screw it back in. Hurry up!"

John lay on his stomach, too, and discovered that he could just reach the screw. He took a deep breath. Then he fitted the tip of the Swiss Army knife screwdriver into the slot on the screw and, as Abigail struggled to hold the piece in place, began to screw it into the hole that some-one had pulled it out of.

And now I suggest you get out those smelling salts.

"Hey! What are you *doing*?" someone yelled.

Down on the stage, Porter Shorter was glaring up at them. All around him, actors and members of the chorus had assembled in their places, waiting for the curtain to go up. A member of the scenery crew was hustling past. Porter Shorter grabbed him by the arm, pointed at the twins, and snarled, "Get them down from there. NOW." He shoved the crew member toward the catwalk ladder.

Suddenly the music reached a grand closing chord and stopped. The rainlike sound of the audience applauding flooded into the stage area and up to the twins. John gave the screw a final slow turn. "Got it."

"It's not strong enough," Abigail said. "The lens is too heavy!" She pointed toward the control box cover. "Use one of those!"

John realized that he had been clutching the two screws from the control box cover. In fact, his left hand had been gripping them so tightly they had made an imprint in his palm. He put one between his lips so he could use both his hands and began to try to fit the other screw into an empty hole on the mount. If he could screw it in that hole—or even just jam it in—it would take some of the weight off the other screw.

He stopped to wipe sweat from his eyes with the back of his fist, and—

Suddenly everything went quiet.

*Everything.* The orchestra, the audience, the little last-second chatter and buzz backstage: All ceased, as the stage lights came up full and the curtain rose.

To the twins it was like awakening *into* a dream. The lights above the stage where the twins were silently flared into burning life. The twins could feel their heat radiating from every direction. Looking down, John and Abigail could see they were now suspended above a space much brighter than noon on a sunny day, a gigantic box of brilliance and motion. Hovering just beyond it was a hazy black void: the audience. You couldn't see them, but you could sense that they were there, watching and listening.

"Hurry up!" Abigail whispered.

"Ac—" John abruptly stopped talking but it was too late. By trying to speak, he had, of course, opened his mouth. This allowed the screw he had been holding to plummet onto the stage. He looked down in time to see it land harmlessly without hitting anyone.

But Abigail wasn't looking at her brother. She was looking back down the catwalk, where the stage crew member was now striding toward them.

"You two! Up! Let's go!" he said.

"Wait—" Abigail began.

"Are you KIDDING? Is this some kind of PRANK?"

"We're *fixing* it," she hissed.

"It doesn't need fixing. They already checked it out."

"That was yesterday! We just—"

"LET'S. GO."

Abigail was about to protest further when, to her surprise, John stood up and said to her, "He's right. Let's go." He held out his hand.

Abigail took it and stood up. As they moved across the catwalk Abigail said, "Is it okay?" She couldn't hear his answer.

When they climbed down the ladder to the stage, Porter Shorter was there. But he was listening to his headset and could only say to the twins, "I'll deal with you two later."

The twins traded a look and, as though sharing the same thought (which they were), they ran out of the wings and down a hallway to a door, banged through it outside, hurried around to the front of the theater, and went back inside.

All the seats were filled. Even the rear area of the theater was crowded with people standing. The lead actor seemed to be reaching the climax of his opening song, about his hopes and dreams. The audience applauded. But the music kept going very softly in the background, as the leading lady joined him. Then the lights dimmed to about a third of their normal brightness as the lead actor stepped forward—and the Live Performance Horizontal-Tracking Individual Close-Up Lens began to descend from above the stage.

The audience gave a little gasp as the giant upside-down lollipop moved slowly down until its big, clear, round glass lens was positioned right in front of the leading man's face, which instantly seemed to expand to fill the entire area of the lens. Where, a moment before, his face had been a tiny, inexpressive blur on a stage a hundred feet away, it was now five or six times its normal size, his every expression easily seen.

The twins turned to each other and whispered at exactly the same time, "It's like Manny's glasses!"

The actor now sang a new part of the song. And even though this moment was thrilling and triumphant, the new part of the song was quiet, thoughtful, and slow. Everyone could see the little changes in expression that crossed the actor's face as he voiced one thought and feeling and then another. A thousand people held their breath and stared as the leading man quietly sang.

Then he began to move.

He stepped slowly across the stage in order to sing to other characters. The lens moved with him. Another sigh of pleasure rippled through the audience. He skipped quickly across to his right, and the lens moved with him. Then he walked more thoughtfully back to the left, and the lens kept pace.

Finally the slow part of the song led back into the main part of the song. The chorus joined in. The music got louder and more complicated and more victorious. At the final, triumphant chord, all the actors struck their poses, their faces and their gestures all pointing toward the lead actor, whose arms were raised and whose expression—of joy, hope, and determination—was magnified by the lens and could be seen clearly in the last row of the balcony.

The place went nuts.

As you know, I don't usually write sentences like "The place went nuts." Normally, everything I write is intelligent and dignified, such as, "The audience burst into loud applause and cheers." But in this case, I have decided there is no better way to describe the initial public response to the Professor's invention than to draw attention to the nutsiness of the crowd's response.

The entire audience leaped to its feet, clapping and cheering like mad as the actors held their poses, panting and sweating but unable to keep themselves from smiling with delight. In the orchestra pit, the conductor and the musicians were applauding. (The violinists tapped their bows on their violins, which is a string player's way of indicating "yay.")

Abigail and John applauded as hard as they could. People yelled and whistled. John even thought that at one point he heard a dog barking. And then, as the lights from the lens gently dimmed and then went out, and the device rose up and out of sight and the normal stage lighting swelled back, something caught his eye. He tapped Abigail urgently on the shoulder and pointed.

Two people, a man and a woman, were storming up the aisle toward the exit. The man held the woman lightly by the arm, because she walked with a limp. They both looked angry.

They also looked familiar.

## FOR FURTHER STUDY

1. How often do you sing about your hopes and dreams?

   a. Every day.
   b. Once a week.
   c. On the first day of National Hopes and Dreams Week.

2. Do you have plans to sing about them in the near future?

   a. Yes.
   b. No.
   c. It is none of your business.

3. Write an essay on the theme, "I will be terribly hurt if the Narrator declines to listen to me sing about my hopes and dreams." Illustrate it with crude cave paintings.

CHAPTER 17

# THE TEMPLETON TWINS ACTUALLY MEET STEVE STEVENSON

T he twins watched the couple brusquely exit through a door about twenty feet away. John looked at Abigail. Abigail looked at John. Their glances said, wordlessly, "We know darn well who those two are, and it confirms all our suspicions and we're not letting them get away with it." The twins charged through the exit door nearest to them, hustled through the lobby, and burst out onto the steps.

The couple were making their way down the broad steps in front of the auditorium. The twins chased after them. John yelled, "Hey!"

The couple stopped. The twins ran up to them.

"We knew you'd try something," Abigail said.

"I *beg* your pardon," the woman said in a low, throaty voice. She was tall and somewhat bony and wore amazingly heavy, colorful makeup. Her black dress did not fit well, and there was something about her body that looked out of alignment.

"We haven't tried anything!" the man said. He had a big beard and wore sunglasses. "Plus we don't know what you're talking about."

"Oh, come on," Abigail said. "We know it's you." She pointed to the man and said, "You're Dan." She said to the woman, "And you're Dean D. Dean."

"I most certainly am *not*," the woman said. "That is a man's name. A man who I am not. Because, as you can see, I am a woman of the female variety. Now excuse me. My brother, I mean, my husband and I are late for an appointment elsewhere. Come, uh—" she waved her hand around as though trying to think of something. "—Bill."

The couple started walking. The twins walked with them.

"We know what you did, Dan," Abigail said.

"You climbed up when no one was looking and unscrewed the device so it would fall and break and maybe hurt somebody," John said.

"He did no such thing," the woman said. "I should know. Because he is my husband."

"And that's why you're both here now," Abigail said. "You wanted to make sure it fell and broke."

The woman stopped walking and gritted her teeth and looked furious for a second, but then replied, "I deny every word of this. I don't want to make sure of anything."

"But we fixed it," John said. "So it's not going to break."

The woman turned to the man and said, "Tom, these children are upsetting me."

"I thought my name was Bill," the man said.

"All *right*! *Bill*. These children—"

"The question isn't who did the sabotage," Abigail said. "Because we know it was you. The question is, who is Steve Stevenson? Do you guys know him?"

"We are not 'guys,'" the woman said in a sniffy manner. "We are an adult woman and a man with a beard."

"But do you know him?" John said.

"Of course not," the man said. "I mean, just regular 'no.' Not 'of course.' Just 'no.' Now leave us alone. We just came to watch the show."

"Then why are you leaving?" John said.

"Because, uh, I think we don't feel good."

Abigail suddenly frowned and wrinkled her brow, as though she had just had an important thought, which she had. "Wait a second," she said. "You did the sabotage. But how did that student know to tell us about it?"

John shrugged. "Steve Stevenson told him."

"Right. And how did *he* know?"

"Nobody knows how anybody knows anything!" the woman said. She grabbed her companion's arm. "Come, Harold."

"Bill."

"Yes! Fine! Bill! Good-bye, you obnoxious twins," she said. "We hope we never see you again."

She began to lead him away. But the twins dashed around in front of them and blocked their way. "Wait! We're not finished figuring this out yet," Abigail said.

John said to the couple, "Steve Stevenson knew you did the sabotage. That means either he spied on you when you did it, or you told him about it."

The woman drew herself up indignantly and said, "No one spied on anyone and no one told anyone about anything."

"Well," John began, "It has to be one of those—"

"No, it doesn't."

Everyone looked at Abigail in surprise. She said, "There's a third explanation. I can't believe I didn't think of it until now." She turned to her brother and began ticking things off on her fingers. "We know Dan did the

sabotage. We also know that the sabotage in the lighting booth was really simple to find and really easy to fix. So we're pretty sure that it was *meant* to be found."

"Um, honey?" the man said to the woman. "I think we should go."

"No," the woman said in a chilly tone. "I've changed my mind. I want to hear what they think they know."

"No one has ever seen Steve Stevenson except that student. And no one knows Steve Stevenson," Abigail said. "The only thing Steve Stevenson has ever actually done, in any of this, is to tell that student to tell us about the sabotage—"

"—which Dean and Dan wanted us to know about," John added. "It's like Steve Stevenson was *helping* the Deans make sure we found it."

"Right. And what did that student say? That guy who actually *met* Steve Stevenson? He said Steve Stevenson had a beard and sunglasses." She looked at the man. "Like you're wearing right now."

**"BWA HA HA HA!"** the woman laughed, or pretended to. "What of it? Everyone wears sunglasses."

"At night?" John asked.

"Well, no," the woman admitted. "But people have beards at night. A great many, many people. But not me, you will notice. That's because I am a *woman*, you horrible twins. Women don't have beards, and I don't have a beard, which proves I am a woman."

Abigail ignored all this and said to her brother, "Why didn't Steve Stevenson come in and tell us himself about the sabotage? Why did he only tell that student to tell us?"

John thought for a second. "Because he was in a hurry?"

"I don't think so," she said. "I think it's because he was afraid we would recognize him. Because we actually *do* know him."

"You don't know anyone!" the woman cried. "I've heard enough. Come, Will."

Abigail pointed to the man and said to John, "*This* is Steve Stevenson."

"WHAT A STRIKING AND PROVOCATIVE THEORY YOU HAVE JUST ADVANCED, MY DEAR SISTER," John did not say. Instead he conveyed essentially the same thing by saying, "Huh." Then he added, "But this is Dan."

## DAN D. DEAN IS STEVE STEVENSON!

Abigail said excitedly.

"That's preposterous!" the woman said. "Tell them, Phil."

"Yes, um, that's preposterous," the man said without much conviction.

"You've been sneaking around here the whole time *in disguise*," Abigail said to the man. "Telling everyone you're Steve Stevenson. And if anyone talks to you, you tell them you're in someone else's department. That's why everyone thinks you work for someone else. Meanwhile—"

"Meanwhile," John said, catching up, "you were wearing a beard the first day we saw you. When we were taking a tour of the campus and you left Papa that note in his office. But why? You didn't know we were going to see you that day. Why did you bother to wear a disguise?"

For a couple of seconds, no one spoke. Even the couple seemed curious to see if anyone would be able to answer John's question. Suddenly Abigail gave a big hoot of laughter. "Because they're *twins*, John! Dan looks

like Dean! If someone had seen Dan without the beard, they'd say, 'Hey, you look exactly like Dean D. Dean. Are you sure your name is Steve Stevenson?'"

"I've heard enough," the woman said. "Come, Bob."

Throughout this exchange, the man had begun to look nervous. Now he said, "Look, Dean—"

"I'm not Dean!" the woman yelled. "No one is Dean!"

"What if they call the cops *again*?"

"Let them!" The woman's voice had abruptly changed into a man's voice. "We haven't done anything!"

"We almost killed people!"

"No one knows that, you idiot!" Dean D. Dean shouted at his brother.

"We do," John said.

The woman glared at him—and then "she" ripped off her wig, confirming (as if anyone had had any doubt) that "she" was, in fact, Dean D. Dean. "Yes, you do, don't you." He suddenly drew up close to John and grabbed him by his shirt, actually lifting him off the ground. "So we'll have to do something about that."

"Hey!" Abigail launched herself at Dean D. Dean and started hammering him with her fists. "Let him go!"

"Do something!" Dean D. Dean yelled at his brother.

Sighing, Dan D. Dean moved forward and grasped Abigail's arms and pulled her off. "Now what?" he said.

"Bring them," his brother said. "We'll think of something."

"Think about THIS!" a fourth voice said.

## FOR FURTHER STUDY

1. How much more frequently do you think people would wear sunglasses at night if the sun came out more at night?

   a. Much more frequently.
   b. Somewhat more frequently.
   c. About the same amount, but in an exciting new array of designer styles.

2. Why do men wear beards?

   a. Because they forget to shave.
   b. To remind themselves that they are not women.
   c. Because their chins get cold.

3. Were you surprised to learn that Dan D. Dean was, in fact, Steve Stevenson? Hint: Yes.

CHAPTER 18

# THE THWARTING
# OF THE BAD GUYS

F| rom out of nowhere a figure appeared and, crouching low, charged headfirst at Dean D. Dean, who barely had time to drop John before the figure tackled him. Dean D. Dean lay on his back on the broad concrete walkway and struggled to catch his breath.

Suddenly there was barking.

Ten feet away, standing pert and upright and wagging her little tail in delight and looking thrilled to be taking part in whatever was going on, was Cassie the even-more-ridiculous-than-usual dog. She wore her collar and leash.

"All right, that's enough!" Dan D. Dean said. He shoved Abigail aside and began to advance on the person who had tackled Dean D. Dean. But Abigail, rather than retreating from Dan D. Dean, actually went back up to him (can you believe it!?), turned her back to him, and pushed herself backwards into his arms, calling, "Help! Cassie! He's got me! I can't get away!"

When she heard Abigail's call for help, Cassie darted forward and positioned herself in front of Dan D. Dean, crouched into a hunting position, bared her sharp teeth, and began to growl. It wasn't cute. It wasn't even ridiculous. John leaped forward and grabbed Cassie's leash but didn't tell her to stop growling.

Finally the person who had tackled Dean D. Dean stood up. I am going to permit you to guess who it was. Thanks to my highly skilled narration, it should be fairly easy. Still, if you need a hint, here is a partial list of who it wasn't:

1. Leonardo da Vinci
2. Clarence Birdseye, the Inventor of Frozen Food
3. The San Francisco 49ers
4. Dora the Explorer
5. Vasco de Gama the Explorer

This should be sufficient to enable you to guess who tackled Dean D. Dean and now stood before the twins.

"Manny!" the twins cried out at the same time.

"Look," Dan D. Dean said, indicating his brother. "I'm just going to help my brother up, and then we're going to leave. Okay?"

The twins traded a look that said, wordlessly, "We know what they did, but we probably can't prove it. And the only person hurt in this whole thing was Dean D. Dean. So let's let them go so we can get on with things."

John said, "Good girl, Cassie! It's okay." The dog stopped growling and John gently pulled her away from Dan D. Dean, who ran over to his brother and helped him to his feet. Dean D. Dean glared over at the twins and started to say something.

"Dean?" Dan D. Dean said. "Just drop it."

Dean D. Dean snorted but said nothing. He put his arm around his brother's shoulder and the two of them hobbled off toward the parking lot.

"Come on!" Manny said.

"Where?" John said.

"To watch the rest of the show!"

The cast party for *Let's Live Life!* was held in the banquet room of the main administrative building of the Thespian Academy of the Performing Arts and Sciences. Everyone who had worked on the show was there: actors, crew, the creative team, musicians, publicity people, and all of their husbands and wives and boyfriends and girlfriends and friends of the Academy. The feeling was one of triumph and joy.

Of the almost one hundred people in attendance, only six of them knew the disaster that had been averted by the quick thinking and brave actions of the Templeton twins. The twins knew, of course, and they had told their father and Manny Mann. The stage crew person who had chased them off the catwalk knew. And Porter Shorter, the stage manager, knew.

But none of them wanted to distract or steal attention from the cast and crew and orchestra, all of whom had performed brilliantly. So they kept that knowledge to themselves, and joined in the big celebration of the show and of the successful use of the Live Performance Horizontal-Tracking Individual Close-Up Lens.

It was about an hour into the party, during which the twins had consumed a million little egg rolls and drunk an unlimited amount of soda, when John looked up and said "Uh-oh," and Abigail looked where he was looking and she said, "Oh boy."

Gwendolyn Splendide floated over to them. (By this, I do not mean that the lady actually left the floor and flew through the air. I mean she moved as though floating, gracefully and smoothly and, if you must know, a little tipsily from having drunk several glasses of champagne.) She had somehow managed to change from the clothes she had worn at the opening performance. Now she wore a deep-red pantsuit over a jet-black blouse and a number of gold earrings, bracelets, necklaces, and a large gold pin depicting the (twin) faces of mirthful Comedy and agonized Tragedy.

"And *here* they are," she announced, although it was not clear to whom she was speaking. "I salute you, Arleta." She executed a pretend little bow and extended her hand to Abigail. Then she did the same toward John. "And Geoffrey. As I salute your *brilliant* father."

The twins shook her hand. "Um, thank you," Abigail said.

"Because—can you keep a secret? I know *I* can't, but you surely can—*entre nous*, my darlings, I don't *know* what the Academy would have done without your father's genius invention.[30] Of course, I suppose I deserve *some* credit for having hired him. Oh, but enough about me. As it is, his creation will be in demand all *over* the world, and our future is secure." She glanced around and someone caught her eye. "Now excuse me. It's that *dreadful* woman who reviews plays for the local paper. I must make her feel important."

---

30. "Entre nous" is, you will be unsurprised to learn, French. It's pronounced "AHN-truh NEW." It means "between us" or "between ourselves." You say it when you want the person to whom you're talking to keep secret what you're about to tell them. Saying "entre nous" makes an excellent impression on people, and I urge you to use it in your daily life.

Gwendolyn Splendide drifted off. The twins made their way to the dessert table, where there were ten thousand little cupcakes. They were somewhere between their third and fourth ones when the Professor joined them. He looked tired but happy. He—

I will tell you what happened next, but first I have several things I wish to say.

It will come as no surprise if I tell you that this story—this narrative—is almost over. If you are reading it in book form, you can obviously see that there are barely any pages left. And even if you are listening to it being read, or are reading it in some mysterious invisible electronic form which has no "pages," I am sure that you can *sense* that it's almost over.

I know this realization saddens you beyond words, but I couldn't be happier. As I said at the beginning, in order to tell this second story about the Templeton twins, I have had to write *an entirely new group of words*, completely different from those I wrote in the first story. One can scarcely overstate how arduous this has been.

True, these words are just as new to you as they are to me, and you have had to read (or listen to) them. But reading is as different from writing as eating is from cooking. I think we can all agree that this is an excellent analogy,[31] and that the activity of writing (and cooking) is much more demanding than that of reading (or eating).

I hope, therefore, that you appreciate all the work I've done during the past 255 pages. If you do, you need say nothing. If you don't, I invite you to write a letter to me, in care of the publisher of this book. I will almost certainly ignore it.

The Professor and the twins gazed across the floor and watched as Manny Mann said something to one of the actresses, who burst into laughter as Manny stood there with a little smile on his face. The Professor turned to the twins and said, "By the way, children, I've been meaning to ask you. That complicated eyeglass helmet you made for Manny—why did you go to all that trouble?"

---

31. What is an "analogy"? It is when you describe one thing in terms of another. You might wish to say, "The Narrator is brilliant," but instead of simply saying that (although there is nothing wrong with saying that, especially since it is true), you might choose to say, "The Narrator is to narrating as Albert Einstein is to physics" or "The Narrator is the Albert Einstein of narrating." You will have thus *made an analogy* between the Narrator and Albert Einstein.

Abigail and John traded a look of surprise. John said to his father, "Because he kept bothering us with all his ideas. His funny ideas, and his serious ideas—"

"We thought if we could get his glasses to stay on, he'd be able to read and do homework and leave us alone," Abigail said.

"Mmm, I'm not so sure that's it," the Professor said. "We could have made him understand that he shouldn't distract you while you were doing homework. I think there was another reason." The twins looked expectantly at their father. "I think you like him," the Professor said. "He's a friend. You did a nice thing for a friend."

"He's our nanny," Abigail said. "How can your nanny be your friend?"

"Why not?" the Professor said. The twins looked across the room. Manny waved at the Templetons, and then took the hand of the actress he'd been speaking to and began to pull her over to introduce her to them. "And he feels the same way. Don't you think?" The twins nodded. "Yes, you put in a lot of hard work to solve a problem for a friend. I think that's great."

Then Manny and the actress made their way over to the twins, the Professor was called away to discuss his triumphant invention with many of his admirers, and things got loud and full of laughter. And so it wasn't until the ride home that the Professor was able to say, "By the way, children, I got an interesting letter this morning from another university . . ."

Abigail, in the front passenger seat, turned toward John, who was in the backseat. The Templeton twins shared a look that said, wordlessly, "Here we go again . . ."

But that is most definitely another story. In any case, *this* one is over. Do not expect any additional narration from me. I cannot, in spite of what you may believe, entertain you all the time. Entertain *yourself*. Go do

something interesting. Or go to sleep, and then get up and *then* do something interesting. I am sure that, when you do, you will want to call me up or come to my house to thank me for suggesting it. Please. Don't bother.

## FOR FURTHER STUDY

1. "If the Narrator is the Albert Einstein of narrators, then Albert Einstein is the Narrator of physicists." Discuss these two analogies, preferably with another person.

2. Now that this book is over, don't you feel sorry for me, and for how exhausted I am?

3. Even if you don't feel sorry for me, and for how exhausted I am, you certainly have to admit that this has been a splendid experience for everyone, and another top-notch example of excellence in narration. Don't you? Oh, please. You certainly do.

**W**elcome to the Appendix. I know I said that here you would be able to read a concise summary of the first book about the Templeton twins, so as to be better informed as to who they are and who everyone else is. But once I sat down to write the Appendix, I changed my mind.

I think—and, really, don't you think, too?—that it would be better for everyone if you simply obtained the first book and read it yourself. (Or, if you already have it and have read it but forgotten it, then read it again.) For[32] only in doing so will you be able to learn the Complete Story.

In fact, I feel so strongly about this that I hereby refuse to tell you that, in the first book, the twins are born on the very same day that Professor Elton Templeton gives Dean D. Dean (who at that time was twenty-one years old, and the Professor's student at Elysian

---

32. I like this use of the word "for" as a fancy way to say "because." From now on, if your parent, greengrocer, investment adviser, or bodyguard asks, "Hey, why didn't you finish your homework?" tell them, "For I didn't feel like it." Please note that I am not responsible for whatever consequences may follow therefrom, which is a fancy way of saying, "Don't blame me for what happens next."

University) an "F" in a course, thereby causing Dean D. Dean to flunk out of college, to be angry at the world, and to hate Professor Templeton until further notice.

Nor will I reveal that, twelve years later, Dean D. Dean and his brother, Dan D. Dean, show up at the Tickridge-Baltock Institute of Technology, where the Professor is teaching, and kidnap John and Abigail and their new (ridiculous) dog, Cassie, so as to force the Professor into signing over to them the rights to his recent invention, the Personal One-Man Helicopter (POMH).

I am equally determined not to disclose that the twins, through the use of cleverness, intelligence, physical bravery, and the lessons they learned from their hobbies (which are playing the drums [John] and doing cryptic crossword puzzles [Abigail]), manage to thwart (yes, "thwart") the Dean twins, rescue their father, and generally save the day.

I have decided not to reveal any of the background information concerning the Templeton twins here in the Appendix, although it occurs to me, upon further review, that I have in fact done so. Well, all right. But that's it. I'm done.

# SENSE OF
# EVIL

BANTAM BOOKS BY KAY HOOPER

*The Bishop Trilogies*
STEALING SHADOWS
HIDING IN THE SHADOWS
OUT OF THE SHADOWS

TOUCHING EVIL
WHISPER OF EVIL
SENSE OF EVIL

*The Quinn Novels*
ONCE A THIEF
ALWAYS A THIEF

*Romantic Suspense*
AMANDA
AFTER CAROLINE
FINDING LAURA
HAUNTING RACHEL

*Classic Fantasy and Romance*
ON WINGS OF MAGIC
THE WIZARD OF SEATTLE
MY GUARDIAN ANGEL
(anthology)
YOURS TO KEEP
(anthology)

# KAY HOOPER

# SENSE OF
# EVIL

BANTAM BOOKS

SENSE OF EVIL
A Bantam Book / August 2003

Published by Bantam Dell
A Division of Random House, Inc.
New York, New York

Book design by Lynn Newmark

Library of Congress Cataloging in Publication Data
Hooper, Kay.
Sense of evil./Kay Hooper.
p. cm.
ISBN 0-553-80300-X
I. Title

PS3558.O587 S46 2003
2003056270
813/.54 21

Manufactured in the United States of America
Published simultaneously in Canada

BVG    10   9   8   7   6   5   4   3   2   1

This one is for Jeff and Tommy,
my shopping buddies.
Mostly because they didn't believe
I'd put them in a book.
Hey, guys!

# ACKNOWLEDGMENTS

This time out, Bishop and his Special Crimes Unit owe even greater thanks than usual to the fantastic Team Bantam, whose members worked above and beyond the call of duty to put this story into your hands.

A grateful author wishes to thank Irwyn Applebaum and Nita Taublib, Bill Massey and Andie Nicolay, Kathy Lord, and all the other hardworking professionals in production who made this book possible.

Words aren't enough, but they'll have to do.

Thanks again.

# PROLOGUE

THE VOICES WOULDN'T leave him alone.

Neither would the nightmares.

He threw back the covers and stumbled from the bed. A full moon beamed enough light into the house for him to find his way to the sink in the bathroom.

He carefully avoided looking into the mirror but was highly conscious of his shadowy reflection as he fumbled for a drinking cup and turned on the tap. He drank three cups of water, vaguely surprised that he was so thirsty and yet . . . not.

He was usually thirsty these days.

It was part of the change.

He splashed his face with the cold water, again and again, not caring about the mess he was making. By the third splash, he realized he was crying.

*Wimp. Spineless coward.*

"I'm not," he muttered, sending the next handful of water to wet his aching head.

*You're afraid. Pissing-in-your-pants afraid.*

Half-consciously, he pressed his thighs together. "I'm not. I can do it. I told you I could do it."

*Then do it now.*

He froze, bent over the sink, water dribbling from his cupped hands. "Now?"

*Now.*

"But . . . it's not ready yet. If I do it now—"

*Coward. I should have known you couldn't go through with it. I should have known you'd fail me.*

He straightened slowly, this time looking deliberately into the dim mirror. Even with moonlight, all he could make out was the shadowy shape of his head, dark blurs of features, faint gleam of eyes. The murky outline of a stranger.

What choice did he have?

*Just look at yourself. Wimp. Spineless coward. You'll never be a real man, will you?*

He could feel water dripping off his chin. Or maybe it was the last of the tears. He sucked in air, so deep his chest hurt, then let it out slowly.

*Maybe you can buy a backbone—*

"I'm ready," he said. "I'm ready to do it."

*I don't believe you.*

He turned off the taps and walked out of the bathroom. Went back to his bedroom, where the moonlight spilled through the big window to spotlight the old steamer trunk set against the wall beneath it. He knelt down and carefully opened it.

The raised lid blocked off some of the moonlight, but he didn't need light for this. He reached inside, let his fingers search gingerly until they felt the cold steel. He lifted the knife and held it in the light, turning it this way and that, fascinated by the gleam of the razor-sharp, serrated edge.

"I'm ready," he murmured. "I'm ready to kill her."

The voices wouldn't leave her alone.

Neither would the nightmares.

She had drawn the drapes before going to bed in an effort to close out the moonlight, but even though the room was dark, she was very conscious of that huge moon painting everything on the other side of her window with the stark, eerie light that made her feel so uneasy.

She hated full moons.

The clock on her nightstand told her it was nearly five in the morning. The hot, sandpapery feel of her eyelids told her she really needed to try to go back to sleep. But the whisper of the voices in her head told her that even trying would be useless, at least for a while.

She pushed back the covers and slid from her bed. She didn't need light to show her the way to the kitchen, but once there she turned on the light over the stove so she wouldn't burn herself. Hot chocolate, that was the ticket.

And if that didn't work, there was an emergency bottle of whiskey in the back of the pantry for just such a night as this. It was probably two-thirds empty by now.

There had been a few nights like this, especially in the last year or so.

She got what she needed and heated the pan of milk slowly, stirring the liquid so it wouldn't stick. Adding in chocolate syrup while the milk heated, because that was the way she liked to make her hot chocolate. In the silence of the house, with no other sounds to distract her, it was difficult to keep her own mind quiet.

She didn't want to listen to the whispering there, but it was like catching a word or two of an overheard conversation and *knowing* you needed to listen more closely because they were talking about you.

Of course, some people would call that paranoia. Had called it. And at least part of the time, maybe they weren't wrong.

But only part of the time.

She was tired. It got harder and harder, as time went on, to bounce back. Harder for her body to recover. Harder for her mind to heal.

Given her druthers, she would put off tuning in to the voices until tomorrow. Or the next day, maybe.

The hot chocolate was ready. She turned off the burner and poured the steaming liquid into a mug. She put the pan in the sink, then picked up her mug and carried it toward the little round table in the breakfast nook.

Almost there, she was stopped in her tracks by a wave of red-hot pain that washed over her body with the suddenness of a blow. Her mug crashed to the floor, landing unbroken but spattering her bare legs with hot chocolate.

She barely felt that pain.

Eyes closed, sucked into the red and screaming maelstrom of someone else's agony, she tried to keep breathing despite the repeated blows that splintered bones and shredded lungs. She could taste blood, feel it bubbling up in her mouth. She could feel the wet heat of it soaking her blouse and running down her arms as she lifted her hands in a pitiful attempt to ward off the attack.

*I know what you did. I know. I know. You bitch, I know what you did—*

She jerked and cried out as a more powerful thrust than all the rest drove the serrated knife into her chest, penetrating her heart with such force she knew the only thing that stopped it going deeper still was the hilt. Her hands fumbled, touching what felt like blood-wet gloved hands, large and strong. The hands retreated immediately to leave her weakly holding the handle of the knife impaling her heart. She felt a single agonized throb of her heart that forced more blood to bubble, hot and thick, into her mouth, and then it was over.

Almost over.

She opened her eyes and found herself bending over the table, her hands flat on the pale, polished surface. Both hands were covered with blood, and between them, scrawled in her own handwriting across the table, was a single bloody word.

### HASTINGS

She straightened slowly, her entire body aching, and held her hands out in front of her, watching as the blood slowly faded until it was gone. Her hands were clean and unmarked. When she looked at the table again, there was no sign, now, of a word written there in blood.

"Hastings," she murmured. "Well, shit."

R AFE SULLIVAN ROSE from his crouched position, absently stretching muscles that had begun to cramp, and muttered, "Well, shit," under his breath.

It was already hot and humid even just before noon, the sun burning almost directly overhead in a clear blue sky, and he absently wished he'd had his people put up a tarp to provide some shade. The effort wouldn't be worthwhile now; another half hour, and the coroner's wagon would be here.

The body sprawled at his feet was a bloody mess. She lay on her back, arms wide, legs apart, spread-eagled in a pathetically exposed, vulnerable position that made him want to cover her up—even though she was more or less dressed. Her once-white blouse was dull red, soaked with blood and still mostly wet despite the heat, so that the coppery smell was strong. The thin, springlike floral skirt was eerily undamaged but blood-soaked, spread out around her hips, the hem almost daintily raised to just above her knees.

She had been pretty once. Now, even though her face was virtually untouched, she wasn't pretty anymore. Her delicate features were contorted, eyes wide and staring, mouth open in a scream she probably never had the chance or the breath to utter. From the corners of her parted lips, trails of blood ran down her cheeks, some of it mixing with the golden strands of her long blond hair and a lot of it soaking into the ground around her.

She had been pretty once.

"Looks like he was really pissed this time, Chief. Bit like the first victim, I'd say." Detective Mallory Beck made the observation dryly, seemingly unmoved by the gory scene before them.

Rafe looked at her, reading the truth in her tightened lips and grim eyes. But all he said was, "Am I wrong, or did this one fight him?"

Mallory consulted her notebook. "Doc just did the preliminary, of course, but he says she tried. Defensive injuries on the victim's hands, and one stab wound in her back—which the doc says was probably the first injury."

Shifting his gaze to the body, Rafe said, "In the back? So she was trying to turn—or run—away from him when he stabbed her the first time. And either he turned her around so he could finish her face-to-face or she turned herself trying to fight him."

"Looks like it. And only a few hours ago; we got the call on this one earlier than the others. The doc estimates the time of death as around five-thirty this morning."

"Awfully early to be up and out," Rafe commented. "Caleb opens his office between nine-thirty and ten as a rule. She was still his paralegal, right?"

"Right. Normally went to the office around nine. So she was

out very early. What I don't get is how he was able to lure her this far away from the road. You can see there are no drag marks, and two sets of footprints—we have good casts, by the way—so she walked out here with him. I'm no Daniel Boone, but I'd say from her tracks that she was walking calm and easy, not struggling or hesitating at all."

Rafe had to admit that the ground here looked remarkably calm and undisturbed, for the most part, especially considering the violence of what had been done to the victim. And after last night's rain all the tracks were easily visible. So this murder scene, like the last one, clearly illustrated what had happened here.

From all appearances, twenty-six-year-old Tricia Kane had gotten out of her own car around dawn at an unofficial rest spot off a normally busy two-lane highway and then walked with a companion—male, according to all likelihood as well as an FBI profile—about fifty yards into the woods to this clearing. And then the companion had killed her.

Brutally.

"Maybe he had a gun," Rafe suggested, thinking aloud. "Or maybe the knife was enough to keep her docile until they got this far."

Mallory frowned. "You want my hunch, I say she didn't see that knife until they reached this clearing. The instant she saw it, she tried to run. That's when he got her."

Rafe didn't know why, but that was his hunch too. "And it's the same way he got the other two. Somehow he persuaded these women to leave their cars and walk calmly into the woods with him. Smart, savvy women who, from all accounts, were way too careful to let any stranger get that close."

"Which means they probably knew him."

"Even if, would *you* leave your car and just stroll into the woods with some guy? Especially if you knew two other women had recently died under similar circumstances?"

"No. But I'm a suspicious cop." Mallory shook her head. "Still, it doesn't make sense. And what about the cars? All three women just left their cars on pull-off rest areas beside fairly busy highways and walked away from them. Keys in the ignition, for Christ's sake, and not many do that even in small towns these days. And we don't know whether he was with them when they stopped or somehow flagged them down and *then* persuaded them to come with him. No tracks out at the rest stop to speak of with all that hard dirt and packed gravel."

"Maybe he pulled a Bundy and claimed to need their help."

"Could be. Although I still say that would have worked loads better if they knew who was asking. This guy isn't killing strangers. I think the profilers got that one right, Chief."

With a sigh, Rafe said, "Yeah, me too. I hate like hell the idea that this bastard is local rather than some insane stranger passing through town, but I don't see any other way to explain how he's getting these women to go with him."

"Unless he's some kind of authority figure they'd be inclined to trust and obey on sight. Like a cop."

"Oh, hell, don't even suggest that," Rafe responded so instantly that Mallory knew the possibility had already been in his mind.

She studied him unobtrusively as he scowled down at the body of Tricia Kane. At thirty-six, he was the youngest chief of police ever in Hastings, but with a solid background in law enforcement both in training and experience, nobody doubted Rafe Sullivan's qualifications for the job.

Except maybe Rafe himself, who was a lot smarter than he realized.

Mallory had wondered more than once if his tendency to

doubt himself and his hunches had anything to do with his looks. He wasn't exactly ugly—but she had to admit that his self-described label of "thug" pretty much fit. He had a harsh face, with very sleepy, heavy-lidded eyes so dark they tended to make people uncomfortable. His nose had been broken at least twice, he had a sharp jaw with a stubborn jut to it, and his high cheek-bones marked him indelibly with his Celtic ancestry.

He was also a very big man, several inches over six feet tall and unmistakably powerful. The kind of guy you wanted on your side no matter what the fight was about. So he definitely looked the part of a cop, in or out of uniform—and it was mostly out, since he disliked uniforms as a rule and seldom wore his. But any-one, Mallory had long ago discovered, who had him pegged as all brawn and no brain or who expected the stereotypical dense, cud-chewing Southern cop was in for a surprise, sooner or later.

Probably sooner. He didn't suffer fools gladly.

"That's three murders in barely three weeks," he was saying, dark eyes still fixed on the body at their feet. "And we're no closer to catching the bastard. Worse, we've now officially got a serial killer on our hands."

"You thinking what I'm thinking?"

"I'm thinking it's time we yelled for help."

Mallory sighed. "Yeah, that's what I'm thinking."

Quantico

Isabel Adams made her voice as persuasive as she possibly could, and her well-rehearsed arguments sounded damned impressive if she did say so herself, but when she finally fell silent she wasn't surprised that Bishop didn't respond right away.

He stood at the window gazing out, only his profile visible to

Isabel. In deference to the fact that he was actually on FBI territory, he was dressed more formally than was usual, and the dark suit set off his dark good looks and powerful build admirably. Isabel looked at Miranda, who was sitting on Bishop's desk, idly swinging one foot. Even more of a maverick than her husband and far less deferential to the FBI in any sense, she was wearing her usual jeans and sweater, the casual outfit doing nothing to disguise startling beauty and a centerfold body that turned heads wherever she went.

She gazed at Bishop now, seemingly waiting as Isabel waited for his answer, but her electric-blue eyes were very intent, and Isabel knew there was communication between the two of them on a level that didn't require speaking aloud. Whatever Bishop's decision turned out to be, he would arrive at it only after Miranda's views and recommendations were added to his own; although Bishop had far greater seniority in the Bureau and in the unit he had created and led, no one doubted that his partnership with Miranda was equal in every possible sense of the word.

"It's not a good idea," he said finally.

Isabel said, "I know all the arguments against my going."

"Do you?"

"I've gone over all the material that police chief sent when he requested a profile after the second murder. I even got on-line and read the local newspaper articles. I think I've got a very good feel for the town, for what's happening down there."

Miranda said, "Your basic powder keg, just waiting for a match."

Isabel nodded. "Small town on the teetering edge of panic. They seem to have a lot of faith in their police, especially the chief, and pretty fair medical and forensics facilities for a small town, but this latest murder has everybody jumping at shadows and investing in security systems. And guns."

She paused, then added, "Three murders makes this a serial killer in Hastings. And he's showing no signs of stopping now. Chief Sullivan just officially requested the FBI's help, and he's asking for more than an updated profile. Bishop, I want to go down there."

Bishop turned at last to face them, though instead of returning to his desk he leaned back against the high windowsill. The scar on his left cheek was visible now, and Isabel had been with the unit long enough to recognize, in its whitened appearance, that he was disturbed.

"I know what I'm asking," she said, more quietly than she might otherwise have spoken.

Bishop glanced at Miranda, who immediately looked at Isabel and said, "From all indications, this is the sort of killer that local law enforcement can handle with very little outside help. Maybe a bit more manpower to ask questions, but it'll be inside knowledge that catches this animal, not an outsider's expertise. The profile marks him as nothing out of the ordinary. He's local, he's killing local women he knows, and he's bound to make a mistake sooner rather than later."

"But it wasn't an SCU profile," Isabel pointed out. "None of us developed it."

"Special Crimes Unit can't develop all the requested profiles," Bishop reminded her patiently. "We barely have the manpower to handle the cases we do get."

"We didn't get the call on this one because this killer is so seemingly ordinary, I know that. Around a hundred serial killers active in this country on average at any time, and he's one of them. Nothing raised a red flag to indicate that our special abilities are needed in the investigation. But I'm telling you—there's more to the case than the official profile picked up on. A lot more." She paused, then added, "All I'm asking is that you take a look at the material for yourselves, both of you. Then tell me I'm wrong."

Bishop exchanged another glance with Miranda, then said, "And if you're right? Isabel, even if the SCU took on this investigation, given the circumstances in Hastings you're the last agent I'd want to send down there."

Isabel smiled. "Which is why I have to be the agent you send. I'll go get the file."

She left without waiting for a reply, and as Bishop returned to his desk and sat down, he muttered, "Goddammit."

"She's right," Miranda said. "At least about being the one who has to go."

"Yeah. I know."

*We can't protect her.*

*No. But if this is what I think it is . . . she'll need help.*

"Then," Miranda said calmly, "we'll make sure she has help. Whether she likes it or not."

**Thursday, June 12, 2:00 PM**

"Chief, are you saying we *don't* have a serial killer?" Alan Moore, reporter for the Hastings *Chronicle,* had plenty of practice in making his voice carry without shouting, and his question cut through the noise in the crowded room, silencing everyone else. More than thirty pairs of expectant eyes fixed on Rafe.

Who could cheerfully have strangled his boyhood chum. With no particular inflection in his voice, Rafe answered simply, "We don't know what we have as yet, except for three murdered women. Which is why I'm asking you ladies and gentlemen of the press not to add unnecessarily to the natural anxiety of our citizens."

"In this situation, don't you think they should be anxious?" Alan glanced around to make certain all attention was on him, then added, "Hey, I'm blond, and even I'm nervous. If I were a twenty-something blond *woman*, I'd be totally freaked out."

"If you were a twenty-something blond woman we'd all be freaked out," Rafe said dryly. He waited for the laughter to subside, fully aware of the fact that it was as much nervous as amused. He was good at taking the pulse of his town, but it didn't take any particular skill to feel the tension in this room. In the town.

Everybody was scared.

"Look," he said, "I know very well that the women here in Hastings are worried—whether they're blond, brunette, redhead, or any shade in between—and I don't blame them a bit. I know the men in their lives are worried. But I also know that uncontrolled speculation in the newspaper and on the radio and other media will only feed the panic."

"Uncontrolled?"

"Don't start yelling censorship, Alan. I'm not telling you what to print. Or what not to print. I'm asking you to be responsible, because there is a very fine line between warning people to be concerned and take precautions, and yelling fire in a crowded theater."

"Do we have a serial killer?" Alan demanded.

Rafe didn't hesitate. "We have three murders we believe were committed by the same person, fitting the established criteria for a serial killer."

"In other words, we have a lunatic in Hastings," somebody he didn't recognize muttered just loud enough to be heard.

Rafe responded to that as well, still calm. "By definition a serial killer is judged conventionally if not clinically to be insane, yes. That doesn't mean he'll be visibly any different from you or me. And they seldom wear horns or a tail."

The reporter who'd made the lunatic comment grimaced. "Okay, point taken. Nobody is above suspicion and let's all freak out." She was blond.

"Let's all take care, not freak out," Rafe corrected. "Obviously, we would advise blond women in their mid to late twenties to take special care, but we have no way of knowing for certain if age and hair color are factors or merely a coincidence."

"I say err on the side of factor," she offered wryly.

"And I can't say I'd blame you for that. Just keep in mind that at this point there is very little we can be sure of—except that we have a serious problem in Hastings. Now, since a small-town police department is hardly trained or equipped to deal with this type of crime, we have requested the involvement of the FBI."

"Have they provided a profile?" This question came from Paige Gilbert, a reporter with one of the local radio stations. She was more brisk and matter-of-fact than some of the other women in the room had been, less visibly uneasy, possibly because she was brunette.

"Preliminary. And before you ask, Alan, we won't be sharing the details of that profile unless and until the knowledge can help our citizens. At this stage of the investigation, all we can realistically do is advise them to take sensible precautions."

"That's not much, Rafe," Alan complained.

"It's all we've got. For now."

"So what's the FBI bringing to the table?"

"Expertise: the Special Crimes Unit is sending agents trained and experienced in tracking and capturing serial killers. Information: we will have access to FBI databases. Technical support: medical and forensics experts will study and evaluate evidence we gather."

"Who'll be in charge of the investigation?" Alan asked. "Doesn't the FBI usually take over?"

"I'll continue to head the investigation. The FBI's role is assistance and support, no more. So I don't want to read or hear any BS about federal officials superceding states' rights, Alan. Clear?"

Alan grimaced slightly. He was a good reporter and tended to be both fair and even-handed, but he was close to phobic about governmental "interference," especially from the federal level, and was always loud in protest whenever he suspected it.

Rafe took a few more questions from the assembled reporters, resigned rather than surprised to find that several of the people were from TV stations in nearby Columbia. If the investigation was getting major state coverage now, it was only a matter of time before it went national.

Great. That was just great. The last thing he wanted was to have the national press looking over his shoulder and second-guessing every decision he made.

Bad enough he had Alan.

"Chief, do you believe this killer is local?"

"Chief, has anything else turned up linking the victims?"

"Chief . . ."

He answered the questions almost automatically, using variations of "no comment" or "we have no reliable information on that" whenever possible. Even though he had called the press conference himself, it was only because he'd gotten wind of some pretty wild speculation going on and hoped to head off the worst of it before it was in print or other media, not because he had any real progress to report.

He was concentrating on the crowd in front of him as he answered their questions, but even as he did, he felt an odd change in the room, as if the very air had somehow sharpened, freshened. Cleared. It was a weird feeling, like waking suddenly from a dream thinking, *Oh, that wasn't real. This is real.*

Something had changed, and he had no idea if it was for better or worse.

From the corner of his eye, he caught a glimpse of movement and was able to turn his head just a bit, casually, so that none of the reporters picked up on his suddenly diverted attention.

Still, he was surprised that no one else seemed to have observed her entrance, even though she came into the room from the hallway, behind the flock of reporters. Rafe doubted she went unnoticed very often. He saw her pause to speak briefly to one of his officers, producing what appeared to be an I.D. folder, saw Travis's visible surprise and undoubtedly stuttering response, then saw her move past him and take up a position near the door. She scanned the crowd of reporters and their tangle of cameras, a small half smile that was not so much amused as it was rueful playing around her mouth. She was dressed casually and for the weather in jeans and a sleeveless top, her hair pulled up into a neat ponytail. She could easily have been one of the reporters.

She wasn't.

When her gaze met his fleetingly across the crowded room, Rafe was conscious of an instant certainty that made him go cold to his bones.

No. The universe couldn't hate him that much.

"Chief, could you—"

He cut off the question abruptly. "Thank you all very much for coming today. When there are further developments, you'll be notified. Good afternoon."

He stepped away from the podium and went straight through the crowd to the other side of the room, ignoring the questions flung after him. When he reached her, his statement was brief and to the point.

"My office is across the street."

"Lead the way, Chief." Her voice was as extraordinary as the rest of her, one of those smoky, husky bedroom voices a man would expect to hear if he called a 900 sex-talk line.

Rafe wasted no time in leading the way past his still-goggling officer, saying merely, "Travis, make sure nobody bothers the mayor on their way out."

"Yeah. Okay. Right, Chief."

Rafe started to ask him if he'd never seen a woman before, but since that would have resulted in either stuttering incoherence or else a lengthy explanation that would have boiled down to "Not a woman like this one," he didn't bother.

He also didn't say a word as they left the town-hall building and walked across Main Street to the police department, although he did notice that she was a tall woman; wearing flat sandals she was only a few inches shorter than he was, which would put her at about five-ten.

And her toenails were polished red.

With most of his people out on patrol, the station wasn't very busy; Mallory was the only detective at her desk in the bullpen, and though she looked up with interest as they passed, she was on the phone, and Rafe didn't pause or greet her except with a nod.

His office looked out onto Main Street, and as he went around behind his desk he couldn't help a quick glance to see whether the reporters had left the town hall. Most were still clustered out in front, some obviously recording spots for today's evening news and others speaking to each other—speculating, he knew. It didn't bode well for his hopes of keeping things calm in Hastings.

An I.D. folder dropped onto his blotter as he sat down, his visitor taking one of the chairs in front of his desk.

"Isabel Adams," she said. "Call me Isabel, please. We're pretty informal. Nice to meet you, Chief Sullivan."

He picked up the folder, studied the I.D. and federal badge inside, then closed it and pushed it across the desk toward her. "Rafe. Your boss saw the profile, right?" was his terse response.

"My boss," she answered, "wrote the profile. The updated one, that is, the one I brought with me. Why?"

"You know goddamned well why. Is he out of his mind, sending *you* down here?"

"Bishop has been called crazy on occasion," she said in the same pleasant, almost careless tone, not visibly disturbed by his anger. "But only by those who don't know him. He's the sanest man I've ever met."

Rafe leaned back in his chair and stared across the desk at the special agent sent by the FBI to help him track and capture a serial killer. She was beautiful. Breath-catching, jaw-dropping gorgeous. Flawless skin, delicate features, stunning green eyes, and the kind of voluptuous body most men could expect to encounter only in their dreams.

Or in their nightmares.

In Rafe's nightmares.

Because Isabel Adams was also something else.

She was blond.


The voices were giving him a pounding headache. It was something else he was getting used to. He managed to unobtrusively swallow a handful of aspirin but knew from experience it would only take the worst edge off the pain.

It would have to be enough.

Have to.

Still exhausted from the morning's activities, he managed to do his work as usual, speak to people as though nothing out of the ordinary had happened. Nobody guessed, he was certain of that.

He'd gotten very good at making sure nobody noticed anything out of the ordinary.

*You think they don't all see? Don't all know?*

That was the sneering voice, the dominant one, the one he hated most and heard most often. He ignored it. It was easier to do that now, when he was drained and oddly distant from himself, when the only thing for him to do, really, was wait for his next opportunity.

*They know who you are. They know what you did.*

That was more difficult to ignore, but he managed. He went about his business, listening whenever possible to the nervous gossip. Everybody was talking about the same thing, of course. The murders.

Nobody talked of anything else these days.

He didn't hear much he hadn't already known, although the speculation was amusing. Theories, most of them absurd, abounded as to why the killer was targeting blondes.

A hatred of his mother, for Christ's sake.

Rejection by a blond girlfriend.

Idiots.

The pharmacist downtown told him there'd been a run on hair color, that those women trying blond as an option were going back to their natural colors.

He wondered if the natural blondes were considering changing, but thought probably not. They liked the effect, liked knowing men were watching them. It gave them a sense of power, of . . . superiority.

None of them could imagine dying because of it.

He thought that was funny.

He thought that was funny as hell.

2

R AFE SAID, "Please don't tell me the general idea is for
you to be bait."

"Oh, I'm probably too old to tempt him."

"If you're past thirty, I'll eat my hat."

"Salt and pepper?"

Rafe stared at her, and she chuckled.

"I'm thirty-one. And, no, that isn't the idea. I'll do a lot for
king and country, but I don't have a death wish."

"Done anything to piss off this Bishop of yours?"

"Not lately."

"Has the profile changed?"

"Not as far as this animal's fixations go. He's still after white
females with blond hair, and he's likely to stay within the age
range of twenty-five to thirty-five. He apparently likes them

smart and savvy as well as strong, which is an interesting twist on the stereotypical image of helpless dumb blondes as victims."

Rafe said something profane under his breath.

Ignoring that, Isabel went on briskly, completely professional now. "He's someone they know or at least obviously believe they can trust. Possibly an authority figure, maybe even a cop—or impersonating one. He's physically strong, though he won't necessarily look it; he might even appear effeminate."

"Why effeminate?" Rafe was listening intently, his eyes narrowed.

"These women were killed brutally, with a viciousness that suggests both a hatred of women and doubts or fears about his own sexuality. All three were sexual crimes—deep, penetrating wounds and targeting the breasts and genitals are classic signs of a sexual obsession—and yet none of the women was raped. That, by the way, will probably be his next escalation, raping as well as killing."

"And if he's impotent? This sort of killer often is, right?"

Isabel didn't hesitate. "Right. In that case, an object rape, possibly even with the murder weapon. And it will be postmortem; he doesn't want his victim to see his possible sexual failure. In fact, he'll probably cover her face, even after he kills her."

"So he's a necrophiliac as well."

"The whole nasty bag of tricks, yeah. And he will be escalating, count on it. He's got the taste for it now. He's enjoying himself. And he's feeling invulnerable, maybe even invincible. He's likely to begin mocking us—the police—in some way."

Rafe thought about all that for a moment, then asked, "Why blondes?"

"We don't know. Not yet. But it's very possible that his first victim—Jamie Brower, right?"

"Right."

"Twenty-eight-year-old real-estate broker. It's very likely, we believe, that something about her was the trigger. Maybe something she did to him, that's possible. An emotional or psychological rejection of some kind. Or something he saw, something she made him feel, whether or not she was aware of doing so. We believe she was a deliberate choice, not merely a random blonde."

"Because she was the first victim?"

"That, plus the uncontrolled violence of the attack. According to the crime-scene photos and ME's report you sent us, she was riddled with stab wounds."

"Yes." Rafe's lips tightened as he remembered.

"The wounds were ragged, multiple angles, but virtually all of them so deep the hilt or handle of the knife left bruises and imprints in her skin. He was in a frenzy when he killed her. With the second and third victims, except for some minor defensive injuries, most of the wounds were concentrated in the breast and genital areas; Jamie Brower had injuries to her face and wounds from her neck to her lower thighs."

"It was a bloodbath."

"Yes. That sort of fury usually means hatred, very specific, very personal hatred. He wanted to kill *her*. Not just a blonde, not just a representation of his killing fantasy. Her. We believe that by focusing the investigation on the life and death of Jamie Brower, we're likely to uncover facts or evidence that will help us to identify her killer."

"Focusing on her how? We've accounted for all her movements the week before she was killed."

"We'll have to go further back than that. Months, maybe even years; the pressure built inside him for a while before he acted, and during that time their paths crossed."

"If she was the trigger."

24

Isabel nodded. "If she was the trigger."

"And if she wasn't?"

Isabel shrugged. "Still a valid, even critical, investigative approach, knowing who the victim was. Who all of them were. We won't understand him until we understand the women he's killing. Something more than superficial appearance connects them."

"They were all unusually successful at their jobs," Rafe said, relaying the information without the need to consult any file or notes. "Jamie had been Broker of the Year with her company the past three years; Allison Carroll had been recognized both locally and statewide as an outstanding teacher; and Tricia Kane not only had a very good job as a paralegal to one of our most successful attorneys but also was a very talented artist gaining regional recognition."

"It might be the public recognition of their abilities as much as their success that drew his interest," Isabel mused. "They stood in a spotlight, lauded for their achievements. Maybe that's what he likes. Or doesn't like."

"You mean he could be punishing them for their success?"

"It's a possibility. Also a possibility that he was attracted to them because of their success and was rejected by them when he expressed his interest."

"Men get rejected all the time. They don't turn to butchery."

"No. The vast majority don't. Which is a good thing, don't you think?"

Rafe frowned slightly, but she was going on before he could comment.

"It means this particular man has some serious, deep-seated emotional and psychological problems, which have apparently lain dormant or at least were hidden here in Hastings until about three weeks ago."

"Hence the trigger."

Isabel nodded. "There's no question about that, not as far as we're concerned. Something *happened*. To him, in his life. A change. Whether it was an actual event or a paranoid delusion on his part remains to be seen. But something set him off. Something definitive."

Rafe glanced at his watch, wondering if there was time today to visit all three crime scenes.

"Starting with the actual crime scenes," Isabel said, "would probably be the best way to go. According to the map I studied, they're within a five-mile area. And it's still hours till sunset, so we have time."

"Where's your partner?" Rafe asked. "I was told there'd be at least two of you."

"She's settling in. Wandering around, getting a feel for the town."

"Please tell me she isn't blond."

"She isn't." Isabel smiled. "But if you're wondering, she doesn't resemble the conventional FBI *suit* any more than I do. The SCU really is an unusual unit within the Bureau, and few of us conform to any sort of dress code unless we're actually on FBI grounds. Casual and understated are sort of our watchwords."

Rafe eyed her but decided not to comment on that. "And do you normally show up unarmed?"

"Who says I'm unarmed?" She lifted one hand and gently wiggled her fingers, each one adorned with a neat, but hardly understated, red-polished oval nail.

Hearing the faint note of mockery in her voice, Rafe sighed and said, "Let me guess. Martial-arts expert?"

"I've trained," she admitted.

"Black belt?"

"Got that when I was twelve." She smiled again. "But if it

makes you feel better, I'm also wearing a calf holster—usually my backup, since my service automatic is worn in a belt holster. Our unit doesn't break all the rules, just some of them; on duty, we're expected to be armed. Since I was taking a casual look around town, a visible weapon would have been a bit conspicuous, I thought."

Rafe had noticed that her jeans were very close-fitting from waist to knees, so he couldn't help asking, "Can you get to that weapon in a hurry if you have to?"

"You'd be surprised."

He wanted to tell her he wasn't sure he could take too many more surprises but instead said only, "We've set up a conference room here as a base of operations, so all the reports, evidence, and statements are there. Couple of good computers with high-speed Internet access, plenty of phones. Standard supplies. Anything else that's needed, I'll get."

"In a situation like this, the city fathers generally say to hell with the budget."

"Which they pretty much did."

"Still, you and I both know it'll come down to basic police work, so the budget is likely to go toward overtime rather than anything fancier. As for the crime scenes, I really would like to take a look at them today. And it would help if it's just you and me out there this time. The fewer people around me when I'm studying a crime scene, the better."

"Fewer distractions?"

"Exactly."

"We've kept the scenes roped off," Rafe said, "but I'd bet my pension that at least a dozen kids have tramped all over them despite the warnings. Or because of them."

"Yeah, kids tend to be curious about crime scenes, so that's to be expected."

More than a little curious himself, Rafe said, "It's rained since we found Tricia Kane's body on Monday; what do you expect to find?"

"I'm not likely to find anything you and your people missed," Isabel replied, her matter-of-fact tone making it an acknowledgment rather than a compliment. "I just want to get a sense of the places, a feel for them. It's difficult to do that with only photographs and diagrams."

It made sense. Rafe nodded and rose to his feet, asking, "What about your partner?"

"She may want to take a look at the scenes later," Isabel said, getting up as well. "Or maybe not. We tend to come at things from different angles."

"Probably why your boss teamed you up."

"Yes," Isabel said. "Probably."

Caleb Powell wasn't a happy man. Not only had he lost his efficient paralegal to the killer stalking Hastings, he had also lost a friend. There hadn't been the slightest romantic spark between Tricia and him, particularly since she was almost young enough to be his daughter, but there had been an immediate liking and respect from the day she first began working for him almost two years before.

He missed her. He missed her a lot.

And since the temp he had hired was still trying to figure out Tricia's filing system—and kept coming to him with questions about it—his office wasn't exactly his favorite place to be right now. All of which explained why he was sitting in the downtown coffee shop sipping an iced mocha and staring grimly through the front window at the media-fest still going on across the street at the town hall.

"Vultures," he muttered.

"They have their jobs to do."

He looked at the woman seated at the next table, not really surprised she had responded to his comment because people did that in small towns. Especially when there were only two customers in the place at the time. He didn't recognize her, but that didn't surprise him either; Hastings wasn't *that* small.

"Their jobs stop when they cross the line between informing the public and sensationalizing a tragedy," he said.

"In a perfect world," she agreed. "Last time I checked, we didn't live in a perfect world."

"No, that's true."

"So we have to cope with less than the ideal." She smiled faintly. "I've even heard it said that the world would be better off without lawyers, Mr. Powell."

Just a bit wary now, he said, "You have me at a disadvantage."

"Sorry. My name is Hollis Templeton. I'm with the FBI."

That did surprise him. An attractive brunette with a short, no-fuss hairstyle and disconcertingly clear blue eyes, she looked nothing at all like a tough federal cop. Slender almost to the point of thinness, she was wearing a lightweight summer blouse and floral skirt, an outfit eerily like the one Tricia had reportedly worn the day she was killed.

His disbelief must have been obvious; with another faint smile, she drew a small I.D. folder from her purse and handed it across to him.

He had seen a federal I.D. before. This one was genuine. Hollis Templeton was a Special Investigator for the FBI.

He returned the folder to her. "So this isn't a coincidental meeting," he said.

"Actually, it is." She shrugged. "It was hot as hell outside, so I came in for iced coffee. And to watch the circus across the street. I recognized you, though. They ran your photo in the local paper Tuesday after Tricia Kane was killed."

"As you noted, Agent Templeton, I'm a lawyer. I don't really appreciate impromptu interviews with federal officials."

"But you do want to find out who killed Tricia."

He noticed that she didn't deny it was an interview. "I also don't appreciate typical law-enforcement tactics and questions designed to *encourage* me to talk carelessly to a cop."

"Take all the care you like. If a lawyer doesn't know how much is . . . safe . . . to disclose, nobody does."

"I think I find that offensive, Agent Templeton."

"And I think you're awfully touchy for a man with nothing to hide, Mr. Powell. You know the drill better than most. We'll be talking to everyone who knew Tricia Kane. You were her employer and her friend, and that puts you pretty high up on our list."

"Of suspects?"

"Of people to talk to. Something you know, something you saw or heard, may be the key we'll need to find her killer."

"Then call me in to the police station for a formal interview or come see me at my office," he said, getting to his feet. "Make an appointment." He left a couple of dollars on the table and turned away.

"She liked tea instead of coffee, and took it with milk. You always thought that was odd."

Caleb turned back, staring at the agent.

"She always felt she had disappointed her father by not becoming a lawyer, so being a paralegal was a compromise. It gave her more time for her art. She had asked you to pose for her, but you kept putting her off. And about six months ago, you offered her a shoulder to cry on when her relationship with her boyfriend ended badly. You were working late at the office when she broke down, and afterward you drove her home. She fell asleep on the couch. You covered her with an afghan and left."

Slowly, he said, "None of that was in the police report."

"No. It wasn't."

"Then how the hell do you know?"

"I just do."

"How?" he demanded.

Instead of replying to that, Hollis said, "I saw some of her work. Tricia's. She was talented. She might have become very well known if she'd lived."

"Something else you *just* know?"

"My partner and I got into town last night. We've checked out a few things. Tricia's apartment, for one. Nice place. Really good studio. And some of the paintings she'd finished were there. I . . . used to be an artist myself, so I know quality work when I see it. She did quality work."

"And you read her diary."

"She didn't keep one. Most of the artists I know don't. Something about images as opposed to words, I guess."

"Are you going to tell me how you know what you know?"

"I thought you didn't want to talk to me, Mr. Powell."

His mouth tightened. "What I think is that alienating me is not at all a good idea, Agent Templeton."

"It's a risk," she admitted, not noticeably disturbed by that. "But one I'm willing to take if I have to. You're smart, Mr. Powell. You're very, very smart. Too smart to play dumb games. And at the end of the day I'd really rather not have you as an enemy, never mind the fact that you know all the legal angles and could keep us at arm's length for a long time."

"You think I'd do that? Potentially put other lives in danger by withholding information?"

"You tell me."

After a moment, Caleb crossed the few feet separating them and sat down in the second chair at her table. "No. I wouldn't. And not only because I'm an officer of the court. But I don't know anything that could help you find this killer."

"How can you be so sure of that? You don't even know what questions we want to ask you." She shook her head slightly. "You aren't a suspect. According to Chief Sullivan's report, you have a verifiable alibi for the twenty-four hours surrounding Tricia Kane's murder."

"What the thrillers like to call a cast-iron alibi. I spent the weekend in New Orleans for a family wedding and didn't fly back here until Monday afternoon. I got the news about Tricia when Rafe called me at my hotel around noon."

"And a companion places you in your hotel room from just before midnight until after eight that morning," Hollis said matter-of-factly. "She's positive you never left the room."

Without at all planning to, Caleb heard himself say, "A former girlfriend."

"Former?" Her voice was wry.

A bit defensive despite himself, he said, "We also happen to be old friends, what my father used to call scratch-and-sniff buddies. We see each other, we end up in bed. Happens about twice a year, since she lives in New Orleans. Where we both grew up, and where she practices law, which makes her highly unlikely to perjure herself. Any other nuggets you want to mine from my personal life, Agent Templeton?"

"Not at the moment."

"Too kind."

She didn't react to his sarcasm except with another of those little smiles as she said, "About Tricia Kane. Do you think her ex-boyfriend might have wanted to hurt her?"

"I doubt it. She never said he was violent or in any way abusive, and I never saw any signs of it. Besides, unless he slipped back into town in the last three weeks, he's out of the picture. They broke up because he thought his pretty face could earn him screen time in Hollywood and he didn't want Tricia along for what he was convinced was going to be a wild and award-winning ride."

"Sounds painful for her."

"It was. Emotionally. She went home for lunch that day and found him packing to leave. That's when he told her he was going. Until that moment, she'd believed they would end up married."

"Since then had she ever talked about a particular man?"

"I don't think she was even dating. If so, she never mentioned it. She was concentrating on her painting when she wasn't at the office."

"Do you know if anything unusual had happened lately? Strange phone calls or messages, someone she'd noticed turning up wherever she went, that sort of thing?"

"No. She seemed fine. Not worried, not stressed, not upset by anything. She seemed fine."

"There was nothing you could have done," Hollis said.

Caleb drew a deep breath and let it out slowly. "Oh, I have no illusions, Agent Templeton. I know how quickly random acts of violence can snuff out lives, no matter how careful we think we are. But those acts tend to be committed by stupid or brutal people, for stupid and brutal reasons. This is different. This bastard is pure evil."

"I know."

"Do you?"

She smiled an odd, twisted smile, and her blue eyes had an equally strange, flat shine to them that made Caleb feel suddenly uneasy. "I know all about evil, Mr. Powell, believe me. I met it up close and personal."

Isabel stood gazing around the clearing where Tricia Kane's body had been found. It was mostly in shade now that the sun was no longer directly overhead, which she appreciated since the day was hot and humid. She was conscious of Rafe Sullivan's scrutiny, but she had been at this too long to allow him to distract her.

Much.

Both the blood and the chalk used to mark body position and location had been washed away by the rain, but she didn't need either to know exactly where Tricia Kane had suffered and died. She looked down just inches from her feet, her gaze absently tracing the shape of something—someone—that was no longer there.

She had been here, in this sort of place, so many times, Isabel thought. But it never got any easier. Never.

"He got her in the back," she said, "then jerked her around by the wrist and began driving the knife into her chest. The first blow to her chest staggered her backward, the second put her on the ground. She was losing blood so fast she didn't have the strength to fight him off. She was all but gone when he began stabbing her in the genital area. And either her skirt came up when she fell, or else he jerked it out of the way when he began stabbing her, since the material wasn't slashed. He pulled the skirt back down when he was done. Odd, that. Protecting her modesty, or veiling his own desires and needs?"

Rafe was frowning. "The ME says she died too fast to leave any bruises, but he told me privately he felt she'd been jerked around and held by one wrist. It wasn't in his report."

34

Isabel looked at him, weighing him for a moment, then smiled. "I get hunches."

"Yeah?" He crossed powerful arms over his chest and lifted both eyebrows inquiringly.

"Okay, they're a little more than hunches."

"Is this where the *special* in Special Crimes Unit comes in?"

"Sort of. You read the Bureau's brief on our unit, right?"

"I did. It was nicely murky, but the gist I got is that the unit is called in when a judgment is made that the crimes committed are unusually challenging for local law enforcement. That SCU agents use traditional as well as *intuitive* investigative methods to solve said crimes. By *intuitive* I gather they mean these *hunches* of yours?"

"Well, they couldn't very well announce that the SCU is made up mostly of psychics. Wouldn't go over very well with the majority of cops, considering how . . . um . . . levelheaded you guys tend to be. We've discovered through bitter experience that proving what we can do is a lot more effective with you guys than just claiming our abilities are real."

"So why're you telling me?"

"I thought you could take it." She lifted an eyebrow at him. "Was I wrong?"

"I'll let you know when I make up my mind."

"Fair enough."

"So I gather you don't normally inform local law enforcement of this?"

"Depends. It's pretty much left up to our judgment. The assigned team, I mean. Bishop says you can't plan some things in advance, and whether or not to spill the beans—and when—is one of them. I've been on assignments where the local cops didn't have a clue, and others where they were convinced, by the time we left, that it was some kind of magic."

35

"But it isn't." He didn't quite make it a question.

"Oh, no. Perfectly human abilities that simply don't happen to be shared by everyone. It's like math."

"Math?"

"Yeah. I don't get math. Never have. Balancing my checkbook stresses me out like you wouldn't believe. But I always liked science, history, English. Those I was good at. I bet you're good at math."

"It doesn't stress me out," he admitted.

"Different strokes. People have strengths and weaknesses, and some have abilities that can look amazing because they're uncommon. There aren't a lot of Mozarts or Einsteins, so people marvel at their abilities. Guy throws a hundred-mile-an-hour fastball and puts it over the plate three out of five pitches, and he's likely to be set for life, because very few people can do what he does. Gifts. Rare, but all perfectly human."

"And your gift is?"

"Clairvoyance. The faculty of perceiving things or events beyond normal sensory contact. Simply put, I know things. Things I shouldn't be able to know—according to all the laws of conventional science. Facts and other bits of information. Conversations. Thoughts. Events. The past as well as the present."

"All that?"

"All that. But more often than not it's a random jumble of stuff, like the clutter in an attic. Or like the chatter of voices in the next room: you hear everything but really catch only a word or two, maybe a phrase. That's where practice and training come in, helping make sense of the confusion. Learning to see the important objects in that cluttered attic or isolate that one important voice speaking in the next room."

"And you use this . . . ability? In investigating crimes, I mean."

"Yes. The Special Crimes Unit was formed to do just that. For most of us, becoming a part of the unit was the first time in our lives that we didn't feel like freaks."

Rafe thought that much, at least, made sense. He could understand how people with senses beyond the "normal" five might feel more than a little alienated from society. Having a useful and rewarding job and a place where they were considered entirely normal had probably changed their lives.

Isabel didn't wait for his response, just went on in that slightly absentminded tone. "There's been very little study into the paranormal, really, but we've built on that with our own studies and field experience. We've developed our own definitions and classifications within the SCU, as well as defined degrees of ability and skill. I'm a seventh-degree clairvoyant, which means I have a fair amount of ability and control."

Rafe watched as she knelt down and touched the ground, no more than an inch or so from where Tricia Kane's blond hair had lain. "Touching the ground helps?" he asked warily.

"Touching things sometimes helps, yeah. Objects, people. It's better when the area is contained, enclosed, but you work with what you've got. The ground is pretty much the only thing left out here, so . . ." She looked up at him and smiled, though her eyes held a slightly abstracted expression. "Not magic. Maybe we're just a lot more connected to this world and to one another than we think."

*It was hot, the way it is now. But barely light. She could smell the honeysuckle. But that's all* . . . all she could get about the murder, at least. That and her certain sense of something dark and evil crouching, springing . . . But only that. Isabel wasn't really surprised. This place was wide open, and they were always the toughest.

He watched her intently. "What do you mean?"

He had very dark eyes, she thought. "We leave footprints when we pass. Skin cells, stray hairs. The scent of our cologne lingering in the air. Maybe we leave more than that. Maybe we leave energy. Even our thoughts have energy. Measurable electromagnetic energy. Today's science admits that much."

"Yeah. And so?"

"Our theory is that psychics are able to tap into electromagnetic fields. The earth has them, every living thing has them, and many objects seem to absorb and hold them. Think of it as a kind of static electricity. Some people get shocked more often than others. I get shocked a lot."

"Are you getting shocked now?"

Isabel straightened and brushed the dirt off her hand. She was frowning slightly. "It'd be easier if the clairvoyant bits came in neon, but they don't. That cluttered attic. That noisy party in the next room. In the end it's usually just a jumble of information, stuff I could have read or heard or been told."

Rafe waited for a moment, then said, "Except?"

"Except . . . when the information comes in the form of a vision. That *is* in neon. Sometimes in blood."

"Not literally?"

"Afraid so. It's rare for me, but it does happen from time to time. In the case of a murder, it's as if I become the victim. I see or hear—or sometimes feel—what they do. While they're being killed. I'm told it's a bit startling to watch. Don't freak out if it happens, okay?"

"You're telling me you actually *bleed*?"

"Sometimes. It fades away pretty fast, though. Like I said, don't let it bother you."

"Don't let it bother me? Cops see blood, Isabel, we tend to freak out. In a controlled, professional manner, of course. We take it as a signal that it's time to do our job."

Her eyes sharpened abruptly, and she smiled. "Well, if you see blood on me, resist your instincts. Chances are, it'll belong to somebody else."

"In Hastings, chances are it'll be yours. Unless you want to color your hair for the duration."

"Wouldn't help. He already knows."

"Knows what?"

"He's already seen me, Rafe. One of the clairvoyant bits I've picked up. I'm on his A-list."

# 3

GODDAMMIT, YOU TOLD ME being bait for this bastard wasn't the idea."

"It wasn't the plan. It was always a possibility, of course, but it wasn't the plan."

"Isabel—"

"Besides, it isn't that clear-cut. I said I was on his A-list, but I'm not next. He gets to know his victims before he kills them, Rafe. He doesn't know me. Not yet. And he won't come after me until he does. Or thinks he does."

"Are you willing to bet your life on that?"

She didn't hesitate. "To catch this bastard? Yes."

Rafe took a step toward her. "Have you reported it to your boss? Does he know you're on the A-list?"

"Not yet. I'm scheduled to report in later today. I'll tell him then."

"Will you?" His doubt was obvious.

Isabel chuckled. "Rafe, our unit is made up of psychics. You don't keep secrets, or withhold vital bits of information, when half the team can read your mind. Very few of us have been able to keep anything important from Bishop no matter how far away we were."

"Have you?"

Isabel took a last look down at the ground where Tricia Kane had died, then started toward him with a slight gesture to indicate they might as well walk back to his Jeep. "I thought so once. Just after I first joined the unit. I thought I was being very clever. Turned out he'd known all along. He usually does."

Rafe didn't say anything else until they were in the Jeep and he had turned the air-conditioning on full-blast. "The simplest thing to do," he said, "is to have you recalled and somebody else sent down here. Somebody who won't draw this bastard's attention."

"The simplest thing," Isabel said, "is not always the smartest thing."

"I am not going to stand by while you're dangled on a god-damned hook."

"I told you, I'm not next on his hit parade. But somebody else is. Some woman is walking around in your town right now, Rafe, and a killer is stalking her. My partner and I are up to speed on this investigation. Bishop thought we were the best team to send down here, and his success rate, *our* success rate as a unit, is over ninety percent. We can help you catch him. Send me back, and the next team has to start from scratch. Do you really want to waste that time, especially when this killer is averaging a victim a week so far?"

"Shit." He stared at her grimly. "I'm taking a hell of a lot on faith here. This psychic stuff."

"At least you didn't call it bullshit," she murmured. "That's usually the first reaction."

Ignoring that, he said, "I'm supposed to be okay with you being on our killer's list because you assure me you aren't *next*. That we have time while he stalks his next victim and, not incidentally, finds out enough about you to feel that he knows you. So he can kill you."

"That pretty much sums it up, yeah."

"Convince me. Convince me that this *clairvoyant* knowledge you have is genuine. That it's something I can trust."

"Parlor tricks. It always comes down to parlor tricks."

"I'm serious, Isabel."

"I know you are." She sighed. "You sure you want to do this?"

Suddenly wary again, he asked, "Why wouldn't I be?"

"Because the best way for me to convince you is to open up a connection between us and tell you things about yourself, your life, your past. Things I couldn't possibly know any other way. You might not find that very comfortable. Most people don't."

"Women are dying, Isabel. I think I can endure a little psychic reading."

"Okay. But when we speak of this later—and we will—just remember that I tried to warn you. I get bonus points for that."

"Fine."

She held out a hand, palm up, and Rafe hesitated only an instant before placing his hand on hers. He nearly jerked away when their flesh touched, because there was a literal, visible spark and a definite, if faint, shock. But her fingers closed over his strongly.

Matter-of-factly, she said, "Well, that's new."

Rafe wanted to say something about static, but he was busy having another of those strange feelings, just as he'd had when she walked into the press conference, but much, much stronger.

That a door had opened and a fresh breeze was blowing through. That everything around him was in sharper focus, more real than it had been before. That something had changed.

And he still didn't know if it was a good change or a bad one.

Isabel didn't go into some kind of trance or even close her eyes. But her eyes did take on that abstracted expression he had noticed before, as if she were listening to some distant sound. Her voice remained calm.

"You have an unusual paperweight on your desk at home, some kind of car part encased in acrylic. You prefer cats over dogs, though you don't have either because of your long working hours. You're allergic to alcohol, which is why you don't drink. You're fascinated by the Internet, by the instant communication of people all over the world. You're a movie buff, especially interested in science fiction and horror."

Isabel smiled suddenly. "And you wear a particular style of jockey shorts because of a commercial you saw on TV."

Rafe jerked his hand away. "Jesus," he muttered. Then, getting back on balance, he added somewhat defensively, "You could have found out any of that. All of it."

"Even the jockey shorts?"

"Jesus," he repeated.

She was looking at him steadily, her eyes still faintly abstracted, distant. "Ah, now I understand why the idea of an FBI unit made up of psychics didn't throw you. Your grandmother had what she called 'the sight.' She knew things before they happened."

Rafe looked at his hand, which he had been unconsciously rubbing with the other one, then at her. "You aren't touching me," he noted in a careful tone.

"Yeah, well. Once a connection is made, I tend to pick up stuff from then on."

"Jesus Christ," he said, varying the oath somewhat.

"I tried to warn you. Remember, bonus points."

"I still don't— You could have found out most of that some other way."

"Maybe. But could I have found out that your grandmother told you on your fifteenth birthday that your destiny was to be a cop? It was just the two of you there at the time, so nobody else knew. You believed it was weird, she was weird, because you hadn't thought of being a cop. The family business was construction. That's what you were going to do, especially as you'd been swinging a hammer since you were twelve."

Rafe was silent, frowning slightly.

"She also told you . . . there would come a point in your life when you would have to be very, very careful." Isabel was frowning herself now, head slightly tilted, clearly concentrating. "That there was something important you were meant to do as part of the destiny she saw for you, but it would be dangerous. Deadly dangerous. Something about . . . a storm . . . a woman with green eyes . . . a black-gloved hand reaching . . . and glass shattering."

He drew a breath. "Vague enough."

Isabel blinked, and her green eyes cleared. "According to what our seers have told me, visions often come that way, as a series of images. Sometimes they prove to be literal, other times it's all symbolic. The green-eyed woman could be a jealous woman or someone who resents you or someone else. The black-gloved hand a threat. The storm, violence. Like that."

"Still vague," he insisted. "Any of that is something a cop deals with regularly."

"Well, we'll see. Because I have more than a hunch that what your grandmother saw was this point in your life—otherwise I probably wouldn't have picked up her prediction."

"What do you mean?"

"Patterns are everywhere, Rafe. Events touch other events like a honeycomb, connecting to one another. And seeming coincidences usually aren't. I may pick up some trivial information unrelated to what's going on at present, and not all the stuff I get could even be called hits, but I'm focused on this investigation, this killer—and when that's the case it almost always turns out that most of what I get is relevant to what's going on around me at the time."

"Want to use a few more qualifiers?"

She smiled at his exasperation, though it was more rueful than amused. "Sorry, but you've got to understand we're in frontier territory here. There aren't a whole lot of absolute certainties. Conventional science pretty much sneers at psychic ability, and those who were brave enough to test and experiment found themselves dealing with an unfortunate commonality among psychics."

"Which is?"

"Very few of us perform well under laboratory conditions. Nobody really knows why, that's just the way it is." Isabel shrugged. "Plus, the tests tended to be poorly designed because, to begin with, they didn't know what they were dealing with. How can you effectively measure and analyze something without even knowing how it works? And how do you figure out how it works when you can't *make* it work within a controlled situation?"

"Somebody must have known, or you wouldn't be here. Would you?"

"The SCU wouldn't exist if Bishop hadn't been highly motivated and exceptionally driven to figure out how to use his own abilities to track and capture a serial killer years ago. Once he was able to do that, he believed other psychics could be trained, that we could learn to use our abilities as investigative tools. And that those tools would give us an edge. We're proving it works.

Slowly, carefully—and with setbacks now and then. We're also learning as we go.

"What we've found through sheer trial and error in the field is that our abilities function best when we're focused on something compelling—such as a murder investigation. But that doesn't mean we can flip a switch and get exactly the piece of information we need. As with everything else in life, we have to work for it. It's still trial and error."

"So, bottom line, your best guess is that because you *picked up* what my grandmother told me over twenty years ago it means what she saw has something to do with what's happening in my life today. This investigation."

"It's a good bet, based on how my abilities have worked so far. Plus, logically this'll probably be the toughest case of your career, assuming you don't move to a big city and deal often with violent killers. And though I can't speak to the specifics of your grandmother's vision—yet—I can tell you it's going to be dangerous as hell tracking and catching this killer."

Listening to her tone as well as the words, Rafe said, "You picked up something else out there where Tricia Kane was killed, didn't you? What was it?"

She hesitated just long enough to make the internal debate obvious, then said, "What I picked up out there confirmed something I suspected even before I came to Hastings. This town is just his latest hunting ground."

"He's killed before?"

"In at least two previous locations. Ten years ago, he butchered six women in Florida. And five years ago, six women in Alabama."

"Blondes?" Rafe asked.

"No. Redheads in Florida. Brunettes in Alabama. We have no idea why."

"And nobody caught him then."

"Lots tried. But he hit quick—one victim every week, just like here—and then he vanished. Typical serial killer cases, if there is such a thing, usually drag on months, years, and it takes time to get law enforcement organized once a pattern is even noticed. But this monster hit and vanished before the task forces could even get up and running. And he didn't leave so much as a hair behind to help I.D. him, so they had almost nothing to work with."

"Then how do you know it's the same killer?"

"The M.O. The profile. The fact that Bishop himself worked on the second set of murders—one of his very few unsuccessful cases."

"I wasn't told about any of this in the initial profile."

"No. The first profiler wasn't a member of the SCU. And even though the two earlier sets of murders came up on the computer as possibly connected, he discounted them because it was believed at the time that the most likely suspect was killed trying to escape police in Alabama. His car went off a bridge. But they never found the body."

"So do you and Bishop believe he didn't die—or that the suspect the police were chasing wasn't the killer?"

"We believe the latter, actually. The man the police were after had a few violent crimes on his rap sheet, but neither Bishop nor I was convinced he had the right psychological makeup to be the clever serial killer we were after."

"So he kills his six victims, lays low for five years, and then starts up all over again. That's a hell of a cooling-off period."

"And unusual. We believe he uses the time to relocate and get to know the people around him. We also believe there's always a trigger, as I said. Something sets him off. Something *always* sets him off."

47

Again, Rafe heard a note in her voice that made him wary. "There's another reason you believe this is the same killer. What is it?"

Isabel answered without hesitation. "Standing where Tricia Kane was murdered, I felt him. Just the way I felt him five years ago when I first encountered Bishop and joined the team. And the way I felt him ten years ago when he killed a good friend of mine."

It was nearly midnight when Mallory Beck pulled herself reluctantly from bed and began getting dressed. "Dammit. Where on earth did my bra get to?"

"Over there by the bookcase. You could stay, you know. Spend the night."

"I'm back on duty at seven," she said. "First big meeting of our task force, FBI agents included, starts at eight. That's off the record, Alan."

"Mal, I've told you before, anything you say to me privately is off the record." His voice was patient. He propped himself up on an elbow and watched her dress. "I'm not going to cross that line."

She was reasonably sure he wouldn't. But only reasonably sure.

"Okay. But I still need to go home. I won't sleep much if I stay here, and I want to be rested tomorrow."

"You don't have anything to prove, you know. To these FBI agents, I mean. Or to Rafe. You're a damned good cop, everybody knows that."

"Yeah, well, being a good cop hasn't been enough so far, has it?"

He frowned a little as he watched her, wondering as he so often had in the last few months if he would ever really know her. It was undoubtedly part of the attraction as far as he was concerned, he knew that very well; there was so much of her beneath the surface, and his instinct was to dig, to explore and understand.

She wasn't making it easy for him.

Maybe that was part of the attraction as well. Plus the mind-blowing sex, of course. Either it was sheer natural talent, or else Alan had to take his hat off to the men in her past, because Mallory was something else in bed.

*Addictive* was the word that came to mind.

"You can't blame yourself," he said finally.

"*To Protect and Serve.* It says that on the sides of our cruisers and Jeeps. It's what we get paid for. Our entire reason for being, so to speak."

"It's not a one-woman police force, Mal. Let some of the others carry the weight."

"They do. Especially Rafe."

"Yeah, give him his due. He wasn't too proud to yell for help."

Mallory sat down on the bed to put her socks and shoes on, eyeing her lover. "We've both known him a long time. Pride is never going to be his downfall."

"No. But failing to trust himself might be."

Since she'd had the same thought herself, Mallory could hardly disagree. But she felt uncomfortable on several levels discussing her boss with Alan, so she simply changed the subject. "I'm sorry I missed the press conference today. I hear you cracked up the room."

"Rafe did—with a joke at my expense. I gather that gorgeous blonde he left with is one of the FBI agents?"

"Mmm. Isabel Adams—and I better not see that name printed in the paper unless and until it's released officially."

"You won't, dammit." Still, Alan couldn't stop asking questions. "She's not down here alone?"

49

"No, she has a partner. Another woman. I haven't met her yet."

"Did it occur to anybody at the Bureau that sending a blond female agent down here at this particular time might be a little dicey?"

Mallory shrugged. "They wrote the profile. I have to assume they know what they're doing."

"I bet Rafe is pissed."

"You'll have to ask him about that."

"Jesus, you're pigheaded."

"It'd be more polite to call me stubborn."

"And less accurate. Mal"—he leaned over to grasp her wrist before she stood up—"is something wrong? I mean, aside from the obvious maniacal-killer-stalking-Hastings thing."

"No."

That mild syllable didn't give him much room to maneuver, but he tried. "I know you're preoccupied. Hell, we all are. But sometimes I get the feeling you're not even here."

"I didn't hear you complaining a little while ago. Even though I always wonder when a guy calls out God's name instead of mine."

Refusing to be sidetracked, Alan said, "You barely caught your breath before you were up and dressing."

"I told you. I have to go to work early."

"If you'd leave some stuff here, you could spend the night occasionally and still get to work early." He heard the note of frustration in his own voice, and the familiar resentment prickled inside him. *Why does she make me do this?*

"Alan, we've been over this. I like my own space. I never leave any of my stuff at a man's apartment. I don't like sleepovers except for vacation trips out of town. And I'm not *real* comfortable being in bed with a reporter in the first place. *Conflict of interest* rings a rather ugly bell."

Her patient tone grated, but he managed to keep his own voice calm. Even careless, around the edges. "It's that last that really bugs you, and don't think I don't know it. You don't trust me, Mal. You don't believe I can separate my work from my personal life."

"Why should you be different from the rest of us?" she asked dryly, pulling away from him and rising to her feet. "My job is in my head twenty-four seven. And so is yours. We're both career people. We live on takeout and caffeine. Half the time our socks don't match, and when we realize it we just buy new socks. We do our laundry when we run out of clean clothes. And when the biggest, baddest bad to ever hit Hastings rears its ugly head, both our careers kick into high gear. Right?"

"Right," he agreed reluctantly.

"Besides, let's not kid ourselves. Neither one of us is looking for anything more than a few hours of stress-busting sex every week." She smiled down at him. "Don't get up. I'll let myself out. See you."

"Good night, Mal." He remained where he was until he heard the front door of his apartment close. Then he fell back against the pillows and muttered a heartfelt "Shit."


Outside Alan's apartment building, Mallory stood on the sidewalk for a moment breathing in the slightly breezy but otherwise mild night air. It was a well-lighted sidewalk close to downtown Hastings, and Mallory shouldn't have felt particularly threatened.

The breeze intensified suddenly, blowing an empty soft drink can across the sidewalk a few feet away, and Mallory nearly jumped out of her skin.

"Shit," she muttered.

She could hear the trees whispering softly as the wind stirred their leaves. Hear the occasional swish of a car passing a block or so away. Crickets. Bullfrogs.

Her name.

Not that she really heard that, of course. It was just that she had the uneasy feeling she was being watched. Even followed sometimes.

She'd been conscious of it for some time now, days at least. At odd moments, usually but not always when she was outside, like now. If she were a blonde, she would have been getting really nervous about it; as it was, the sensation just made her wary and a lot more careful.

And jumpy as hell.

She had to wonder if this killer, like so many she'd read about in the police manuals, kept an eye on the cops as they investigated his crimes. Was that it? Was some wacko watching gleefully from behind the bushes, congratulating himself on his cleverness and their incompetence?

If so, maybe it made sense that he'd concentrate on one—or more—of the female officers rather than the guys. She made a mental note to herself to ask some of the other women in the department if any of them had been aware of this creepy feeling. And if they had, or maybe especially if they hadn't, she'd have to ask the FBI profiler about it.

The gorgeous female blond FBI profiler.

Mallory knew Rafe was pissed and unhappy about that; he'd never been a man to hide his feelings. But she also knew that Isabel Adams had somehow managed to persuade him to accept her presence in the investigation.

And it hadn't been by batting her baby greens at him either.

No, there was a lot more to this than sex appeal; she knew Rafe too well not to feel sure that his reasons for accepting Isabel were logical and completely professional. She was still here because he believed she was an asset to the investigation. Period.

Which wasn't to say he was immune to the effects of a beautiful face, green eyes, and a body that looked really good in clingy summery clothing. He was a man, after all.

She half laughed under her breath but kept a wary eye on her surroundings as she unlocked her car and got in. Then again, she thought, maybe she wasn't being quite fair to Rafe. Maybe having her own man problems at the moment made her overly sensitive to undercurrents.

Not that Alan was being particularly subtle. Mallory was somewhat bemused to find herself, for the first time in her adult life, on the traditionally male side of things in their relationship: she was the one who was perfectly happy with casual sex a couple of times a week, no strings or promises.

Alan wanted more.

Sighing, Mallory started the car and headed off toward her own apartment on the other side of town. It was relatively easy to push Alan and the various problems he presented to the back of her mind, at least for the moment, because in the forefront there was still the vague but persistent feeling that she was being watched.

All the way home, she couldn't shake the feeling, even though she didn't see anyone following her. Or anyone in the vicinity of her apartment building. She parked her car carefully in its slot in a well-lighted area and locked it up, then kept her key-chain pepper spray in one hand and her other hand resting on or near her weapon all the way inside and up to her apartment.

Nothing.

No one.

Just this nagging feeling that someone was watching every move she made.

Once inside, Mallory leaned back against her locked apartment door and softly muttered, "Shit."

"Let me get this straight." Isabel rubbed the nape of her neck, staring at her partner. "You met Caleb Powell in that coffee shop on Main Street, and you spilled all that stuff I picked up at Tricia Kane's apartment?"

"Not all of it." Hollis shrugged. "Just some . . . selected bits. I told you, he didn't want to talk to me. And from the jut of his jaw, I'd say he wouldn't have been willing to talk to any of us. So I got his attention. What's wrong with that?"

"Did he ask you how you obtained this information?"

"Yeah, but I distracted him. More or less."

"Hollis, he's a *lawyer*. They don't get distracted, as a rule. Not for long, anyway. What happens when he starts asking questions?"

"I don't think he will. He wants to find out who killed Tricia Kane. Besides, you told Chief Sullivan."

"As closely as we'll have to work with Rafe and his lead investigator on this case, he had to know. So will she. But a civilian?"

Hollis sighed, clearly impatient with the discussion. "Somehow I don't think a lawyer finding out we're psychics is going to be our major problem. I'm new at this whole thing, and you might as well have a bull's-eye target on your back. In neon." She stood up. "Since we have that early meeting in the morning, I think I'll go back to my own room and get some sleep, if you don't mind."

Without protest, Isabel merely said, "I'll be up and ready for breakfast at seven if you want to meet me here." The small inn where they were staying didn't provide room service, but there was a restaurant nearby.

"Okay. See you then."

"Good night, Hollis."

When she was alone in her room again, Isabel got ready for bed, brooding. Just as the night before, she barely noticed the uninspired, any-hotel-in-any-town-U.S.A. decor, and out of habit she filled the silence by having the air-conditioning on high and the TV tuned to an all-news network.

She hated silence when she was in an unfamiliar place.

She had put off calling Bishop, undecided despite what she'd told Rafe as to what she intended to report. So when her cell phone rang, she knew who it was even without the caller I.D. and answered by saying, "This is supposed to be one of those lessons you're always saying we have to learn, right? A reminder from the universe that we don't control anything except our own actions? When we're able to control them, that is."

"I don't know what you're talking about," Bishop replied, calm and transparently unconvincing.

"Yeah, yeah. Why team me with Hollis? Answer that."

"Because you're the one most likely to help her through this first real test of her abilities."

"I'm not a medium."

"No, but you understand how it feels to be forced suddenly to cope with abilities you never even dreamed were possible."

"I'm not the only other team member who wasn't born a psychic."

"You're the best adjusted."

"That's an arguable statement. Just because this stuff no longer scares the hell out of me doesn't necessarily mean I'm all that well adjusted."

"I didn't say well adjusted. I said best adjusted."

"Which only proves my point. I would think you'd want somebody well adjusted to help Hollis."

"You're going to keep arguing about this, aren't you?" Bishop said.

"I thought I might."

"Are you asking me to recall Hollis?"

Isabel hesitated, then said, "No. Dammit."

"You can help her. Just listen to your instincts."

"Bishop, we both know mediums are fragile."

"And we both know how difficult it's been for us to find a medium for the unit. They're rare, for one thing. And, yes, they're emotionally fragile. Most can't handle the job, and those who can tend to burn out quickly."

"So far," she reminded him, "we haven't found a single one who was able to gain information for us by contacting murder victims. I mean an agent. Bonnie did it, but she wasn't an agent. When she grows up, though—"

"She still has a lot of growing to do. Right now, she's preoccupied with being a teenager. It's not the easiest time of life, remember? Especially when you're gifted."

"Or cursed. Yeah, I remember. Bonnie aside, the few mediums we've found and tried to bring into murder investigations have either been terrified of opening that particular door or else didn't have enough strength or control to do it in any way helpful to us."

"Which is another reason you're teamed with Hollis and why she's in Hastings. She's strong enough to handle the work, and her control has been steadily improving."

"Maybe, but her field experience is zilch. And she's not ready to open that door, not yet. Strong or not, she's one of the scared ones. She doesn't show it, unless you count the chip on her shoulder, but she's terrified of facing death."

"Can you blame her? She fought like hell to keep death at bay on her own account hardly more than six months ago. Willingly opening that door and confronting what's on the other side is going to be the hardest thing she'll ever have to do."

"Yeah, which is one reason I don't think she's ready for this job, not yet. Look, I'm as sympathetic as anyone about what Hollis has been through, but—"

"She doesn't need sympathy. She needs to work."

"She isn't ready to work, if my opinion counts for anything."

"She believes she is ready."

"And what do you believe?" Isabel challenged.

"I believe she needs to work."

Isabel sighed. "This killer is vicious. The attacks have been vicious. If Hollis is even able to nerve herself to open the door, she's going to find a hell of a lot of terror and pain barreling through at her."

"I know."

"I can't push her, Bishop."

"I don't want you to."

"Just be here to catch her when she falls?"

"No. Don't focus on that. It's not what this is about. You investigate your case. Hollis is intelligent, curious, intuitive, and observant, and that plus the training we've given her means she'll be an asset to the investigation. If she's able to use her psychic abilities, we'll find out in a hurry whether she can handle the fallout."

"And whether I can. She could end up a basket case."

"Possibly, but don't count her out. She's exceptionally strong." Bishop paused, then added dryly, "The more imperative problem, I'd say, is that this killer you and I are both all too familiar with has noticed you this time around. For all we know, he may remember you. In any case, you're on his hit list."

"Damn," Isabel said.

H E WOKE UP with blood on his hands.
It wasn't an instant realization. The alarm was droning on and on, and he had the vague notion that he had overslept. Again. He'd been doing that a lot lately. The bed-clothes were tumbled, tangled around him, and it took a consider-able amount of effort just to roll himself over and slap at the irritating alarm clock to stop the damned noise.

He froze, hand on the now-silent clock.

His hand was . . . there was blood.

He pushed himself slowly up on an elbow and looked at his hand, at both hands. Reddish stains covered the palms. Dried stains, not wet. But now that they were close to his face, he could smell the blood, sharp and metallic, so strong it made his stomach heave.

The blood.

Again.

He fought his way out of bed and hurried to the bathroom. He stood at the sink, washing his hands over and over until there was no sign of the red. He splashed water on his face, rinsed his mouth, trying to get rid of the sour taste of fear.

He raised his head and stared into the mirror, hands braced on the sink.

A white, haggard face stared back at him.

"Oh, Christ," he whispered.

**8:00 AM**

Isabel wasted no time, at the first meeting of the four lead investigators of their combined police and FBI task force, in explaining to Detective Mallory Beck what made the SCU team "special."

Mallory, like Rafe the previous day, took the news quite calmly, saying only, "I'd call that a pretty unusual sort of unit for the FBI."

Isabel nodded. "Definitely. And we exist as a unit only as long as we're successful."

"Like that, is it? Politics?"

"More or less. Not only are we unconventional in too many ways to count, but the Bureau can't use us and our success to improve their own image; what we do too often looks like magic or some kind of witchcraft rather than science, and that is *not* something the FBI wants to publicize no matter how high our success rate is. We're becoming quietly well known within other law-enforcement organizations because of our successes, but there are still plenty of people inside the Bureau who'd love it if we failed."

"So you haven't yet?"

"Debatable point, I suppose." Isabel pursed her lips. "A few got away. But the successes have far exceeded the failures. If you call them failures."

"You don't?"

"We don't give up easily. Bishop doesn't give up easily. So . . . just because a case goes cold doesn't mean we forget about it or stop working on it. Which brings me back to this case." She explained their belief that they were dealing with a killer who had terrorized two previous towns and had a dozen murders under his belt even before he came to Hastings.

"I think we're gonna need a bigger task force," Mallory said dryly.

Even though he smiled faintly, Rafe's response was matter-of-fact. "Technically, we have one. Every officer and detective we have will be working on some aspect of the investigation. Overtime, more people to handle the phones, whatever it takes. But only you and I know about Hollis's and Isabel's psychic abilities. That's the way it stays. The last thing I want is for the press to turn this thing into a carnival sideshow."

"And they will, given the chance," Isabel said. "We've seen it happen before."

*Great,* Mallory thought, *one more thing I have to hide from Alan.* Out loud, she said, "I don't know much about ESP, unless you count commercials from those psychic hotlines, but I gather neither of you can just I.D. our perp for us like snapping your fingers?"

"Our abilities are just another tool," Isabel told her. "We use standard investigative techniques like every other cop, at least as much as possible."

Mallory was more resigned than scornful. "Yeah, I figured that would be the deal."

"It can't be too easy," Hollis said. "The universe has to make us work for everything."

"So how will your abilities help us, assuming they do?" Mallory asked. "I mean, what specifically is it that you're able to do?"

"I'm clairvoyant," Isabel said, explaining the SCU's definition of the term.

"So you have to touch something or someone to pick up information about them?"

"Touching helps, usually, because it establishes the strongest connection. But I also get information randomly sometimes. That tends to be trivia."

"For instance?" Mallory was clearly curious.

Without hesitation, Isabel said, "You had a cinnamon bun for breakfast at home this morning and you feel guilty about it."

Mallory blinked, then looked at Rafe.

"Spooky, isn't it?" he said.

Mallory cleared her throat and, without commenting on Isabel's statement, looked at Hollis. "And you?"

"I talk to dead people," she replied with a wry smile. "Technically, I'm a medium."

"No shit? That must be . . . disconcerting."

"I'm told you get used to it," Hollis murmured.

"You're told?"

"I'm new at this."

Rafe frowned. "You weren't born with it?"

"Not exactly." Hollis looked at Isabel, who explained.

"Some people possess latent—inactive—paranormal abilities. For most of those people, the abilities remain unknown and unused their entire lives. They may get hunches, flashes of knowledge they can't logically explain, but they generally ignore it or dismiss it as coincidence."

"Until something changes," Rafe guessed.

"Exactly. Every once in a while, something happens that

causes latent psychics either consciously or subconsciously to tap into the previously dormant ability and actually begin using it."

"What could do that?" Mallory asked warily.

"The most common, and most likely, scenario is that a latent becomes an adept—our term for a functional psychic—due to a physical, emotional, or psychological injury. A head injury is the most common, but almost any severe trauma can do it. Generally speaking, the greater the shock of the awakening, the stronger the abilities tend to be."

"So Hollis—"

"Both of us. Both of us survived a traumatic event," Isabel said matter-of-factly. "And became functional psychics because of it."

**9:00 AM**

Officer Ginny McBrayer hung up the phone and frowned down at the message pad for a moment, debating. Then she got up and went around the corner to Travis's desk. "Hey. Is the chief still in that meeting?"

On the phone himself, but obviously on hold judging by his propped-up feet, bored expression, and only semicontact between the receiver and his ear, Travis replied, "Yeah. Not to be disturbed unless it's an emergency. Or 'relevant,' I think he said."

"This might be." Ginny handed over the message slip. "What do you think?"

Travis studied the slip, then searched his cluttered desk for a minute, finally producing a clipboard. "Here's the list we already have going. Women of the right general age reported missing within a fifty-mile radius of Hastings. We're up to ten in the last three weeks. It was twelve, but two of them came home."

62

Ginny looked over the list, then picked up her message slip again and frowned. "Yeah, but the one I just got the call about is local, from that dairy farm just outside town. Her husband really sounded upset."

"Okay, then tell the chief." Travis shrugged. "I'm waiting for the clerk at the courthouse to get back to me about all that property Jamie Brower owned. She's got me on hold. Remind me to tell them they need some new canned music, okay? This shit is giving me a headache."

"I don't want to interrupt the chief's meeting," Ginny said, ignoring the irrelevant information he'd offered. "What if this is nothing?"

"And what if it's something? Go knock on the door and report the call. Better for him to be mad at an interruption than to be mad because he wasn't told something he should have been."

"Easy for you to say," Ginny muttered. But she turned away from the other cop's desk and headed for the conference room.

"Neither of you was born psychic?" Mallory said in surprise. "But—"

Isabel smiled, but said, "Understandably, neither one of us is all that eager to talk about what happened to us, so if you two don't mind, we won't. We're both trained investigators, of course, and I'm a profiler. Plus we have the full backing of the SCU and the resources of Quantico. But anything Hollis and I are able to glean from our abilities or spider sense will have to be considered a bonus, not something we can count on."

Rafe eyed her. "Spider sense?"

"It's not as out there as it sounds." She smiled. "Just our informal term for enhanced normal senses—the traditional five. Something Bishop discovered and has been able to teach most of us is how to concentrate and amplify our sight, hearing, and other senses. Like everything else, it varies from agent to agent in terms of strength, accuracy, and control. Even at its best it isn't a huge edge, but it has been known to help us out from time to time."

"I have a question," Mallory said.

"Only one?" Rafe murmured.

"Shoot," Isabel invited.

"Why you? I mean, why did this Bishop of yours pick you to come down here? You fit the victim profile to a T, unless there's been a change I don't know about."

"It gets worse," Rafe told his detective, his voice grim. "Isabel believes our killer has already spotted her. And added her to his list of must-kill blondes."

"Well, I can't say I'm all that surprised." Mallory lifted a brow at the blond agent. "So why're you still here? Bait?"

"No," Rafe said immediately.

Isabel said, "We have some time before it becomes an issue. This bastard gets to know his victims before he kills them, or at least has to feel that he knows them, and he doesn't know me. In any case, the reason why I'm here is much more compelling than any risk I face as a possible target."

"And that reason is?"

"As I told Rafe yesterday, patterns and connections are every-where, if we only know how to look for them." Isabel spoke slowly. "I have a connection with this killer. He killed a friend of mine ten years ago, and five years ago I was involved in the inves-tigation in Alabama of the second series of murders."

Mallory was frowning, intent. "Are you saying you know him? But if you know him, doesn't that mean he knows you? Knows you the way he has to know his victims? That thing that's rapidly becoming an issue?"

"No. I wasn't in law enforcement when my friend was killed,

I was just another shocked and grieving part of her life—and her death. And I was on the fringes of the official investigation in Alabama; by the time I was officially involved, he'd already murdered his sixth victim and moved on. So it's at least as likely as not that he won't even know I was involved in the previous investigations."

"But you're on his hit list."

"On it, but I'm not next in line. I'm not local, so it won't be easy for him to find information about me, especially since I don't plan to become too chatty with anyone outside our investigation."

"What about inside?" Mallory asked. "We've had at least the suspicion that the perp could be a cop. Has that been ruled out?"

"Unfortunately, no. Our feeling is that we're not dealing with a cop, but there are some elements of the M.O. that make it at least possible."

"For instance?" Rafe was frowning slightly. "We haven't seen the updated profile," he reminded her.

"I have copies here for both of you," Isabel replied. "Not a lot has changed from the first profile as far as the description of our unknown subject is concerned. We have revised his probable age range upward a bit, given the time frame of at least ten years as an active killer. So, he's a white male, thirty to forty-five years old, above-average intelligence. He has a steady job and possibly a family or significant other, and he copes well with day-to-day life. In other words, this is not a man who's obviously stressed or appears in any way at odds with himself.

"Blondes are only his latest targets; in the earlier murders, he killed first redheads in Florida ten years ago, and then, five years ago, brunettes in Alabama. Which, by the way, is another reason he wouldn't have noticed me then even if he'd seen me; he's always very focused on his targets and potential targets, and I had the wrong hair color for him both times before."

"What about the elements that could indicate he's a cop?" Rafe asked.

"The central question of this investigation—and the two before this one—is how he's been able to persuade these women to calmly and quietly accompany him to lonely spots. These are highly intelligent, very savvy women, in several cases trained in self-defense. None of them was stupid. So how did he get them to go with him?"

"Authority figure," Rafe said. "Has to be."

"That's what we're thinking. So we can't rule out cops. We also can't rule out someone who appears to be a member of the clergy, or any other trustworthy authority figure. Someone in politics, someone well known within the community. Whoever he is, these women trusted him, at least for the five or ten minutes it took him to get them alone and vulnerable. He looks safe to them. He looks unthreatening."

Mallory said, "You said earlier that he'd killed a dozen women before coming to Hastings. Exactly twelve?"

"Six women in six weeks, both times."

"So it is just women," Mallory said. "Bottom line, he hates women."

"Hates, loves, wants, needs—it's probably a tangle. He hates them for what they are, either because they represent what he wants and can't have or because he feels somehow emasculated by them. Killing them gives him power over them, gives him control. He needs that, needs to feel he's stronger than they are, that he can master them."

"A manly man," Hollis said, her mockery both obvious and hollow.

Isabel nodded. "Or, at least, so he wants to believe. And wants us to believe."

Alan Moore had always thought that calling the central work area of the *Chronicle* offices "the newsroom" must have been someone's idea of irony. Because nothing newsworthy ever happened in Hastings.

Or hadn't, until the first murder.

Not that there hadn't been killings in Hastings before, of course; when a town had been in existence for nearly two hundred years, there were bound to be killings every now and then. People had died out of greed, out of jealousy, out of spite, out of rage.

But until the murder of Jamie Brower, no one had been killed by pure evil.

Alan hadn't hesitated to point that out in his coverage of the murders and their investigation. And not even Rafe had accused him—publicly or privately—of sensationalizing the tragedies of those murders.

Some things damned well couldn't be denied.

There was something evil in Hastings, and the fact that it was walking around on two legs passing itself off as human didn't change that fact.

"How many times have I told you to pick up your own damned mail, Alan?" Callie Rosier, the *Chronicle*'s only full-time photographer, dumped several envelopes on his already cluttered desk. "It's in a little box with your name on it right on the other side of that wall. You can't miss it."

"I just said you could pick up mine while you were getting yours, what's wrong with that?" Alan retorted.

"What is this 'while you're up' thing with you men?" She continued to her own desk, shaking her head as she sat down. "You sweat your brains out running miles every morning and lifting weights in the gym so you'll look good in your jeans but pester other people to get stuff for you when it's in the same damned room. Jesus."

"Don't you have film to develop?" The question was more habit than curiosity, and absentminded to boot since he was leafing through his mail.

"No. Why are all these places offering me credit cards?"

"The same reason they're offering them to me," Alan replied, tossing several into his overflowing trash can. "Because they haven't checked our credit records." He eyed his final bit of mail, a large manila envelope with no return address, and hesitated only an instant before tearing it open.

"I think these telemarketers are morons," Callie said, studying the contents of one envelope marked URGENT! "They don't even bother to be accurate in who they're sending this stuff to anymore. I ask you, does the name Callie sound like it belongs to a man? This one should have been addressed to you. Take a little blue pill and get another inch or two. I'm sure you'd like another inch or two. And more staying power, says here."

"I'll be a son of a bitch," Alan said.

"Aren't you usually?"

He looked at her, saw that she was focused on her own mail and not even paying attention to the conversation. With only an instant's pause, Alan said casually, "Oh, yeah, always." Then he looked back down at his mail and, this time under his breath, repeated, "I'll be a son of a bitch."


Rafe accepted the message slip, absently introduced Officer McBrayer to the federal agents, then read the information she had offered. "Her husband says she's been gone since Monday?"

"He thinks since Monday." Ginny made an effort to sound as brisk and professional as she could, even though she was nervous and knew it showed. "He didn't see her that afternoon, and with two cows calving he was out in his barns all night. He says it could have been Tuesday; that's when he realized she wasn't in the house. He thought she'd gone to visit a friend in town, since it's something she often does, but when she didn't come home, he checked. She wasn't there. Isn't anywhere he could think to check. I think it only slowly dawned on him that maybe he should be worried."

"Yeah," Rafe muttered, "Tim Helton isn't the sharpest pencil in the box."

"Understatement," Mallory offered. "The way I heard it, he once decided that moonshine would work just as well as fuel in his tractor. Dunno if he got a bad batch or what, but it blew the sucker all to hell and nearly took him with it."

"Moonshine?" Isabel asked curiously. "They still make that stuff?"

"Believe it or not. We've had the ATF out here a few times over the years because of illegal brew. Seems like a lot of trouble to go to, if you ask me, but the bootleggers seem to feel it's worth it. Either that or they just don't want to pay The Government a cent more than they have to."

Rafe said, "And there's at least one survivalist group in the area. They consider it the norm to make everything they need themselves. Including booze." He made a note on the pad before him, then handed the message slip back to his officer. "Okay, standard procedure, Ginny. I want a detective out there to talk to Tim, and let's get a list of places she might possibly be. Friends, relatives, anybody she might be visiting. From now on, we treat every missing person, man or woman, as if he or she could be a murder victim."

"Yes, sir."

When the young officer had hurried from the room, Isabel said, "Is this people starting to panic? I mean, is this an unusual increase in women reported missing?"

He nodded. "Oh, yeah. In the past three weeks, we've seen the reports jump tenfold. Most come home within twenty-four hours or are discovered visiting relatives or talking to divorce attorneys, or just at the grocery store."

"Most. But not all."

"We still have a few missing in the general area, but we haven't yet been able to rule out a voluntary absence in any of the cases."

"We'll probably see even more of this," Isabel commented.

"Problem is," Mallory said, "we have to treat every report seriously, just as Rafe said. So we'll waste a lot of manpower searching for women who aren't really missing or who ran off and don't want to be found. Lady last week cussed me out good for *finding* her."

"Motel?" Isabel inquired sapiently.

"Uh-huh. Not alone, needless to say."

"Still, we have to look for them," Hollis said.

Rafe nodded. "No question. I'm just hoping it won't muddy the water too much. Or deplete resources needed elsewhere."

"In the meantime," Isabel said, "those of us in this room at least have to focus on what we know we've got. Three murdered women."

Rafe said, "You told me there's always a trigger. Always something specific that sets him off."

"There has to be," Isabel responded. "You said yourself that five years is a hell of a long cooling-off period for a serial killer; it is, especially after a fairly frenzied six-week killing spree. A gap that long usually means either that murders in another location have gone unnoticed or at least weren't connected to him, or that he's in prison somewhere or otherwise unable to keep killing."

"I gather you're certain that isn't the case here."

"When he hit in Alabama five years ago, we combed through police files of unsolved murders from coast to coast. Nothing matched his M.O. except for the series of murders five years before that. We were convinced he had been inactive during that five-year gap, yet there was also no even remotely likely suspect we could find who had been in prison for exactly that length of time. And according to all the information gleaned from databases we had Quantico double-check yesterday, he's also been inactive in the five years since Alabama. Until he started killing in Hastings a little over three weeks ago."

Mallory rubbed her temple, scowling. "So something sets him off and he kills six women in six weeks. Then, apparently sated for the time being, vanishes before the cops can even get close to catching him. Why six women?"

"We don't know," Isabel replied. "The number has to be important, since it's been exactly the same twice before, but we don't know how or why. We can't even be absolutely positive he'll stop at six this time. He could be escalating. Most killers of this sort do sooner or later kill more or get more viciously creative in the killing itself."

Mallory shook her head. "Great. Because we didn't have enough to look forward to. So he kills at least six women. Moves on to a new location. Then waits five years—it's not exact, is it?" she interrupted herself to ask.

Isabel shook her head. "Not to the day, no. The gap between the first and second set of murders was actually four years and ten months. The gap between the last set and this one was five years and one month. Give or take a few days."

"Okay. But he moves somewhere new after his six-week

killing spree, settles down, settles in. Which has to mean we're looking for someone who's been in Hastings no more than five years, right?"

"Or someone who used to live in the area and has moved back. Or someone who works in Hastings but lives outside the town—or the other way around. Or someone who takes long vacations every few years; that's at least possible."

"Goes on vacation to kill people?"

"We've encountered stranger things. He could scout out his hunting grounds in advance, maybe start picking his victims, and return later for the actual kill." Isabel shook her head. "Honestly, if you look at a map, the two previous hunting grounds and Hastings are all within a day's drive, despite being in three different states. So we can't even rule out the idea that he lives in an area central to his hunting grounds and has just somehow managed to spend enough time in each to get to know his victims."

"Oh, hell, I was hoping we could narrow down the possibles at least a little bit."

Hollis said, "The universe never makes it easy, remember? Probably the only people we can even begin to rule out are those who have lived continuously in Hastings during the last fifteen years at least. And I mean continuously: no vacations longer than, say, two weeks; no going away to college; no out-of-town visits, no day trips fitting the right time periods."

Mallory grimaced. "Which is just not possible. Even those of us who've lived here our whole lives tend to go away to school or travel or something. And day trips? Lots of good shopping in Columbia, Atlanta, other places within a day's drive."

"I was afraid of that," Isabel said with a sigh.

With a nod, Mallory said, "That sort of thing is so common I doubt we could find anybody who was absent or took weekly day trips out of town during those six-week stretches specifically, not without questioning every soul in town and probably not then. Who remembers specific dates from years ago? And like I said, people travel on vacations or for business, go away to school. I was away in Georgia three years finishing college. It was four for you, wasn't it, Rafe?"

"Yeah. And I went to Duke, in North Carolina." He sighed. "It's like Mal said, we've all traveled, been away from Hastings, most of us more than once. And people do take regular day trips, even out of state, for shopping or business. I get the feeling this isn't going to help us narrow the list all that much."

"Probably not," Isabel agreed. "Although if we get lucky enough to find a suspect or two, we have some concrete questions to ask . . ."

Hollis didn't intentionally tune out the discussion. She didn't want to; despite the repetition of details she already knew, she was still new enough to the investigative process itself to find it interesting, even fascinating.

She wasn't even aware at first that Isabel's voice had faded into a peculiar hollow silence. But then she realized the discussion around her had gone distant, deadened. She felt the fine hairs on her body rise, her flesh tingle.

It was not a pleasant sensation.

She looked around the table at the others, watching their mouths move and hearing only a word now and then, muffled and indistinct. And they themselves appeared different to her. Dim, almost faded. They seemed to be growing ever more distant moment by moment, and that frightened her.

Hell, it terrified her.

She opened her mouth to say something, or try to, but even as she did, a new and unfamiliar instinct urged her to turn her head toward the doorway. Again without meaning to, without wanting to, she looked.

Standing near the doorway was a woman.

A blond woman.

She was clearer than the people around Hollis, brighter somehow, and more distinct. She was beautiful, with perfect, delicate features. Her hair was burnished gold, her eyes a clear, piercing blue.

Eyes fixed on Hollis.

Her lips parted, and she started to speak.

A chill swept through Hollis and she quickly looked away, instinctively trying to close the door, to disconnect herself from the place from which this woman had emerged.

It was a cold, dark place, and it terrified Hollis.

Because it was death.


Mallory rubbed her temple again. "Okay, back to what sets him off. What sets him off?"

Isabel answered readily, if not too informatively. "Something specific, but we don't know what that is, at least not yet. The gaps between his killing sprees can and might be explained by his need to get to know these women."

"Might," Rafe said. "But you aren't sure?"

"I'm sure he has to feel he knows them. For whatever reason, they can't be total strangers to him. Maybe in getting to know them, he discovers something about them—at least the initial victim—that sets him off, something that pushes his button. Or maybe he has to win their trust; that could be part of his ritual, especially since these women appear to be leaving their cars and going willingly with him."

"He doesn't pick out all six women before he starts killing, right? Otherwise you wouldn't have made his list."

"Good point." Isabel nodded. "It's also a point that he is able to look beyond the woman he's currently stalking in order to take note of, and even choose as a future victim, another woman. Even though this guy's actual killings are frenzied, it's becoming clear that he's quite able to think coolly and calmly right up until the moment he kills them."

"We have to find her."

They all looked at Hollis. Her voice had been tight, and her face showed visible tension. She was chewing on a thumbnail, which, Rafe noticed, was already bitten short.

"He's stalking her even now. Watching her. Thinking about what he's going to do to her. We have to—"

"Hollis." Isabel spoke quietly. "We'll do all we can to find her before he gets to her. But the only way we have of doing that is by starting with the women he's already killed. We have to find out what they all have in common besides the color of their hair. What connects them to each other. And to him."

Hollis looked at her partner almost blindly. "How can you be so calm about it? You know what's going to happen to her. We both know. We both know how it feels. The helpless terror, the agony—"

"*Hollis.*" Isabel's voice was still quiet, but something in it caused her partner to blink and stiffen in her chair.

"I'm sorry," Hollis said. She pressed her fingertips briefly to her closed eyes, then looked at them again. "It's just that—" This time, no one interrupted her.

But something did.

She turned her head abruptly as if someone had called her name, staring toward the closed door of the room. Her eyes dilated until only a thin rim of blue circled the enormous pupils.

Rafe sent a quick glance toward Isabel and found her watching her partner intently, eyes narrowed. When he looked back at Hollis, he saw that she was even more pale than she had been before, and trembling visibly.

"Why are you here?" she whispered, looking at nothing the others could see. "Wait, I can't hear you. I want to. I want to help you. But—"

Softly, Isabel said, "Who is it, Hollis? Who do you see?"

"I can't hear her. She's trying to tell me something, but I can't hear her."

"Listen. Concentrate."

"I'm trying. I see her, but . . . She's shaking her head. She's giving up. No, wait—"

Rafe was a bit startled to feel his ears pop just an instant before Hollis slumped in her chair. He told himself it was his imagination, even as he heard himself ask, "Who was it? Who did you see?"

Hollis looked at him blankly for a moment, then past him at the bulletin board where they had posted photos and other information about the victims.

"Her. The first victim. Jamie Brower."

EMILY BROWER WOULDN'T have admitted it to a soul, but she was a horrible person. A horrible daughter. A really horrible sister. People kept coming up to her with shocked eyes and hushed voices, telling her how sorry they were about Jamie, asking her how she was holding up.

"Fine, I'm fine," Emily always replied.

Fine. Doing okay. Holding up. Getting on with her life.

"I'm okay, really."

Being there for her grieving parents. Allowing people she barely knew or didn't know at all to hug her while they whispered their condolences. Writing all the thank-you cards to people for their cards and flowers, because her mother couldn't do anything except cry. Dealing with all the phone calls from Jamie's college friends as the news rippled out.

"I'm getting through it."

*I'm a hypocrite.*

They had never been close, she and Jamie, but they had been sisters. So Emily knew she should feel something about Jamie being dead, being horribly *murdered,* something besides this slightly impatient resentment.

She didn't.

"I don't know what she was doing those last few weeks," Emily told Detective Mallory Beck in response to the question she'd asked. "Jamie had her own place, a job that kept her busy, and she liked to travel. She came to Sunday dinner a couple of times a month, but other than that . . ."

"You didn't see much of her."

"No. She was six years older. We didn't really have anything in common." Emily tried not to sound as impatient as she felt, even as she stole glances at the tall blond FBI agent who was across the living room standing before the shrine.

"So you don't know who she might have been dating?"

"No, I already told you that." Emily wondered what the FBI agent found so fascinating in all the photos and trophies and awards littering the built-in shelves on either side of the fireplace. Hadn't she ever seen a shrine before?

"Do you know if she had an address book?"

Emily frowned at Detective Beck. "Everybody has an address book."

"We didn't find one in her apartment."

"Then she must have kept it at her work."

"The one in her office held business information and contacts only."

"Well, then I don't know."

"She had a good memory," Agent Adams said suddenly. She looked back over her shoulder and smiled at Emily. "There are awards here for spelling and science—chemistry. Jamie didn't have to write things down, did she?"

"Not usually," Emily admitted grudgingly. "Especially numbers. Phone numbers. And math. She was good at math."

Agent Adams chuckled. "One of those, huh? My sister was good at math. I hated it. Used to turn numbers into little cartoons. My teachers were never amused by that."

Emily couldn't help but laugh. "I always tried to make faces out of the numbers. My teachers didn't like it either."

"Ah, well, I've found there are numbers people and words people. Not a lot who do well with both." She reached out and lightly touched a framed certificate that was part of the shrine. "Looks like Jamie was one of the rare ones, though. Here's an award for a short story she wrote in college."

"She liked telling stories," Emily said. "Made-up ones, but stuff that happened to her too."

"You said she traveled; did she tell you any stories about that?"

"She talked about it sometimes at Sunday dinner. But with Mom and Dad there, she only talked about the boring parts. Museums, shows, sightseeing."

"Never talked about any of the men she met?"

"Nah, to hear her tell it she was a nun."

"But you knew the truth, naturally. Was she seeing anybody, locally?"

"She didn't talk to me about her private life."

Agent Adams smiled again at Emily. "Sisters don't have to talk to know, do they? Sisters always see what's there, far more than anybody else ever does."

Emily wavered for a moment, but that understanding, conspiratorial smile combined with the stresses and strains of the last few weeks finally caused her resentment to escape.

"Everybody thought she was so perfect, you know? It all came so easy to her. She was good at everything she tried, everybody loved her, she made loads of money. But underneath all that, she was scared. It really showed in the last few weeks before she died. To me, anyway. Nervous, jumpy, rushing around like she had too much to do and not enough time. She was scared shitless."

"Why?" Detective Beck asked quietly.

"Because of her big secret. Because she knew how upset and disappointed our parents would be, other people would be, how horrified. It's just not something you do in a little town like Hastings, not something people could accept. And she was always scared they'd find out. Always."

"Scared they'd find what out, Emily?" Agent Adams asked.

"That she was gay." Emily laughed. "A lesbian. But not just any sort of lesbian, mind you, that's not the part she was terrified people would find out. Lovely, sweet, talented, good-at-anything-and-everything Jamie was a dominatrix. She dressed in shiny black leather and stiletto heels with fishnet stockings, and she made other women crawl and fawn and do whatever she wanted them to."

Agent Adams didn't seem in the least surprised. "Are you sure about that, Emily?"

"You bet I'm sure. I've got pictures."


As they got into Mallory's Jeep a few minutes later, she said, "Did you know about Jamie Brower going in or pick up something there in the room?"

"Picked it up while I was there. That house was practically screaming at me."

"Really? Amazing how much people can keep hidden. Because we didn't get any of this before, and both Rafe and I talked to Emily several times. And Jamie's parents, friends, coworkers. Not so much as a hint that Jamie led any kind of unconventional life sexually."

"Yeah, I read the statements you guys collected. Jamie even dated local men, and at least two claimed fairly recent sexual relationships."

Mallory started the Jeep but didn't put it in gear, turning her head to frown at Isabel. "They weren't lying about that. I'd bet my pension on it."

"I think you're right. Just the fact that they were willing to admit to intimate relationships and put themselves in that police spotlight makes it fairly certain they were telling the truth. But I don't believe Jamie was truly bisexual, that she enjoyed sex with men *and* women."

"Then why sleep with the men? Just to keep her secret life secret?"

"I'd say so. Emily was right; in a small town like Hastings, any successful woman like Jamie would hesitate to come out of the closet. Especially if that closet contained whips, chains, and black leather. She wouldn't have wanted that image in a client's mind while she was trying to sell them real estate."

"Hell, I don't want the image in my head. But it's there now."

Isabel smiled wryly. "I know. The question is, how important is this information? Is it what triggered our killer's compulsion? Did he find out he could never possess Jamie Brower the way he needed to? Did he discover her secret and find himself unable to bear it for some other reason?"

"Or," Mallory finished, "is it just an extraneous fact completely unconnected with Jamie's murder."

"Exactly."

Mallory put the Jeep in gear and headed toward the end of

the Browers' circular driveway. "Well, it's a new fact for us, at any rate. Lucky you could get chummy with Emily about the trials of sisterhood."

"I never had a sister," Isabel said.

After a beat, Mallory said, "Ah. You used what you picked up psychically from Emily to encourage her to talk. The cartoon numbers she drew in school. Being lousy at math when her sister was so good at it. You used the knowledge to be sympathetic, be on her side so she'd feel comfortable talking to you. So that's how your abilities can be used as investigative tools."

"That's how," Isabel said. "An edge that sometimes makes all the difference. But something else I learned in there is that Emily was all but invisible in that family. Which is why she knew about Jamie's secret life. Why she saw more than anyone else realized. And why there's a good chance she saw something that could get her killed."

"What?"

"Her sister's murderer."

**3:30 PM**

Isabel closed the folder and looked at Rafe with a sigh. "Just like I remembered. As far as we could determine both times, the twelve women killed before he came to Hastings were all straight. No secret sexual closet, with or without whips and chains. And the second and third victims here, Allison Carroll and Tricia Kane, were straight as well, according to the information you got. Right?"

"Right."

"Still, I'm going to ask Quantico to reopen those old files, maybe send an agent to the towns in Florida and Alabama to double-check, particularly the lives of the primary victims just

82

before they were killed. With Jamie's secret life staring us in the face, we have to be sure whether or not it has anything to do with what triggers his killing rage."

"Makes sense to me. Could be, he got the kind of rejection he couldn't take. Rejection as a man, for being a man."

"That is entirely possible."

Rafe looked down at the three small in-living-color photographs of Jamie Brower in full dominatrix gear: a silver-studded, black leather bustier, fishnet stockings held up by garters, stiletto heels—and a whip. In each shot, there was another woman, crawling, fawning, or in some clearly submissive pose, just as Emily had said.

And while Jamie's face was unmasked and highly visible, her companion was completely unidentifiable due to a black leather hood and mask.

He lined up the photos on the table and studied them intently. "I'd say this is the same woman in all three shots."

Isabel nodded. "And I'd guess all three shots were taken on the same day. Same . . . session. Though all the details of costume and . . . um . . . accessories being exactly the same could be part of their whole ritual, so we can't assume too much."

"Can I assume the second woman is nobody I know personally? Please?"

Isabel smiled wryly. "It is unsettling, isn't it? Other people's secrets."

"This sort of secret, at least. I guess you never really know about people."

"No. You don't." There was something oddly flat about Isabel's response, but she went on before Rafe could question it. And her voice was easy once again. "That outfit the other woman is wearing shows a lot of skin, but considering how tight and rigid it is, it's also doing a dandy job of disguising her true body shape.

So are her positions; we can't even realistically estimate how tall she is. Her face is never turned to the camera, so not even her eyes are visible. And her hair's caught up under that hood."

Rafe cleared his throat. "And since she's shaved . . ."

Isabel didn't seem at all embarrassed or disturbed, and nodded matter-of-factly. "Not uncommon in S&M scenarios, according to the list Quantico sent us, but pubic hair would at least have given us a hair color, and probably natural. I didn't see a birthmark, tattoo, even a blemish that might help us I.D. her."

She paused, then added, "Several things interest me about this little twist. We don't know if any or all of Jamie's playmates lived here in Hastings, though my guess is that more than one isn't very likely."

"A few weeks ago," Rafe said, "I would have said investigating a serial killer in Hastings would be the next thing to impossible. A few S&M games seem fairly tame by comparison. Hell, almost innocent."

"Yeah, but not innocent to Jamie. If she was so afraid of discovery, it could well have been because her partner—at least the most recent one—lives here and maybe isn't as good at keeping secrets as Jamie was. That might explain what Emily saw as Jamie's increasing worry and fear. Another thing is that we don't know where these photographs were taken, and though Emily claims she *borrowed* these three from a photo box full of them, your people found no sign of the box at Jamie's apartment when they did an intensive search."

"I'm surprised Emily found it," Rafe said. "This is not the sort of thing you'd leave lying around, I'm thinking."

"Oh, you can bet Emily snooped. She said she caught a glimpse of the corner of the box under her sister's bed and was curious, but she had to be looking for secrets. She knew her sister was afraid of something, and she wanted to know what that was. It was the first chink she'd seen in Jamie's armor."

"Why take these?" Rafe wondered.

"Proof. Even if she never planned to show them to anyone— including Jamie—she had something that proved to her that Jamie wasn't as perfect as her family believed she was. That was probably enough for Emily; she doesn't strike me as a black- mailer or the vindictive type."

"Yeah," Rafe said, "I'd agree with you there."

Isabel shrugged. "I'm also willing to bet that she left the box just enough out of place to make Jamie uneasy about it. If it really was filled with photos, then she couldn't be sure any were miss- ing. But she had to wonder if her sister found the box. That's probably why we haven't found it."

"Because she hid it somewhere safer."

"I would have. The question is, where? Your people checked her office thoroughly, but I wouldn't have expected to find some- thing like those photographs there anyway. Did she have a safe- deposit box?"

"Yeah, but the only items in it were legal documents. Insur- ance policies, deeds to some property she owned, stuff like that. I've got some people putting together a list of the properties, what they are, where they are, but nothing else in the box provided anything in the way of a lead."

Mallory came into the room in time to hear that, and said, "Jamie's lockbox? I just double-checked, and that's the only one she had. No other bank has her on their customer list."

"At least not under her real name," Rafe said.

Mallory sighed. "I can go around to all the area banks and show them a picture of her. Or, better yet, send a few of the guys out on Monday to do that, since it's too late to get a decent start today. Although you'd think someone would have come forward after seeing all the pictures of her in the newspapers."

"People generally don't," Isabel said. "Don't want to get involved, or honestly don't believe they have any knowledge of value."

"And secrets of their own to protect," Rafe noted.

"Definitely. It's amazing how many people get nervous about some little transgression they're afraid we'll be interested in."

"Transgressions can be entertaining," Mallory noted.

Isabel grinned, and said, "True enough. But in this case, we hardly have time for them. Pity we can't make that announcement publicly. It'd probably save us time."

"And trouble," Rafe agreed.

"Yeah. Anyway, if Jamie had a lockbox under another name, she may well have worn a disguise of some kind when she visited. Just a wig, most likely, something that wouldn't have looked too phony. You probably won't have much luck showing her photo, but it's something that needs to be done. And we might get lucky."

Rafe nodded. "We do need to do whatever we can to make sure we've covered all the bases. But I'm not holding out much hope either. Especially after finding out she was pretty good at keeping secrets."

"Maybe a lot more secrets than we've yet discovered," Isabel said. "I know she made very good money, but she's also invested quite a bit in properties in the area, and she lived very well. I'm thinking that maybe the S&M stuff wasn't all fun and games for Jamie."

"Shit," Rafe said. "Mistress for hire?"

"Lots of people, apparently, willing to pay to be humiliated. Jamie was a smart businesswoman, so why wouldn't she charge for *all* her talents?"

———

Cheryl Bayne had been working hard on her career, doing all the frequently boring and certainly fluffy junk demanded of baby reporters—and female reporters. Especially when they worked for fourth-place TV stations. Dumb filler pieces on what the society ladies were wearing this season, or the mayor's daughter's birthday party, or the baby lion cub born at the zoo.

She was really sick of fluff.

So when her producer had offered her the chance to come to Hastings and cover this story—because a woman would play better, he'd said, and she was brunette, after all—Cheryl had jumped at it.

Now she was mostly just jumping at shadows.

Presently, on this Friday afternoon, she felt relatively safe standing in front of the town hall under the shade of a big oak tree. Her cameraperson was off getting background shots of the town, but she wasn't really alone, since the area was crawling with media.

"This is getting old." Dana Earley, a more experienced reporter for a rival Columbia station, sidled closer, studying the police department across Main Street with a slightly jaundiced eye. "Whatever they know over there, they aren't anxious to share."

"At least the chief called that press conference yesterday," Cheryl offered.

"Yeah, and told us squat." Dana reached up to tuck a strand of blond hair behind one ear. She looked at Cheryl, hesitated, then asked, "Have you had the feeling you were being followed, watched, especially at night? Or it is just us blondes?"

A little relieved to be able to talk about it, Cheryl said, "Actually, yeah. I thought it was my imagination."

"Umm. I've been asking around, and so far every woman I've

KAY HOOPER

talked to has had the same feeling. Including, by the way, a couple of female cops who refused to speak on the record. I'd say it was just paranoia if it was only one or two of us, but all of us?"

"Maybe it's just . . . nerves."

Bluntly, Dana said, "I think he's watching us. And I have a very bad feeling about it."

"Well, you're blond—"

Dana shook her head. "I just got a peek at a list of women missing in the general area. And very few of them are blondes. Watch your back, Cheryl."

"I will. Thanks." She watched the blond reporter walk away, hearing the hollowness in her own voice when she added half under her breath, "Thanks a lot."

"Jesus," Mallory muttered.

"She wouldn't have considered it prostitution," Isabel pointed out. "Merely a fee-for-services-provided arrangement. Especially since she was the one in charge, the one making all the rules. No emotional involvement to clutter up her life, yet she gets the satisfaction of dominating other women. Maybe men as well. We don't *know* all her lovers—or clients—were women, after all. We only have Emily's word for it, and even she claims she didn't look through all the photos in that box."

"Do you believe her on that point?" Rafe asked.

"I think she saw more than she's admitted, but I didn't get a good sense of just how much."

"Every answer we get just opens up more questions," he said with a sigh.

Isabel, who was sitting at the end of the conference table near him, reached over and turned one of the photos so that she could

88

study it. "Par for the course in serial-murder investigations, I'm afraid. In the meantime, does either of you have a clue where this room might be? It doesn't look like a room at the inn, and I doubt it's any other local hotel or motel. Anything about it look familiar to either of you?"

Mallory sat down on the other side of Rafe and leaned an elbow on the table, staring at the photos. "Not to me. There's not a lot there to go by. Bare paneled walls, what looks like an old vinyl floor, and a—yuck—stained mattress on a plain wooden platform. I guess comfort wasn't the point."

"The opposite, if anything," Isabel said with a grimace. "Have you *tried* stilettos? I have. It's a hideous thing to do to a foot."

Rafe looked at her with interest. "Stilettos? My God, how tall are you in them?"

"The ones I was wearing put me at about six-four. Note the past tense. I will never wear them again."

Curious, Mallory said, "Why did you wear them once? Or would that be sharing too much?"

Isabel chuckled. "Business, not pleasure, I promise you. Bishop believes our law-enforcement training should be varied and extensive, so at one point I worked for a while with a narc squad. Naturally, when they needed somebody to pose as a hooker . . ."

"You got the call."

"And the makeup and big hair and skanky outfit—and the stilettos. I gained a whole new respect for hookers. Their job is *hard*. And I mean just the walking around on the streets part."

Rafe cleared his throat again and tried to clear his mind of the image of Isabel dressed as a hooker. He tapped one of the photos in front of him. "Getting back to this room . . ."

Mallory grinned, but then sobered and said, "Maybe it's a

basement, but look at the shaft of light on the floor; that doesn't look like it's artificial light. There's a window in that room, and not a little basement window, I'm thinking. High, though."

"A walk-out basement could have full-size windows," Rafe noted almost absently. "I don't know, though, it doesn't look like a basement to me. The angle of the camera gives us a floor-to-ceiling view, and that ceiling's too high for most basements I've seen. Might even be something like a warehouse."

"Could be. And, judging by how fixed the positioning is, I'm guessing the camera was on a tripod and taking timed shots; neither woman is paying particular attention to it. So no third person was present. Probably."

"Maybe the submissive isn't even aware there is a camera," Rafe suggested.

"The submissive?" Mallory eyed him with faint amusement. "Did you take a crash course in S&M, or is the lingo a lot more standard than I thought it was?"

"I should refuse to answer that," Rafe said, "but in my defense I have to say we spent time about half an hour ago gathering and downloading information on the S&M scene from Quantico. Your tax dollars at work. I am now much more informed on the subject."

"I'll just bet you are."

"They sent plain facts, Mal, not pages from a magazine or some how-to manual."

"Ah. Learn anything interesting?"

"Nothing helpful."

"That wasn't what I asked."

"That's what I answered."

"Do you two do parties?" Isabel asked.

Rafe sighed. "Sorry."

"Oh, don't apologize. In a case like this one, I'd much rather laugh when I can. The chuckles tend to be few and far between."

Mallory said, "We've already had a few moments of gallows humor here and there. And I have a feeling this dominatrix stuff is going to provide a few more. Hard to take it seriously, you know? I mean, hard to imagine somebody you knew dressing up and making another woman lick her foot. What's *that* about?"

"In this context, a need to be in control and a high level of insecurity. Or, at least, that's my reading of Jamie Brower."

"Your psychic reading?" Rafe asked.

"From what I picked up at her parents' home and from Emily, yeah. Also a fair psychological stab in the dark. I'd like to check out her apartment, though, and try to get a better sense of her."

"I'd rather do that than keep staring at these damned pictures," Rafe said frankly. "I'd also rather not post them on the board, if it's all the same to you."

Knowing that virtually every cop in the place had access to the conference room and the boards set up with victim information, Isabel agreed with a nod. "We'll keep them in the Eyes Only file."

"We have one of those?" Mallory asked.

"We do now. I have a feeling there'll be more stuff for it as we go along, but for now I'd just as soon keep these photos and Jamie's secret between us. If this particular avenue of pursuit turns out to be a dead end, I don't see any reason for us to be the ones to out Jamie. Especially posthumously."

"Emily will probably take care of that," Mallory said.

"Or," Isabel said, "she'll keep it to herself and feel superior knowing her sister's dirty little secret. Could go either way, I'd say."

Mallory said, "You suggested to me that Emily might have caught the attention of her sister's killer; how serious were you about that?"

Isabel leaned back in her chair, absently rubbing the nape of her neck. "I don't have anything concrete, no evidence to support it. Not even a clairvoyant sense, really. Emily just barely fits the victim profile; she's blond, but on the young side for our killer. Not especially successful in any career, since she's still in school, but she's smart and observant."

"But?" Rafe said.

"It's just . . . a feeling I got in that house. Emily was actively snooping in Jamie's life during the weeks before she was killed, and we can be reasonably sure that during that period our killer was involved in Jamie's life, that he crossed her path. Which means he probably crossed Emily's path as well."

"And maybe she noticed him," Rafe said.

"Maybe. It's just a theory, but . . . it might not be such a bad idea to have your people keep an eye on Emily, at least when she's out of the house."

"Done. I'll assign a patrol. Plainclothes or uniformed?"

Isabel debated silently for a moment. "Let's not try to be subtle. Uniformed. Tell them to be casual but stay alert. If nothing else, focusing on the family member of a victim may lead the killer to think we're on the wrong track."

"Or on the right one," Mallory murmured.

"If he is after her, yeah. And, if so, a police escort may cause him to think twice. Worth the risk, I think."

Rafe nodded. "I agree. I'll assign the patrol on our way out and then go with you to check out Jamie's apartment. Mal, Hollis is at Tricia Kane's office; why don't you go over Jamie's office one more time? Just to make sure."

"Her boss is already pissed that we've taped the door to her office so none of his other agents can use it. Can I release it to him if I don't find anything this time?"

"Yeah, might as well. Unless the FBI has an objection?"

"Nope." Isabel shook her head. "But if you find anything at all that seems out of place to you, bring it back here."

"Gotcha."

Rafe watched as Isabel opened her briefcase and pulled out a bottle of ibuprofen. She swallowed several pills with the last of her coffee, then added cheerfully, "I'm ready when you are."

"Headache?"

"Usually," she confirmed, still cheerful. "Shall we?"

"It's getting late," Caleb Powell said.

Hollis looked up from her position behind what had been Tricia Kane's desk and nodded. "Yeah. I do appreciate you pretty much shutting down the office for a couple of hours today so I could go through her desk."

"Not a problem. I haven't felt much like working this week anyway. Find anything?"

"Nothing useful, as far as I can tell." Hollis pressed slender fingers to her closed eyes briefly in what he was beginning to recognize as a characteristic gesture, then studied the small pile of items on the neat blotter.

"Nothing new, I'd say," Caleb observed, wondering if she was as tired as she seemed. Telling himself he shouldn't take advantage.

Hollis agreed with a nod. "The police have already photocopied and gone through every page of the day planner: everything in it is purely work related. What few personal effects she kept in the desk are the usual, innocuous sort of thing any woman would keep at work. Extra compact and lipstick, small bottle of perfume, emery board and nail clippers, a ripped-in-half photo of the ex-boyfriend she clearly wasn't quite ready to throw away."

Caleb grimaced. "I caught her looking at that once or twice. She said just what you did, that she wasn't quite ready to toss it."

"It takes time for some people to let go."

He decided not to comment on that. "So there's nothing helpful here in the office."

"Nothing I can see." Hollis rose to her feet. She glanced past Caleb toward the front door and for an instant went still, eyes widening.

Caleb looked back over his shoulder, then at her. His first, instinctive reading of her posture and expression was that she had received a shock but was almost immediately back in control of whatever emotions that shock had caused.

"What?" he asked.

She blinked, her gaze returning to him. "Hmm? Nothing. It's nothing. Listen, Mr. Powell, confidentially, the focus of the investigation is going to shift back to the first victim. We believe something about that victim or that murder is most likely to help us identify the killer."

He thought she was a little pale, but what she'd told him pushed that awareness out of his mind. "So Tricia's murder goes on the back burner."

Gravely, Hollis said, "In the conference room at the police department where we'll work every day, there are bulletin boards sectioned, so far, into thirds. Each third is filled with photos and information on each victim. Time lines of the last weeks of their lives. Habits, haunts, events that might or might not have been important. Every day, we look at those boards. Every day, we look at the pictures of those women. And every day, we'll discuss their lives and the people who knew them and try to figure out who killed them. Every day."

Caleb drew a breath and let it out slowly. "Sorry. It's just that . . . she was my friend."

"I know. I'm sorry." Her blue eyes gazed past him for another moment, briefly. "Just know that nobody is going to forget Tricia. And that we'll get her killer."

"You seem so certain of that."

Hollis looked faintly surprised. "We won't give up until we do get him. It's only a matter of time, Mr. Powell."

"Caleb," he said, "please. And thank you for your efforts, Agent Templeton."

She smiled wryly. "Hollis. Especially since I'm not a full agent yet. *Special Investigator* is a title the SCU gives its members who lack a background in law or law enforcement. I've only been with the unit a few months."

"But you're a trained investigator?"

"Recently trained, yeah. In my . . . previous life . . . I did something else." Hollis came out from behind the desk, adding in a slightly preoccupied tone, "My partner, on the other hand, has a solid background in law and law enforcement, as well as years of experience, so you don't have to worry that the Bureau sent two rookies down here."

"I wasn't worried, actually." Realizing she was about to leave, and reluctant to let her go, he said quickly, "I remember you saying something about being an artist."

"Used to be."

"Used to be? Does a creative person ever stop being creative?"

For the first time, Hollis was clearly uncomfortable. "Sometimes things happen that change your whole life. I—uh—need to get back to the police station. Thank you very much for your cooperation, Mr.—Caleb. I'll be in touch."

"I'll be here."

"Thanks again. Bye."

He didn't try to stop her, but for several minutes after she left, Caleb gazed after her, frowning, wondering what had happened to change Hollis Templeton's entire life.

*"I know all about evil, Mr. Powell, believe me. I met it up close and personal."*

He hadn't thought she'd been speaking literally.

Now he was very much afraid she had been.

5:00 PM

When Rafe and Isabel were in one of the department Jeeps and on their way to Jamie Brower's apartment, he said, "I notice you haven't suggested that Hollis visit any of the crime scenes."

"Since what happened earlier, you mean?" Isabel shrugged. "You've obviously also noticed Hollis is a bit . . . fragile."

"It's a little hard to miss."

"She has a lot of potential. But becoming a medium cost her a trip to hell you wouldn't believe, and she hasn't completely dealt with that yet.

"But despite being afraid, despite her not reaching out, not trying to make contact—she did. Which is an indication of just how much potential she has."

Rafe sent his companion a glance. "You really believe there was a ghost in the room with us?"

"I believe the spirit of Jamie Brower was there, yes."

"But you didn't see her? It?"

"No, I can't see the dead." Isabel's voice was utterly matter-of-fact. "Or hear them, for that matter. But I can sometimes feel them near me. The very air in the room changes, maybe because they aren't supposed to be a part of this dimensional plane. You felt it yourself."

This time, Rafe kept his eyes on the road. "My ears popped. It happens."

"All the time," she agreed mildly.

"Look, if Jamie was really there, why didn't she say or do something to help us find her killer?"

"She was trying. Trying to speak to Hollis, the only one in the room with the ability to hear her. Unfortunately, Hollis isn't ready to listen."

"I don't suppose Jamie could just scribble us a note, huh? *X killed me.*"

Isabel answered the question seriously. "So far, none of us has encountered a spirit or noncorporeal force with enough focus and power to physically touch or move objects. Unless they were inside a host, of course. Or controlling one."

# 6

*S*HE'LL TELL. *You know she'll tell.*

He listened to the voice this time because he wanted to. Because he enjoyed this part of it so much. Watching them. Following. Learning their routines.

Hunting.

*Like the others. Just like them.*

The voice was right about that. She was just like all the rest. Laughing behind his back. So eager to tell his secrets. He had to stop her before she could do that.

*You've done three. Only three more. And then you can rest. Then you can be.*

"I'm tired," he murmured, still watching her. "This time, I'm tired."

*That's because you're changing.*

"I know." He moved carefully, staying in the shadows as he

followed her. This one was tricky; she was aware of her surroundings, watchful. Uneasy. They were all beginning to act that way, he'd noticed. Part of him loved that, that he made them so uneasy.

But it made things more difficult.

*You can do this. You have to. Or she'll tell. She'll tell them all about you.*

"Yes," he murmured, easing a little closer despite the risk that she would see him. "I have to. I can't let her tell. I can't let any of them tell."

Rafe pulled the Jeep abruptly to the curb and parked. They were still in the downtown area, not even halfway to Jamie's apartment. He continued to stare through the windshield, his rugged face completely unreadable. "A host."

Isabel didn't have to be clairvoyant to know he had just about reached the end of his willingness to believe in the paranormal. Or even to accept that it might be possible.

Or possibly he had simply reached the end of his rope.

Hard to blame him for that.

"A host," he repeated, his deep voice still extremely calm. "You want to explain that?"

Matching his tone, Isabel replied, "When it's a spirit, the simple truth is that some of them refuse to accept what's happened to them when they die. Whether it's unfinished business or simply an unwillingness to move on, they want to stay here."

"I guess that explains haunted houses." He was trying hard to keep his voice matter-of-fact.

"Well, only partly. Some houses really do contain the spirit or spirits of people who didn't want to move on. But some of what people call hauntings are just place memories."

"Place memories?"

"Yeah. When people report seeing the same *ghost* repeat the same actions again and again, that's likely a place memory. A good example is the Roman soldiers so many people have seen marching on their battlefield, endlessly. Or other battlefields, like Gettysburg. We don't believe those poor men keep reenacting the battles that killed them; we believe the places remember what happened there."

"How?"

"We can only theorize. Either because those particular areas have a specific energy of their own or possibly just the ability geographically or topographically to contain energy better than other places do. We believe that the extreme psychic—electro-magnetic—energy of such horrific, tragic events literally soaked into the earth at places like that.

"And sometimes there's a buildup of pressure and those 'memories' are discharged in the form of energy, like static. If anybody happens to be around, especially a functional or latent psychic, what's seen is what that place remembers. An image of what happened there."

"That actually makes a kind of sense," Rafe said, sounding both reluctant and bemused.

"Yeah, most of this does, if you consider possible scientific explanations. Which we always do. All based on some form of energy."

"So explain this host thing."

"Well, like I said, some people who die don't want to be dead. If they're desperate enough, or angry enough, sometimes they're able to muster enough power to . . . find and inhabit a physical host. Another person."

"Possession. You're talking about possession?" He was beginning to sound incredulous again.

Isabel waited until he finally looked at her, then said, "Not in the . . . Hollywood . . . sense of the word. This isn't some pea-soup-spewing demon a priest could exorcise. Often, they aren't even negative, or bad, spirits. They just want to live. It's a case of a stronger mind and spirit overpowering a weaker or otherwise vulnerable one."

"You're telling me this has actually happened?"

"We believe it has, although I can't offer you any proof. Bishop and Miranda actually fought the spirit of an insanely determined serial killer once. Quite a story there."

Rafe blinked, but said only, "Who's Miranda?"

"Sorry. Bishop's wife and partner. Years ago, Miranda touched several mental patients who were being treated for severe schizophrenia. She definitely felt, in each case, that there were two distinct and separate souls fighting for possession of those people. It convinced her. It convinced us, even before we duplicated the experiment and got the same results in three out of the five diagnosed schizophrenic mental patients we tested."

"This is a little hard to swallow," Rafe said finally.

"I know. Sorry about that." She might have been apologizing for bumping him in a crowd.

He stared at her, then pulled the Jeep away from the curb and continued on their way. "So, worst-case scenario in a situation like that, the host goes nuts and ends up in a mental institution being *treated* for a mental disease he doesn't have."

"I can think of worse things that might happen, but, yeah, we do believe that has happened. Theoretically, if the host mind and spirit were really weak, the invading spirit would just take over. You'd have a person who appeared to suddenly develop a whole new personality." Isabel reflected, then said, "Which, I suppose, could explain teenagers."

Rafe didn't smile. "What happens to the host's spirit?"

"I don't know. We don't know. Withers away, maybe, like an unused limb. Gets booted out and passes on to whatever awaits all of us when we leave this mortal coil." Isabel sighed. "Frontier territory, remember? We have a lot of theories, Rafe. We have some personal experiences, war stories we can tell. Even a few nonpsychic if not unbiased witnesses to testify to things they've seen and heard. But scientific data to back us up? Not so much. For most of us, we believe because we have to. Because it's us experiencing the paranormal. Hard to deny something when it's part of your everyday life."

"And the rest of us have to take it on faith."

"Unfortunately. Unless and until you have your own close encounter with the paranormal."

"I'd rather not."

Isabel's smile twisted a bit. "Yeah. Well, let's hope you get your wish. But don't count on it. Maybe it's just because we psychics are present to pull in and focus the energy, but people around us do tend to experience things they never would have imagined before. Fair warning."

"You keep warning me."

"I keep trying."

It was Rafe's turn to sigh, but all he said was, "You made a distinction earlier between a spirit and a—what did you call it?—a noncorporeal force? What the hell is that supposed to be?"

"Evil."

He waited a moment, then said, "Evil as in . . . ?"

"As in the force opposing good, the negative to offset the positive. As in the precarious balance of nature, of the universe itself. As in worse than you can imagine, breath smelling like brimstone, glowing red eyes, straight-out-of-a-fiery-hell evil."

"You're not serious?"

When he glanced over at her, he found something in her green eyes older and wiser than any woman's eyes should ever have held. Than any human eyes should ever have held.

"Didn't you know, Rafe? Hadn't you even considered the possibility? Evil is real. It's a tangible, visible presence when it wants to be. It even has a face. Believe me, I know. I've seen it."

Alan had every intention of taking the note to Rafe and the federal agents. Just not right away.

He wasn't stupid about it, of course. He made a copy and put the original in a clear plastic sleeve to protect it. And then he spent a lot of time staring at the note. The words. Trying to figure out what the author was trying to tell him.

And trying to decide if the author was the killer.

Despite his sometimes provocative attitude in print, Alan wasn't a big fan of conspiracy theories, so his natural inclination was to believe that the note had been written by the killer. It was the simplest explanation, and it made sense to him. What didn't make sense was that someone in town knew who the killer was and had done nothing to stop him.

Unless that someone was very, very afraid.

And if that was the case . . . how could Alan flush him or her out of hiding?

It would be such a coup. And stop the killings, of course.

But how to bring that person, if he or she existed, out of the woodwork?

Musing over that question, Alan left the original of the note securely locked in his desk, but took the copy with him when he left the office—a bit early—for the day. He didn't go straight home but stopped by the town-hall building, which had become the unofficial hangout for most members of the media.

There were quite a few hanging around, but most were

talking companionably, with the relaxed posture that came of having passed the deadline for the six o'clock news. The pressure was off, at least for most of them and for the moment.

Dana Earley, the only blond female in the bunch, was also the most obviously tense. Understandably. She was also the only TV reporter still present today, and kept her cameraman close.

Alan doubted it was because she liked the guy, who was skinny, clearly bored, and appeared to be about seventeen.

*Some protection he'd be,* Alan thought.

"You," Dana said to him, "are looking far too smug. What do you know that the rest of us don't?"

"Oh, come on, Dana. You think I want a Columbia TV station to scoop me?"

Her brows disappeared up under her bangs. "Scoop you? What old movies have you been watching?"

Refusing the bait, Alan merely said, "It'll be dark soon. I think if I were a blond TV reporter, I'd want to be inside. Behind a locked door. With a gun. Or at least some muscle." He eyed the cameraman sardonically.

"I hear you have some muscle of your own," she retorted. "Police muscle. Sleeping with a cop, Alan?"

"If I am, it's hardly newsworthy," he said dryly, showing no outward sign of an inward flinch. Mallory was not going to like it if this *news* was common knowledge, dammit. "Unless your station prefers tabloid gossip over substantive news."

"Don't sound so superior. You were the first print journalist to use the phrase *serial killer,* and however you intended it, it sounded gleeful and excited in your article."

"It did not," he found himself countering irritably.

"Go back and read it again." She tucked an errant strand of blond hair behind her ear, smiled at him gently, and wandered off toward a magazine journalist here to research serial killers.

"Here you go, Alan."

He jumped, and frowned at Paige Gilbert, who was holding out a tissue to him.

"Jesus, don't sneak up on people. And what's that?"

"I thought you might need it. For the spit in your eye."

For just an instant, he was blank, but then he glanced after Dana and scowled as he looked back at the radio reporter. "Ha ha. She was just being all superior because she's a talking head on the six o'clock news."

"Not today she wasn't," Paige murmured.

"None of us has had much to report today," he reminded her.

"True. But you might as well have canary feathers smeared all around your mouth. Come on, Alan, give it up. You know we'll find out sooner or later."

Alan made a mental note to stop playing poker with Rafe and a few other of their friends; obviously, his serious lack of a poker face was why he had lost so much imaginary money to them.

"I'm done for the day," he informed Paige. "And even though this is your first really big story, if you want some advice from a veteran, you should go home and get some sleep as well. You never know when you'll get that call that pulls you out of bed at two in the morning."

Paige gazed after him, then jumped slightly herself when Dana said at her elbow, "He knows something."

"Yeah," Paige said. "But what?"


The rented car she and Isabel were sharing was parked near Caleb Powell's law office, so Hollis was able to make it that far. Once locked inside, though, engine and air-conditioning running, she sat behind the wheel and watched her hands shake.

Bishop had warned her that until she learned to fully control her abilities, the door that devastating trauma had created or activated in her mind was likely to open up unexpectedly. And that the experiences were apt to be particularly powerful ones in the midst of a murder investigation when several people had died recently and violently.

But all the months spent in the relative peace of Quantico, learning how to be an investigator, learning about the SCU, plus learning all the exercises in concentration, meditation, and control, had given her a false sense of security.

She had thought she was ready for this.

She wasn't.

First seeing Jamie Brower in the conference room, and now this. Seeing Tricia Kane standing near the desk where she had worked in life, less clearly visible than Jamie had been, oddly dreamlike but obviously trying to say something Hollis hadn't been able to hear.

Why couldn't she hear them? Before, it had been a voice in her head and only the sense of a presence, at least until the very end. Not . . . this. Not these misty images of people—souls—trapped between worlds. No longer alive, but not yet gone, standing in the doorway between this life and the next, the doorway Hollis's own traitorous mind kept opening for them. Talking to her.

Trying to talk to her.

Hollis hadn't expected this.

Not this.

She didn't know how to cope with this. She didn't know if she wanted to even try to learn to cope.

She wanted to run, that's what she wanted to do. Run and hide, from the dead and from—

The ringing demand of her cell phone jarred her from the

panic, and she took a deep breath to try and steady her voice before she answered it. "Templeton."

"What happened?" Isabel asked without preamble.

"I checked out Tricia Kane's office, but—"

"No, Hollis. What happened?"

She'd already had a few unsettling experiences with other SCU members and their easy connections with one another, so Isabel's obvious awareness of Hollis's state of mind didn't surprise her all that much. It still unsettled her, however.

"I saw Tricia Kane," she said finally, baldly.

"Did she tell you anything?" Isabel's voice was calm.

"She tried. I couldn't hear her. Like before."

"How long did it last?"

Hollis had to stop and think about that. "Not long. Not as long as in the conference room. And not as clear. She was . . . the image was fainter. Wispy. And it didn't feel as spooky."

"Powell didn't notice anything?"

"I don't think so."

"You're out of the office now?"

"Yeah."

"Okay. It's getting late. Why don't you go back to the inn and soak in the tub, have a hot shower, something like that. Relax. Order a pizza. Watch something mind-numbing on TV for a while."

"Isabel—"

"Hollis, trust me. Take the time while you can, and chill. Just chill. Sleep if you can. Don't think too much. We're just getting started here, and it's only going to get harder."

"I have to learn how to handle this."

"Yes. But you don't have to learn everything today. Today you just have to get some rest and get centered again. That's all. I'll be back at the inn myself in a couple of hours. I'll check, see if you feel like company. If not, that's cool, I'll see you at breakfast. But if you want to talk, I'll be there. Okay?"

"Okay. Thanks."

"Don't mention it, partner."


Rafe watched Isabel close her cell phone and return it to the belt pack she wore in lieu of a purse. They were standing in the living room of Jamie Brower's apartment, but they had barely arrived before Isabel reached for her phone, saying without explanation that she had to call Hollis.

"She was in trouble," Rafe guessed, watching Isabel.

"She saw another of the victims. Tricia Kane. It freaked her out a bit." Isabel shrugged, frowning slightly. "Still couldn't hear what Tricia was trying to tell her, so no help for us."

"You knew she was in trouble before you called her. How?" Before Isabel could answer, Rafe did himself. "Connections. A psychic connection. She's your partner."

"A connection she finds more unnerving than reassuring at this point," Isabel said wryly. "I'm sure you can relate." She began walking through the very nice apartment, looking around her with interest.

Rafe followed. "What do you mean by that?"

"I make you nervous. Admit it."

"I've known you barely twenty-four hours," Rafe retorted. "That isn't enough time to get used to a woman's perfume, let alone the fact that she knows without looking what kind of shorts you happen to be wearing."

Isabel chuckled. "Okay, you win that round."

Rafe thought it was about time he won one. "Is Hollis all right?"

"She will be, I think. This time. But if she doesn't get a handle on her abilities pretty fast, things are just going to get harder for her."

"I'd think talking to dead people would never get easier."

"No, from all I'm told, that part doesn't. It takes an exceptionally powerful medium with a strong sense of self to open that door and yet remain detached—and protected—from all the emotional and spiritual energy pouring through."

"Protected?"

Isabel paused in the kitchen, running a hand lightly along the immaculate granite countertops. The usual small appliances were scattered about: toaster, blender, coffeemaker. "She didn't cook much."

"Not according to what her family and friends said, no. A lot of takeout. What do you mean about a medium needing to protect herself?"

"Or himself. It's not a gender-specific ability, you know."

"I stand corrected. *Are* there any gender-specific abilities?"

"Not as far as we know."

"Okay. What did you mean about the medium protecting him- or herself?"

Isabel left the kitchen and went down the short hallway to the bedroom. She stood in the center, looking around. "A medium is the most vulnerable of all psychics to what you called possession. They're the ones who open the doors angry or desperate spirits usually need in order to return to this plane of existence. And the nearest potential host when the spirit comes through."

"*Usually* need?"

"We've theorized that an unusually powerful spirit could make its own doorway, if it were determined enough. So far, though, our experience has been that mediums or latent mediums provide the doorways."

"I can't believe I'm talking about this. Listening to this."

She looked at him, smiling faintly. "This stuff has always been with us, always been a part of our lives. For most of us, it was simply a case of not seeing what was there. Who knew there were protons and electrons until we found them? Who knew germs were responsible for illnesses until somebody figured it out? Who knew even fifty years ago that we had a chance in hell of mapping the human genome?"

"I get the point," Rafe said. "Still, this is—or at least feels—different."

"It's human. And one day, eventually, science will catch up, figure out a way to define, measure, and analyze, and make us legit."

"It's just . . . it's difficult to wrap my mind around it."

"I know, but you have to." Isabel walked over to the bed and rested a hand on it, frowning. "There are more things in heaven and earth, Horatio. Get used to it. Here endeth the lesson."

Rafe accepted the mild rebuke with a nod. "Okay. Though I do reserve the right to ask questions if anything unusual happens right in front of me."

"I wouldn't expect anything else."

He had to smile a little at her dry tone. "Picking up anything useful here?"

*Touch me there . . . like that . . .*

*Harder . . .*

*Christ, you feel good . . .*

Years of practice enabled Isabel to keep her face expressionless, but it was unexpectedly difficult with Rafe's eyes on her. He had very dark eyes, and there was something very compelling in them. She hadn't expected that.

Hadn't expected him.

"This is where she kept her sex straight. A few male lovers over the years. No women."

"So you think the room in the pictures was hers? One of the

properties she owned? A place she kept separate and secret for those . . . encounters?"

"Seems likely. She led a very traditional life here, so obviously her secret life was kept a thing apart. Really a thing apart; there are no secrets at all here. In fact, I'm more than a little surprised Emily found the photo box in this apartment."

"Unless Jamie had lost her most recent lover and hadn't yet found another. In that case, she might have needed to look at those pictures."

Isabel smiled. "You'd make a fair profiler, know that?"

Rafe was more than a little startled. "I was just guessing, that's all."

"What do you think profilers do? We make guesses. Mostly educated guesses, and for some of us occasionally psychic ones, but at the end of the day they're still guesses. Speculation based on experience, knowledge of criminals and how their minds work, that sort of thing. A good profiler probably gets sixty to seventy-five percent right if he or she is especially tuned in to a particular subject. A good psychic with solid control gets, maybe, forty to sixty percent in hits."

"Is that your percentage?"

She shrugged. "More or less."

He decided not to try to pin her down on that; he had a feeling it was one he wouldn't win. He hadn't known Isabel Adams an hour before reaching the conclusion that she was extremely unlikely to let slip by accident anything she didn't want him to know.

Isabel said, "We have to find the box or that room. Both, preferably. I need to know how Jamie felt about her secret life, really felt about it. And I'm getting nothing about that here."

"So you're getting no sense of a secret hiding place my people missed?"

"No sense of anything secret. I mean at all; this lady obviously knew how to compartmentalize her life. This was her public self, what the world was allowed to see. All bright and shiny and picture-perfect. We know her public self. We need to know her private self."

Rafe frowned as he followed her from the room. "Do you believe Jamie was targeted because of her sexual preferences? Because she was a dominatrix?"

"I don't know. It's about relationships, I'm sure of that. Somehow, it's about relationships. I'm having a hard time seeing Jamie's sexuality, or even the S&M games, as the trigger, that's all. Given his history. But it's the only thing hidden in Jamie's day-to-day life, and that means we have to be sure how much it means."

"Makes sense."

"So we need to find that room. And we need to find it quickly. It's been four days since he killed Tricia Kane; even if he waits a full week between murders, we only have three days to find him and stop him before another woman dies."

And before Isabel moved up on the hit list, Rafe thought but didn't say.

"You think he's stalking her now?" he asked instead.

"He's watching her. Thinking about what he's going to do to her. Imagining how it's going to feel. Anticipating." She was surprised that after all these years and so many similar investigations, it could still make her skin crawl.

But it wasn't just the fact of this killer, she knew that. It wasn't even what he had done to his victims. It was him. What she felt in him. Something twisted and evil crouching in the shadows, waiting to spring forward.

She could almost smell the brimstone.

Almost.

"Isabel—"

"Not now, Rafe." For the first time, there was a hint of vulnerability in her slightly twisted smile. "I'm not ready to talk about that evil face I saw. Not to you. Not yet."

"Just tell me this much. Does it have something to do with you becoming psychic?"

"It had everything to do with it." Her smile twisted even more. "The universe has an ironic sense of humor, I've noticed. Or maybe just an innate sense of justice. Because sometimes evil creates the tool that will help destroy it."

Cheryl had planned to drive back to Columbia for the night, especially after Dana's warning, but something was bugging her. It had been bugging her all day, ever since she'd noticed it early this morning.

She had her cameraman wait for her in the van and went to check it out, telling herself she'd be safe; it wasn't even dark yet, for God's sake. Of course, telling herself was one thing, and feeling it something else entirely.

Every time the breeze stirred it felt like somebody touching her with a ghostly hand, and she caught herself looking back over her shoulder more than once.

Nothing there, naturally. No one there.

The whole thing was just her imagination, probably. Because it didn't make sense, not if she'd seen what she thought she had. Not if it meant—

A hand touched her shoulder, and Cheryl whirled around with a gasp. "Oh, Jesus. Scare a person, why don't you?"

"Did I? Sorry about that."

"You of all people should know—"

"I do. Like I said, sorry. What're you doing out here?"

"Just following up a hunch. I'm sure the rest of you saw it, but it's been bugging me, so . . . here I am."

"You really shouldn't be out by yourself."

"I know, I know. But I'm not a blonde. And I hate it when something bugs me. So it seemed like a risk worth taking."

"Just for a story?"

"Well," Cheryl said self-consciously, "that's part of it, sure. The story. And maybe to stop him. I mean, it would be so cool if I could help stop him."

"Do you really believe your hunch could do that?"

"You never know. I could get lucky."

"Or unlucky."

"What're you—"

"Not a blonde. But nosy just like they are. And you'll tell. I really can't let that happen."

Cheryl saw the knife, but by the time understanding clicked into place in her head, it was too late to scream.

Too late to do anything at all.


**Friday, 11:30 PM**


Just occasionally, whenever her day had been particularly stressful, Mallory was so wild in bed that it took everything Alan had just to keep up with her.

Friday night was like that.

She held him with her arms, her legs, her body, as though he might escape her. The pillows were shoved off the bed, and the sheets tangled around them, and still they wrestled and rolled and held on to each other. They finished, finally, with Mallory on top, riding him fiercely, one hand on his chest and the other

114

braced behind her on his leg, grinding her loins to his in a hard, hungry, rhythmic dance.

He held her hips, surging up to meet her, his gaze fixed on the magnificence of her face taut in primitive need, her eyes darkened, her lithe, toned body glowing with life and exertion.

When she finally came with a cry, shuddering, he spent in almost the same instant, feeling her inner muscles spasming, milking him dry.

Usually, at that point Mallory rolled off him to lie at his side, however briefly, but this time he held on and shifted their bodies himself so that they lay on their sides, facing each other. He kept his arms around her.

"Good," she murmured, relaxed at least for the moment. "That was . . . good."

Drained himself, Alan nevertheless consciously tried to control the moment, his hand stroking her back in a soothing motion, enjoying the sensation of her warm breath against his neck. "More than good." He knew better than to comment on her passion, knowing from experience that it would only cause her to draw away, to start making excuses for leaving.

He had never figured out if it was the intimacy of the act that bothered Mallory when she allowed herself to think about it, or was reminded of it, or if it was her own lack of control that disturbed her. Either way, he was careful not to push that particular button.

He had learned.

"Long day," he murmured finally, intentionally keeping his voice as easy and soothing as his hands.

"Very long." She sounded a little sleepy. She moved just a bit against him, but closer, and sighed. "And a longer one tomorrow. God, I'm tired."

He didn't say anything, but continued to stroke her back gently even after he knew she had fallen asleep. He held her close and caressed her warm, silky skin, and felt her heart beat against his. And it was enough. For now.

A storm woke him before dawn, and Mallory was gone.

She hadn't even left a note on the fucking pillow.

# 7

H E WOKE UP with blood on his hands.
Wet blood.
Fresh blood.

The pungent, coppery smell of it was thick and heavy in the room, and he gagged as he stumbled from the bed and into the bathroom. He didn't bother to turn on the light even though the room was dim, just turned on the taps and fumbled for soap, washing his hands in the hottest water he could stand, soaping again and again.

The water, first bright red and then rusty-colored, swirled around the drain and slowly, so slowly, grew fainter and fainter. Like the smell.

When the water ran clear and he couldn't smell the blood anymore, he turned off the taps. For a long moment he stood there, hands braced on the sink, staring at his shadowy reflection in the mirror. Finally, he went back into the bedroom and sat on the side of the tumbled bed, staring at nothing.

Again.

It had happened again.

He could still smell the blood, though there was no sign of any on the sheets. There hadn't been before either. There never was, on anything he touched.

Just his hands.

He leaned forward, his elbows on his knees, and stared at his hands. Strong hands. Clean hands. Now.

No blood. Now.

"What have I done?" he whispered. "Oh, Christ, what have I done?"

Travis Keech yawned widely as he sat up in bed and vigorously rubbed his head with both hands. "Jesus. It's after eight."

"It's dawn," Alyssa Taylor said sleepily. "And it's Saturday, so who cares?"

"I care. I have to. I'm supposed to work. The chief said we could come in later if we've worked late—which I did last night—but we're all working overtime."

"I suppose it's taking all of you to investigate these murders."

"You can say that again."

"And I suppose you've got leads to follow."

Her voice still sounded sleepy, but Travis looked down at her with a tolerant smile. "You know, just because you're convinced I'm a yokel with straw in my hair doesn't mean you're right."

"I don't know what you're talking about." Sounding less sleepy now, she stretched like an elegant cat. The position showed him a nice expanse of bare skin already wearing a light summer tan, which really set off her gleaming dark hair and pale eyes.

"Oh, come on, Ally. I don't normally end up in bed with gorgeous women just hours after meeting them in our one little excuse for a bar. Unless, of course, they happen to be TV reporters from the big city and I happen to be involved in a serial-killer investigation."

"Don't underrate yourself," Alyssa told him. "And don't measure my morals with your yardstick, if you don't mind. I didn't set out to sleep with a cop, and I don't go after stories on my back."

"A lot of reporters do, I hear."

"I'm not one of them."

The sheet had slipped to show him most of one generous breast, and Travis decided he didn't want to offend her. "I never said you were," he protested, lying back down beside her and reaching underneath the covers. "But you could have had any guy in that bar and you came home with me. What else was I supposed to think?"

"That I thought you were sexy?" She didn't exactly pout, but her body was just the slightest bit stiff when he pulled her into his arms. "That I was bored and didn't want to go back to my hotel room alone? That I like guys in uniform?"

"Which was it?" he asked, nuzzling her neck.

"All of the above." She sighed and relaxed in his embrace, her arms slipping around his middle and her hands sliding downward. "And you've got a cute ass too."

He made an urgent sound, his body responding instantly to her caress, and she thought with faint, fleeting amusement that there was a lot to be said for catching a guy in his early twenties and at the peak of his sexuality.

A lot to be said.

She murmured, "I thought you had to go in to work."

"Later," Travis said.

It was nearly half an hour later when he finally, reluctantly pulled himself out of the bed. "I've gotta get to work. Want to join me in the shower?"

Alyssa stretched languidly. "Are you kidding? That tiny stall isn't even big enough for you. I'll wait my turn, thanks. I can shower while you're shaving."

"Okay, suit yourself."

Alyssa waited until she heard the water running, then slipped from the bed and gathered her scattered clothing from the floor. She had to follow a trail halfway to the front door to get it all, which amused her yet again. Her purse had been left carelessly on a chair near the front door, something that made her shake her head.

Not smart. Not at all smart.

Could be she was slipping.

"Nah," she murmured in response to that idea.

Returning to the bedroom, she laid the clothing out on the bed and then got her cell phone from the purse. She turned it on and punched in a number, keeping her gaze fixed on the half-open bathroom door.

"Hey, it's Ally." She kept her voice low. "I've found that source we talked about. A pretty good one. He's already told me more than he realizes. He must have had half a dozen strong drinks last night, and no hangover this morning. Oh, to be twenty-four again."

She listened for a moment, then said, "Yes, *my* head hurts. Well, I had to at least seem to keep up with him, didn't I? Never mind. He's going in to work, and the plan is to get him to meet me for lunch."

A question made her laugh under her breath. "No, I don't

think there'll be any problem persuading him to meet me. And I have a . . . hunch . . . that he'll be perfectly happy to have me sticking close for the duration. So I should have a fair idea of what's going on inside the department. Yeah. Yeah, I'll check in at least twice a day, as arranged."

**10:05 AM**

The third property they checked turned out to be an old commercial building off what had once been a busy two-lane highway until the bypass opened years before. Several companies had lost most of their customers, and more than one derelict office building or small store now stood abandoned and slowly falling into ruin. But a few, like the one Jamie Brower had owned, had been converted to have some kind of a useful life not dependent on passing customers.

"She was ostensibly using it for storage," Rafe noted as they stood just inside the front door. The early sunlight slanted through the dusty front windows so that the interior of the front part of the building was easily visible to them.

"Just barely ostensibly," Isabel agreed, looking around at a half dozen or so large pieces of old furniture in obvious need of restoration or repair, and a few crates labeled STORAGE. "Only enough stuff so that anybody looking in the front window would assume that was what she was using it for."

"The real story is in the back," Mallory called from a doorway about thirty feet from the front door and roughly halfway down the length of the building, where a wall divided the space. "The tools the locksmith gave us worked on this door and the rear entrance—which is conveniently hidden from the road. Great place to park your car if you don't want anybody to know you're

121

here. And there are signs quite a few cars have been parked back there in recent months."

"Why does that not surprise me?" Hollis wondered aloud.

"It's about time we got lucky," Rafe said as he, Isabel, and Hollis joined Mallory, all of them stepping into the half of the building that was quite obviously the reason Jamie had bought this place.

It was the room in the photographs.

"The submissive did know she was being photographed," Rafe said, gesturing toward the camera set up on a tripod several yards from the bed platform. "There's no place in here to hide that thing. The distance and angle look just right."

Hollis, wearing latex gloves, as they all were, went to examine the camera. "Yeah, it's set up to work on a timer. No cartridge or disk," she said. "Whatever last photos she took weren't left in the camera."

"No, I'd expect her to be more cautious than that," Isabel said, looking slowly around. "The really interesting thing is the question of whether the camera was part of the ritual. If she really does have a box full of photos, as Emily said, then it's likely most if not all of her partners were photographed."

Rafe kept watching her instead of studying the room, bothered by something he couldn't quite put a finger on. He thought Isabel was somehow uncomfortable or uneasy here. Her posture seemed a bit stiffer than usual, and something about the very calm of her features was almost masklike.

So when he spoke, it was absently. "It's all about control. And submission. Being photographed probably was part of the ritual, one of Jamie's rules. Her partners had to submit completely to her and her rules, even to the extent of having their secret needs and desires, their humiliation, recorded on film—and left in the hands of the dominant."

Mallory had located a large built-in closet or storage area on the right-hand wall and was working on the padlocked double doors with the ring of all-purpose tools provided by the locksmith. "Just for the record," she said, "I don't ever want to want anything that much."

"I'll second that," Rafe said. He was still watching Isabel, and directed his question to her. "Picking up anything?"

"Lots," she answered. "I don't know yet how much of it will be important, though. Or even relevant."

Her voice had been completely serene, but Rafe found himself frowning nevertheless. He glanced at Hollis and saw that she was also watching her partner intently, a crease between her brows indicating worry or unease.

Isabel walked over to the bed platform and bent slightly to place her gloved hand on the bare, stained mattress. Her face remained expressionless, though her mouth seemed to firm.

"I guess the latex doesn't interfere with psychic contact," Rafe said.

It was Hollis who replied, "No, it doesn't seem to. Although some of the SCU psychics say it has a slight muffling quality. Like everything else, it varies from person to person."

"Got it," Mallory announced suddenly. She unfastened the padlock and opened the two doors. "Christ."

"The toy box," Hollis murmured.


Dana Earley would have been the first to admit that being in Hastings at this particular time was making her extremely nervous. It had always been easy in the past for her to blend in, become a part of the background until she was ready to step in front of the camera and report the news.

This time, she was afraid of *becoming* the news.

"You shouldn't be out here," one male citizen of the small town scolded her in front of the coffee shop when she attempted to interview him about his feelings.

"I'm not alone," Dana said, gesturing toward Joey.

The man gave her cameraman the same scornful look Alan had offered the previous day. "Yeah, well, he might drop his camera on the killer's toe before he cuts and runs, but I wouldn't count on it if I were you."

"I resent that," Joey said sullenly.

They both ignored him.

"You should at least protect yourself," the man told Dana earnestly. "The police department is offering pepper spray to any woman who asks. I got some for my wife. You need to go get some for yourself."

"What about you?" Dana asked, making a mental note about the pepper spray. "Aren't you worried the killer might start going after men?"

He glanced from side to side warily, then opened his lightweight windbreaker to show her a pistol tucked into his belt. "I hope the bastard does come after me. I'm ready. A lot of us are ready."

"Looks like," she offered brightly, trying not to show him how much it frightened her to see guns in the hands of people other than the police. Especially angry and very nervous people. "Thank you very much, sir."

"No problem. And you watch it, you hear? Stay off the streets as much as you can."

"Yes. I will." She watched him walk away, then stood gazing around at Main Street, where there was less than normal activity for a lovely Saturday morning in June. And where there were far too many men just like the one she'd interviewed, walking around with windbreakers half-zipped and wary, watchful expressions on their faces.

"Can we go now?" Joey whined.

"I wish we could," Dana said, half-consciously reaching up to touch her hair. "I really wish we could. Hey—have you seen Cheryl?"

"Nah. Saw their van parked near the town hall this morning. Why?"

Dana bit her lip, hesitated, then said, "Let's head back toward the town hall."

"Ah, jeez."

"You're getting paid," she reminded her cameraman.

"Not enough," he muttered, following behind her.

"It could be a lot worse," she told him irritably. "You could be a blond woman. The way I hear it, the surgeon wouldn't have to cut off much to make that happen."

"Bitch," he grunted under his breath.

"I heard that."

He gave her the finger silently, reasonably sure she didn't have eyes in the back of her head.

"And I saw that," she said.

"Shit."


Inside the large storage closet of Jamie's playroom was, neatly arranged on shelves and hanging on hooks, all the paraphernalia necessary for sadomasochistic games. Whips, masks, padded and unpadded handcuffs, an extremely varied selection of dildos and vibrators, ropes, chains, and a number of unidentifiable objects, some quite elaborate.

Also a tasteful selection of leather bustiers, garters, and

stockings, including, seemingly, the outfits Jamie and her partner had worn in the photographs.

"I'm no expert," Hollis said, "but I'm thinking at least a few of those gadgets are meant to be used on a man."

Rafe could see the ones she meant. "I'd say so. And given that, it's beginning to look more and more like Jamie was . . . an equal-opportunity mistress. She may not have enjoyed sex with men, but it looks like she enjoyed dominating them."

"Men and women," Hollis said. "She really did want to be boss, didn't she? I wonder what would happen if she ran into somebody who wanted to be boss even more than she did?"

"A trigger, maybe," Isabel said in an absentminded tone.

"His trigger?" Rafe asked. "He wanted to be the one on top—so to speak—and it wasn't a position Jamie was willing to allow him to assume?"

"Maybe." Isabel's tone was still abstracted. "Especially if we find out the other two primary victims from the earlier murders were unusually strong women. Dominant women. That could be his trigger, his hot button. Finding himself interested in women literally too strong for him."

"Some men just prefer their women to be sweet and submissive, I guess," Hollis said dryly.

"Jerks," Mallory said, then lifted a brow at Rafe. "Forensics?"

"Yeah, get them out here," Rafe said. "But only T.J. and Dustin with their kits, not the van. I'd still like to keep this quiet as long as we've got a hope in hell of it."

"Right." She pulled out her cell phone.

Rafe walked over to Isabel, still uneasily sensing that something wasn't right with her. She was no longer touching the mattress but was gazing off into space with that distant expression he was beginning to recognize in her eyes. But this time she seemed to be looking so far away that it sent a chill through him.

"Are you okay?" he asked.

"There is," she said slowly, "a lot of pain in this room."

"You don't feel it, do you?"

"No. No, I'm not an empath. I feel during the visions, but not this. I just . . . I just know there's a lot of pain in this room. Physical. Emotional. Psychological." She reached both hands up and rubbed the nape of her neck. Her hair was in its accustomed neat, high ponytail, and Rafe could see how hard she was kneading the tense muscles of her neck. But before he could ask about that, she went on in the same level tone.

"Jamie was strong. Very strong. But she'd spent her life being the good girl. Pretending to be what everybody wanted her to be. Hiding inside that shell. But this part of her life . . . this is where she could be in control. Really in control. Where she could be herself and be respected—demand respect—for who she really was."

Hollis stepped closer, her frown deepening. "Isabel—"

"This is where she called the shots. Her partners, male or female, were never her lovers, never close to her emotionally; they were . . . validation. That she was strong and certain. That she was the one in control. They did anything she told them to do. Everything. No matter what, no matter how wild she got. No matter how much she hurt them."

When Rafe realized that Isabel's nails were literally digging into her own skin despite the gloves she wore, he stripped his own gloves off and reached up and grasped her wrists, ignoring the again visible and audible flash that was a hell of a lot stronger than any static shock he'd ever felt. He pulled her hands away from her neck.

"Wow," Hollis murmured. "Talk about sparks."

Rafe ignored her. "Isabel."

She blinked, those vivid green eyes still distant but seemingly focusing on him. "What?"

"You've got to stop. Now."

"I can't."

"You have to. This is hurting you." He wasn't entirely sure she knew who he was. She was looking at him, he thought, as though he were the only Technicolor object in a black-and-white universe. Puzzled and wondering.

"It always hurts," she said matter-of-factly. "What difference does that make?"

"Isabel—"

"Bad things happened here, you know. It's been going on for years. Years. But Jamie was always in control. She had to be. Always. At least until . . ."

She frowned. "They sold insurance here, and before that—no, after that—somebody sold bootleg whiskey out of here for nearly a year. Moonshine, just like you said. How strange. And a preacher spent some time here, a few weeks. Except that he wasn't a preacher anymore, because he'd been caught in bed with a deacon's wife and it hadn't been the first time. He thought God had abandoned him, but it was the other way around . . ."

Hollis said, "Take her outside. There are too many secrets in this place. Too much pain. Too much information for her to sort through all at once."

Rafe didn't wait for a more complete explanation; Isabel was pale, he could feel her shaking, and it didn't require anything more than common sense to know she was very close to some kind of collapse. So he took her outside.

Isabel didn't really protest, although once they were outside she did mutter under her breath, "Shit. I *hate* it when this happens."

He put her in the passenger seat of his Jeep and got the engine and air conditioner running, then dug into his first-aid kit and pulled out a gauze pad.

"What's that for?"

He tore open the wrapping and reached over to place the pad against the nape of her neck, again ignoring a strong shock.

"Ouch," she said.

"You drew blood," Rafe told her. "Even with the gloves on. Jesus, does this happen often?"

Isabel looked down at her hands with a faint frown, then stripped off the gloves. "Oh . . . from time to time. Bishop keeps telling me I should wear my nails short. Maybe I'd better start listening to him. Got any aspirin in that box?"

"Ibuprofen."

"Even better. If I could have a couple? Or . . . a dozen?" She reached up to hold the pad in place herself while he got the pain reliever and then a bottle of water from the cooler he kept in the Jeep.

By the time she had swallowed four capsules, the faint scratches had stopped bleeding, and Rafe used an antiseptic pad to wipe the nape of her neck while she sat with her head bowed and eyes closed.

Every time he touched her, the shock was definite, but she didn't react or comment and Rafe thought he was getting used to it. In fact, it seemed to clear his head.

Which was more than a little unnerving.

Her pale gold hair felt even silkier than it looked and seemed to want to cling to the back of his hand as he worked on her neck. Static, of course. Had to be. He concentrated on treating the scratches she had inflicted on herself, though he admitted silently that it took him longer than was strictly necessary.

"Thanks."

"Don't mention it. Are you going to be okay?"

She nodded slightly, still without opening her eyes. "When the painkillers kick in. And as long as I don't go back in there right away."

129

"Isabel—"

"Look, I know you have questions. Can we save them for a while, please?" She raised her head and opened her eyes finally, looking at him. The distant expression was gone, but she looked incredibly tired. "For now, your forensics team should be here any minute; why don't you go back inside and get everybody doing their thing? Hollis may be able to help. I felt something weird in there."

Rafe thought there had been a lot of weird in there, but all he said was, "Meaning?"

"That increasing nervousness and fear Emily had been seeing in her sister. I don't think it was just because Jamie was afraid her secret life would be exposed. I think she had another secret, a far worse one. And a much greater fear. I think something went wrong in there. I think she went too far."

"What are you saying?" He asked the question, even though he knew what she would answer.

"Have your team look for signs of blood. A lot of blood."


"No sign of that box," Mallory said after both women had thoroughly searched the back room. "No sign of anything she wanted to keep hidden—outside that closet, I mean."

Hollis nodded. "There's an attic, but it's wide open and empty."

"Um . . . on another subject, I gather from your reaction that it isn't normal for somebody touching Isabel to literally strike sparks?"

"I've never seen it happen before, though I've only known her a few months." Hollis frowned. "I was given a pretty thorough knowledge of the other SCU members, and that definitely wasn't mentioned. Could be something new for her, caused by this particular situation."

"Or it could be Rafe."

"Or it could be Rafe, yeah. Don't quote me on this, because I'm certainly no expert, but I guess if the right two energy signatures came in contact, there could be something like those sparks."

"Don't tell me this is what all the poets wrote about," Mallory begged.

Hollis smiled in response, but said, "Who knows? Maybe it's as much an emotional connection as it is literal energy fields. In any case, those two are reacting to each other, and on a very basic level."

"Is that a good thing or a bad thing?"

"I have no idea. But it might explain why Isabel seems to be having a rougher than usual time with this investigation."

"What might explain it?" Rafe asked, entering in time to hear the statement.

"You."

"Come again?"

"Hey, I'm just guessing," Hollis told him. "And I'm a long way from being an expert on any of this stuff, as I just told Mallory. But I was taught at Quantico that sometimes electromagnetic fields—those of individual people or places—come together in a particular way that tends to change or enhance a psychic's natural abilities. Or at least alter the limitations of those abilities. I have never seen Isabel so wide open, and as far as I can tell it's all been hits. No misses. That is very unusual. I'm thinking that sparking thing between you two has something to do with it."

"We can't be sure everything she's picked up is factual, not yet," Rafe said without commenting on the sparking thing.

"I wouldn't bet against her."

"Well, I sure as hell hope she's wrong about one thing. She thinks one of Jamie's little games got out of hand. We're now looking for evidence of a death here."

"Shit." Mallory stared at him. "You mean separate from our serial killer?"

"God knows. Hollis, are you getting anything?"

"I haven't tried." From the slightly stubborn set of her jaw, it didn't appear she planned to anytime soon.

After seeing what had happened to Isabel, Rafe wasn't about to push either psychic, but he was still curious. "Isabel never seems to try. I mean, it doesn't seem to be an effort for her."

"It isn't. For her."

He waited, brows raised.

After a moment, Hollis said, "You know the bit about me not being able to hear what these victims have tried to tell me? So far, I mean."

Somewhat warily, Rafe said, "Yeah, I think I get that."

"There's a barrier, something virtually every psychic has. We call them shields. Think of it as a bubble of energy our minds create to protect us. Most psychics have to consciously make an opening in that shield in order to use our abilities. We have to reach out, open up, deliberately make ourselves vulnerable."

"You didn't seem to be doing it deliberately," Rafe noted.

"I'm new at this. My control isn't as strong as it should be yet, so sometimes I reach out—or at least open a door or window in my shields—without meaning or wanting to. Usually when I'm tired or distracted, something like that. Eventually, they tell me, I should be able to shut this stuff out unless and until I very specifically want it. Most psychics can do that. Isabel is the very rare one who can't."

"You mean—"

"I mean she lacks the ability to shield her own mind. She's always wide open, always picking up information. Important stuff. Trivia. Everything in between. All that stuff always coming at her, crowding into her mind, like the voices of hundreds of people all talking at once. It's a miracle she can make sense of it at all. Hell, it's a miracle she isn't locked up in a padded room somewhere, screaming her guts out."

Hollis drew a breath. "When she told you she couldn't stop it, she meant it literally. She can't shut it off, ever."

Isabel sat in the cool Jeep and stared down at her hands. Watching them shake.

"Okay," she murmured, "so this one was bad. You've had bad ones before. You've heard all the ugly voices before. You can handle them. You can handle this."

She heard the ghost of a laugh escape her. "But *not* if you keep talking to yourself."

She laced her fingers together in her lap and raised her head, staring through the windshield at the building where Rafe and the others were.

It was where she should be, dammit, and never mind the pain. In there trying to sort through all the impressions, listening to the voices still echoing too loudly in her head. Even the ugly ones. Maybe especially the ugly ones.

Doing her job.

Isabel drew in a deep breath and let it out slowly, trying to focus, to soothe raw nerves and regain control of her senses, all her senses. Control. She had to find control.

Jamie had liked controlling people.

And that preacher . . .

*God, my God, why have you abandoned me?*

133

*Obey your mistress! Crawl!*

*Just three quarts more, and—*

*Bones bend before they break, you know. Bones bend—*

*Blood . . . so much blood . . .*

Her shaking hands lifted to cover her face, fingertips massaging her forehead and temples hard, and Isabel drew another breath, fighting to close out the voices. Not that she could.

Not that she'd ever been able to. Still, she tried.

Concentrate.

Focus.

Don't listen to them.

*She tempted me, that's what it was. Tempted me down the road to damnation. I was weak. I was . . .*

*I can make the rope tighter. I can make the rope much tighter. You want me to, don't you? You want me to hurt you. You want me to hurt you until you scream with the pain.*

*Bones bend . . .*

*And Bobby Grange, over to Horton Mill, he wants enough to fill a keg. Must be having a party, I guess. Guys like him keep me in business, that's for sure. And it ain't my business, what else they do. It just ain't any of my affair.*

*It wasn't my fault! She tempted me!*

*Do you know what happens when you feel all the pain you can feel? When your nerve endings are hot and raw, and your voice is gone from screaming? Do you know what it feels like to go beyond pain? Let's find out . . .*

*Bones bend before they—*

*Isabel.*

*Iss . . . a . . . belll . . .*

Her hands jerked away from her face, and Isabel stared all around her, a bit wildly at first. There it was. A different voice. Male. Powerful. Crouching in the darkness . . .

But . . . there was no one. No one. Her head was pounding, her heart pounding, and the voices were only whispers now. Only whispers, none of them calling her name.

"Okay," she said aloud, shakily, "that was new. That was different."

That was terrifying.

# 8

T.J. MCCURRY FINISHED spraying an area of the floor about two feet from the bed platform and said, "Kill the lights."

They had already draped the high window, so when T.J.'s partner, Dustin Wall, turned off the lights in the room, they could all see the eerie greenish-white glow.

"Bingo," Dustin muttered, and began photographing the evidence.

T.J. said, "Lotta blood here, Chief. There are some older spatters in other areas of the room, especially there around the bed, but here's the only place where somebody bled like a stuck pig."

"Bled enough to die?"

In the glow of the Luminol, T.J.'s round face looked peculiarly gaunt. She shrugged and looked down at the old vinyl floor covering. "Somebody's done a fair job of cleaning, but you can see how strongly the Luminol is reacting. I'm betting that when we pull up this floor covering, we'll find even more soaked into the concrete underneath. This is the old style of vinyl that was put down in tiles, not in a solid sheet, so the blood would have found all the crevices."

"T.J., did somebody die here?"

"You know I can't be absolutely certain about that, Chief. But if you want an educated guess, I'd say somebody did. Either that or a lot of somebodies bled a little bit here at different times—which, given the obvious purpose of the room, is entirely possible. We'll sort it out, get a blood type or types for you, DNA if you want."

"I want. Especially since I don't have a body."

Dustin said, "The state crime lab has cadaver dogs, if you want to start looking."

"Not yet. Not without more information. As edgy as this town is, the last thing we need is to have people and dogs out looking for another body, unless we're very sure one is actually out there." Rafe didn't say anything about psychic help, and he didn't look at Hollis, who was standing only a couple of feet away from him. "T.J., can you tell me if there's a blood trail out of this place?"

"I'll work on it. Dustin, do you have the shots? Then let's get the lights back on so we can see what we're doing."

Rafe left her to it, admitting silently that he was relieved when the lights came back on. He'd seen Luminol used before, and it always struck him as chilling. Invisible to the eye until the chemicals in the Luminol reacted with it, the blood was a silent, ghostly accusation.

He joined Hollis, saying, "Would I be out of line in suggesting that Isabel go back to the inn and call it a day?"

"Arguable point, I suppose, but she won't go, so it hardly matters."

137

He sighed. "You people are a very stubborn lot."

Hollis didn't ask whether he meant FBI agents or psychics; she knew the answer to that one. Instead, she said, "There are only a handful of team leaders in the SCU, agents Bishop trusts to head up investigations. Isabel is one of them, and has been from the beginning."

"You said it was a miracle she hadn't gone insane." Rafe kept his voice low.

"Yes. But she didn't go insane, that's the point. She is an exceptionally strong lady. She lives her life and she does her job, whatever the effort or the cost. What you saw happen in here is a rare thing, but similar things have happened before. It hasn't stopped her in the past, and this won't stop her now. If anything, the strong connection will probably make her even more determined to put all the puzzle pieces in place and get this killer."

"He's gotten away from her twice before," Rafe said, more to himself than to Hollis.

But she nodded. "Yeah, it's personal. How could it not be? It was her best friend he killed ten years ago, in case you didn't know that. She and Julie King grew up together, practically sisters. Isabel was only twenty-one when it happened, in college, trying to decide what to do with her life. Taking the most amazing variety of subjects, like classical Latin, and computer science, and botany. Nerdy stuff."

Hollis shrugged. "She was drifting, mostly. Getting by with good grades because of a good mind, not effort. Sort of . . . shut in herself, detached, uninvolved. From all I've been told, Julie's murder changed her completely."

"That isn't what . . . triggered her psychic ability?" It wasn't really a question.

"No. That had already happened." Hollis didn't offer to elaborate.

Rafe wasn't surprised. "But her friend's murder more or less started her life as a cop."

"I'd say so. In the beginning, she just wanted to find out who had killed Julie. That's what motivated her, what began to shape her life and future. By the time he surfaced again in Alabama five years later, she had a degree in criminology under her belt and worked for the Florida State Police. She apparently did routine searches of law-enforcement databases on her own time, waiting for the killer to strike again. Just after he killed the second victim in Alabama, Isabel took a leave of absence and turned up there. That was when she met Bishop."

"And turned in her state badge for a federal one."

"Pretty much, yeah."

Rafe drew a breath and let it out slowly. "So now she uses her knowledge, training, and psychic abilities to try and ferret out killers. Especially this one. Tell me something, Hollis. How many more times can she go through what she did in here before it breaks her?"

"At least one more time." Hollis grimaced at his expression. "I know it sounds harsh. But it's also the truth; we take this stuff one . . . experience . . . at a time, and none of us can be sure when the end will come. Or how."

"Wait a minute. You're telling me you guys *know* this stuff you do is going to kill you one day?"

"I'd call that a radical interpretation of the text," she murmured.

"Hollis."

"We're not the only stubborn ones, I see."

"Answer my question."

"I can't." She shrugged, more than a little impatient now. "Rafe, we don't know. Nobody really knows. We're all checked out medically after assignments, and the doctors have noted some changes in some agents. They don't know what that means, *we* don't know what it means. Maybe nothing."

"Or maybe something. Something fatal."

"Look, all I can tell you is that for some agents, there's a price for using their abilities. Some, like Isabel, live with pain most of the time, usually headaches. Some finish up assignments so exhausted it takes them weeks to fully recover. I know one agent who eats constantly during a case, and I mean constantly; it's like her abilities cause her metabolism to shoot into high gear and she has to fuel her body continually in order to do her job. But there are other agents who never seem affected physically by what they do. It varies. So, no, I can't tell you using our abilities is going to kill us one day. Because we just don't know."

"But it's possible."

"Sure, it's possible, I guess. It's also possible—more than possible, really—that we'll be killed in the line of duty by a regular old bullet or knife or explosion of some kind. The risk comes with the job. We all know the potential hazards, believe me. Bishop is very careful to make certain we understand what we might be risking, even if it's only a theoretical possibility. Anyway, Isabel made the decision that was hers to make, to use her abilities this way. She's been doing it for years, and she knows her limits."

"I don't doubt that. What I doubt is that she'll stop before those limits are reached."

"She's dedicated" was Hollis's only response.

"Yeah, I get that."

"You face risks in your job. Why keep doing it?"

Rafe didn't answer, just shook his head and said, "T.J. and Dustin will be a while, and there's really nothing more you and Isabel can do here. Is there?"

It was Hollis's turn to avoid the direct question. "We can go back to the station, work there while you guys finish up here. Get the information on the two previous series of murders posted on the boards."

"Good idea," Rafe said.

Hollis took the first chance she got to call in, which turned out to be about an hour later, when Isabel left the conference room to make copies of a stack of paperwork.

The number was still a bit unfamiliar, but her cell phone's address book had been carefully programmed, so it was easy to find the number and make the call.

As soon as he answered, Hollis said, "I didn't like doing that. Isabel's business is her own. She wouldn't talk about me behind my back, not that sort of personal stuff."

"He needed to know," Bishop said.

"Then Isabel should have been the one to tell him."

"Yes, but she wouldn't. Or, at least, wouldn't tell him right now. He needs to know now."

"And why is that, O wise Yoda?"

Bishop chuckled. "I'm guessing 'Because I say so' is not going to be a satisfactory answer for you."

"I didn't accept that even from my father; it definitely won't work for you."

"Okay. Then I'll tell you the truth."

"I appreciate that. The truth being?"

"The truth being that certain things have to happen in a certain order if we're to avert a catastrophe."

Hollis blinked. "And we know that catastrophe lies ahead because . . . ?"

"Because some of us occasionally catch a glimpse of the

future." Bishop sighed. "Hollis, we can't fix everything. We can't make the future all bright and shiny just because we know before they happen that there are troubles and tragedies waiting there for us. The best we can do sometimes, the absolute best, is to chart a careful path somewhere between bad and worse."

"And that path requires that I spill part of Isabel's story to Rafe."

"Yes. It does. This time. Next time, you may be asked to do something else. And you'll do it. Not because I say so, but because you can trust in the fact that Miranda and I would never do anything to injure or betray any member of the team—even to save the future."

Hollis sighed. "I wish that sounded melodramatic, but since I know the stories and I've seen a few things myself, I'm afraid it's the literal truth. The saving-the-future business, I mean."

"We have to do what we can. It's seldom enough, but sometimes the right word or the right information at the right moment can change things just a bit. Shift the balance more toward our favor. When we can even do that much. Sometimes we can't interfere at all."

"Going to tell me how you know that this is one of the times you can interfere?"

"Miranda sees the future and takes me along for the ride. Sometimes we see alternate futures; that's when we know we can change things. Sometimes we see only one future. We see what's inevitable."

"That's when you know you can't."

"Yes."

"And the future I just changed by telling Rafe some of Isabel's past?"

"Was a future in which he died."

---

"So why hasn't her cameraman reported her missing?" Isabel asked Dana Earley.

"I think he's ashamed of himself. Apparently, she told him to wait in the van while she went to check something out. He claims he doesn't know what. Anyway, she hadn't been gone ten minutes before he was asleep. And he didn't wake up until Joey and I banged on the side of the van about half an hour ago."

"That's a long nap."

"He says he's been running short on sleep for days. Probably true; a lot of our technical people get fascinated with their toys and keep the weirdest hours you can imagine."

Isabel frowned. "You've checked with her station, with the other media people across the street?"

Dana nodded. "Oh, yeah. The last anybody saw of Cheryl was just before dark last night. Dammit, I warned her to watch her back, brunette or not."

"Why?"

"Because I think the spotlight on a small town like Hastings can get pretty uncomfortable, and I wouldn't be surprised if this maniac targeted a journalist just to get us to back off."

Isabel rested a hip on the corner of an unoccupied desk, where the conversation was taking place. "That's not a bad theory, assuming he isn't too far gone to think logically. Off the record."

Dana nodded again, this time somewhat impatiently. "And I'm no profiler, but I'd expect him to target somebody who doesn't fit his clear preferences so far, just to make a statement."

"You're not the one I want, but you're in my way. Nobody's safe," Isabel murmured. "Go away."

"It makes sense, doesn't it?"

143

"Unfortunately, yes. Thanks for filing the report, Ms. Earley."

"If there's anything I can do to help look for that kid—"

"The best way you can help her and us is not to get yourself added to our missing-persons list. Don't go anywhere alone. I mean anywhere, unless it's into a locked room you know damned well is safe. Pass the word to the other journalists, will you?"

"Will do."

"Male and female journalists," Isabel added.

Dana nodded wryly and left.

Isabel remained where she was for several minutes, frowning at nothing. She was tired. Very tired. And worried.

If this bastard *had* grabbed a brunette journalist, *had* been angry enough to stray so far from his preferences, then why hadn't Isabel felt it?

"What's wrong with me?" she murmured.

There was no answer, except for the feeling she had of something crouching in the darkness. Watching.

Waiting.

When Rafe walked into the conference room just before four that afternoon, he wasn't especially happy to find Alan Moore there with Isabel.

"Hollis and Mallory are out running down a couple of leads," she told him, without going into detail. She seemed none the worse for what had happened in Jamie Brower's secret playroom, though something about her eyes told him she was still suffering a pounding headache.

Rafe nodded without commenting on either her info or his own hunch, and said to Alan, "Please tell me you have a reason other than idle curiosity for being here."

"My curiosity is never idle."

"I should have warned you about him, Isabel. You can only believe about half of what he says. On a good day."

"See, this is what happens when you grow up with a guy who becomes a cop," Alan said. "He turns into a suspicious bastard right before your eyes."

"Not without reason," Rafe retorted. "You've been a pain in my ass since I was appointed."

"I've been doing my job."

Isabel intervened before they could begin rehashing past offenses, saying, "Alan received something a bit unexpected in yesterday's mail."

Rafe stared at Alan. "And you're just now bringing it in?"

"I've been busy."

"Alan, one of these days you're going to go too far. Consider this a warning."

Despite the calm tone, Alan was perfectly aware that his boyhood friend was deadly serious. He nodded, not really having to fake the sheepish expression. "Noted."

Without commenting on the byplay between the men, Isabel handed Rafe a single sheet of paper in a clear plastic evidence bag. "I've already checked it. No prints, except his."

The note, block-printed yet virtually scrawled in a bold, dark hand on the unlined paper, was brief.

MR. MOORE, THE COPS HAVE GOT IT
ALL WRONG. HE ISN'T KILLING THEM BECAUSE
THEY'RE BLONDES.
HE'S KILLING THEM BECAUSE THEY'RE NOT

"Not blondes?" Rafe said, looking at Isabel.

"Yeah, but they were," she said. "At least, Jamie and Tricia were natural blondes; Allison Carroll used hair color."

145

"But she—" He stopped himself.

Isabel finished the comment for him. "She matched top and bottom. But the lab results are in, and they say she used hair color. It's not all that uncommon for a woman to dye her pubic hair, especially when the change is so drastic and she's at a stage in her life when looking good naked is a major goal. In any case, Allison's natural hair color was very dark."

Rafe met Alan's interested gaze, and said, "This is off the record, you realize that?"

"Yeah, Isabel's already warned me. Giant red federal warning, accompanied by flags, stamps, sealing wax, oaths of secrecy, and appropriate threats of being transported to Area 51 and turned into a lab rat."

Isabel smiled but said nothing.

"Just as a point of interest," Alan commented, "Cheryl Bayne is a brunette."

"Cheryl Bayne," Isabel said, "is missing. As are others on an unfortunately lengthy list. We don't know that anything has happened to any of them."

"Yet."

"Yet," she agreed.

Alan eyed her, then continued, "Anyway, when all is said and done and you've got the guy, I reserve the right to inform the public that I was contacted by the killer."

"Were you?" Isabel murmured.

"Third person," Rafe noted, studying the note. "*He* isn't killing them because they're blondes. This could have been written by someone who knows the killer. Knows what he's doing."

"Or maybe," Alan offered, "he's schizophrenic and believes it's not really him killing these women."

"You just want this to be the killer," Rafe said in an absent tone.

"Well, yes. This story could be my Watergate."

Isabel pursed her lips. "No. Your Ted Bundy or John Wayne Gacy. Not your Watergate."

"It could make my career," Alan insisted.

"Yeah?" Isabel was politely interested. "And do you happen to remember the name of the journalist who was supposedly contacted by Jack the Ripper?"

Alan scowled. "Shatter a man's dreams, why don't you?"

"Do you remember?"

"It was over a hundred years ago."

"And the most famous serial killer of modern times. Countless books have been written about him. Movies made about him. Theories as to his identity endlessly debated. And yet the name of that journalist doesn't exactly spring readily to the tongue, does it?"

"Do you know it?" Alan challenged.

"Of course. But then, I specialize in serial killers. More or less. Everybody in the business has studied the Ripper case. It's practically Murder 101 in Behavioral Science at Quantico. Everybody wants to be the one to solve it."

"Including you?"

"Oh, I don't think it'll ever be definitively solved. And I don't believe it should be. Some things should remain mysteries."

"You don't really believe that."

"Yes, I do. We should never, ever believe life—or history—holds no surprises for us. That way lies arrogance. And arrogance can blind us to the truth."

"Which truth?"

"Any truth. All truth." Her voice was solemn.

Alan sighed and got to his feet. "Okay, before you start calling me Grasshopper, I'm going to leave."

"I'm sure I have a pebble around here somewhere, if you want to stay and test your readiness," Isabel said, still solemn.

"Somehow, I don't think I'm fast enough," Alan said, not without a note of honest regret. He offered them both a casual salute, then left the conference room, closing the door behind him.

"Good job of distracting him," Rafe said.

"Maybe. With any luck he'll spend at least the next few hours on the Internet or in the library reading up on Jack the Ripper— just so he can tell me the name of that journalist the next time I see him. It'll occupy his mind a little while." She leaned back in her chair and rubbed the nape of her neck with one hand, frowning slightly.

"Still got that headache?"

"It comes and goes. So far, there's no sign of Cheryl Bayne; her station has backed up Dana Earley's missing persons report with one of their own. And Hollis and Mallory are checking out the rest of the properties owned by Jamie Brower."

"You still want to find that box of photos."

"I want to find whatever is there. Speaking of which, your forensics team confirmed blood in Jamie's playhouse, I gather. A lot of blood."

He nodded. "Yeah, you were right about that. And a faint blood trail to the door. T.J. figures the body was wrapped in plastic. I'm guessing it was put into a car and hauled somewhere. They're going over Jamie's car now, but we didn't find anything when we checked it bumper to bumper after she was killed."

Isabel shook her head. "She wouldn't have panicked, and she was too smart to transport a body in her own car. It would have been her playmate's car. And I'm betting she got rid of it afterward. Very rid of it. Like maybe sank it to the bottom of one of the lakes in the area. With or without the body inside."

"That," he agreed, "is all too likely." He hesitated, then added, "Did you pick up anything from Alan?"

"No, he's a very closed book. Not uncommon for a journalist;

they keep a lot of secrets, as a rule. Most of us find it difficult to read them, even the telepaths."

"You think his guess about the killer being schizophrenic was right?"

"I think it's at least as likely as any other theory we have. Maybe more than likely." She drew a breath and spoke rapidly. "One school of thought proposes four different types of serial murderers: visionary, mission-oriented, hedonistic, and control-oriented. The mission-oriented is out to eliminate a particular group he feels is unworthy of living. Common victims for this type of killer are those easily categorized: prostitutes, the homeless, the mentally ill. Or—plumbers."

Rafe blinked. "Plumbers?"

"I'm just saying. Mission-oriented serial killers target groups. Unless our guy is out to kill all women, or at least all successful women—a task even a madman would have to find daunting— then I don't believe he's mission-oriented."

"Sounds logical to me. Next?"

"The hedonistic killer is after pleasure or thrills when he kills. He may get his jollies from the kill itself, from the arousal and gratification of what's basically a lust murder; he may enjoy the planning stages, the stalking of his prey. Or he may find pleasure in the consequences of the kill if, for instance, he gains a kind of freedom by killing family or people he perceives as tying him down somehow."

"Control-oriented type?"

"His thing is having power over the victim, especially the power of life and death. If he rapes, it's for control and domination, not thrills. And this type generally doesn't kill his victims immediately. He likes to torture, both physically and psychologically. He wants to draw it out, savor his power over them, watch their helplessness and terror."

"You must have hellacious nightmares," Rafe said.

She looked at him with a little half smile. "Oddly enough, no. My nightmares tend to come while I'm awake."

Rafe waited a moment, giving her an opening, but it was obvious she didn't intend to take it. "So our guy is not likely to be control-oriented, or at least not driven by that, since he doesn't waste any time at all in killing his victims. And the visionary type of serial killer I'm assuming is the nail Alan may have hit on the head?"

"Umm. Alan . . . and the note sent to him." She tapped a red fingernail against the plastic-sleeved note Rafe had placed atop the stack of papers on the conference table in front of her. "This makes me wonder, it really does. If it's not purely a ruse designed to throw us off track—and we have to assume that's at least possible—then this note could tell us a lot about our killer. I'll need to make a copy for us and send the original to Quantico, by the way. The handwriting experts may be able to tell us something. As for what the note says . . ."

"He wants us to stop him?"

"If we accept this as written, and as written by the killer, then some part of him does. The sane part." Isabel paused, frowning. "The least common type of serial killer is the visionary, someone who sees visions or hears voices commanding him to kill."

"As in Son of Sam."

"Yeah. He usually attributes the voices to God or some kind of demon and feels himself helpless to disobey them. He's not in control, the voices are. They tell him to kill, who to kill, when to kill. Maybe why those particular people have to be killed. He may hear the voices from childhood, or it may be a sudden psychosis brought on by stress or trauma. Some people believe a chemical change in the brain is responsible, but, as I said, we don't know a whole hell of a lot about how the brain really works.

"In any case, the visionary killer feels he's controlled by something alien, something that is no part of himself. Sometimes he ignores or fights the voices or visions for years before they finally overpower his will. Bottom line, he's a puppet with someone else—or something else—pulling his strings."

"Okay," Hollis said, studying the notes in her hand and then looking up as Mallory pulled the police Jeep to the curb and parked. "This should be it. Last place on Jamie's list of properties."

"What're we expecting to find here?" Mallory wondered, eyeing the boarded-up front window of what had once, years before, been a gas station. "According to her broker, Jamie planned to sell this place."

"Yeah, but he also said that wasn't the original plan. She bought this property meaning to raze what's here and build a nice little place to fit in with the boutiques popping up at this end of town. It would have vastly increased the value of the property. Then she very suddenly decided to just sell out."

"But she made that decision about several of the properties we've looked at. And the broker didn't say suddenly, he said somewhat unexpectedly."

"Somewhat unexpectedly about three months ago. Isabel says that fits the time frame; it's when Jamie started showing signs of nerves. Deciding to unload so much of her property virtually all at once even if it meant taking a loss was out of character, and when people do things out of character there's usually a good reason behind the actions."

"Like she accidentally killed a lover, maybe. But what was the plan after she sold out? Did she mean to get her hands on all the cash she could so she could leave town?"

"Could be. Isabel thinks there's a possibility."

"Then why are we checking out these places? She wouldn't have hidden the photo box—or any other keepsake—in a place she was going to sell. You don't think we're going to find a body in there?"

"Well, you know as well as I do, the state crime network coughed up a list of at least three women of roughly the right age reported missing in this general area at about the same time Jamie got nervous. The police in each district believe all three women did not leave of their own free will, which makes homicide at least a possibility. And . . . if things did get out of hand in one of Jamie's little games, she had to do something with the body."

"Hide it in a building she owned herself and was planning to sell?"

"I wouldn't call it a smart thing to do. Unless she figured out a way to completely destroy the body or completely hide it even if the building came down. Or unless she planned to be far away and living under an assumed name or something by the time anything was discovered."

"Interesting possibilities," Mallory agreed. "Okay. Grab your flashlight and let's check it out."


Isabel turned her gaze to the bulletin boards across the room, which had, Rafe noted, acquired what looked like canvas drop cloths that could be conveniently lowered to cover the boards whenever unauthorized persons were present.

The cloths were lowered now, presumably because Alan had been in the room.

Absently, she said, "Mallory thought the drop cloths would be a good idea, so she fixed them. We can keep the boards covered most of the time, unless we're in here working. Less chance of too much information leaking out."

"Isabel? Could a visionary killer gain control over his voices for years between killing sprees? Could he live normally during those years?"

"That would be . . . unusual."

"But would it be possible? Could it be? Are we dealing with a killer who really isn't responsible—at least legally—for what he's doing?"

"That might depend on the trigger—and the reason or reasons behind all this."

"What do you mean?"

"I mean the human mind, the human psyche, is a very complicated beast. Generally speaking, it knows how to protect itself, or the most fragile aspects of itself. If he's hearing voices or seeing visions, and they're commanding him to do things utterly alien to his nature, then sure—he could forget about them the moment the voices or visions stop."

"For years on end?"

"Maybe. And then something happens in his life to trigger this psychosis, and his sick and twisted alter ego comes out to play."

"For six weeks. Six women. Six murders."

"The number, the time period, both have to be relevant, either tied to an event somewhere in his past or tied to the psychosis. To his voices."

"Which is your guess?"

Isabel thought for a moment, then said, "Childhood. The majority of the traumas that affect us most deeply occur in childhood. It's when we're most vulnerable."

"What about the idea that he's schizophrenic?"

"There are schizophrenics able to function, with medication and other treatment. No pharmacy within a hundred miles has filled a prescription for the sort of medication that would be needed."

Rafe lifted his brows. "Already checked that out?"

"Well, the profile noted the possibility of schizophrenia, so it seemed prudent. An inquiry from the Bureau tends to carry a bit of weight, and since we weren't asking for specific patient information or identification, all the pharmacies were happy to cooperate."

"Okay. So we can be pretty sure he isn't being treated for schizophrenia."

"Which doesn't rule out him having it. Or that he's getting psychiatric treatment without medication. We haven't checked with doctors."

"Because they wouldn't disclose the information."

"Not willingly. They have a responsibility to report it if they believe a patient has committed or is about to commit a violent crime, but that sort of treatment can take years before the doctor truly begins to understand his or her patient."

"And understand what the voices are making him do."

"Exactly. In any case, my guess is that our guy isn't getting treatment of any kind. Whether he's aware of being sick is an open question; whether he knows what he's done is another one. From the information we've gathered so far, there's just no way to be certain."

"Earlier, you said some schizophrenics were, literally, possessed by another person, another soul trying to take over. Is that possible in this case?"

Isabel shook her head. "So far, we've never encountered a person in that condition who wasn't in a mental institution and under restraints or drugged into a stupor. We don't believe such a person could function normally under any conditions—far less something like this. There's just too much violence going on in the brain itself to allow even the appearance of normalcy."

"And our killer appears normal."

"Yes. No matter how screwed up his childhood may have been, or how many voices he might be listening to, he's able to function normally to all outward appearances."

After a moment, Rafe said, "I think I'd prefer an evil killer who knows exactly what he's doing, sick as it is. At least then it would be . . ."

"Simpler," she agreed wryly. "Black and white, no shades of gray. No agonizing over who or what is really responsible. No reason to hesitate or regret. But you know as well as I do that it's seldom that easy."

"Yeah. As Hollis said, the universe never seems to want to play it that way. Listen . . . we aren't talking about a psychic killer, are we?"

"Christ, I hope not." With a sigh, she returned her gaze to his face. "True visionary killers are delusional, Rafe. They believe they hear the voices of demons or the voice of God. They're being commanded to do things they wouldn't ordinarily do, for reasons the sane among us would find completely nuts. They aren't psychic; what they're experiencing isn't real except inside their own twisted minds."

# 9

IT HADN'T TAKEN ALAN long to find the information he was looking for on Jack the Ripper, and he was somewhat chagrined to see just how much information was readily available via the Internet on the case.

Just as Isabel had said.

She hadn't exactly thrown a gauntlet at his feet, but Alan nevertheless felt challenged to somehow best the federal agent. And Rafe, of course. It would be nice, he thought, to get the upper hand with Rafe.

Just once, for Christ's sake.

The problem was, Alan hardly had access to the sort of data-bases of information the police and feds could command. But there was one thing he did have, and that was knowledge of this town and its people.

The question was, could he use that?

He wasn't able to speak to Mallory as he left the station, since she wasn't there, so he didn't know whether to expect a visit from her tonight. After last night, he figured he probably wouldn't see her for days; whenever she showed him any signs of vulnerability—falling asleep in his arms would definitely be listed in that column, he knew—she tended to retreat for a while both literally and figuratively.

In any case, he had learned the hard way not to plan his days or nights around her. He got in his car at the station and checked his watch, debating silently, then started the car.

It was time he tapped *all* his sources.

**4:45 PM**

Rafe had a hunch Isabel's explanation contained a *but*, so he asked. "But?"

"But . . . we've encountered serial killers before who also happened to be psychic, so the two aren't exactly mutually exclusive. In fact, some researchers believe that serial killers and psychics have something in common: an unusual amount of electromagnetic energy in the brain."

"Which means?"

"Which means we are or could be kindred spirits, scary as that sounds. The *excess* energy in a psychic seems to activate an area of the brain most people don't appear to use, an area we believe controls psychic abilities. The energy in a serial killer tends to sort of go wild, building up in different areas of the brain, especially in the rage center, and since it has no way to be channeled, you end up with synapses misfiring right and left. Burned-out or overloaded areas of the brain could trigger the compulsion to kill."

157

"So that's one theory."

"One of many. And that theory holds something else to be a possibility. That a serial murderer can also become psychic. Which comes first in that case, the psychic ability or the insanity, is still an open and much debated question."

"Does it matter?"

"Well, yeah, for some of us." Her voice was light. "I hear voices, Rafe, remember?"

"Voices you don't attribute to God or a demon. Voices that don't command you to kill."

"Not even on the worst day yet, I'm happy to say. So far, so good." She shook her head slightly. "But returning to the point—a psychic killer is possible."

"Would you know? I mean, could you tell if that were the case?"

"Not necessarily. Psychics can often recognize each other as psychic, but not always."

"Shields," he said, remembering what Hollis had told him. "Yet another instance of the mind protecting itself."

"Hollis said she mentioned that." Isabel didn't seem disturbed by it. "And it is one reason we don't always recognize each other. Also, nonpsychic people frequently develop shields of their own, for privacy or protection, especially in small towns where everybody tends to know everybody else's business. It's a lot more common than you might think. Hell, I could talk to the killer every day, never knowing he's the murderer and never picking up psychic ability—or psychotic voices in his head."

For the first time since he'd returned, she sounded tired, and it made him say, "How close are Mallory and Hollis to finishing up?" He was about to suggest calling one of them, but Isabel automatically used a more direct line of communication.

"They are . . ." She frowned, concentrating. ". . . at the last property on the list, I think. What used to be a gas—" Her face changed, tightened.

Watching her, Rafe was conscious of the same uneasiness he'd felt in Jamie's "playhouse." She was somewhere else, somewhere distant from here. He wanted to reach over and touch her, anchor her here somehow.

She came abruptly to her feet. "Oh, Christ."

"You know, for a gas station, this is a huge building." Mallory's voice echoed.

They were in the rear area, which was divided into at least three separate rooms, all apparently cavernous; the one they were presently exploring had a concrete floor and high windows so dirty they admitted almost no light. Rusted pieces and parts from old cars still hung on hooks and racks on the cinder-block walls, and piles of junk lay everywhere.

Every time Mallory moved the beam of her flashlight, it seemed to catch something metallic and glare back at her, like something springing out of the shadows.

Unsettling.

"Tell me about it. I'm guessing it didn't start out life as a gas station." Hollis pointed her flashlight into a dark corner and jumped when an unexpectedly shiny chrome bumper glinted brightly. "Jesus."

Mallory jumped in the same instant, but in her case it was because something skittered across her foot. "Shit. I hate rats, but I hope that's what just ran across my foot."

Hollis didn't care for rats herself, but she was standing before what looked like a solid steel door that held her interest at the moment. The door was padlocked. "Never mind the rats. Take a look at this."

159

Mallory joined her. "I can't never mind rats. I hate rats. And I'm going to throw these shoes away. Yuck." Her flashlight beam joined Hollis's. "Is that a new lock?"

"I'd say so. Hold on a minute." She juggled her flashlight briefly before tucking it under her arm as she dug into the waist pack she was wearing. She put on a pair of latex gloves, then produced a small, zippered leather case.

Mallory watched with interest. "Burglar's tools? You didn't bring those out at Jamie's playhouse."

"I didn't have to, you had the locksmith's tools." Hollis smiled suddenly. "I've been hoping there'd be an opportunity for me to try out my lock-picking skills. They haven't been field-tested yet." She selected a couple of tools and bent to begin working on the lock.

"You learned this at Quantico?"

"From Bishop. It's sort of fascinating which skills he determines to be most important to a new agent. Handling a gun without shooting myself in the foot and with reasonable accuracy—check. Being able to use a form of autohypnosis and biofeedback to focus and concentrate—check. Ability to talk to the dead—a major plus. Being able to pick various and sundry locks—check. Or, at least, so I hope."

Mallory laughed under her breath. "You know, I'd really like to meet this Bishop of yours. He sounds like a very interesting man."

"He certainly is. Damn. Shine your light right here, will you?"

Mallory complied.

"Wait—I think—" There was a soft click, and Hollis opened the padlock with a flourish. "Ta-da. What do you know, I can do this. I wasn't at all sure I could."

"Congratulations."

"Thank you." She put away the tools, then had to put her

shoulder against the door to push it inward. And the moment it was open a few inches Hollis immediately stepped back. "Oh, shit."

The two women looked at each other, and Mallory said, "I haven't had the misfortune to stumble across a decomposing human corpse, but I'm guessing that's what one would smell like. Please tell me I'm wrong."

Breathing through her mouth, Hollis said, "I'm pretty sure that's what it is. Part of the training I got was a visit to the body farm—where students and forensics specialists study decomposition. It's not an odor you easily forget."

Mallory stared at the partially open door. "I'm not looking forward to seeing what's inside there."

"No, me either." Hollis eyed her. "Want to wait and call in reinforcements?"

"No. No, dammit. With a padlocked door and that smell, there's obviously nothing dangerous in there. Nothing alive, I mean. We have to open the door and look, make sure it's not some dead animal in there. Then call it in."

Hollis braced herself mentally and emotionally—and did her best to shore up her psychic shields. Then she and Mallory shouldered the door all the way open and stepped inside.

"Jesus," Mallory whispered.

Hollis might have echoed her, if she could have forced words past the sick lump in her throat.

It was a bare room, for the most part, with only a few shelves along one wall to show it had been used at least once for storage. The high windows admitted just enough illumination, from the southwestern corner of the building and the hot sun low enough in the sky, to provide mote-filled beams of light focused on the center of the room.

On her.

One end of a thick, rusted chain was wrapped around a steel I-beam overhead, while at the other end of the chain a big hook jutted from between her rope-bound wrists. She dangled, literally, from the hook, her feet several inches above the floor. There was nothing beneath her except rusty stains on the concrete.

Thick, dark hair hung down to mostly obscure her face. The clothing she had worn, a once-demure blouse and skirt, had been shredded, but very neatly, methodically, almost artistically. The material provided a fringe that almost hid what had been done to her body.

Almost.

"Jamie didn't do this," Mallory whispered. "She couldn't have done this."

"Nothing human could have done this," Hollis responded, her own voice thin. "It's like he was curious to see what color her insides were."

Mallory backed out of the room, gagging, and Hollis didn't have to follow to know the other cop was throwing up everything she'd eaten today.

Her own stomach churning, Hollis reached for her cell phone, her gaze fixed on the dangling and decomposing body of a woman who'd been gutted like a fish.

**6:00 PM**

The medical examiner for the county, Dr. David James, was a normally dour man, and a scene like this one didn't make him any more cheerful.

"She's been dead at least a couple of months," he told Rafe. "The fairly cool, dry conditions in here probably slowed decomp a bit, but not much. I can't be positive, of course, but from the

162

bruising on her neck I'm guessing strangulation, probably with a rope of some kind. Whoever cut her did it postmortem, probably days afterward; there was almost no bleeding from those wounds."

"Anything missing?" Rafe kept his own voice as level as the doctor's, but it required a tremendous effort.

"I'll be able to tell you more when I get her on the table, but it does look like one kidney is gone, some of the intestines, part of her stomach."

"Christ."

"Yeah. I may be able to get you prints from her, and it looks like she's had some dental work done, so we have a fair shot at an I.D. if she's one of the missing women on your list. Get this guy, Rafe. What he did to the other women was bad enough, but this . . . He's worse than a butcher."

Rafe didn't comment on the doctor's assumption that the same killer was responsible for this woman's death. "We're doing our best."

"Yeah. Yeah, I know." Dr. James hunched his shoulders a little, weariness in the gesture. "My guys are standing by to bag her as soon as yours are finished."

"Right."

"I'll get the report to you ASAP."

Rafe watched the doctor make his way back toward the front of the former gas station, then returned his gaze to the activities in the back room. T.J. and Dustin were working methodically, their faces grim. Off to one side, Isabel stood with Hollis as they studied the dead woman.

If he'd been asked to guess, Rafe would have said that Hollis was feeling queasy and Isabel was exhausted. He was pretty sure both hunches were on the mark.

Mallory joined him in the doorway and nodded toward the

federal agents, saying, "They still believe she was one of Jamie's playmates, the one accidentally killed."

"But they don't believe Jamie did this," Rafe said, a statement rather than a question.

"No."

"Which begs the question . . ."

"Who did. Yeah. Didn't Doc say she died two months ago at least?"

Rafe nodded. "Before the murders started. Isabel?"

She and Hollis immediately walked over to join them at the doorway.

"The doc says she didn't bleed to death," Rafe said to Isabel without preamble.

She nodded. "Yeah, I missed that one. I'm guessing the lab work from Jamie's playhouse will come back showing several people bled in that spot over a long period of time. Some of her clients, probably, but others as well. There might even have been a murder there a long time ago."

"That blood trail to the door," he noted.

"Possibly. Or one or more of Jamie's clients." Isabel shrugged. "In any case, I missed."

Mallory said dryly, "All will be forgiven if you just help us get this bastard."

"Was this his trigger?" Rafe asked.

"I don't know," Isabel replied.

"An educated guess?"

"If you want that . . . then maybe. Maybe he saw this woman die accidentally at Jamie's hands, and maybe it pissed him off. Or maybe he got his hands on a cold body and wondered what a warm one would feel like. Or maybe she was just a toy he played with because she happened to be handy."

"You're not picking up anything?" He kept his voice low.

She grimaced slightly. "Lot of old, old stories; this building has been here a while. Arguments, mostly, but . . ."

Whispers.

*Jesus, George, we have to do it in the backseat?*

*I told you I can't afford a motel room.*

*Yeah, but . . .*

*Hide the stuff inside the hubcap. I'm tellin' you, the cops'll never find it there . . .*

*That Jones bitch wants her car done by tomorrow or she won't pay . . .*

*You're fired, Carl! I'm fucking sick and tired of . . .*

*Bones bend before they break.*

*She's all colors inside.*

*Isabel.*

*Isss . . . a . . . bellll . . .*

"Isabel?"

She blinked and looked at Rafe. "What? Oh. Just old stuff, mostly. But he was here. A day or two ago."

"How do you know that?"

There was no way Isabel was going to tell Rafe that their killer had been looking at this poor woman and thinking about what he wanted to do to Isabel.

No way.

So all she said was, "He . . . looked at her. Thought about how she had deserved to die because she was bad."

Rafe frowned. "Bad?"

"I get the sense he saw her with Jamie. Watched them. And what they did together bothered him on a very deep level. Sickened him, believe it or not."

Something in the dark, crouching, waiting.

Watching.

Isabel shivered. "It feels cold here. Really cold."

He was a little surprised. "Cold?"

"Yeah." Her arms were crossed beneath her breasts, the goose-flesh on her skin actually visible. "Chilled, cold. Like a gust of icy air blowing through me. Yet another fun new experience."

"You said you weren't an empath."

"I'm not. I have no idea why I'm beginning to feel things rather than simply know them. Until now, feelings, sensations, only came with visions. Now ..." She shivered. "No visions. But, man, I'm cold. I'm thinking that's not normal for June, never mind it not being normal for me."

"Maybe you're coming down with something," Rafe suggested prosaically.

"I sort of doubt it."

"It's just in here?" Hollis asked.

"Seems to be. Outside, I was fine."

"Then you should be outside."

"We both should," Isabel said. "You feel the cold too." She gestured slightly, and they all saw the goose bumps on Hollis's bare arms.

Rafe looked at both agents, then said to his detective, "Mal, would you mind staying to supervise until T.J. and Dustin are finished and the body is removed?"

"No problem."

"Thanks. I'll be right back." Rafe gestured slightly, and the two other women walked with him toward the front of the building. "It's after hours for most of the businesses around here, so there's not too much traffic in the area, but I've posted a few of my people on the block to stop the curious from gathering. Or, at least, from gathering close by."

When they stood out on the sidewalk, Isabel could indeed see both uniformed cops and passersby at a perimeter about half a block away.

"Great," she muttered. "Well, at least the icy breeze stopped blowing." She rubbed her upper arms briefly with both hands, relaxing visibly.

To Hollis, Rafe said, "I gather you didn't pick up anything helpful in there either?"

"No."

He couldn't tell whether it was because there'd been nothing for her to pick up or because she hadn't tried. He decided not to ask.

"I was about to suggest we call it a day before Hollis and Mallory found the body. It still sounds like a good idea. First thing tomorrow we'll have a preliminary forensics report, and if I know Doc we'll have the postmortem as well. We'll have a decent shot at making an I.D. of the body, and we can start trying to piece together what happened to this lady. Between now and then there isn't much we can do. Except get some rest for tomorrow."

"I will if you will," Isabel said.

He eyed her, but before he could say anything, Hollis was speaking calmly.

"I, for one, would just as soon start fresh tomorrow. I want to shower about six times, watch something funny on television, and maybe call my mother. If I ever feel like eating again, I'll order a pizza. You two want to be gluttons for punishment, have at it. I'm going back to the inn."

Isabel grimaced slightly. "A shower definitely sounds like a good idea; nobody wants to smell like death. But I'm way too restless to call it a day." She looked at Rafe, brows lifting inquiringly. "Buy you dinner?"

He checked his watch but didn't hesitate. "I'll pick you up at eight."

"See you then." Isabel walked with Hollis back to their rental and got in the driver's seat. Hollis got in beside her and didn't say anything for about half a mile.

167

Then she spoke slowly. "He's blocking you, isn't he? No—he's shielding you."

Isabel gave her partner a surprised glance, then fixed her gaze on the road again. "Bishop said you picked up on things quickly. Once again, he wasn't wrong."

Absently, Hollis said, "You relax a bit whenever Rafe is nearby, as if some of the strain is lifted. Maybe I see it because I used to be an artist. It started in Jamie's playroom, didn't it? When he put his hands on your wrists."

"Yeah."

"You felt something?"

"The shock first. And then a muffling quality. Didn't shut out the voices, just . . . quieted them a bit, as though I were suddenly insulated. Just enough for me to notice. Out in the Jeep, when he was putting disinfectant on my neck and sitting so close, the voices were barely whispers. When he left to go back inside, they got louder again."

"And just now, back there?"

"If he was within five feet of me, all I heard were whispers. Creepy whispers, but whispers. And felt that goddamned icy breeze; he doesn't seem to have had any effect at all on that."

"So what does it mean?"

"I don't know. I seem to have been saying that a lot today. I don't like saying it, for the record."

Hollis looked at her. "What do you hear now?"

"Usual background hum. Like listening to a party in the next room. That's normal."

"Headache?"

"Dull throb. Also normal."

"Rafe shielding you—is it getting stronger as time goes on?"

Isabel shrugged. "Hard to say, since it just started hours ago. I'll have to wait and see. It could get stronger. Or it could go away entirely. God knows." She smiled suddenly, wryly. "But if it turns out he can silence the voices, if only for a while, I may just have to move in with the man. Or at least take vacations with him."

"It would be nifty to have that quiet place to go to from time to time," Hollis said seriously. "A refuge."

Shaking her head, Isabel said, "Something else you'd better catch on to: the universe never offers something for nothing. There'll be a price tag. There always is."

"Maybe it's a price you can pay."

"And maybe it's a price he'll have to pay instead of me. Or would, if we went in that direction. It's the sort of thing the universe demands. Cosmic irony."

"Doesn't seem fair. And you don't have to remind me that the universe isn't about fairness."

"No, it's about balance."

"Then maybe that's what Rafe is, for you. Balance. Maybe the universe is offering you a refuge because you push yourself so hard."

"Yeah, and what's it offering him? A clairvoyant, career-driven federal agent who reads up on serial killers for fun, travels all over the country on a regular basis to get shot at and *talk* about serial killers, not to mention meeting a few of them in deadly situations, and, oh, by the way, hasn't had a successful romantic relationship in her entire adult life?"

"Great breath control," Hollis murmured. "The meditation exercises must really work."

Ignoring that, Isabel said, "I'm fairly sure Rafe hasn't pissed off the universe enough to be offered that little *balance* for his life."

"Maybe there are qualities in you he needs for his own balancing act."

"And maybe," Isabel said, "it's just a chemical or electromagnetic thing. Energy fields, nothing more. Basic science, emotions and personalities not involved."

169

She didn't have to be psychic to know she was being warned off, so Hollis didn't say anything else until her partner pulled the car into the parking lot of the inn. And then all she offered was a mild "I hear there's a surprisingly good Mexican place here in Hastings. You like Mexican, don't you?"

"I do."

"And does Rafe?"

Isabel hesitated, then said with clear reluctance, "Yes. He does."

As both agents got out of the car, Hollis said, again mildly, "Handy to already know so much about him. Likes and dislikes, habits, background. Sort of shortens the getting-to-know-each-other dance."

"For me. Not for him."

"Oh, I don't know about that. I have a hunch Rafe Sullivan already knows most of what he needs to about you. Except for one thing, I guess. And sooner or later, you're going to have to tell him."

"I know," Isabel said.


Special Agent Tony Harte scowled at the window as lightning flashed, then said, "Why is it that we always get the lousy weather, you want to tell me that?"

"Just lucky, I guess," Bishop responded absently as he worked at his laptop.

"This is not lucky. This is The Universe Hates Me. Me, personally. Who got a flat tire in the rain last night? Me. Who got grazed by a bullet when a pissed-off guy who wasn't even our suspect got even more pissed off and started shooting? Me. Who had to observe what was without doubt the most gross autopsy on record? Me."

"Who has to put up with your bitching? Me," Bishop said.

"And me," Miranda said as she came into the room. "What's he going on about now?"

"Usual," Bishop replied. "The universe hates him."

"Persecution complex."

"Yeah, that was my diagnosis."

"You two are not nearly as funny as you think you are," Tony informed them.

"Neither are you," Miranda said, then smiled. "Kendra will be fine, Tony."

"I hate it when you do that. Here I am, working up a really good, strong mad to let off steam, and you pat me on the head—metaphorically—and tell me, there, there, sit down and be a good boy."

"I did no such thing. I just said Kendra would be fine. And she will."

"She's in *Tulsa*," Tony said witheringly. "Setting aside the deranged killer she's looking for, they have tornadoes out there. Did you see today's weather?"

"Must have missed it." Miranda sent a glance toward the window, where another flash of lightning showed the heavy rain battering Spokane. "There was so much weather here that I didn't bother."

"There's a storm cell," Tony fretted. "Big, nasty one. Bearing down on Tulsa."

"Tony. Kendra will be fine."

He eyed her cautiously. "Are you just saying that, or do you know?"

"I know."

Looking up from his laptop, Bishop said mildly, "That's breaking the rules."

"You really want to listen to him bitch for the next few hours?"

"No."

"Well, then."

Tony was staring at Bishop in some indignation. "You knew? You knew Kendra would be fine and just sat there without easing my mind?"

"I thought you wanted to let off steam."

"There wouldn't have been any steam to let off if you'd told me Kendra would be all right. Dammit."

"See what you started?" Bishop said to his wife.

"Sorry. I just came in for—"

Whatever she'd come in for, what she got was a vision.

Even though he was relatively accustomed to seeing it happen, Tony nevertheless felt a little chill go through him as both Miranda and Bishop paled and closed their eyes, perfectly in sync. He waited, watching them, his own extra senses telling him this was a strong one, a painful one.

Finally, they opened their eyes, each reaching up to massage one temple. Miranda sat down across from her husband, and they looked at each other, both wearing an expression Tony had never seen before.

It caused another chill to go through him.

"We can't interfere," Bishop said. "We've done all we can do."

"I know. She'd probably ignore a warning anyway."

"Probably. She's stubborn."

"That's one word for it."

Tony cared about all the members of the SCU, not only his absent fiancée, and he was anxious. "What is it?" he demanded. "What did you see?"

Slowly, still gazing at her husband, Miranda said, "If it's literal and not symbolic, then Isabel is about to make a choice that will change her life. And put her on a very, very dangerous path."

"What's at the end of the path?"

Miranda drew a breath and let it out slowly. "The death of someone she cares about."

# 10

CALEB HEARD THE NEWS about a fourth woman's body being found when he stopped by the coffee shop for a cup to take home. The girl behind the counter—he couldn't figure out how on earth they could be called "sales associates" when they worked in a coffee shop—was only too happy to fill him in on the latest details while she prepared his latte.

Gory details.

"And you know the worst part?" she demanded as she put a lid on the cup.

"Somebody died?" he suggested.

She blinked, then said anxiously, "Well, yeah, but I heard she'd been dead for months."

Caleb resisted the impulse to ask what the hell difference that made. Instead, he said, "And the worst part is?"

"She was brunette," Sally Anne, sales associate for the coffee shop and a brunette herself, whispered.

"Ah."

"So none of us is safe. He's not just going after blondes now, he's—he's going after the rest of us."

Caleb paid for his coffee and said with ruthless sympathy, "If I were you, I'd leave town."

"I might. I just might. Thanks, Mr. Powell. Oh—can I help you, ma'am?"

"One iced mocha latte, please. Medium."

Caleb turned quickly, surprised to find Hollis there. "Hi."

"Hi." She looked tired and also more casual than he'd yet seen her, in jeans and a black T-shirt that demanded to know if the hokey-pokey was *really* what it was all about.

"You're not still working?"

"No, we've pretty much called it a day." She shrugged. "Can't do a lot in the way of investigating the body Sally Anne just told you about until we get forensics and a postmortem."

Something about her wry tone made him say, "You didn't expect the news to *not* get around, did you?"

"No. But this town sets the land speed record for gossip, I've realized that much. The unfortunate thing is that it tends to be so damned accurate."

"I'll say. I didn't grow up here, but when I started my practice fifteen years ago, it took less than a week for everyone in town to know that my parents were dead and my younger brother had gotten his girlfriend pregnant and married her literally at the business end of her daddy's shotgun." He paused, then added, "I told no one, absolutely no one."

Hollis smiled slightly and paid Sally Anne for her coffee. "They do seem to find out what they want to know. Which begs the question . . ."

174

"How can a killer walk among us, unseen?"

"Oh, not that question. Killers always have walked among us unseen. No, the question I'm asking myself is: how is it possible that a woman's decomposing body hung inside a derelict gas station less than three blocks from the center of town for months without anybody noticing?"

Sally Anne uttered a choked little sound and rushed toward the back of the shop.

Hollis grimaced. "Well, that was definitely indiscreet. To say the least. I must be more tired than I thought. Or, at any rate, that'll be my story."

Caleb shook his head slightly. "Look, I know you've had a hell of a day, but can we sit down here and talk for a while? There's something I want to ask you."

She nodded and joined him at one of the small tables by the front window.

"Have you eaten?" Caleb asked. "The sandwiches here aren't bad, or—"

Hollis shook her head, almost flinching. "No. Thank you. I'm reasonably sure the coffee will stay down, but only because I was practically breast-fed the stuff. I'm not planning to eat anything for the foreseeable future."

It was Caleb's turn to grimace. "So I take it Sally Anne's gory details about the body were on the mark?"

"Oh, yeah."

"I'm sorry. That had to be rough."

"Not destined to be one of my more pleasant memories. But I was warned what to expect when I signed on for this gig." She sipped her latte, adding, "You wanted to ask me something?"

"Why *did* you sign on for this gig?"

Surprised, Hollis said, "I . . . didn't expect a personal question."

"I didn't expect to ask one," he confessed.

175

She smiled. "I thought lawyers always rehearsed what they said."

"Not this one. Or, at least, not this time. If it's too personal, we can forget I asked. But I'd rather not."

"Why so curious?"

Even experienced as he was at reading juries, Caleb couldn't tell if she was stalling or really wanted to know. "That explanation would undoubtedly involve a lot of me backpedaling and trying to justify my curiosity to myself, let alone you, so I'd just as soon skip the attempt. Let's just say I'm a curious man and leave it at that."

She gazed at him for a long moment, blue eyes unreadable, then said in a queerly serene voice, "I was assaulted. Beaten, raped, stabbed, left for dead."

Not what he had expected. "Jesus. Hollis, I'm sorry, I had no idea."

"Of course not, how could you?"

He literally didn't know what to say, and for one of the very few times in his life. "That's . . . why you became an agent?"

"Well, my old life was pretty much in tatters, so it seemed like a good idea when I was offered a chance at a new one." Her voice retained that odd tranquillity. "I was able to help—in a small way—stop the man who had attacked me and so many other women. That felt good."

"Revenge?"

"No. Justice. Going after revenge is like opening a vein in your arm and waiting for somebody else to bleed to death. I didn't need that. I just needed to . . . see . . . him stopped. And I needed a new direction for my life. The Bureau and the Special Crimes Unit provided that."

Tentatively, because he wasn't sure how far she would be willing to go in talking about this, he said, "But to devote your life to a career that puts you face-to-face on a regular basis with violence and death—and evil? How healthy can that be, especially after what you've gone through?"

"I guess it depends on one's reasons. I think mine are pretty good, beginning with the major one. Somebody has to fight evil. It might as well be me."

"Judging by what I've seen in my life, it'll take more than an army to do it. No offense."

Hollis shook her head. "You don't fight evil with an army. You fight it with will. Yours. Mine. The will of every human soul who cares about the outcome. I can't say I thought much about it until what happened to me. But once you've seen evil up close, once you've had your entire life changed by it, then you see a lot of things more clearly." Her smile twisted, not without bitterness. "Even with someone else's eyes."

He frowned, not getting that last reference. "I can understand feeling like that after what you went through, but to let it change your whole life—"

"After what I went through, it was the only thing I *could* do with my life. I not only saw some things more clearly, I also saw things differently. Too differently to ever go back to being an artist."

"Hollis, it's only natural to see a lot of things differently after such a horribly traumatic experience."

A little laugh escaped her. "No, Caleb, you don't understand. "I *saw* things differently. Literally. Colors aren't the same now. Textures. Depth perception. I don't see the world the way I used to, the way you do, because I can't. The connections between my brain and my sight are . . . man-made. Or at least man-forged. Not organic. The doctors say my brain may never fully adjust."

"Adjust to what?"

"To these new eyes I'm wearing. They weren't the ones I was

177

born with, you see. When the rapist left me for dead, he took a couple of souvenirs. He took my eyes."

By the time Mallory got back to the station, it was nearly eight and she was tired. Tired as hell, if the truth be known. Also queasy, depressed, and not a little anxious.

"Mallory—"

"Jesus."

"Oh, I'm sorry," Ginny McBrayer said. "I didn't mean to make you jump."

"These days, everything is making me jump." Mallory sighed. "What is it, Ginny?"

"You asked me to check with the other women in the department and find out if anybody had the sense of being watched lately."

"Yeah. And have any of them?"

Ginny shrugged. "It's sort of hard to say. Everybody's jumpy. Two or three said they'd gotten the feeling of being watched at least a couple of times in the last few weeks, but even they admitted they weren't sure of anything. Of course, now that I've brought up the subject, everybody's talking about it, the guys too."

Mallory sat down at her desk and rubbed her eyes wearily. "Well, hell. Dunno if that helps."

"We'll all be alert, anyway. Have you talked to the FBI agents about it?"

"Not yet. Need to, though, I suppose." She sighed. "The dairy farmer's wife; she turn up yet? And what is her name, anyway? Helton. What Helton?"

"Rose Helton. Not a sign of her. And we still have two other women reported missing in Hastings during the past month, not counting that news reporter who vanished last night. Sharona Jones and Kate Murphy. Plus the dozen or so missing from the general area outside Hastings in the same time period."

"I know Sharona—she doesn't fit the profile, she's black. She's missing?"

"Well, her boyfriend claims she is. But her dog is also missing, as well as her car and a lot of her clothes, and her mother says she's always wanted to see the world, so we're thinking she might have upped and left."

"If Ray Mercer was my boyfriend, I'd up and leave too." Mallory sighed again. "Still, we have to make sure, so keep everybody on it. What about Kate Murphy?"

"More troubling, in that she *does* fit the profile. Late twenties, blond, successful; she owns one of those new little boutiques on Main Street. Was doing pretty well with it too. Didn't show up for work on Monday, so her assistant manager has been running the shop."

"We've checked out her house or apartment?"

"Uh-huh. No sign she's been taken—but no sign she left voluntarily either. Her car is in its slot at her condo, and far as we can tell it's clean. Haven't found her purse or keys, though. She didn't—doesn't—have any pets, and no family in Hastings. We're trying to track down relatives now."

"And still no sign of Cheryl Bayne."

"No. The station in Columbia has sent another reporter, this one male, to cover this new . . . angle."

"How caring of them."

Ginny nodded. "Yeah, even the other reporters are being pretty scathing about that."

"While doing their own reports."

"Uh-huh."

Mallory shook her head in disgust. "Okay. Let me or the chief know if anything changes."

"Right."

When she was alone again, Mallory sat for a moment with her elbows on her desk and her hands cupping her face, fingers absently massaging her temples. She should stay, but Rafe had made it plain she was to go home as soon as the body had been taken from that old building and the forensics team finished.

Both of which had been done.

Mallory was tired but also curiously wide awake. She didn't want to go home. Didn't want to be alone. She wanted something to get the image of that poor woman out of her head.

With only a slight hesitation, she picked up her phone and called Alan's cell. "Hey, are you home?" she asked without preamble.

"Headed that way. Pulling into the parking lot now, as a matter of fact."

"Have you eaten?"

"Nothing you could truthfully define as food," he replied. "There was something a charitable person might have called a sandwich hours ago, but it may have been just a figment of my imagination. Are you offering?"

"I'm offering takeout Chinese. I'll even pick it up on my way to your place. Deal?"

"Deal. Stop for wine if you feel like that. My place is dry as a bone. Oh—and I have a splitting headache, so if you could pick up some aspirin as well? I don't think I have any."

"Okay. See you in a few minutes." Mallory hung up, telling herself this wasn't a bad idea at all. So what if she had spent most of the previous night in his bed? It didn't mean anything. It didn't have to mean anything. Alan could be an amusing and entertaining companion, and he was good in bed.

Very good, in fact. And she couldn't deceive herself into believing she wasn't looking forward to a little body-on-body comfort, because she was. Two clean, healthy, sweaty bodies tangled together in the sheets sounded like a dandy way to affirm that both of them were alive.

Alive. Not hanging from a beam like a weeks-old gutted fish. Not lying in a boneless, bloody sprawl in the woods off some highway. Not laced into an impossibly tight leather corset and smothered with a hood while a woman with a whip and chains tortured—

"Christ," she muttered. "I've gotta get out of here."

It took a few minutes, of course, to do what she had to in order to leave for the night, but she took care of things quickly and bolted before anyone could come up with anything that required her continued presence at the station.

She called and ordered the food on her way to the restaurant, so it'd be ready and waiting for her, and did stop for wine even though she wasn't usually much of a drinker. She even remembered Alan's aspirin. Still, it was barely half an hour after she talked to him when Mallory entered his apartment with one bag full of little cardboard cartons and another holding the wine and aspirin.

"You look jumpy as hell," he commented as soon as she walked through the door.

"It's a jumpy time." Mallory knew the way to the kitchen, of course, and lost no time in getting the wine out and hunting through his cupboards for glasses. "Jesus, Alan, not a single wineglass?"

"Housewares aren't a priority with me. Sue me."

"My life has come down to drinking wine from jelly glasses. Could this day get any better?"

Alan had swallowed several aspirin dry, then began setting out the cartons on his breakfast bar, where they normally ate. He paused to look at her intently. "I heard. Couldn't have been much fun, finding that body."

"No."

"Want to talk about it?"

"No." She poured wine into one of the glasses and immediately took a swallow. "I intend to drink at least half this bottle, part of it while I shower away the assorted smells of today, then choke down some shrimp and vegetables. After that, unless you object, the plan is to adjourn to your bedroom and fuck like bunnies. Possibly all night. Unless you still have your headache, of course. Tell me you won't."

"I expect the aspirin to work any minute," Alan replied. "And that plan suits me just fine."


The Mexican restaurant wasn't crowded despite the fact that Saturday night was usually one of the busiest. As the owner had told them mournfully when he escorted them personally to a cozy table back in the corner, people were going out less at night since the murders had started. And after what had been found today, undoubtedly most of his usual patrons were home with their doors locked.

So if Rafe and Isabel didn't have the restaurant to themselves, they did have their own secluded corner of it. With quiet music playing in the background and an attentive but unobtrusive waiter, they were almost in their own world.

Almost.

"You still believe Jamie didn't mutilate Jane Doe?" Rafe

asked as they were finishing up the main course. They had been talking generally about the murders and the investigation, both with too much experience as cops to allow either the clinical details of brutal death or the bloody images they had seen all too recently to affect their appetites. And both shying away from anything more personal.

"I'm positive. My guess is, he was watching Jamie and saw her put the body into the trunk of Jane Doe's car. I don't know if she drove the car to wherever she planned to leave it, or if he did—and when she came back either to the playroom or to the car for some reason and didn't find the body, that was when she really freaked out. In any case, I think he put the body in that old garage. And amused himself with it."

"That's sickening," Rafe said.

"Definitely. He's very twisted, our boy."

"So his reasons for picking Jamie as his first victim in Hastings were probably twisted as well."

"Well, it may have been about Jamie being a dominatrix rather than a lesbian. Her wielding so much power over other women, power he wanted and didn't have. Maybe sheer jealousy was the trigger. Or envy. Maybe he couldn't stand the fact that she could control the women in her life."

"And he couldn't control the women in his."

"Maybe. Or it could have been the fact that her partners came to Jamie, willingly put themselves into her hands, submitted to her. And no matter how hard he tried, he couldn't get that response from women. Ironic, really. He always goes for the smart, successful ones, the ones least likely to allow themselves to be dominated in a relationship, and yet to dominate women is what he desperately wants."

"So for him it really is the unattainable."

"Unless his taste in women changes, yeah." Isabel's voice was wry. "He'll never get what he wants—except by killing them. It's only when they're dying and then lifeless that he's the one in control, stronger than them.

"In killing Jamie, he could have achieved a particular sort of satisfaction, because she was a dominatrix. For the first time, he was able to dominate a woman whose specialty was dominating others. Even if he had to kill her to do it."

"She possessed traits he wants to destroy?"

"That's usually the case with a sexual sadist."

"But not this time? Not our guy?"

Isabel frowned. "Targeting the breasts and genitals is a classic sign of a sexual obsession. But this guy, our guy, the sense I get is that he seems to be . . . punishing them for being women. So maybe he is trying to destroy the feminine traits in his nature. Or maybe he's furious with them because they're too female for him, literally too much woman for him to handle."

"And that isn't a sexually driven motivation?"

"Not really. More a question of identity. His."

"This is fascinating," Rafe said.

Isabel stared at him for a moment, then sat back in her chair with a sigh. "See, this is why my social life sucks. I always end up talking about killers."

"My fault. I did ask."

"Yeah, but the subject sprang to mind. Doesn't say much about my sex appeal."

Rafe eyed her. "It says we're in the middle of a murder investigation. And so."

"That's a handy excuse. Can't you tell when a woman is fishing?"

"You're not serious? Isabel, you have to know you're gorgeous."

"My mirror tells me all the pieces fit together nicely, but that

184

doesn't mean I'm your type. Lots of men prefer petite redheads, or very slender brunettes. Or—women who don't carry guns and know a dozen different ways to *really* hurt a guy if he pisses her off."

He had to laugh. "I admit that last bit is enough to give any man pause, but you don't see me taking to my heels, do you?"

"No, but since we sort of have to work together—"

"We don't have to go out to dinner together. Isabel, I'm here because I want to be, period. Just for the record, I don't prefer petite redheads or slender brunettes. And I never figured you for the insecure type."

"And here I was thinking I was coming on too strong."

Their attentive waiter appeared to clear the plates and take their order for coffee and dessert, and Rafe waited until he'd gone again to respond to her somewhat mocking comment.

"So what happened today?"

Isabel blinked. "You know what happened today."

"What don't I know? What's got you so rattled that you're pushing yourself to . . . make a different kind of connection with me when you're not sure it's what you want?"

"Who says it's not what I want?"

"I do. Hell, you do. Look at your body language, Isabel. As soon as you decided to end the shop talk and get into more personal territory, you leaned back. Away from me. That's not as good as a sign, that *is* a sign. Your words say you're interested, but your body says stay away."

"Dammit," she muttered. "What was that I said earlier about you making a fair profiler? I'm changing my assessment. You'd make a very good one."

"So I'm on target?"

"Well, let's just say you're not far off it. I am just not very good at this sort of thing."

Rafe had to smile at her disgruntled tone. "You're a very confident woman, Isabel—almost always. Very sure of yourself. But right now, at this moment, you're scared. Why?"

She was silent, frowning down at the table.

"Something happened. What was it?"

"Look, this investigation is . . . different, that's all. Odd things are happening. My abilities seem to be changing. And I don't quite know what do to about it."

"Have you reported this to Bishop?"

"No. Not yet."

"Why not?"

"Because . . . I don't know why not. Because I want to figure it out for myself."

"And making a move on me seemed like a good way to do that?"

"Stop rubbing it in."

"What?"

"My failure."

Dryly, he said, "Who says you failed? Isabel, I realized I wanted you sometime yesterday. Early yesterday. Or possibly about ten minutes after we met. I also realized it was going to hellishly complicate the entire situation, so I've been doing my best not to think about it."

"Maybe thinking about it would be good," she said earnestly. "And doing something about it even better."

"You're still leaning back in your chair," he pointed out.

"I can lean forward." But she didn't. She frowned again, honestly baffled.

"See?" Rafe said. "Conflicting signals. Even consciously, you're not sure what you want."

With a sigh, she said, "Trust me to find myself attracted to the one man who isn't willing to take what he's offered, no questions asked. Keep this up, and I'll have to start believing in lep-rechauns. And unicorns."

"Sorry about that. But I'm not a kid, Isabel. I'm a twenty-year veteran of the sexual wars, and I've learned a few things along the way. One being if you're going to get involved with a complicated woman, you'd better damned well know what the complications are. Ahead of time. Before you trip over them."

"That does sound like bitter experience."

"It was. Not bitter, really, but I learned a hard lesson. And it's more or less my own fault. You said the sort of energy that makes you psychic is something you have in common with our killer; well, I have something in common with him too. I like strong women. With strong, I've discovered, comes complicated, which can cause problems. Unless I know about the complications going in."

"Okay. Well, I hear voices. There's that."

"Uh-huh. And?"

"I need coffee in the morning before I'm human. And corn-flakes. I like cornflakes. I take really hot showers, always, so I tend to steam up the room. I hate silence in strange places, so I travel with a sound machine. Ocean waves. I have to have air-conditioning on full blast even in the dead of winter to sleep well. Oh—and I hate moonlight shining in the bedroom."

"Isabel."

"Not those sorts of complications, huh?"

"No."

"Dammit."

"If I *were* a profiler," he said slowly, "making an educated guess, I'd say that your breezy manner and humorous attitude cover up a lot of pain. And I'm not talking about the headaches your voices give you. That evil face you saw—it really did change your life, didn't it?"

Their waiter placed coffee and dessert on the table and went silently away again, and still Isabel said nothing. She picked up a spoon and poked at her dessert, then put it down again.

"Still not ready to tell me?" He fixed his coffee the way he liked it, his gaze remaining on her face, trying to make his own posture and expression as relaxed and unthreatening as possible.

She sipped her coffee, then grimaced and dumped cream and sugar in before trying a second sip.

"Isabel?"

Abruptly, as if against her will, she said, "It was beautiful."

"What was?"

"The face evil wore. It was beautiful."

It was late when Ginny left the police station, much later than usual for her. And after talking to the other women and hearing how jumpy they were, she made a point of walking out to her car in the company of a couple of male officers who were also leaving. Though none of the guys had said anything openly to the female officers, Ginny had noticed that in the last week or so all the women had an escort coming or going.

She doubted any of the women were complaining. She certainly didn't; anytime she was outside alone, she tended to spend a lot of time looking back over her shoulder and jumping at shadows.

By tacit consent, neither of the men left her until her car was unlocked, the door open, and the interior light showing them all an empty, unthreatening little Honda.

"Lock your doors," Dean Emery advised.

"You bet. Thanks, guys." She got in and immediately locked the doors and started the car, absently looking after them until both reached and safely entered their own cars.

Not that the guys had to worry, really.

So far, anyway.

Ginny was hardly a profiler, but she did have a semester of Abnormal Psychology under her belt, and she vividly recalled the section about serial killers, especially since it had given her nightmares for weeks.

Very few serial killers murdered both men and women. There had been killers who targeted both male and female children or young people, but when the targets were adults, they were almost always one sex.

A homosexual serial killer targeted men or young males, and a heterosexual killer targeted women or girls, as a rule. Though some homosexual killers, or men who were insecure sexually and feared they might be homosexual, had been known to target women out of sheer rage. They didn't want to be whatever they were, and they blamed women for it.

The very rare female serial killers went after men, or apparently had so far—except in the rather frighteningly common cases of women poisoning children or other family members, when they tended not to differentiate between the sexes.

Have some soup, dear. Oh, it tastes funny? That's just a new spice I'm trying out.

Jesus.

The things people got up to.

Ginny pulled her car out of the lot and headed for home, still pondering, mostly because her mind refused to let go of the subject.

What did he look like? Did she pass him on the street every day? Did she know him? He was strong, very strong; the medical report on Tricia Kane said that he'd driven a large knife into her chest to the hilt.

Ginny shivered.

What kind of rage did it take to do something like that? And how had Tricia aroused it in him? Just by being blond and successful? Just by being female?

Just by being?

When Ginny had colored her bleached hair back to something approximating its natural dark brown a week or so before, not a soul at the station had laughed or even commented, and her friends said it was wise of her. No reason to take stupid chances, after all, not when she was a cop in the thick of things.

Her mother had been visibly relieved.

Her father had said at least it made her look less like a whore.

As she pulled her car into the driveway, Ginny felt all her insides tighten. He was home, and judging by the crooked way his car was parked, he had, as usual on a weekend, spent the afternoon drinking.

Shit.

Still in the car, she removed her holster and locked it securely away in the glove compartment. When she got out, she locked the car up as well.

She never took the gun with her into the house. Never.

It was too tempting.

She went up the steps and used her key to let herself in, silently telling herself for the hundredth time that she had to get her own place, no matter what. And soon.

"Hey, little girl." His voice was slurred, his mouth wet. "Where you been?"

Her own voice deadened, Ginny replied, "At work, Daddy," and pushed the door closed behind her.

ISABEL LOOKED AT RAFE with a faint smile. "You didn't expect that, did you? That evil could be beautiful." She wondered if he understood. If he could even begin to understand.

"No."

"Of course not. It should be ugly, that's what everyone expects. Red eyes, scaly flesh, horns and fangs. It should look like it was born in hell. At least that. At least. It should breathe fire and brimstone. It should burn to the touch."

"But it doesn't."

"No. Evil always wears a deceptive face. It won't be ugly, at least not until it really shows itself. It won't look like something bad. That would be too easy to recognize. Too easy for us to see. Because the important thing, the thing evil does best, is deceive."

"And it deceived you."

She laughed, the low sound holding no amusement. "It wore a handsome face, when it first showed itself to me. A charming smile. It had a persuasive voice, and it knew all the right words to say. And the touch of it was kind and gentle. At least in the beginning."

"A man. Someone you cared about."

Isabel crossed her arms beneath her breasts, unconsciously adding yet another barrier between them, but she continued speaking in a toneless voice.

"I was seventeen. He was a little older, but I'd known him all my life. He was the boy in the neighborhood everybody depended on. If an elderly widow needed her yard mowed, he'd do it—and refuse payment. If anybody needed furniture moved, he'd offer to help. Stuck for a baby-sitter? He was there, always reliable and responsible, and all the kids—all the kids—adored him. The parents trusted him. Their sons considered him a buddy. And their daughters thought he walked on water."

"Deceiving everyone."

She nodded slowly, her gaze fixed on the table now, eyes distant. "The weird thing is, after taking all the time and trouble to deceive everybody around him for such a long, long time, when it came right down to it, it didn't take much at all to start revealing the beast inside."

Rafe was very much afraid he knew where this was going, and it required an effort to hold his voice steady when he asked, "What did it take?"

"*No*. Just that. Just one little word." She looked up, focused on him. "That was the beginning. He asked me to a school dance, and I said no."

"What did he do, Isabel?"

"Nothing then. I told him I didn't feel like that about him, that he was more of a brother to me. He said it was a shame, but he understood. A few days later, I saw him in the bushes outside my house. Outside my bedroom. Watching me."

"You didn't call the cops," Rafe guessed.

"I was seventeen. I trusted him. I thought he was just . . . taking the rejection badly. Maybe I was even a little bit flattered on some level of myself, that it mattered so much to him. So I just closed the curtains. And kept them closed. But then he started . . . turning up wherever I was. Always at a distance. Always watching me. That was when I started to be . . . just a little bit afraid."

"But you still didn't report it."

"No. Everybody loved him, and I think I was half afraid nobody would believe me. I confided in my best friend. She was envious. Said he had a crush on me, and I should be flattered." She laughed, again without humor. "She was seventeen too. What do you know, at seventeen?

"I tried to feel flattered, but it was getting more and more difficult to feel anything but scared. I could take care of myself, I knew self-defense, but . . . there was something in his eyes I'd never seen before. Something angry. And hungry. And I didn't understand why, but it terrified me."

Rafe waited, unable to ask another question. He wished they were somewhere more private yet had a strong hunch that, if they had been, Isabel wouldn't have been willing—or able—to confide in him about this. He thought she needed the insulation of a semi-public place for this. There were people here, even if not close by. Food and music and an occasional quiet laugh from another part of the room.

Normality here.

He thought Isabel was afraid she wouldn't be able to hold it together enough to talk about this if they were alone. Either that or she had chosen, quite deliberately, to tell him this without even a shadow of intimacy. With a table between them in a public place, where the ugliness could be softened or blurred or even dis-carded at the end with a game shrug and a bland *But it happened years ago, of course.*

Depending on his reaction to what she was telling him.

Depending on how well *he* held it together.

"Of course, it wasn't talked about so much in those days, stalking." Her voice was steady, controlled. "I mean, that was something that happened to celebrities, not ordinary people. Not seventeen-year-old girls. And certainly not involving boys they'd known their whole lives. So when I finally did tell my father, he did the logical thing in his mind. He didn't call the police—he confronted the boy. Very reasonably, no yelling, no threats. Just a friendly warning that I wasn't interested and he should, really, stay away."

"His trigger," Rafe muttered.

"As it turned out, yes. My father couldn't have known. No-body could have known. He'd hidden his true face all too well. If my father had gone to the police and everyone had taken the threat seriously, maybe the ending would have been different. But after it was all over, they told me . . . it probably wouldn't have. Delayed things, maybe, but he hadn't actually done any-thing, and he was such a *good* boy, so they couldn't have held him for long. So it probably wouldn't have changed anything if I had acted differently, if my father had. Probably."

"Isabel—"

"It was a Wednesday. I came home from school, just like al-ways. Rode with a friend, because my father didn't believe I was old enough to have a car yet. She let me out, and then she headed home while I went into the house. As soon as I closed the front door behind me, I knew something was wrong. Everything was wrong. Maybe I smelled the blood."

"Oh, Christ," Rafe said softly.

"I went into the living room and . . . they were there. My parents. Sitting on the couch, side by side. They were holding hands. We found out later from the note he'd left that he had forced them in there at gunpoint. Sat them down. And then he shot them. Both of them. They hadn't even had time to get really scared; they just looked . . . surprised."

"Isabel, I'm sorry. I'm so sorry."

She blinked, and for just an instant her mouth seemed to quiver. Then it steadied, and she said calmly, "The story could have ended there. If it had, maybe I wouldn't have come out of it psychic. I don't know. Nobody knows.

"But that was really just the beginning. I turned—to run or call the police, I don't know. And he was there. He said he'd been waiting for me. He had the gun, a silenced automatic; that's why the neighbors hadn't heard. I was too scared to scream at first, too shocked, but then he told me he'd kill me if I made a sound. So I didn't. All during those hours, all night long, I never made a sound."

Rafe wished he could drink. He wished he could stop her from finishing the story. But he couldn't do either.

"Looking back, knowing what I know now, I think if I had made a sound he might not have gotten so crazy. I think that's what maddened him, that no matter what he did to me, he couldn't get me to scream. Or even to cry. Without even understanding how or what it would mean, I was taking away his power.

"He—right there on the living-room rug, in front of my dead parents, he tore my clothes off, and he raped me, holding the gun jammed against my neck. He kept saying I was his, I belonged to him, and he'd make me admit it.

"He did things to me I didn't even know were possible. I was just seventeen. Just a kid, really. I was a virgin. I'd never had a

195

boyfriend serious enough to—to do more than kiss. I wasn't ignorant about sex, but . . . I couldn't understand why I didn't die, why what he was doing didn't kill me. But it didn't. I bled. And I hurt. And as the hours passed, the beautiful face he'd worn for so long got uglier and uglier. He started cursing me. Hitting me. He took the gun and—hurt me with that too."

She drew a breath and let it out slowly. "Cracked ribs, a fractured jaw and wrist, a dislocated shoulder. Too many bruises to count. Raw inside. At the end, he was sitting astride me, both hands holding my head as he slammed it against the floor, over and over again. Screaming that I was his and he'd make me admit it."

Isabel didn't shed a tear, but her eyes were very bright, and her voice was very soft when she finished. "And his touch burned. He had red eyes, and horns, and scaly flesh, and his breath smelled of brimstone."

Travis was more pleased than he wanted to admit—or show her—when he found Ally waiting for him outside the police station after work. Waiting on the hood of his car, actually, and wearing a very short skirt.

"You shouldn't be out alone this time of night," he told her, trying not to stare at long legs that looked great even under garish outside lights.

She lifted an eyebrow at him, amused. "I'm in a brightly lit parking lot. At the police station. Other than being inside the building, I doubt there's a safer place right now."

"Maybe not. Some of our female officers think they've been watched, maybe even followed."

"Really?" She slid off the car's hood and shrugged. "Well, I'm not a blonde. And I can take care of myself."

"It might not be just blondes, you know. Or didn't you hear about the body we found today?"

"I heard. Also heard she'd been dead a couple months or thereabouts. So maybe it was a different killer."

Travis didn't want to admit that he wasn't so close to the inner circles of the investigation that he was up on the latest theories, so he merely shrugged and said, "Still, we've got other women missing in the area, and not all of them are blondes. You really should be careful, Ally."

"It's so sweet that you're worried about me."

He grimaced. "Don't make it sound like that."

"Like what?"

"Like you're amused. I'm not some toy you're playing with, Ally. Or, if I am—"

"If you are, what?" She stepped closer and slipped her arms up around his neck.

"If I am . . . then tell me before I make a goddamned fool of myself," he said, and kissed her.

She laughed. "Believe me, sweetie, you are not a toy. I like my men with plenty of muscle and minds of their own. You fit that bill, right?"

"I'd better."

"Great. And now that we both understand that—how about a drink or two to unwind after a tough day?"

He groaned. "I've gotta be up at the crack of dawn. Why don't we just pick up a pizza on the way to my place?"

"Or we could do that," Ally agreed. She smiled at him and kept smiling as he put her into the passenger seat of his flashy sports car and went around to the driver's side.

She wondered how soon she could find a few minutes alone to call in and report what Travis knew.

Before he figured out what she was up to.

Without a word, Rafe placed his hand on the table between them, palm up.

For the longest time, Isabel didn't move. Then, finally, at last, she leaned forward and put her hand in his. The shock this time was almost a crackle, as if it should have been white-hot and burned them. But it didn't. It just felt warm, Isabel thought.

He said, "I can't even begin to imagine how you survived that. And then to survive, sanity intact—only to find yourself hearing voices. That's what happened, isn't it?"

She nodded. "The worst of it, at first, was that I was in the hospital with my jaw wired shut." A shaky little laugh escaped her. "Left-handed, and it was the left wrist that was fractured. So I couldn't even write to the doctors and tell them what I was hearing. I just had to lie there and listen."

"A combination of the head injury and the other shocks and trauma. That woke up your latent abilities."

"With a vengeance. At first, I just thought I was going nuts. That he had damaged my mind even worse than he had my body. But slowly, while I healed physically, I began to realize that the voices were telling me things. Things I shouldn't have been able to know. A nurse would come in to check on me or whatever, and I'd know she was having trouble in her marriage. Then later, I'd hear her out in the hallway talking to another nurse—about having trouble in her marriage. Things like that. Sometimes voices, as though another person were saying something to me conversationally, sometimes . . . I'd just know."

"And when you could finally speak again? You didn't tell anyone, did you?"

"Not even the trauma expert—shrink—I saw for nearly a year

afterward. I went to live with an aunt while I finished high school. Another school, needless to say. In another neighborhood."

"Where no one knew."

Isabel sighed. "Where no one knew. My aunt was very kind, and I loved her, but I never told her about the voices. At first because I was afraid they'd lock me up. Then, later, when I began reading up on what little information I could find on psychic abilities, because I didn't think anyone would believe me."

"Until you met Bishop."

"Until I met Bishop. By then, the only thing I was sure of was that there had to be a reason I could do what I did, a reason why I heard the voices. A reason why that evil hadn't been able to destroy me, hard as it tried."

"A reason you had survived."

"Yeah. Because there had to be a reason. They call it survivor's guilt. You have to get through that, find some purpose in your life. Figure out how you lived when those around you died. And why. I didn't know those answers.

"I drifted through college until my friend was killed. Julie. She died horribly, suddenly. There one day, gone the next. Before I could even begin to grieve for her, more women were dead and their killer had vanished."

"The second traumatic event in your life," Rafe said. "And the second time you encountered evil."

Isabel nodded. "I hadn't seen it coming then either, that was what hit me hardest. These voices that told me things never told me I was going to lose my best friend. That was when I decided to become a cop. I still didn't know how to channel or use the voices—or how to keep myself from being locked away in a padded cell somewhere if I did. But I knew I had to try. I knew I had to look for that evil face. And destroy it when I found it."

Dana had finally grown tired of Joey's whining and sent him back to Columbia—but she had also ordered him to make the drive back to Hastings on Sunday morning. And when he whined about *that,* she reminded him that news was a twenty-four-seven business and if he didn't like it he could go use his supposed camera skills elsewhere.

As for Dana herself, she had elected to keep her room at the inn. There were several women staying there, including the federal agents, and it felt safer there.

If anywhere could feel safe in Hastings.

Dana didn't apologize even to herself for being so jumpy, especially since Cheryl Bayne had disappeared. If this maniac was killing anybody who got in his way, anybody who offered a threat to him . . . then Dana now had two strikes against her. She was blond and she was media.

It was enough to make any woman jumpy, and never mind the additional worry of too many guys prowling around town with guns stuck in their belts, also jumpy as hell—

"Hi."

Dana nearly came out of her skin. "Christ, don't do that!"

"Sorry." Paige Gilbert shrugged apologetically. "Like you, I just came out for ice." She was holding an ice bucket in one hand.

Dana looked at her own bucket and sighed, continuing around the corner of the hallway to the alcove where the ice machine lived on this floor of the inn. "Why're you staying here?" she asked the other woman. "You live in Hastings, don't you?"

"I live alone. So I thought I'd stay here at the inn for the duration."

Dana scooped ice, then eyed Paige. "But you aren't a blonde."

"Neither was—is—Cheryl Bayne. And then there's the body they found today."

Wary, Dana said, "I know they found one. Been dead a while, I heard."

"Yeah." Paige scooped ice into her bucket and straightened, adding, "My sources claim she was brunette."

"Brunette."

"Yeah."

"Did your source also say she was . . . tortured?"

"Mangled."

"The difference being?"

Paige hesitated, then said, "Tortured means she was alive when it happened. Mangled means she was dead."

"Oh, shit."

"I've got a bottle of scotch in my room. Want some?"

Dana didn't hesitate. "Bet your ass I do."


Rafe didn't push his luck by asking too many questions. He knew Isabel had been exhausted even before the evening began, and by the time she'd confided the unspeakable tragedies in her life, it was obvious what she needed more than anything was sleep and plenty of it.

So he took her back to the inn, some instinct urging him to maintain the physical contact between them as much as possible. He was still holding her hand when they walked up the steps to the wide, old-fashioned porch.

Absently, she said, "This place couldn't decide what it wanted to be when it grew up—a bed and breakfast or a hotel. I've never seen a hybrid quite like it."

"Rocking chairs on the front porch, but no central dining

room," he agreed. "Strange. But nobody has to share a bathroom, and there's cable."

Isabel smiled faintly, looking at him in the yellow glow of the front porch lights. "I think Hollis and I, and a few of the news-people, are the only guests."

"Hastings was never a favored tourist destination, just a little town on the way to Columbia. Nothing much to see. But if we manage to stop this guy here, before he slips away again, I have a feeling it'll put us on the map. For all the wrong reasons, unfortu-nately." His fingers tightened around hers. "Isabel . . . that first evil face you saw. He killed himself, didn't he? After he thought he'd killed you."

She nodded. "Left that note I mentioned earlier, explaining what he'd done and why. Then blew his brains out. They found his body draped across my bed. How did you know?"

"Because you never went after him. Once you healed and be-fore your friend was killed, if he hadn't already been dead, you would have gone looking for him."

"Maybe."

"No maybe about it. You would have."

Her smile went a little crooked. "You're probably right. And I probably would have gotten myself killed doing it. Anger and vengeance as motives never offer a happy ending. So it's all for the best that he did the job for me, that evil is as *self*-destructive as it is destructive. Tips the scale a bit toward the good guys on those rare occasions when evil consumes itself with little or no help from us."

"That balance thing."

"Yeah. That balance thing." She looked down at their clasped hands. "Rafe . . . what happened to me is something I recovered from, eventually. Physically, even psychologically. I've had a few relationships in recent years. Not very successful ones, but that's probably due as much to my dedication to my job as to any lingering . . . emotional scars. Or maybe it's the voices that men along the way haven't been able to deal with. I do come with lots of baggage."

"You don't want me to be afraid to touch you."

"Stop being so perceptive. It's unnerving."

Rafe smiled. "The only thing I'm afraid of, Isabel, is that you still don't know what it is you want. From me. For yourself. And until you do, taking the wrong step could be the worst possible choice. For the record, I don't think either of us is the type to consider a quick roll in the hay as a great way to de-stress."

"No."

"And neither one of us is a kid. At our age, we should know what we want—or, at least, know what we're risking by getting involved with each other."

Isabel eyed him, not without a certain humor. "I've always been impulsive as hell. Jump, then look for a place to land. Obviously, you look before you jump."

"They do say opposites attract."

"They certainly do." She sighed. "You're right, I don't know what I want. And I have been feeling rattled all day because of the changes in my abilities. Not the best time to make this sort of decision, I guess."

"No. But for what it's worth . . ." He leaned over and kissed her, his free hand lifting to the side of her neck, his thumb stroking her cheek. There was nothing especially gentle in the action, nothing in the least tentative; he wanted her, and left her in no doubt of that fact.

When she could, Isabel said, "Okay, that wasn't fair."

Rafe grinned at her and stepped back, finally releasing her hand. "See you tomorrow at the office, Isabel."

"Bastard."

"Night-night. Sleep tight."

"If you say don't let the bedbugs bite, I'll shoot you."

Rafe chuckled and turned away.

She stood there on the porch and gazed after him until he returned to his Jeep, then shook her head and went into the inn's lobby, still smiling.

"Good evening, Agent Adams," the desk clerk said cheerily.

Isabel glanced back over her shoulder at the mostly glass front door and very well-lighted front porch, then at the clerk's face. She looked like the soul of discretion.

Which undoubtedly meant she was already making a mental list of people to call with the latest tidbit of gossip.

Sighing, Isabel said, "Good evening, Patty."

"We provide a continental breakfast on Sunday morning, Agent Adams. From eight to eleven. In case you and your partner didn't know that."

"I'll be sure to tell her. Have a nice night, Patty."

"You, too, Agent Adams." She sounded consoling, sympathetic, obviously since Isabel was going to bed alone.

Isabel escaped up the stairs, hoping that glass front door was, at the very least, soundproofed. She stopped by Hollis's room and knocked softly, reasonably sure her partner was still up but not sure she wanted company.

But Hollis opened the door immediately, saying, "I actually ordered a pizza a couple of hours ago. And ate some of it. Does that mean I'm taking a step closer to becoming accustomed to dead bodies?"

"It means your own body is healthy and needs sustenance, mostly," Isabel replied, stepping into the room. "But, yeah, it's a good sign you can handle the more gross aspects of the job. I'd put it in the plus column."

"Good. I need more checks in the plus column. I was beginning to feel horribly inadequate." Hollis invited her in with a gesture, adding, "I have an extra Pepsi here. Or did you get enough caffeine with dinner?"

"Enough. Plus, I really need a good night's sleep." Isabel frowned slightly, but said, "The plan is to meet up at the station by nine-thirty. Patty, downstairs, says the inn offers a continental breakfast on Sunday morning. We can go down between eight and eight-thirty, if that's okay with you."

"Sure." Hollis studied her thoughtfully as she went to sit on her bed beside a closed pizza box. "You look sort of . . . disconcerted. Rafe?"

"He's a little more complicated than I bargained for," Isabel admitted, wandering around the small bedroom somewhat restlessly. "Even the clairvoyant stuff I picked up didn't warn me about that. Dammit."

"You told him?"

"My horror story? Yeah."

"And?"

"He . . . handled it really well. Didn't freak out, didn't act like I was suddenly a leper. Compassionate and understanding and very discerning." She frowned again and added in a dissatisfied tone, "Also a cautious man."

Hollis grinned. "Wasn't ready to just jump into bed, huh?"

"Now, what makes you think—"

"Oh, come on, Isabel. As soon as we talked earlier, I could see the wheels turning. You saw a potential emotional complication looming and, characteristically, your response was to charge toward it head-on. If he was going to be a problem in any way whatsoever, you intended to deal with it *now*. Whether he was ready or not."

"Why is everybody else suddenly so perceptive as to my motives?" Isabel demanded. "I'm supposed to be the clairvoyant one. Look, I wasn't after a one-night stand. Necessarily. It's just . . . things are simpler when the physical stuff is out of the way, that's all."

Shaking her head, Hollis said, "Well, now I can understand why your past relationships weren't entirely successful, if that's your attitude about sex. Just something to get over and done with?"

"I didn't say that."

"Yes, you did. You're a lot of things, Isabel, but subtle isn't one of them. You probably as good as told the man you wanted to sleep with him so you wouldn't be distracted having to think about it anymore."

"I was not that blunt."

"Maybe not, but I'm sure he got the gist of it."

Isabel sat down in the chair in the corner of the bedroom and scowled at Hollis. "The SCU therapist says I have a few emotional issues about giving up control."

"No, really?"

"It's not a big thing. I just . . . prefer to make the first move whenever possible."

"Because the last guy you allowed to make the first move turned out to be a twisted, evil bastard. Yeah, I get that. I imagine Rafe gets it as well."

"I don't like having transparent motives," Isabel announced. "It makes me feel naked."

Hollis smiled. "Don't snap at the messenger. I'm not telling you anything you don't already know."

Isabel sighed. "It's about control. I know it's about control. Even after all these years, I can't help feeling . . . wary. Not of men in general, just of men who might—possibly—mean something to me. Especially if they're obviously very strong men. Don't you? We both went through similar experiences, after all, and yours was just a few months ago."

"I had Maggie Barnes," Hollis reminded her. "That empathy thing of hers did a dandy job of taking away a lot of the pain and healing the trauma. Even though what happened to me was just months ago, it feels more like years. Decades. Distant, unimportant, almost as if it happened to someone else. Almost. Do I know if I can feel a normal, healthy desire for a man? No idea. Not yet anyway. Haven't met a man I felt that sort of interest in so far."

Isabel lifted an eyebrow. "You seemed a bit drawn to Caleb Powell, I thought."

"A bit," Hollis admitted with a shrug. "But . . . a big-city-caliber attorney lives and works in a small town for a reason. He wants a simple life. Had one, too, until a lethal killer began stalking his nice little town, and his employee and friend was horribly murdered. Now, like it or not, I'm part of that gruesome series of events that's turning his simple, peaceful existence upside down."

"You're one of the good guys."

"Yeah, points in the positive column for that. But not enough to balance it, I'm afraid. Especially since I have my own horror story."

"Did you . . ."

"Tell him? Yeah. I met him in the coffee shop earlier, by chance, and we talked for a while. He asked questions, so I answered them. He didn't take it all that well. Sort of freaked, actually. In a very quiet, controlled, lawyerish kind of way. But I saw his face. And he certainly didn't offer to drive me home." Her smile was wry. "It was the eye thing that finally got to him. Up until then, he was more or less okay, but that was a bit too much to take."

"Hollis, I'm sorry."

"Oh, don't worry about it. Some things aren't meant to be, you know? I mean, if he couldn't accept a little thing like an eye transplant, then it's a cinch he'd never be comfortable with me talking to dead people."

"No, probably not."

"Some people just . . . can't think outside the box. You're lucky Rafe can."

Isabel was frowning again. Her head tilted a bit, the frown deepening. Absently, she said, "Yes. Yes, I guess I am. The psychic stuff doesn't throw him at all, and he was more than okay with the rest."

"So if you can just deal with these control issues of yours, and always assuming we get this killer before he decides to add you to his blonde collection, maybe the universe really is offering you something special. A man who knows what you've been through, what you are, and doesn't mind all the baggage you have to drag around with you."

"Maybe."

"At least accept the possibility, Isabel."

Isabel blinked at her. "Sure. Yes. I can always accept possibilities."

It was Hollis's turn to frown. "Are you thinking about the long-term complications of him being settled here and you at Quantico?"

"No. I haven't gotten that far. I mean, I haven't really looked past now."

Hollis studied her. "So what's bothering you?"

"It's just . . . I'm tired. Really tired."

"I'm not surprised. You need a good night's sleep."

Still frowning, Isabel said, "I know I do. I can't remember ever being this tired. So that's probably why, right?"

"Why what?"

Softly, Isabel said, "Why I don't hear the voices. At all."

# 12

GINNY HUNG UP the phone and frowned at the clock on the wall. Three times. Three times she'd tried to call Tim Helton, hoping his wife might have come home and he just hadn't thought to report in.

It was after ten-thirty; dairy farmers got up at dawn, she knew that much. Even on Sundays. And Tim Helton wasn't a churchgoer. Maybe he was out with his cattle. Except he'd given her his cell-phone number and said he always kept it with him. And a body would think he'd be eager to hear whatever the police might have to say about his missing wife. Unless she'd come home.

Or unless he knew she wasn't going to.

Travis wasn't at his desk, so Ginny couldn't ask him, as she usually did, what she should do. This would have to be her call, her decision.

Surprising herself somewhat, Ginny didn't hesitate. She got to her feet and headed for the closed door of the conference room.

Rafe shut the folder and shoved it toward the center of the conference table. "Okay, so neither the post nor any forensic evidence gathered at the scene has told us much more than we knew yesterday."

Mallory said, "Well, the doc's sure she wasn't bound in any way when she died, and there are absolutely no defensive wounds, so we can reasonably infer she didn't put up a fight."

"Yeah," Rafe said, "but if she *was* one of Jamie's partners, submissive might have been her natural state."

"So she wouldn't necessarily have fought an attacker," Isabel agreed. "Still, strangling is up close and personal; if somebody was very obviously trying to kill her, the reflexive survival instinct would have kicked in. At the very least, we should have found some skin cells underneath her fingernails. The fact that we didn't lends weight to the idea that she didn't realize what was happening to her until too late."

Hollis said, "And our killer uses a knife, he doesn't strangle. So that's another argument for an accidental death at someone's hands, probably Jamie's."

Mallory added, "Especially since forensics found bits of that old linoleum floor covering embedded in the vic's knees, which places her *in* Jamie's playhouse and in a kneeling, possibly submissive position. Which is, at least, more tangible evidence to confirm what we were pretty sure of but couldn't have proven in court—that this woman was one of Jamie's partners."

"An unlucky one," Rafe noted. "According to the info we have on the S&M scene, strangulation to the point of unconsciousness is fairly common. Supposedly intensifies orgasm."

"Another thing I don't want *that* much," Mallory murmured.

Rafe nodded a wry agreement, but said, "We'll probably never know why Jamie went too far, if it was anger or just a . . . miscalculation. But we need to I.D. this woman. Notify her family."

Isabel said, "A forensic dentist at Quantico is comparing her chart to those we have from women reported missing in the area; we should know in the next hour or so if there's a match."

"But we didn't have charts for every woman," Mallory reminded her. "Either they used dentists we haven't been able to track down, or no dentists. Lots of people are still scared of sitting in that chair."

"And none of the missing women had ever been fingerprinted," Rafe added.

"Is getting an I.D. even going to help us?" Hollis wondered. "I mean, it's closure for her family, which is great, but what's it going to tell us?"

"Maybe if she was a regular client of Jamie's," Isabel said. "We can talk to her relatives and friends, check her bank accounts, hopefully find a diary or journal if we're very lucky. But, yeah, I know what you mean. It's not really likely to put us any closer to the serial killer. Or help us identify and protect the woman he's undoubtedly stalking even as we speak."

"And we're running out of time," Mallory said.

There was a moment of silence, and then a somewhat timid knock at the door preceded Ginny's entry into the room.

"Chief, excuse me for interrupting—"

"You didn't," Rafe told her. "What's up?"

"I've been trying to call Tim Helton, just to check if his wife came home, and I can't get an answer. He doesn't go to church and by all accounts almost never leaves the farm. He should be there."

"If he's out in his barns—"

"He gave me his cell number, Chief, and he said he always wears it clipped to his belt. I tried the house number, too, but there was no answer. And just the machine at the dairy number. It's like the place is deserted out there."

Isabel said, "I don't much like the sound of that. If this killer is escalating, there's nothing to say he might not have decided to change his M.O. and kill somebody in or near her own home. Or just come back later and take out the husband as well."

"What worries me," Rafe said, "is that Tim Helton is the type to get his gun and go looking himself if he feels the police aren't doing enough to find his wife. The detective I sent out there to talk to him said he was angry and just this side of insulting about our efforts so far."

"He has a gun?"

"He has several, including a couple of shotguns and rifles, and his service pistol. He was in the army."

"That's all we need," Isabel murmured. "A scared and pissed-off guy with a gun—and the training to use it."

"No sign of his wife?" Rafe asked Ginny.

"Not so far. Or any hint from anyone who knew her that she might have gone somewhere on her own. In fact, everybody says the opposite, that she was a homebody and quite happy at the farm."

"Solid marriage?" Hollis asked.

"By all accounts."

"No children?"

"No."

Isabel drummed her fingers briefly on the table. "I say we go check it out. There isn't much we can do here for the present, with no new information to go over. And we need to find Tim Helton, make sure he's all right—and not conducting his own manhunt."

Rafe nodded and looked at Ginny. "Anything new on any of the other missing women?"

"Not so far. Still nearly a dozen unaccounted for, if we go back a couple of months and take in the thirty miles or so surrounding Hastings, but only a handful even come close to fitting the profile. The reporter, Cheryl Bayne, is still missing; we tried the dogs, and they lost the trail a block or so from the van."

"Where, specifically?" Rafe asked.

"Near Kate Murphy's store. She's the other woman missing from Hastings. We're drawing blanks everywhere we check in looking for both of them."

"Okay, keep at it."

As the young officer turned to go, Isabel said, "Ginny? Are you okay?"

"Sure." She smiled. "Tired, like everybody else, but otherwise okay. Thanks for asking."

Isabel held her gaze for a moment, then nodded and smiled, and Ginny left the conference room rather quickly.

Absently, Rafe said, "You know, Rose Helton doesn't fit the profile in one very obvious and possibly important way."

"She's married," Isabel said. "So far, in all three series of murders, he's only gone after single white females."

Slowly, Hollis said, "I wonder what would happen if he found himself interested in a married woman? Would he see the husband as a rival? Would that make the chase—the stalking—even more exciting for him?"

"Could be." Isabel rose to her feet.

Mallory got up with the rest, but said, "Since Kate Murphy and Cheryl Bayne are also still missing, I think they should be up there on the priority list too. If you guys don't mind, I think I'll run through the info we have on them and see if I have some luck in either finding them or at least ruling out a voluntary absence."

"Good idea," Isabel said. "The reporter especially worries me; if he's killing to scare off the media or to make a point, then all bets are off. It would mean he's changed in some fundamental way, and we have no way of knowing how or why."

"Or who he could decide to target next," Hollis added.

He wished he could stop the voices. The other things, the other changes, he could deal with. So far, at least. But the voices really were driving him mad. It had become harder and harder to shut them out, turn them off. They told him to do things. Bad things.

Things he'd done before.

Not that he minded doing the bad things. That was the only time he felt real, felt strong and alive. Felt free. It was just that his head hurt all the time now because of the voices, and he hadn't slept through the night since . . . he couldn't remember when.

The whole world looked surreal when you couldn't sleep, he'd discovered.

And blondes were everywhere.

*Tempting, aren't they?*

He ignored the question. The voice.

*They're just asking for it. You know they are.*

"Go away," he muttered. "I took care of the other one. The one you said nearly found us. Leave me alone now. I'm tired."

*Look at that one on the corner. If she swung her ass any harder she'd dislocate it.*

"Shut up."

*Don't forget what they did to you. What they're doing to you. Even now, they're corrupting you.*

"You're lying to me. I know you are."

*I'm the only one who's telling you the truth.*

"I don't believe you."

*That's because they've twisted your thinking, those women. Those blondes. They're making you weak.*

"No. I'm strong. I'm stronger than they are."

*You're a wimp. A useless wimp. You let yourself get distracted.*

"I'm not distracted. She has to be next."

*The other one's more dangerous. That agent. Isabel. She's different. She sees things. We need her out of the way.*

"I can do her later. This is the one I have to do next."

*This one can't hurt us.*

"That's what you think." He watched as she came out of the coffee shop and continued along the sidewalk, an iced mocha in one hand and her list in the other. She always had a list. Always had things to do.

He wondered idly if she had any idea the last item on today's list was to die.

**11:00 AM**

On their way to the dairy farm, Hollis said, "If Rafe hadn't had to stay at the station a few more minutes to deal with a call, would you still have suggested separate vehicles?"

"Probably."

"Still no voices, huh?"

"No. I thought getting away from everybody might help, but it didn't."

"Was anything different when Rafe was close by?"

"No. Just silence, same as when he isn't close by. Exactly the way it's been since last night." Isabel glanced at her partner, mouth twisting slightly. "I'd thought the peace and quiet would be nice. I was wrong. This just feels . . . bad. Not natural. I even miss the damned headache. A part of me has suddenly gone deaf, and I don't know why."

"It must have something to do with the sparking thing between you and Rafe, right?"

"I don't know. As far as I can remember, nothing like this has happened to any psychic. I mean, our abilities can change, but this drastically and suddenly to a reasonably stable and well-established psychic? Not without some . . . trigger. Some cause. It just doesn't make sense."

"You still haven't called Bishop?"

Isabel shook her head. "They're wrapped up in their own investigation out there and don't need a distraction."

"You just don't want him to pull you."

"Well, yeah, there's that. I don't really think he would, not at this stage, but he worries whenever any of us have problems with our abilities. Unforeseen problems, I mean."

Hollis hesitated, then said, "How can you be sure this is an unforeseen problem? I mean, Bishop and Miranda see the future on a fairly regular basis. What if they saw this?"

Isabel considered it, then shrugged and said wryly, "That is more than possible. It wouldn't be the first time they'd seen something ahead in the road for one of us—and just let us stumble forward blindly. Some things have to happen just the way they happen."

"Our mantra."

"More or less. You know, I half expected Bishop to call last night, since he always does seem to know whenever something's gone wrong. So maybe this isn't as wrong as I feel like it is. Or maybe he knows and also knows I have to figure out my own way through it."

"Are you going to tell Rafe?"

"Sooner or later I'll have to. Unless he picks up on it himself. Which is also possible."

"Yeah, he's very . . . tuned in where you're concerned. I mean, it's obvious. I think he knew before I did in Jamie's playhouse that it was going to be too much for you. He kept watching you."

"I know."

"You felt that even with all the voices coming at you?"

"I felt it. Him. He wanted to protect me. To keep me from being hurt."

Hollis lifted both eyebrows. "And now you don't hear the voices. You're protected from them. Coincidence? I sort of doubt it."

"Rafe isn't psychic. He couldn't have done this."

Hollis thought about it, then shook her head. "Maybe not consciously, even if he's a latent. But what if it's a combination of factors?"

"Such as?"

"Such as his desire to shield you and the way his and your electromagnetic fields react to each other. It really could be pure basic chemistry and physics, at least the beginning of it."

Isabel frowned. "Even without a shield of my own, I had the training in how to use one. I know how to reach out, break through a barrier. I know what a shield should be, even if I've never had one. This . . . doesn't feel like a barrier. It's not something I can control."

"It's new. Maybe you have to get used to it before you can. Or maybe . . ."

" . . . it's not mine *to* control," Isabel finished.

"If Rafe is a latent, or was, it could be his to control. You didn't pick up any sense that he might be when you first read him?"

"No."

"Nothing unusual at all?"

"No. At least . . . He's very strong. And not very easy to read except for surface, trivial things. I didn't get the sense he was blocking me, but at the same time I felt there was a lot of him I just couldn't get at."

"Didn't you tell me his grandmother was psychic?"

"Yeah."

"Then if I remember what I was taught in the training sessions, there's a better than average chance he could be a latent."

"In our experience, yes. It often runs in families."

"Isn't that the most likely explanation for all this? That he is, or was, a latent and that the way you two reacted to each other somehow activated it and made him a functional psychic, even if only on an unconscious level?"

"So far, everything we've seen and experienced tells us that activating a latent ability requires a traumatic event."

"Maybe Rafe will add something different to that experience."

"Maybe."

"You could ask him."

"Ask him if he's psychic? Oh, he'll love that."

"If he is, and functional, he needs to know. He needs to begin learning how to control what he can do. Especially since he may be shielding you. That urge to protect you may have him wrapping you in psychic cotton wool. A nice respite for you, at least in theory, but we do need your abilities to help us find and catch this killer."

"Tell me something I don't know."

Hollis pushed her sunglasses to the top of her head and studied her partner thoughtfully. "Maybe when you and Rafe connected, you did it in an unusual way, something every bit as direct and potent as actual physical contact—and magnified by sheer power. That sparking thing we all find so fascinating. Maybe it created a link between you."

218

"It didn't create a shield. I've told you, at first it was just a slight and gradual muffling of the voices. It wasn't until last night that the voices suddenly went silent."

"It *was* sudden? You didn't tell me that. Can you remember exactly what was happening when you lost them?"

Isabel had to think about it, but only for a moment. Slowly, she said, "Actually, it's so clear I don't know why I didn't notice it at the time. Because I was so tired, I suppose. I thought it was that. And the relief."

"Relief?"

"That he didn't draw away. I told him all about my chamber of horrors, and he didn't draw away. In fact, he reached out to me. Physically. And that's when the voices went silent."


"Travis, any luck reaching Kate Murphy's sister in California?" Mallory asked.

Without needing to check the notes on his legal pad, Travis shook his head. "Nada. It's awfully early on a Sunday out there, so you'd think she'd be home, but if so she isn't answering her phone."

"Machine or voice mail picking up?"

"No, it just rings."

"Shit. I thought everybody had voice mail."

"Guess not."

"Well, keep trying." Mallory headed back toward her own desk, pausing as she passed Ginny to ask, "Still nothing new on Rose Helton?"

"I finally got hold of her brother in Columbia, and he says last he heard, Rose was happy on the farm with Tim. No family occasions or visits to other relatives that he knows of. He didn't even know Rose wasn't home. Until he talked to me."

Mallory grimaced. "I hate it when that happens. When we're following up leads or looking for them—and shatter somebody's day, possibly their life, with news they really don't want to hear. That is never fun."

"I'll say. Oh—and for what it's worth, it doesn't seem to have even occurred to Rose's brother that her husband might have had something to do with her disappearance."

"That might be worth a lot. Relatives often know, even if only subconsciously, if there's trouble in a marriage."

"He obviously thinks not. In fact, he asked immediately if we thought it was this serial killer, even though Rose isn't really a blonde."

"Come again?"

"Apparently, the last time he saw Rose at Christmas, she was blond. Trying it out, he said."

Mallory was frowning. "That isn't in the report."

"I know. When Tim Helton gave us a description of his wife, he said brown hair. Just that. The photo he gave us shows a brunette. And none of the people we've talked to in the area described her as blond."

"But she was blond last Christmas."

"According to her brother."

"Shit. Does the chief know?"

"I was just about to call him. He should be getting to the Helton farm any minute now."

"Call him. He needs to know Rose Helton just moved a step closer to the victim profile."

The Helton dairy farm seemed as deserted as the main house when Isabel and Hollis parked their car near the gates to the barn area and got out. Standing at the front bumper of the car, Isabel absently checked her service weapon and then returned it to the holster at the small of her back.

Automatically, Hollis followed suit.

"Storm's coming," Isabel said, pushing her sunglasses up to rest atop her head as she looked briefly at the heavy clouds rolling in. The day had started out hot and sunny; now it was just hot and humid.

"I know." Hollis shifted uneasily. Storms always made her feel especially edgy. Now, at least. It made her wonder if Bishop had been entirely joking when he'd once told her that some people believed storms were nature's way of opening up the door between this world and the next—like a steam valve relieving pressure.

"And this place feels very deserted to me," Isabel added, looking around restlessly.

"You're not picking up anything at all out here? I mean, it's not just no voices, is it? It's nothing the usual five senses can't get?"

"Just the usual five. I'm getting nothing, no sense of anything that isn't visible to me. Dammit. I can't even tell if Helton is anywhere near. He could walk up behind me and I wouldn't feel it. And I've been able to feel that since I was seventeen years old."

"Don't worry, I'm sure it's temporary."

"Are you? Because I'm not."

"Isabel, even without the psychic edge, you're a trained investigator. You'll just have to . . . use the usual five senses until the sixth one comes back."

Eyeing her partner, Isabel said, "Do I detect a certain satisfaction in your voice?"

Hollis cleared her throat. "Well, let's just say I don't feel quite so useless as I did before."

"Fine pair we are. Two psychics who can't use their abilities. Bishop couldn't have seen this one coming."

"Look, we're cops. Federal agents. We'll just *be* federal agents and use our training to look for Helton," Hollis said practically. "When Rafe gets here."

Isabel looked around her, frowning. "Where *is* he? Rafe, I mean. And is it just my internal silence, or is this place way too quiet?"

It really was peculiarly still, the hot, humid air surrounding everything in a heavy, smothering closeness.

"Pretty quiet for a working dairy farm, I'd say. But it's just a guess on my part." Hollis studied the cluster of outbuildings and surrounding pastures. "Maybe all the cows are out in the fields. That's the deal, isn't it? They're milked in the morning, then go out and eat grass all day?"

"You're asking me?"

"Somebody told me you rode horses, so I just figured—"

"What, that I'd know cows? Sorry. You get milk from them; that's all I know." Isabel drummed restless fingers on the hood of the car. "Time to be a federal agent. Okay. We checked the house first and got no answer at the door. At either door. Both doors are locked, and we have no probable cause to enter."

"Can we enter the barns without cause?"

"Being federal agents, we have to walk carefully, at least until Rafe gets here; under the mantle of his local jurisdiction, we can do more." Isabel eyed the cluster of buildings. "The barns that are open are fair game, I'd say. That big central barn looks closed up, though, at least on this end."

Before Hollis could comment on that, they both saw Rafe's Jeep turn in at the end of the long driveway.

"No luck at the house?" he asked as soon as he got out of the vehicle.

"No," Isabel replied. "And haven't heard a sound out here. Is this normal?"

"Well, I wouldn't call it abnormal. The cows will be out in the pastures, so the barns would be quiet. Helton runs this place on his own except for the crew that comes to pick up the milk, and part-time afternoon help, so he has plenty to do around here most of the day. Have you tried yelling for him?"

Without a blink, Isabel said, "We thought your bellow would carry farther."

Rafe eyed her for a moment, then cupped his hands around his mouth and yelled out Helton's name.

Silence greeted the summons.

"Okay," Rafe said, "let's start looking around, before it gets even hotter out here."

"Private property, even if it is a business," Isabel reminded him.

"Yeah, but we've got cause with the wife missing and Helton out of touch. Judge'll back me up on that." He led the way, opening the gate at the end of the drive and allowing it to swing back as they passed through and headed for the cluster of barns and other buildings just a few yards away.

A slight breeze disturbed the heavy closeness of the humid air, giving them all a sense of relief from the heat—and offering a rather ripe olfactory experience.

"I love the smell of manure in the morning," Isabel said. "Smells like . . . shit."

Rafe had to laugh, but said, "Looks like he stopped in the middle of unloading a hay shipment." There was a half-ton truck parked alongside the largest, closed barn and facing in the opposite direction, with its tailgate down and a great deal of loose hay piled all around it. A number of bales of hay remained stacked in the bed of the truck.

"I'll check out the cab," Isabel said, and crunched her way through the hay toward the front of the truck.

Hollis was about to say she'd head in the opposite direction and see if the other side of the barn was open, but something about the way Rafe was looking after Isabel made her pause. Just for something to say, she asked, "Why would he have stopped in the middle of unloading?"

"Maybe that's when he realized his wife was missing. He might have been too distracted since then to worry about unloading hay." Rafe frowned as he looked at her, and lowered his voice when he added, "What's wrong with Isabel?"

"What makes you think something's wrong?" Hollis countered, stalling.

Rafe's frown deepened. "I don't know, just something . . . off. What is it?"

*Something off. Something turned off. Did you do it?*

But she didn't say any of that, of course. Already regretting that she had allowed this, Hollis said as casually as possible, "You'll have to ask her. I should check out the other side of the barn, I guess, and see if there's a door open."

After a moment, Rafe said, "Okay, fine."

Hollis took a step away, then turned back with a genuine question. "Is it just me, or is there a weird smell around this building? Doesn't smell like manure now that the breeze has shifted. Sort of a sweet-and-sour odor."

Rafe sniffed the air, and his rugged face instantly changed. "Oh, no," he said.

"What?"

Before either of them could move, the barn doors burst outward, and a thin, dark man in his thirties stood there between them, one shaking hand pointing a big automatic squarely at Rafe.

"Goddamn you, Sullivan! Bringing feds out here!"

# 13

ALYSSA TAYLOR KNEW damned well there was no good reason for her to hang around near the police station on a Sunday morning. No casual or innocent reason, that is. She couldn't even pretend to sit nonchalantly in the coffee shop near the station, since it wouldn't open until church let out.

She had toyed with the idea of going to church, but Ally found she couldn't be quite that hypocritical.

She also half-seriously feared being struck by lightning if she crossed the threshold.

"You're lurking, too, huh?" Paige Gilbert, who Ally knew was a local reporter for the town's most popular radio station, leaned against the other side of the old-fashioned, wrought-iron light post, as seemingly casual as Ally.

"I bet we look like a couple of hookers," Ally said.

Paige eyed Ally's very short skirt and filmy top, then glanced down at her own jeans and T-shirt, and said, "Well . . ."

"Catch more flies with honey," Ally said.

"I'll just watch them flit past, thanks."

Ally chuckled. "Travis likes my legs. And it's such a little thing to make him happy."

"A very little thing," Paige murmured. "How's the pillow talk?"

"I don't kiss and tell."

"Except on the air?"

"Well, we all have our boundaries, don't we?"

Paige half laughed and inclined her head slightly in a sort of salute. "You're good, I'll give you that much."

"I usually get what I go after."

"Didn't Cheryl Bayne say something like that?"

"She wasn't careful. Obviously. I am."

"Speculation seems to be she stuck her nose in where it didn't belong."

"Occupational hazard."

"For us too."

Ally shrugged. "My philosophy is, no sense being in the game unless you're willing to play all-out. I am. Like I said, I usually get what I go after."

"You get any news on the body they found yesterday?"

Ally's internal debate was swift and silent. "Not a blonde and not a victim of our serial killer. The theory is, she died by accident."

"And hung her own body in that old gas station?"

"No, our resident ghoul probably did that. A nice toy for him, already dead and everything."

"Yuck."

"Well, we knew he was sick and twisted. Now we know he's an opportunist too."

Paige frowned. "If she wasn't one of his victims, how did he get his hands on her?"

"The mystery of the thing. I'm going to go out on a limb and say she had a connection to either him or one of the victims."

"What kind of connection?"

"Dunno. Friend, family, a lover in common—something. She died by accident, he saw or knew and took advantage of the situation."

Paige was still frowning. "There's got to be more to it. How, exactly, did she die?"

"That I don't know. Yet."

"Is it true she'd been dead a couple of months?"

"About that."

"Then she died before the first victim did. Maybe he liked playing with a dead body so much he decided to make a few of his very own?"

"Maybe."

They stood on either side of the lamppost, leaning against it, and gazed across the street at the town hall. The downtown area was practically deserted. It was very quiet.

"I sort of wish I'd gone to church," Paige said finally.

"Yeah," Ally said. "Me too."


Rafe wore his weapon in a hip holster, with the flap fastened; there was no way he could get to it; Hollis, like Isabel, wore her holster at the small of her back, also out of reach. Both she and Rafe stood frozen, their hands a little above waist height with the palms out, by training and instinct showing this dangerously unstable opponent the least threatening posture possible as his gun wavered between them.

"Tim, settle down," Rafe advised calmly.

"Rose said she'd had enough," Helton said, his voice as shaky as his gun hand. "That's it, that's why you're here. She told you. She come and told you, and now you've brought the feds out here."

From her angle, Hollis caught only a glimpse of what she knew Rafe could see more clearly: Isabel, at the rear bumper of the hay truck. Like the other two, she had frozen the moment the doors had burst open, but unlike them, she wasn't visible to Tim Helton.

Unfortunately, he wasn't visible to her either, since the heavy barn door shielded him from her view.

Worse, she was standing knee-deep in brittle, noisy hay; any movement at all would draw his attention and take away whatever hope she had of surprising him.

Standing still, Isabel silently drew her weapon and held it in a practiced, two-handed grip, thumbing off the safety.

Then she looked toward Rafe and Hollis, brows lifting in a silent question.

"Tim, we haven't heard from Rose," Rafe was saying, still calm. He kept his gaze fixed on Helton, though he could see Isabel from the corner of his eye. "That's why we're here, to look for her."

"Liar. I heard them talking out here a while ago—they're feds. Both of 'em. You bring feds out here and think I don't know why? What am I, stupid? Where's the other one? You tell her to come out, Sullivan, and I mean quick. You know I ain't afraid to use this gun."

"Tim, listen," Rafe said. *"Aspice super caput suum."*

Helton blinked in confusion. "Huh? What'd you—"

228

The crack of Isabel's pistol was loud, but before Helton could do more than twitch in surprise, the hay bale that had been hanging several feet above his head crashed down, knocking him to the ground—and out cold.

Rafe immediately moved forward to get the unconscious man's pistol, calling out, "Got him, Isabel. Nice shot."

She came around the barn door even as he finished speaking, crunching through the hay, pistol lowered but ready, and said, "Dead-eye Jane, that's me."

Hollis was staring up at the loft door and the winch designed to lift heavy bales of hay inside the building. "I'll be damned. With the barn painted that wheat color, I didn't even notice that up there."

"Neither did I," Isabel said. "Good thing Rafe did. I gather all this was about moonshine, of all the ridiculous things?"

Rafe nodded. "He's got a still in there. You can smell the stuff. Or, at least, Hollis could. I didn't notice when we got here, unfortunately."

"Easy to smell now. On him. He reeks."

"Yeah, he's drunk. Probably since he noticed his wife was missing, and possibly what drove her to leave him. I don't know how long he's been selling bootleg whiskey, but it's obvious he's been drinking and otherwise using it for years."

"Mallory's tractor story," Isabel said, realizing. "He blew up his own tractor using moonshine instead of fuel."

"Right. I really should have remembered that before bringing two *feds* out here. With that level of paranoia and the amount of raw alcohol in him, he could have shot all three of us and not felt a twinge of regret about it until he sobered up."

"I'm confused," Hollis said. "What did you say to him?"

"Not to him. I told Isabel to look above his head. I knew the only clear shot she had was the winch or rope."

"Nice you trusted me to hit either one," Isabel said, then frowned at him. "But how in hell did you know I'd understand classical Latin? I didn't tell you that."

"No, Hollis did, sort of in passing. I remembered because it so happens that I took it in college as well." He sent a sidelong glance at Hollis. "A fairly nerdy thing to do, I admit, but it has been useful here and there."

"Especially here," Isabel said. "Another few seconds, and this lunatic would have shot one of you. Probably killed you."

Hollis uttered a shaken laugh and, when the other two looked at her inquiringly, said, "Okay, now I'm a believer."

It was nearly five that afternoon when Rafe came into the conference room and found Isabel, for the first time that day, alone. He closed the door behind him.

Sitting on the table studying autopsy photos of the woman found hanging in the old gas station, she said, "Please tell me we finally have an I.D. on her."

"Word just came in from Quantico. They think her name is Hope Tessneer. Age thirty-five, divorced, no children. The dental records are a close, but not exact, match. The record we gave them for comparison is at least ten years old."

"So there's a good chance it's her."

"A very good chance. Mallory's talking to the sheriff's department in Pearson now. That's another small town about thirty miles from here. We'll know more when they give us all the information they have, and when they talk to her family and friends. We do know that Hope Tessneer worked as a real-estate agent."

Isabel looked at him, frowning. "A possible connection with Jamie. How they met, maybe."

"Could be. She's been missing almost exactly eight weeks,

according to her boss. He wasn't all that worried, because she had taken off without warning or explanation at least twice in recent years. Said she wouldn't have come home to a job either time except that she was the best sales associate he had."

"Then she knew how to please people, how to give them what they wanted. That fits."

"For a submissive, you mean."

"Yeah. And a good fit for Jamie. Somebody like that might have been a longtime partner. Someone who wasn't just submissive but really trusted Jamie. It could help explain the lack of defensive wounds."

"That's what I thought."

Still frowning, Isabel said, "I wish we could find that damned box of photos."

"We can't even check for more safe-deposit boxes in the other banks in the area until tomorrow morning."

"I know, I know. I just think it's important. We need to see what's in that box."

"Agreed." Very deliberately, Rafe took a chair on the side of the table where she was sitting. "On another subject . . ."

Her frown vanished, and she smiled. "Where the hell am I, and how do I get to Detroit?"

He smiled slightly in response. "Are you a Richard Pryor fan, or do you just know that I am?"

"Both."

"Any more one-liners you want to throw at me?"

"No. I'll be good."

"Just tell me what's going on, Isabel."

She closed the autopsy file and set it aside, then drew a breath and let it out slowly. "The short, perfectly truthful version is, I don't know what's going on."

"And the long version?"

231

"I'm not picking up anything from anyone. I don't hear any voices. All my extra senses closed up shop last night, and I think it has something to do with you. And I don't know what the *hell* is going on."

**5:10 PM**

Mallory hung up the phone and rubbed the back of her neck as she looked at Hollis, who was perched on the corner of her desk. "They'll get back to us once they've interviewed Hope Tessneer's family and friends. But just from the information they already had on her bank accounts, it looks like she'd been paying for *something* about twice a month for the last year or so. Checks made out to cash, and cashed by her."

"For how much?"

"Always the same amount. Fifteen hundred."

Hollis raised her eyebrows. "I guess Jamie's services didn't come cheap."

"I guess not. If we're right about all this, that's an extra three grand in undeclared cash Jamie was pulling in per month—and from just one client. Who knows how many regulars she had?"

"Where the hell did she hide all that money?"

"There has to be another bank. No unexplained deposits show up in any of the accounts she kept at two banks here in Hastings. Her salary, declared income from real estate and other investments—all documented, everything on the up-and-up. The public part of her life was squeaky clean."

"And the secret part was buried deep."

"I'll say. Buried deep and probably under an alias, at least financially; it's obvious she's been hiding at least some of her financial dealings for a long time, maybe years. Hell, her other bank or banks could be out of state. Or out of the country."

"If so, we may never find them. We've got people set to start checking out all the other area banks tomorrow, right?"

"Yeah. With pictures of Jamie and the information that she could have been disguised and using an alias."

"And it seemed like such a nice little town," Hollis said.

Mallory leaned back in her chair with a sigh. "I always thought so."

"You grew up here, I think you said."

"Yeah. Well, from the time I was about thirteen. Both my parents and a brother still live in the area. I thought about leaving when I was in college, but . . . I like it here. Or did. Never knew how many people kept nasty secrets until I became a cop."

"It's been an eye-opener for me too," Hollis confessed. "Still, this sort of thing has got to be unusual for small towns. I mean, a dominatrix practicing her . . . art . . . for paying clients, while also working as a top real-estate agent?"

"If it's not unusual, I'm moving."

"I don't blame you a bit for that."

"You know, she picked a good public job to hide a private second one," Mallory mused. "Real-estate agents often keep erratic hours, so nobody would question if she wasn't in the office at any given time. She could probably meet clients day or night, accommodate their schedules easily."

"And since she was the dominant," Hollis said, "she could probably take on as many clients as her energy allowed. No need to take a day or week off now and again to allow those ugly bruises and burns to heal. Or whatever else there might be. She'd be the one dealing out the punishment. Jesus."

Hearing the distaste in the other woman's voice, Mallory

grimaced in agreement. "A very twisted way to find pleasure, if you ask me."

Ginny joined them in time to get the gist of the conversation, saying, "The things people get up to behind closed doors. We've found Rose Helton."

"Alive and well, I gather?" Mallory said.

"Definitely alive. I'd say pissed rather than well. When I told her that her husband was sleeping it off in a cell after having waved his gun around at the chief and two federal agents, she said she hoped the judge would throw away the key."

"Where is she?" Hollis asked.

"In Charleston, with a college friend."

"She went to college?" Mallory asked in surprise. "And still married Tim Helton?"

Pronouncing the words carefully, Ginny said, "She said it had been a cosmic karmic mistake. And that she'd already filed for divorce and wasn't coming back here. And, oh, by the way, in case we hadn't found it, there was also a still in an old shed in the back pasture."

"We found it," Hollis murmured.

"Everybody said they were so happy." Mallory shook her head. "Christ, you really don't know about people."

Hollis said, "Well, anyway, we can cross her off the missing list."

"One less to worry about," Ginny agreed.

"How's the rest of the list coming?" Mallory asked her.

"No change. No sign of Cheryl Bayne. Plus, we still have several women missing in the general area, and nothing new on Kate Murphy." Ginny sighed, clearly weary. "It's like she disappeared into thin air. She fits right in with the other victims too."

"But not Cheryl Bayne."

Hollis said, "I think Isabel's probably right about Cheryl. If the killer got her, it wasn't specifically because she was—is—a reporter, but because she somehow got too close. Or he was afraid she had. And if so, it's only going to get more difficult to even try to predict what he might do next."

"Except kill," Mallory offered wryly.

It was Hollis's turn to rub the back of her neck. "And there's something else. Isabel's the profiler, but I've got to say, if Kate Murphy is a victim, why haven't we found her? So far, the rule's been that if he kills them, he does it quick and leaves them out in the open where they're easily found. Assuming he has killed again, or that he has Kate Murphy, why would he change his M.O. now?"

"Our patrols are checking out every highway rest stop," Ginny said. "Most of them two or three times a day."

"Maybe we've spooked him," Mallory suggested. "He could be killing and leaving the bodies in places we aren't keeping under observation."

Hollis glanced toward the closed door of the conference room. "Maybe it's time we discussed that possibility."

Mallory didn't move. "Rafe had a sort of determined look on his face when he closed the door. I'm not so sure I want to be the one to disturb them."

Hollis continued to look at the door intently, focusing, tentatively trying out the spider sense. After a long moment, she said, "Um . . . let's give them a few more minutes."

"You're serious?" Rafe leaned forward and touched her hand, not even reacting now to the spark.

Isabel looked down at their hands for a moment, then back at his face. "Entirely serious. For the first time in more than fourteen years, there's silence in my head."

"That's what's been wrong all day."

"That's it," she said, unsurprised that he had noticed. "The question is: why?"

They both looked down at their touching hands, and Rafe said, "Frontier territory, huh?"

"Yeah. Scary, isn't it?"

"Today, looking at the wrong end of a gun being waved around by a paranoid drunk, was scary. This? This is just a very interesting turn my life has taken."

"You're a very unusual man," she said.

"Which is probably a good thing," he said, "considering that you're a very unusual woman."

There was a part of Isabel that wanted to shy away, to pretend he hadn't said that or that she hadn't understood what he meant. But Isabel didn't let herself shy away, or draw away, or back away. Whatever this was, it was something she had to deal with.

"Rafe, do you realize what this could mean?"

"Static electricity is more important than I thought it was?"

"Electromagnetic energy. And, no, not that."

"Then I don't have a clue what this could mean. Or even what this is."

"Hollis and I have a theory."

"Which is?"

"The theory is, my abilities are still with me, it's just that now there's something standing between me and the great wide world out there."

"You're not saying—"

"We think it might be you."

"You are saying." He frowned at her. "Isabel, how could it be me? I'm not psychic. I wouldn't even know how to *be* psychic."

"We think that might be the problem."

Rafe waited, brows raised.

"When a latent first becomes a functional psychic, there's an adjustment period. The psychic isn't in control of his or her abilities from the get-go. I mean—look at Hollis. She's been a medium for months and still can't open and close that door at will. It takes concentration, and focus, and practice. A lot of practice."

"I'm not psychic." He said it with more wariness than uncertainty.

"Your grandmother was."

"So?"

"So sometimes it runs in families. Your chances of being a latent psychic are much higher than average."

"I still don't—"

"Look. There was a connection between us from the beginning. Call it an attraction, a sense of understanding, simpatico, whatever. It was there. We both felt it."

"I felt that, yes."

"We feel it now," she said, admitting it.

Rafe nodded immediately. "We feel it now."

"And there's the sparking thing. I told you that was something new for me."

"Electromagnetic energy fields. Basic science."

"Yeah, but the way those fields were reacting to each other and the strength of that reaction was something different. Something that might have affected my abilities."

"Okay. But—"

"Rafe. There was this connection, this . . . conduit between you and me. Maybe the energy opened it, or maybe . . . Maybe the energy opened it. And then when I told you about what had happened to me, you reached out. Through the conduit. You wanted the pain to go away. And it did."

Rafe spoke very carefully. "How could I have done anything to . . . put your abilities in a box?"

"Actually, that's a very good description," she noted.

"Isabel."

"Okay. One of the things we've discovered is that the subconscious is often more in control of our abilities than the conscious mind is, especially in a newly functional psychic. One theory is that it's because these are very old abilities—not new ones. They were born out of instinct, when primitive humans needed every possible edge just to survive."

"Makes sense," Rafe said.

"Yes, it does. And if you subscribe to that theory, it also makes sense that our subconscious minds—the deeply buried, primitive id—would not only be able to master psychic abilities but would do so immediately and skillfully. To that part of us, being psychic would be perfectly natural."

"My id put your abilities in a box?"

Thoughtfully, Isabel said, "Has it occurred to you that we have very strange conversations?"

"Constantly. Answer my question."

"Yes. More or less. Rafe, your nature is very protective, and even though you like and respect strong women and are perfectly able to work alongside us on equal terms, deep down inside, you will always want to protect anyone you . . . care about. That is your instinctive response."

"Anyone I care about."

"Yes. And, obviously, the more you care, the more . . . passionate . . . your feelings are, the stronger your protective instincts will be."

His mouth twisted slightly. "Want to stop tiptoeing around that part of it and just say it?"

"Do I have to?"

"We might as well get it out into the open. This is happening because I'm falling in love with you."

Isabel had to clear her throat before she could say, "With or without my extra senses, you keep surprising me. That is very disconcerting."

"What would you have said? That I had a crush on you?"

"Well . . ."

Dryly, he said, "We're talking about my feelings here, Isabel, not yours. I am not trying to corner you, not even asking how you feel about me. So you can stop backpedaling."

"I was not—"

"But I'm guessing honesty on my part is important right now, since I may be—unconsciously—affecting your abilities. Yes or no?"

She cleared her throat again. "Yes. We think so."

"Okay. So despite the reasonable and logical certainty of my conscious mind that you can take care of yourself, and today's ample demonstration that you can also take care of me if the occasion demands, my subconscious thinks you need a shield."

"Apparently."

"And gave you one."

"That's the theory."

"How?"

"That part's a little fuzzy."

"Meaning?"

"We haven't got a clue."

"Shit."

Isabel had to laugh at his expression, even if the sound held virtually no humor. "Frontier territory, remember? We don't know how it happened, *I* don't know how it happened, but it's the only thing that makes sense. I'll tell you now, if we both sur-vive this, Bishop is going to want to study us. Because as far as I know, this has never happened before."

"Never mind Bishop. What do we do about this? You need your abilities, Isabel. Hell, *I* need your abilities. If we don't stop this bastard, he'll murder at least three more women. And you're on his list."

"A fact that makes me far more uneasy today than it did yes-terday."

"Because yesterday you had an edge none of the other women did. You believed you'd see him coming," Rafe said.

*It's time.*

He tried to ignore the voice this time, because there were peo-ple around. People who'd hear.

*Wimp. You really aren't a man, are you? You're worse than a neutered dog, following them around, sniffing at them, unable to do anything else. That's it, isn't it? No balls.*

His head hurt. The voice echoed inside, bouncing off his skull until he wanted to pound it against a wall.

*You know who they are now. The three that matter. You know them.*

Yes, he knew them. He knew all of them.

*And you know they'll tell.*

"But not yet," he whispered, fearful of being overheard. "They won't tell yet."

*That agent will. That reporter will. And the other one, she'll tell too.*

He didn't say it out loud, because he knew people would hear, but it was the other one that worried him most. The other one wouldn't just tell.

240

She'd show.

She'd show it all.


Isabel nodded slowly. "Even though twice before in my life I've been blindsided by evil, I believed I'd see it this time. I believed that this time . . . I'd fight it face-to-face. For some reason, I was sure even before I got here that that's how it would end." She hesitated, then said, "I need to do that, you know."

"Yes. I know."

Isabel was very much afraid he did know. Almost unconsciously, she drew her hand away from his and leaned back a bit, crossing her arms beneath her breasts. "So we need to figure out how to undo this," she said. "How to take away the box, or at least punch a hole or two in it so I can reach out and use my abilities."

After a moment, Rafe leaned back in his chair and laced his fingers together over his middle. "Whether you're right about it or not, the only thing I know about psychic abilities is what you and Hollis have told me. So all I can contribute is willingness to try . . . whatever you think I should try."

She nodded, but said, "Before we try anything, we need to be sure. Sure that psychic ability has been triggered in you and you're a functional psychic."

"I'm beginning to have fewer doubts about that."

"Oh? Why?"

"Because as soon as we stopped touching, your voice became a little muffled."

"As if there's . . . something between us."

Rafe nodded.

"Psychic cotton wool," Isabel said. "That's what Hollis called it."

He looked at her in silence for a moment, then shook his head slightly. "Brave new world. Not something I expected to be part of."

"No. Me either." Before he could say anything to that, she added, "Anyway, we need to know for sure."

"How can we find out?"

Very casually, Isabel said, "It just so happens that there's a telepath in town. A telepath with the ability to recognize another psychic at least eighty percent of the time. That's the highest percentage we've ever found."

"A telepath," Rafe said. "SCU?"

"Yes."

"Undercover, I gather."

"Bishop often sends in a secondary agent or team to work behind the scenes whenever possible. We've found it a very effective method of operation." Her tone was a little wary now, and she watched him uncertainly.

"Waiting for me to blow my stack?" he asked.

"Well, law-enforcement officials we work with tend to get a little upset when they find out they've been left out of the loop. Even for a very good reason. So, let's just say it wouldn't surprise me if you did."

"Then," Rafe said, "your senses really are in a box. And I'm not just talking about the extra ones." His voice was very calm, almost offhand. He got to his feet. "When do I meet this telepath?"

Isabel checked her watch. "Forty-five minutes. We'll have to leave in thirty to make the meeting."

"Okay. I'll be in my office until then."

She watched him leave the room and continued to gaze at the open doorway until Hollis appeared just a minute or two later.

"Isabel?"

"The thing that actually scares me," Isabel said as though they were continuing a conversation begun sometime before, "is that I have this uneasy feeling he's at least three steps ahead of me. And I don't understand how he's doing that."

"The killer?"

"No. Rafe."

Hollis closed the door behind her, then came in and sat down at the conference table. "He's still surprising you, huh?"

"In spades. He just never reacts to things the way I think he's going to."

Mildly, Hollis said, "Then maybe you're thinking too much."

"What do you mean?"

"Stop trying to anticipate, Isabel. Instead of thinking about everything, why not try listening to your instincts and feelings?"

"You sound like Bishop."

Hollis was a little surprised. "I do?"

"Yes. He says I only get blindsided when I forget what my senses are *for.* That I have to accept and understand that what I feel is at least as important as what I think."

"More important," Hollis said. "For you. Especially now, I imagine."

"Why now?"

"Rafe."

Isabel frowned and looked away.

"He reached out to you, Isabel. You wanted him to. You let him. But you couldn't reach back. You weren't quite ready to take that chance."

"I've known the man a grand total of about four days."

"So? We both know time has nothing to do with it. You and Rafe connected in those first few hours. You were wide open because you always are—or were. He was definitely attracted and unusually willing to open himself emotionally, or so it seemed to me. Jesus Christ, Isabel, you two strike sparks when you touch. Literally. Are you telling me you can't see a sign from the universe *that* clear?"

"We're going over old ground here," Isabel said tightly.

"Yes, but you keep missing the point."

"And what is that?"

"Those control issues of yours. You can be flip about them if you want, but we both know they're at the heart of this entire situation."

"Yeah?"

"Yeah. You came into this as confident as always, sure of yourself and your abilities. In control. I don't know, maybe you were a little more vulnerable than usual because it's this particular killer, this old enemy, that you were after. Or maybe that had nothing to do with it. Maybe it was just a case of right place, right person—and really lousy timing."

"I'll agree with that much, anyway," Isabel muttered.

"Doesn't really matter. The fact is, you found yourself losing control, and not just of your own emotions. Your abilities were suddenly different. You were so wide open you didn't have a hope in hell of being able to even filter all the stuff coming at you. You could do that before, I'm told. Filter what came through, exert a kind of control over it even if you couldn't block it out. But once you got to Hastings, once you connected with Rafe, you didn't even have that."

"What happened here was nothing that hadn't happened before, as far as my abilities go."

"No, but the scale of it was different. You've already admitted that much yourself."

Reluctantly, Isabel nodded.

"And there he was, so close. Too close. All of a sudden, you got very spooked. So you opened the door to your chamber of horrors, thinking that would drive him away and things could get back to normal. But it did just the opposite. It brought him even closer, and it strengthened the connection between you two. So much so that he was somehow able to use it himself, even if only unconsciously."

Hollis shook her head slowly. "I guess it was easier for you to just let him be the one in control for a while. Let him do what he wanted to do, needed to do. Protect you, shut out all the pain. Even if it meant shutting off your abilities and blinding you to the evil you know is almost close enough to touch."

# 14

THE POUNDING IN HIS HEAD was almost as rhythmic as his heartbeat, as though his very brain pulsed inside his skull.

The imagery pleased him briefly.

The pain made him reach for yet another handful of painkillers. He'd considered going to a doctor and getting the stronger prescription stuff but was wary of doing anything that might call attention to himself.

That bitch agent, it might occur to her that the change kept him in pain most of the time, and she might start calling doctors, checking for just that.

No, he couldn't take the chance.

But he had a hunch that all the painkillers on top of not being able to eat much these days might be causing other problems. There was a new pain, deep in his gut, a burning. It got better when he was able to eat something, and he knew what that meant. An ulcer, probably.

Was that part of the change? Was it intended that his own digestive acids—helped along by handfuls of painkillers—would eat through the lining of his stomach?

He didn't see how that would help him become what he had to be, but—

*It's punishment, wimp.*

"I haven't done anything wrong." He kept his voice low, so nobody else would hear.

*You're dragging your feet. You haven't done that agent. You haven't done the reporter. Or the other one. What're you waiting for?*

"The right time. I have to be careful. They're watching me."

*I knew I wouldn't be able to count on you to keep it together. You're paranoid now.*

"No—"

*You are. All you should be thinking about is what those women have done to you. Those bitches. You know what they've done. You know.*

"Yes. I know."

*Then there's nothing else to think about, is there? Nothing else to worry about.*

"I just have to kill them. All six of them. Just like I did before."

*Yes. You just have to kill them.*


"I'm not that self-destructive," Isabel said.

"You're that scared."

"And you know that because of your degree in psychology?"

"I know it because I was brutalized too."

After a long moment, much of the tension drained visibly from Isabel and she said, "Yeah. We belong to a very select club, you and I. Survivors of evil."

"It doesn't have to be a lifetime membership, Isabel."

"Doesn't it?"

"No. And if you let it be, then you let him win. You let evil win."

Isabel managed a faint smile. "If this is what Maggie Barnes did for you, then I wish I'd had her around fourteen years ago."

"What Maggie did for me," Hollis said, "was put me in the same place you're in now. As if years have gone by. The memories are still there, the pain is only an echo—and the scars are fear. I can be more objective than you because I'm not the one falling in love."

"And if you were?" It was a tacit admission.

"I'd be scared to death."

"I'll remind you that you said that."

It was Hollis's turn to smile faintly. "Believe me, I'm counting on you to help me through, if it ever happens."

"The blind leading the blind."

"You'll have figured things out by then. You'll have to. As our esteemed leader says, the universe puts us where we need to be. You obviously need to be here, now. With Rafe."

"And a killer."

Hollis nodded. "And a killer. Which is why I think you can't try to ignore or deny your own feelings. Not now, not this time. You don't have that luxury, not with a killer in the equation. You need your abilities at full strength, *plus* whatever Rafe brings to the relationship."

In a slightly suspicious tone, Isabel asked, "Did Bishop tell you anything else about what's happening here? I mean, aside from having you give Rafe just the information he needed to keep that little confrontation at the dairy farm from having a tragic ending?"

"No, but I've been thinking about that."

"I'm almost afraid to ask."

"Oh, it's nothing definitive. You know how Bishop and Miranda are when it comes to seeing the future. Maybe they did see this and knew that Rafe needed to be part of it; maybe that's why they made sure he'd survive Helton's drunken paranoia. But even if they did, they'd hardly tell me anything about it."

"Probably not," Isabel agreed wryly. "They feel very responsible for what they see and the actions they take or don't take, so they don't say a whole lot about it to the rest of us."

"One of these days," Hollis said, "I'd love to talk to them about the whole philosophical question of playing God."

"Good luck."

Hollis smiled faintly, but said, "Getting back to the point I wanted to make, I think there's a very simple reason why you and Rafe reacted to each other so instantly and on a basic chemical and electromagnetic level."

"I guess you're going to tell me even if I don't ask."

"Yes. It's that balance thing the universe tries to keep going. In your case, you needed something outside yourself to be whole, balanced. And so does he. I think you two were meant to be a team, Isabel. Just like Bishop and Miranda. The two of you together are potentially . . . greater than the sum of your parts. A perfect balance, something the universe keeps aiming for and so often misses."

"Hollis—"

"I don't know why I believe that, but I do. Maybe it's the sparking thing. Or just the way you talk to each other, as though you've been close for years. All I know is that I believe what I believe. And I think the only difference between you two and

Bishop and Miranda is that it took them years and a lot of tragedy to figure things out."

"What makes you think I—Rafe and I—can get there any faster or easier?"

"You do. You charge at things head-on, Isabel. It's your instinct as sure as Rafe's instinct is to protect. So stop holding back. Stop being afraid. Trust yourself."

"Easy for you to say."

"Yeah, it is. Like I said, I'm not the one falling in love and trying to cope with all this. But the universe put me here for a reason, too, and maybe it wasn't to talk to dead victims. Maybe it was to talk to you. Maybe it's not time for me to learn to control my abilities."

"That's a handy excuse," Isabel said, not unkindly.

"You don't have to worry that I'll stop trying." Hollis grimaced slightly. "Okay, you don't have to worry that I'll keep on not trying."

"I was beginning to wonder."

"I know I need to learn to control this. And I know I won't be able to if I don't start trying. So I will. You have my word on that. My abilities might be the only edge we've got in this. Especially if it's going to take time for you and Rafe to get this shield thing figured out."

"The thought had occurred."

"So we both have a lot of work to do. And Rafe'll have to get a crash course in being psychic."

Isabel sighed. "Well, after my last little discussion with him, Rafe may not be all that willing, no matter what he said. I don't need any extra senses to know he was not happy with me."

"If I have to say it again, I will. Subtle is not your strong suit, pal."

"It comes of being a platinum blonde almost six feet tall," Isabel said wryly. "Like being a neon sign in human terms, at least according to what the therapists say."

"Since you've never been able to melt into the background physically . . ."

"Exactly. Another reason I—to use your phrase—charge at things head-on. Usually. Everybody tends to be watching me, might as well give them something to see. Never really got much of a chance to practice subtle."

"It shows."

"Yeah, I'm getting that."

"Mmm. In any case, I've got a strong hunch that Rafe will meet you halfway even if he is pissed at the moment. But only halfway. You're the profiler, so consider this: what is it you have that Rafe needs to balance himself—and vice versa? And I'm not talking about the shield thing. Emotionally. Psychologically."

"You obviously think you know the answer."

"Yeah, I think I do. I also think it's something both of you will have to figure out for yourselves."

"Jesus. You really are beginning to sound like Bishop."

Hollis considered a moment, then said, "Thank you."

Shaking her head, Isabel checked her watch, then got herself off the conference table. "I'm taking Rafe for his . . . psychic litmus test."

"Say hello for me."

"I will. In the meantime, the focus of the investigation needs to be on locating that box of photographs and the missing women, *and* trying to figure this bastard out before he kills another one. In other words, same old, same old."

Hollis nodded, then said, "This morning, you asked Ginny McBrayer if she was feeling okay."

"Yeah."

"You saw the shiner, didn't you? It got more obvious as the day wore on, despite her attempts to cover it up."

Isabel sighed. "She did a good job with the makeup, which makes me think it's not the first black eye she's had to hide. What do you know about her home life?"

"I asked Mallory, casually. Ginny still lives at home, with her parents. She's trying to pay off college loans and save for a place of her own."

"Boyfriend?"

"Mallory didn't know. But I can ask Ginny outright. I'm not especially shy."

"I noticed that." Isabel thought about it, then nodded. "If you get the chance, do. She may think we're butting in to something that's none of our business, but there's a lot of tension in this town, and borderline situations can get pushed over the edge really fast."

"An abusive boyfriend or parent could get worse."

"Much worse. Besides, she's got a lot on her plate as a young officer, especially right now, and stress can cause different reactions in people. Like the rest of us, she takes her gun home with her."

"Oh, hell. I hadn't even thought of that."

"Let's hope she hasn't either."

"So, are you still mad at me?" Isabel asked Rafe as they got into her and Hollis's rental car.

"I wasn't mad at you."

"No? Then I guess an arctic cold front swept through the conference room despite all those walls. I nearly got frostbite. Amazing."

"You know," he said as she started the engine, "you don't talk like any other person I've ever met."

"One of a kind, accept no substitutes."

He looked at her, one brow rising. "Where are we going?"

"West. That little motel on the edge of town."

"Great. The only motel in Hastings that charges hourly rates."

"Oh, I doubt anybody will pay attention to us going in, if that's what you're worried about. I took Stealthy 101 at the Bureau."

Rafe's mouth twitched. "You don't play fair either."

"Well, at least we both have our little tricks. You can kiss me until my knees get dizzy, and I can make you laugh even when you're pissed."

He laughed, but said, "I was not pissed. Just . . . annoyed. You are a very difficult woman, in case no one has ever told you that."

"I have been told, as a matter of fact. It doesn't seem to help, knowing about it. Sorry."

He turned slightly in his seat to watch her as she drove, but let a few minutes pass before saying, "Dizzy knees, huh?"

"Oh, don't say you didn't know."

"I knew there was some effect. That was the only reason I didn't get pissed in the conference room when you were so busy backpedaling."

"You weren't supposed to see me backpedaling. Hollis says I don't do subtle real well."

"You don't do subtle at all."

"Then I'll stop trying, shall I?"

He grinned. "So you do have a few buttons."

Isabel got hold of herself. Or tried to. "Apparently. Look, it's not all that much fun to keep hearing how blatant you are. I'm an almost-six-foot blonde, which makes me real visible; I'm a clairvoyant without a shield—usually—which makes me a high-wattage receiver for an amazing range of trivia that tends to come at me like painful bullets, and now I find out I might as well be wearing my heart on my sleeve. Just look for my picture beside the word *obvious* in the dictionary."

"You do defensive very well."

"Oh, shut up."

Rafe chuckled. "You'll feel much better when you just admit it, you know you will."

"I don't know how I'll feel. And neither do you."

"You're wasting a lot of energy, I know that. Want to talk about our primitive instincts? You're a fighter, Isabel; backing away from this isn't doing anything except keeping you rattled and off balance."

"All of a sudden everybody has a degree in psychology," she muttered.

"Just tell me this much. Is it going to make a difference, finding out whether I'm psychic?"

Isabel knew that was a serious question and answered it seriously. "You mean will I love you more if you can provide a shield for me? No. Being shielded for nearly twenty-four hours has taught me I'd rather be without one. I mean, nice place to visit now and then, but I really do feel like I've suddenly gone deaf, and I don't like it."

"So if I am psychic and have somehow put a shield around your abilities, you're going to run to the ends of the earth to escape it?"

"I didn't say that. And no. We'll just figure out a way for one or both of us to control the damned thing, that's all. Having psychic abilities never makes life easier, but the whole point is learning to live with them."

"So you'll love me either way?"

Isabel opened her mouth, then closed it. She allowed the silence to lengthen for a moment before saying, "You're very tricky."

"Not tricky enough. Apparently."

"Here's the place."

Rafe smiled slightly but didn't say anything else as she pulled the car into the motel's secondary drive and around to the back of the building.

It was a somewhat seedy motel, an L-shaped single floor, and the neon VACANCY sign was flickering on the point of going dark. Only two cars were parked at the front; around the back there were half a dozen more scattered vehicles.

Isabel parked the unobtrusive rental beside a small Ford with a dented rear bumper, and they both got out. She went immediately to the room in front of the Ford and knocked quietly.

The door opened. "What, no pizza?"

"I forgot," Isabel said apologetically, stepping into the room.

"You owe me one. Hey, Chief," Paige Gilbert said. "Come on in."

"We're just concerned," Hollis told Ginny quietly.

The younger woman shifted a bit in her chair at the conference table, then said, "I appreciate that. I really do. But I'm fine. In a few more months, I'll have enough saved to move out on my own."

"And until then?"

"Until then I'll just stay out of his way."

"Like you did last night?" Hollis shook her head. "You've had enough training to know better, Ginny. He's mad at the world and you're his punching bag. He won't stop until somebody makes him."

"When I move out—"

"He'll go back to beating your mother."

"I didn't tell you that."

"You didn't have to."

Ginny slumped in her chair. "No. It's textbook, isn't it? He's a bully who beat her up until I got old enough to intervene, and now he hits me. When I'm not fast enough to stay out of his reach, that is. Usually, he's so drunk he passes out or knocks himself out trashing the house, at least now that he's older."

"Your mother?"

"I haven't been able to talk her into leaving him. But once I'm out, I think she'll go live with her sister in Columbia."

"And what will he do?"

"Go down the drain, probably. He hasn't had a regular job in years because of his temper. He's stupid and sullen and—like you said—mad at the world. Because, of course, it's not his fault that his life sucks. It's never his fault."

"It isn't your fault," Hollis said. "But when he goes too far and assaults someone else, or drives drunk and causes an accident, or does something else stupid and destructive, you'll blame yourself. Won't you?"

Ginny was silent.

"You're a cop, Ginny. You know what you have to do. Press charges, see that he's locked up or forced into some kind of treatment program, or whatever it takes to defuse the situation."

"I know. I know that. But it's hard to . . ."

"To take it all public. Yes, it is. Maybe one of the hardest things you'll ever do. But doing it will take away his power. It's his shame you'll be showing the world, not yours. Not your mother's. His."

Biting her bottom lip, Ginny said, "It's mostly the guys here that I think about. I mean, I took the training, I know self-defense, and still he hits me. So what're they going to think? That I'm some weak little girly-girl who needs them to protect me all the time? I wouldn't be able to take that."

"You might get that reaction at first," Hollis admitted. "Not because they think you aren't capable, but because they wouldn't have become cops if they didn't want to help people. Protect people. Especially one of their own. But you'll show them, in time. Earn another marksman's medal or another belt in your karate classes, and they'll notice."

"How did you know—"

"A little birdie told me." Hollis smiled. "Look, the point is that you have friends. And they'll be supportive. But this is not the time to back off, to avoid taking action against your father. With this killer on the loose, everybody's on edge and in full defensive mode. If your father pushes *anybody* the wrong way, he's likely to provoke a situation with a tragic outcome."

"You're right." Ginny got to her feet and managed a smile. "Thank you, Hollis. And thank Isabel for me, will you? If you hadn't said something, I probably would have let this go on, and God knows what might have happened."

"You have friends," Hollis repeated. "Including us. Don't forget that."

"No. No, I won't. Thanks." She went quietly from the conference room.

Hollis sat there frowning in silence for a moment, her gaze fixed on the bulletin boards covered with photographs and reports, then reached for her cell phone and punched in a number.

"Yeah."

"I know this isn't a good time," Hollis said, "but when you've finished up there, ask Rafe about the McBrayer household, will you? He might know just how volatile Hank McBrayer is, how dangerous."

"She's going to press charges?"

"I think so. And I have a very bad feeling about how he might react."

"Okay. Keep her busy there, if you can; she might feel the need to go confront him before she takes official action."

"Shit. Okay, I will. Oh—and we've got a small lead on Kate Murphy; after the latest round of radio announcements asking for help, a witness came forward to report he thinks he might have seen her getting on a bus the day she disappeared. We're checking it out."

"Good. It'd be nice to know we aren't looking for another body. Yet."

"I'll say. How's it going there?"

"I'll fill you in when I get back."

"That bad, huh?"

"*Tense* is the word I'd use. Talk to you later."


"Is who going to press charges?" Rafe asked as Isabel ended the call.

"Tell you later."

He frowned at her. "I am not tense."

Isabel lifted both brows at Paige.

"He's tense," Paige said.

Rafe, sitting on one of the two rather unsteady chairs near the front window, rubbed the back of his neck and stared at the two women warily. "I'm still trying to deal with you being a fed," he told Paige. "And the fact that you've been here longer than Isabel."

Isabel shook her head. She was sitting in the other rickety chair, both of which faced Paige, who sat on the bed. "I'm still pissed at Bishop for that part of it. All the time I was arguing with him about sending me down here, and he already had an agent in place—and had sent her here right after the first murder, even before you asked for a profile."

"Not much gets past him," Paige reminded Isabel. "Neither of them has said, but I get the feeling he and Miranda keep an eye on any investigations that might even possibly involve any of the killers in our cold-case files. Hell, Kendra probably wrote a program for them purely to do that—scan all the police and law-enforcement databases looking for specific details or keywords."

"He might have told me," Isabel said.

"And he might have told Hollis why she was supposed to make sure Rafe knew you understood Latin. Of course, if he had, then she might have been self-conscious about what she was doing, and Rafe might have picked up on the wrong part of the conversation, and you might never have had to bring him to me to find out if he's psychic because he'd be dead."

"If my vote counts," Rafe said, "I vote we let Bishop continue to do things his own way."

"Okay, point taken. But Hollis is right: one of these days, one of us is going to have to sit down and have a long talk with Bishop and Miranda about the philosophical and actual consequences of playing God."

"Later," Rafe said. "Can we please do what we came here to do and find out what's going on inside my head? How *do* we find out, by the way? And does it involve something unspeakable like . . . chicken entrails?"

"What *have* you been reading?" Paige demanded.

"Well, since nobody offered me a copy of the psychic newsletter . . ."

Isabel frowned and looked at Paige. "Isn't that a joke Maggie uses sometimes?"

Paige nodded, her gaze thoughtfully fixed on Rafe. "Yeah.

He's very plugged-in. Aside from Beau, I've never met anybody else who could do that. He's sort of picked up the rhythm of the way you talk too."

"Yeah, I noticed that."

"Ladies, please." Rafe was beginning to look profoundly uneasy.

"Oh, you're psychic," Paige said matter-of-factly.

Rafe had braced himself to be told that, but the abruptness and utter calm of the disclosure threw him more than a little. "You don't have to touch me to make sure?"

"No. I'm not a touch telepath, I'm an open telepath. All I have to do is focus on someone and concentrate. If I can read them at all, I know right away. I can read you, and you're psychic."

"I am?"

"You are." Paige looked at Isabel. "I was pretty sure he was, at that news conference before you showed up on Thursday. When you walked into the room, I was positive."

"That's when everything changed," Rafe murmured. "I felt it."

"I'm not surprised," Paige said frankly. "The hair on the back of my neck stood straight up. It was like an electrical current was let loose in the room."

"Why didn't you tell me?" Isabel demanded. "Then would have been nice, but when I called you today—"

"I reported in to Bishop on Thursday, and he told me to wait. That you and I shouldn't have any contact at all until you called me. On Sunday."

"He knew I'd call today."

"Apparently, yes."

"At least tell me he didn't give you a whole list of things to say to one or both of us."

Paige grinned. "No. He just said you'd call, and it would be safe for us to meet, that I should follow my training and instincts. So that's what I'm doing."

Isabel was looking thoughtful, her irritation with Bishop a fleeting thing. "Wait a minute. Rafe was already a functional psychic before I came into the room?"

"Yeah, but not consciously."

"Then the original trigger was—"

"Dunno. It had to be recent, and probably some kind of emotional or psychological shock."

Slowly, Rafe said, "I don't recall anything like that happening. My life was very ordinary until all this started. Having a serial killer loose in my town was a shock, I admit, but nothing I'm not trained to deal with."

"Could have been some kind of subconscious shock, I suppose, though that's really rare. We're usually completely aware of the jolts we get through life. Whatever it was, I can't get at it; it's behind his shield."

Isabel rubbed her forehead briefly. "Okay, let's try something a little easier. What happened when I came into the room that day?"

Readily, Paige said, "As near as I can tell, you were the catalyst. Or it was a combination of the two of you in close proximity for the first time. On a purely electromagnetic level, it was like energy going to energy. I felt it come through the room between you. Jeez, I could almost see it."

"And what did that do to Rafe's abilities?"

"Same thing it did to yours. Started to change them."

"Wait a minute," Rafe said. "Change them from what? And into what?"

"Here's where we get into educated guesswork," Paige told them. "From what I was getting before Isabel walked into the room, I think your natural ability would have been precognition."

"Seeing the future?"

"Like your grandmother," Isabel said. "She had the sight."

Rafe leaned forward, elbows on knees, and frowned at Paige. "But I'm not precognitive now?"

"No, not actively. When Isabel walked in, everything changed. Her energy added to yours closed that door and opened another one."

"I'm afraid to ask," Rafe said.

"I'm not," Isabel said. "What's behind door number two?"

"Clairvoyance."

Startled, Rafe said, "Like Isabel?"

"Yeah, except that as we all know you have a shield. Dandy one, as a matter of fact. So dandy you've got it wrapped around both of you."

"How is that possible?" Isabel demanded. "He's not consciously controlling any of this."

"That's how it's possible." Paige eyed Rafe thoughtfully. "In case you don't know this, your conscious mind is always second-guessing your hunches and instincts. For most of your life, I gather."

He nodded without comment.

"Well, your instincts are fighting back. Once your abilities became functional, your subconscious took them over. With a vengeance."

Isabel frowned. "Wait a minute. If this shield of his is so powerful it can even enclose my mind—"

"Then how am I able to read him? It's *because* he's doing all this at a subconscious level. Just beneath his conscious mind is a solid wall." Paige lifted her brows at Isabel. "Same one that's just beneath your conscious mind. It's really no wonder you can't hear the voices anymore."

With a sigh, Isabel said, "You know, Bishop was right—as

usual, damn him—to send Hollis with me. She's been pretty much on the mark about all of this."

"Yeah, the rookies often are. Sometimes knowing just the basics can offer you more room to speculate and the imagination to do it," Paige said. "The rest of us tend to get tripped up by our own assumptions."

"I'm still trying to figure out the basics," Rafe told them. To Paige, he said, "So I'm not stripped naked to you, just down to my underwear."

"Pretty good analogy." She smiled. "And accurate, as far as it goes. I'm not picking up thoughts from you—I mean clear thoughts like sentences. It doesn't work that way for me. You could be calling me rude names in your head or worrying about some deep dark secret you don't want anybody to know, and I wouldn't necessarily read either."

"Because you specialize in reading psychic ability in other minds?" he guessed.

Paige nodded. "Exactly. My own energy seems to be tuned for that, picking up on that particular frequency. So I usually know if somebody else is psychic, how they're psychic, and what's going on in that area of their minds. But the human brain is vast, mostly unmapped terrain, and the larger part of it is as alien to me as it is to most everybody else."

Rafe shook his head as he sat back in his chair, but said, "Okay, how do I control this?"

"Simple. Get your conscious mind in control."

"And you're going to tell me how to do that?"

"Wish I could. Sorry. This is the sort of thing almost every psychic has to figure out more or less alone. The only advice I have to offer is that you two work together on it. Clearly, you're meant to."

It was Isabel who said, "So tell us why."

Paige didn't hesitate. "Do me a favor and hold hands for a minute."

Rafe looked at Isabel, then held out his hand. With only a slight hesitation, she put hers in it.

At the spark, Paige's eyes widened. "I'd heard about it but not seen it. Interesting, to say the least." She frowned, obviously concentrating.

But then something really weird happened.

While Isabel and Rafe watched in fascination, Paige's shoulder-length dark hair began to lift and stir as though a breeze had wafted through the room. There was a soft popping and crackling, and a low hum began to fill the silence.

# 15

HOLLIS LOOKED UP as Ginny stuck her head in the conference room to say, "Caleb Powell is here to see you. Should I show him in here, or to one of the offices?"

"In here, I guess. Thanks, Ginny." Hollis went to cover the bulletin boards, then returned to a chair on the far side of the table. She was more than a little surprised that he wanted to see her at all; to seek her out here at the police station, and on a Sunday, definitely made her wonder.

Especially after their last meeting.

"Hi," Caleb said as he came in. He didn't shut the door behind him, and Hollis didn't suggest that he do so.

"Hi yourself. What's up?" With a gesture, she invited him to sit down on the opposite side of the table.

He hesitated, then sat down. "I wanted to apologize."

"For what?"

"You know. I acted like a jerk when you told me about your eyes."

She couldn't help but smile. "You didn't act like a jerk, you were just a little unnerved. I can hardly blame you for that, since I am too. And I've had months to get used to them."

"Still, it was a lousy way for me to act. I'm sorry."

"Apology accepted."

Caleb moved half-consciously in his chair. "Then why do I get the feeling I've damaged . . . something . . . beyond repair?"

Having watched Isabel and Rafe circling each other like a couple of wary cats, Hollis was in no mood to play games. "Caleb, you seem like a nice guy, with a nice, satisfying life here in Hastings. And I hope that after we've done our job and gone away, you get your nice little town back again. I hope we can offer you some sense of closure in Tricia's death by finding the animal who killed her."

"But?"

"But nothing. There isn't anything else. There never was, really."

"There might have been."

Still being honest, she said, "I sort of doubt it. Not because of anything you said or did, but just the timing."

"And there's no use even trying?"

"I think . . . that right now my life and your life are so different we could never even find a bit of common ground to stand on. Honestly. You don't know me, Caleb. The little bit you do know is just the tip of a pretty dark and unsettling iceberg."

He leaned back in his chair with a sigh. "Yeah, I was afraid you'd say something like that."

"Admit it. You're relieved."

"No. No, not relieved. In fact, I have the distinct feeling I'm missing out on something I'll regret one day."

"Nice of you to say so."

He smiled a bit ruefully. "Look, there's something else I came here to tell you. Show you. Something that could possibly be related to Tricia's murder."

Hollis had no problem in shifting from the personal to the professional—which told her a lot. "What is it?"

"I found something in the desk. My desk, not hers. It was in a drawer I never use because it's in an awkward position in the desk layout, and apparently she'd been using it to store work-related things she no longer used. Mostly old notebooks. I went through all of them, and they were all the shorthand notes she'd taken. Dictation, notes about schedules and appointments, that sort of thing."

"What was unusual about that?"

"Nothing. But when I was going through the last notebook—which was actually the one that had been on top, by the way—a slip of paper fell out. I'm guessing it was something she wrote down during a phone call, and the date puts it just before the murders began." He reached into the inner pocket of his jacket, adding, "My prints are all over it, but I figured it didn't really matter. It's clearly a private note, since it doesn't match anything in my schedule, and I doubt it has any value as evidence—except to maybe point the investigation in a different direction." He placed the small piece of paper on the conference table and pushed it across to her.

Out of habit, Hollis nevertheless used the eraser of the pencil she was holding to draw the paper closer so she could study it. "Looks like her handwriting," she said.

"I'm no expert, but I've seen a lot of her handwriting over the years. She wrote that. Plus, that's the sort of doodling she tended to do when her mind was on something else."

The "doodles" were clear enough. A little cat face; a couple of

267

hearts with arrows through them; stairs leading to nowhere; a sun setting off the edge of the paper with its rays beaming; a female eye, with long lashes and carefully detailed iris; and two circles connected by a series of smaller circles.

The paper was clearly from a notepad; it was a neon green, and across the top was printed: *It works in practice, but not in theory.*

"There were other notepads like this one in her desk," Hollis remembered. "The kind with preprinted cartoons or funny sayings on them."

"Yeah. She said they lightened up the serious tone of a lawyer's office, but she only used them for personal or throwaway notes."

Hollis nodded, and studied what Tricia had written in the center of the notepad.

*J.B.*

*Old Hwy*

*7:00 5/16*

It was followed by two large question marks.

"Did Tricia know Jamie Brower?" Hollis asked.

"She never mentioned it, if she did."

"How did she react when Jamie was murdered?"

"Shocked and horrified, just like the rest of us." Caleb frowned. "She did take a few vacation days unexpectedly, now that I think about it."

"Did she leave town?"

"She said she was going to. The time off was because her sister had had surgery, and Tricia needed to go to Augusta and help take care of the kids."

Hollis pushed the note to one side and hunted through the folders stacked on the table until she found the one she wanted.

She looked through several pages, frowning, then paused. "Okay. According to her sister's statement, at the time of Tricia's death she hadn't seen her in more than three months. I thought I remembered reading that."

"Tricia lied to me?" Caleb was baffled. "Why? I mean, it's not like I even asked her why she needed the time off. She had so much vacation and sick time accumulated, I remember telling her to take a week or two if that's what she needed. But she came back to work about . . . four days later."

Hollis looked through the folder for several more minutes, pausing here and there, and finally closed it. "We've backtracked every victim's life for about two weeks prior to their murders, which means we have information that starts tracking Tricia just a few days *after* Jamie was killed."

"So you don't know if she was here in town or went somewhere else."

"No. Shouldn't be too difficult to find out, though. Her apartment manager has been very cooperative, and Tricia was a friendly neighbor, so *her* neighbors noticed her."

"A lesson to all of us not to become too isolated, I guess."

"One way to look at it." Hollis hesitated, then said, "Did Tricia ever show up to work with unexplained bruises or burns, anything like that?"

"No. I told you her former boyfriend showed no signs of abusing her. I never saw a bruise, and since she seldom wore makeup I think I would have noticed."

"True enough." Hollis smiled. "Thanks for bringing this in, Caleb."

He took the hint and rose to his feet. "I only hope it turns out to be helpful."

"I'll let you know," she promised. "That closure we were talking about."

"Thanks, I appreciate it." He hesitated just an instant, then turned and left the conference room.

Hollis was just about to call Ginny in and find out if the younger officer wanted to share a pizza and do some brainstorming when she felt a sudden chill, as if someone had opened a window into winter.

She watched gooseflesh rise on her arms and had to force herself to look up, toward the doorway.

Jamie Brower stood there.

"Oh, shit," Hollis murmured.

She wasn't solid flesh, but neither was she a ghostly, wispy thing; she was definitely clearer and more distinct than Hollis had yet seen her. In this form, anyway.

Her expression was anxious, worried; Jamie said something—or tried to. All Hollis heard was that peculiar hollow silence.

"I'm sorry," she said, trying to hold her own voice steady. Trying not to feel terrified. "I can't hear you."

Jamie moved a step closer to the table and Hollis. Or rather— and very eerily—floated closer, since she didn't seem to actually take a physical step.

Again, she tried to say something.

This time, Hollis could—almost—hear something. Like a quiet voice speaking from the far end of a huge room.

She focused, concentrated. "I can just barely hear . . . Try again, please. What do you need to tell me?"

Jamie's mouth moved as she tried to communicate, the intensity of her need so obvious that Hollis could literally feel it, like something pushing at her.

Unnerved, Hollis lost both concentration and the desire to keep trying. "I'm sorry. I'm really sorry, but I just can't hear you," she said, her own voice unsteady now.

An expression of pure frustration crossed Jamie's lovely face, twisting it, and she threw up her arms in the gesture of someone reaching the end of her limits.

Half the folders on the conference table spewed their contents into the air.

When the rain of paper and photographs had ended, Hollis found herself sitting in the middle of a mess.

Alone.

Ginny came into the room a moment later, looking around in surprise. "Hey, it looks like somebody lost her temper."

"Yes," Hollis said. "Somebody did."


"Okay," Paige said, "getting creeped out here."

Isabel and Rafe looked at each other, then stopped holding hands.

Paige reached up to smooth down her hair, and they could all hear the crackle. "Jesus," she muttered. "I'm going to have to write a detailed report on this one. It's the first time that my ability to tap into other psychics' abilities actually manifested itself physically."

"Some psychic abilities do manifest themselves physically," Isabel reminded her.

"Yeah, but not many. I know your visions do that. Have you had one of those, by the way?"

"Not since I've been in Hastings."

"I wonder if you could now."

"I don't know. I assume not, since the visions are just another aspect of the clairvoyance."

"And both are boxed up inside a shield that might as well be Fort Knox."

"You're serious? It's that tough?"

271

"And then some. Bishop had me test his and Miranda's shield once, and it hit about eight or nine on our scale. Of course, we don't know how consistent that sort of ability is; it may vary widely according to the circumstances—i.e., why the shield is being used by the psychic at that particular moment. When we did the test, they weren't especially motivated or feeling driven to protect themselves. If they had been . . . who knows?"

It was Rafe who said, "So if the reasons were powerful enough, or the—the psychic desperate enough to protect himself or herself from some perceived attack, then the shield would be even stronger than . . . normal." He felt odd just using the word—hell, any of these words. But Paige was nodding, again matter-of-factly.

"The human mind has a hundred ways to protect itself, and it'll use whatever it can whenever it has to. Fear creates energy, just like any other strong emotion does, just like psychic ability itself does. A psychic's mind virtually always uses that extra energy for some kind of wall or shield."

"Except for Isabel."

Isabel shrugged. "We've never been able to figure out why my abilities won't shield themselves."

Rafe looked at her oddly. "No?"

"No." She frowned at him. "Why are you looking at me like that?"

"No reason." But when he looked back at Paige, he lifted his brows slightly.

"Even those of us with extra senses can be incredibly blind to some things," she said. "Keep doing that, by the way. It's working."

Isabel looked from one to the other of them, baffled. "What's he doing?"

"Reaching through his shield."

"He is?"

"I am?"

Paige nodded. "I'm sure you'll both figure it out. Problem is, there's this killer, which doesn't give you a whole hell of a lot of time in which to do it."

"Any advice?" Isabel asked wryly.

"Yeah. Hurry."


Hollis propped her elbows on the table and pressed her fingers against her eyes. "God, I'm tired. What time is it, anyway?"

"Nearly nine," Isabel told her. "I was ready to call it a day hours ago."

Rafe looked at her but didn't say anything, just as he hadn't said much since they'd left Paige at the motel. Isabel had filled the silence—and possibly tried to distract him—by briefly discussing Ginny's situation, a matter Rafe was kicking himself for having completely missed and one he wasn't at all sure how to handle.

Oh, yeah, he was psychic. Sure he was.

In any case, Isabel had offered a few suggestions, and Rafe was more than ready to accept her counsel and approve her plan. He just wished she was as forthcoming with advice regarding this peculiar new ability he supposedly had.

Hell, she hadn't even mentioned it since they'd left the motel, and that bothered him more than he wanted to admit. He knew Isabel was dealing with issues of her own at the moment, and he knew he was a complication in her life. He was even reasonably sure that the simplest thing he could do would be to leave her alone to sort out what she had to.

But as Isabel herself had said, the simplest thing wasn't always the smartest thing.

So what was the smartest thing?

Studiously not looking at him, Isabel said, "Okay, we're agreed that the note doodled by Tricia Kane suggests she was one of Jamie's clients."

"More than suggests," Hollis said. "The only thing on that old highway of any interest is Jamie's playroom."

"Agreed, but that doesn't mean Tricia was a client. We don't know why she was meeting Jamie. Hell, maybe she was painting her."

"There were no sketches of Jamie or anybody who looked like her among Tricia's work. Besides, do you really think Jamie would commission a painting of herself in full S&M ensemble?"

"No."

"Then what other reason could they have for meeting there?"

"Maybe Tricia was interested in buying the building. It was one of those Jamie planned to sell after what happened with Hope Tessneer."

"We checked that out," Mallory said. "At least as far as we could. Jamie kept her official appointments in her date book, and that included appointments to show her own properties during the last couple of months. No appointment listed for May sixteenth."

Rafe spoke finally, saying, "Odds are, Tricia was a client. Or a potential client. You did say at least one of Jamie's partners could have been from Hastings."

Isabel nodded. "I did say that, yes."

Hollis looked from Isabel to Rafe curiously. There had been no opportunity to discuss what they had found out from Paige, since both Mallory and Ginny had been in the room and other officers had come and gone fairly steadily, but it didn't take a sixth sense to feel the tension between them.

Hollis had been debating whether to tell them about the visitation from Jamie, though she had pretty much decided just to tell Isabel later, when they were alone. After all, it wasn't as though she could provide anything new in the way of information or evidence.

Rafe said, "Then Tricia might have been a regular."

"Another Hastings blonde with a secret sexual life?" Isabel leaned back in her chair with a sigh. "And it seemed like such a nice little town."

"I said the same thing," Hollis murmured.

"It was a nice little town," Rafe said. "And will be again. Just as soon as we catch this bastard."

"And all we've got to help us catch him," Isabel reminded the group at large, "is a fairly useless profile and what we know about the victims."

"You haven't revised the profile as you've gotten deeper into the investigation?" Rafe asked Isabel almost idly.

"Not really. This guy leaves so little behind that the only real thing we have to study are the victims he kills. All single white females, all smart and savvy, all successful. Beyond that, and until now, all we really had connecting them was the color of their hair. Cheryl Bayne's disappearance puts the importance of that into question—definitely."

"But even before then," Mallory said, "we found Jamie's secret. And her secret playroom."

Isabel nodded.

"Which could have been an aberration as far as the victims go, having absolutely nothing to do with the killer or his motivations. But then Hope Tessneer's body turned up, having very likely been a . . . toy . . . for our killer after she died, probably accidentally, and probably at Jamie's hands. Connection. And now this note, which is a pretty fair indication that Tricia Kane was or planned to become involved in Jamie's S&M games."

"Another connection," Rafe said.

"But there is absolutely no sign that Allison Carroll led anything but a perfectly traditional sex life. Also no sign that she even knew either of the other victims."

Rafe shook his head. "Maybe we missed something. Or maybe there was nothing there to miss. Maybe she was as good at keeping secrets as Jamie was. As Tricia was."

"Regarding Tricia, there were no regular withdrawals from her bank account in the last few months," Mallory noted. "But that isn't to say she might not have sold some of her sketches or paintings for cash. A couple of her friends mentioned that she'd sold things to them. She could have paid Jamie without leaving any trace of the money."

"Yeah," Isabel said, "but how did she *find* Jamie? I mean, how did she know the services were available? I doubt Jamie advertised in some bondage magazine."

"Word of mouth?" Rafe suggested. "A referral from another client? All these women had something to lose in the sense of not wanting their . . . extracurricular activities to be made public. Jamie could have been pretty sure of their silence."

"Still, she would have wanted to have control—" Isabel broke off with a frown, then continued. "Wait a minute. The photos we have show Jamie unmasked. What if that's the reason Emily took those particular photos? Because they were the only ones that showed Jamie's face?"

Finishing her supposition, Rafe said, "What if Jamie was always masked when she met clients? Except for the client she trusted, the one in the photographs?"

Mallory said, "According to all that info you guys got from Quantico on the S&M scene, that actually makes sense. For the submissive to not know who was dominating her—or him, I guess—could be an important part of the experience. For some of them, it might even be necessary that they not know the identity of their . . . mistress."

"We have got to find that box," Isabel said. "And I want to talk to Emily again first thing tomorrow. The patrol's still watching her, right?"

Rafe nodded. "When she's out of the house, they follow; when she's home, as she was last time I checked, I have a squad car parked across the street from her house. If anybody asks, they're under orders to say they're making sure none of the media bothers the family."

"Good cover story," Isabel said.

"And plausible. Since Jamie was the first victim, the family really has had to put up with a lot of media attention. Allison and Tricia didn't have family in Hastings, so nobody can really know if those families are being watched as well."

"Hey," Ginny said suddenly, "did you guys take a good look at these doodles?"

"I was just looking at the time and place of the appointment," Hollis admitted, unwilling to explain that images often blurred or faded oddly when she looked at them, particularly those drawn two-dimensionally on paper.

"What'd we miss?" Rafe asked his young officer.

Ginny hesitated, then pushed the note across the table to him. "Look at that doodle on the right. The two circles connected with a sort of chain."

Rafe had to look for a moment before he realized what he was seeing. "Jesus. Handcuffs."

"It's about time you got off," Ally told Travis. "I didn't have to hang around the police station waiting for you, you know. I do have other offers."

He grinned at her. "Then why didn't you accept any of them?"

"You're getting too goddamned cocky, I'll tell you that much. Here I am, wandering around downtown on a Sunday evening when the only other women out are brave, and needless to say brunette, hookers—"

"I think those are other reporters, Ally. Hastings doesn't have hookers."

"You sure about that?"

Recalling a certain trip to a certain house when he was about sixteen, Travis felt his face heat up. "Well, not streetwalkers, anyway."

"Don't tell me, let me guess. Your old man took you to a cathouse for your first sexual experience."

"He did not." Travis sighed. "My brother did."

Ally slid off the hood of his car, laughing. "You should send her flowers on every anniversary, pal. She done you proud."

"Thank you. I think." He pulled her close for a long kiss, then said, "Dammit, Ally, it really bothers me that you're wandering around town alone, never mind after dark, especially since Cheryl Bayne disappeared. It's been nearly a week since the last murder; we know we're running out of time. Every other woman in town is jumpy as hell, and you're breezing around like nothing can touch you."

"I'm not blond."

"We don't *know* he's just after blondes. Cheryl Bayne wasn't—isn't—blond. Besides, the other times, he went after brunettes and redheads."

"Other times?"

He grimaced. "You didn't hear me say that."

"Look, I promise I won't report a word until you say it's okay. Scout's honor."

He stared at the fingers she held up. "That's a peace sign, Ally."

"Well, I was never a scout. But that doesn't mean you can't trust me to keep quiet—until I get the word it's okay to report."

He took her arm and escorted her around to the passenger side of his car. "I say we pick up a bag of tacos and head for my place."

"Tacos at this hour? God, you have a cast-iron stomach, don't you? Besides, didn't I see a pizza delivery to the station a couple of hours ago? The poor guy was staggering under the weight of those pizza boxes."

"One of the feds offered to buy," Travis said. "Naturally, we took her up on the offer."

"And you're still hungry?"

"Well, that was a couple of hours ago."

"But tacos? On top of pizza?"

"It's Sunday night in Hastings, Ally; we don't have a lot of choices here."

She sighed and got into his car, waiting until he was behind the wheel to say, "Okay, but only on the condition that you fill me in on the investigation so far."

"Ally—"

"Look, either you trust me by now or you don't. If you don't, please be kind enough to drop me off at the inn."

"So that's it? I talk or it's over?"

"Come on, Travis, give me a break. We're not lovers, we just roll around in the sheets together and have a good time. It's fun and we both enjoy it, but I haven't heard a suggestion that we start picking out china patterns. You're not going to take me home to Mama, and we both know as soon as this maniac is captured or killed, I'm outta here. Right?"

"Right," he said grudgingly.

"So don't get all indignant with me now. I'm having a good time with you, and that's cool, but I also have a job to do. Either I get what I need from you, or I start looking someplace else."

"At least you're up front about it," he muttered.

"I am nothing if not totally honest," she said, lying without a blink.

He eyed her for a moment and then started the car. "Ally, I swear, if you air one single word—or even tell your producer—before I give the okay, I'll figure out a way to throw your ass in jail. Got it?"

"Got it. No problem. So who's Jane Doe, and how did she die?"

"Hope Tessneer, and she was strangled. She lived in another town about thirty miles away."

"And turned up dead here because . . . ?"

"Beats me. I think the chief and the feds know more than they're saying, but they ain't sharing. At least, not with me."

Accurately reading the tone of his voice, she said, "They've brought somebody else into the investigation?"

"Into the inner circle, anyway." He shrugged, trying hard for indifference. "Ginny McBrayer seems to be in their confidence, or at least of the two agents. Figures. You females always stick together."

"Please don't make me call you a sexist pig," Ally requested dryly.

"I'm not. And that's not what I mean. Women talk to each other in ways men just don't. That's all."

Ally looked at him with faint respect. "We do, actually. I'm surprised you noticed."

"I keep telling you I'm not an idiot." He sent her a glance, smiling oddly. "You really should pay attention, Ally."

"Yeah," she said. "Yeah, I guess I really should at that. Where're we going, Travis?"

"The taco place. If I'm going to spill my guts, I'm going to need sustenance first."

"I really wish you'd used a different phrase," Ally said. "Really."

# 16

ISABEL STUDIED THE NOTE and then nodded, passing it on to Hollis and Mallory. "It looks like a sketch of handcuffs to me. Sort of stylized, the way an artist would maybe do it, which could be one reason we missed it. Nice catch, Ginny."

"I should have caught that," Hollis said, more to herself than to the others, and in a tone that struck her own ears as wistful.

"You're just all a little preoccupied," Ginny murmured.

"Good thing you aren't," Isabel told her. "Okay, a paralegal might have doodled handcuffs, I suppose, but having them on this particular note has got to mean something more than absent-mindedness. It's one more indication Tricia Kane was involved, or looking to get involved, with Jamie Brower."

Hollis said, "Any chance Jamie might have trusted Tricia with that box we so badly want to see?"

Isabel started to reply, then looked at Rafe. "What do you think?"

"I'm not the profiler."

"Off the top of your head. What do you think?"

"No," he heard himself reply, and frowned as he went on slowly. "Jamie wouldn't have trusted that box with anyone else—unless it was the partner who saw her unmasked."

"Very good," Isabel said. "And my feeling as well. That box is either stored somewhere Jamie considered safe, or kept by someone she really, really trusted. And we know by now that she didn't trust many people."

Hollis produced the Eyes Only file and opened it to study the photographs. It didn't take long for her to reach a conclusion and close the folder. "This isn't Tricia Kane. For one thing, she had a couple of moles on one arm that would have shown up in the photos. For another, unless the photos were taken months ago, there wouldn't have been time for her hair to grow out."

"But you can't see her hair in the photos because of that hood," Ginny objected. Then she blinked. And blushed. "Oh. That hair."

Isabel smiled at her. "Why don't you go make a few copies of Tricia's note so we can bag the original. And then I really do think we all need to call it a day. Start fresh in the morning."

As soon as Ginny was out of the room, Isabel said to Rafe, "I'm going to go talk to her. Be right back."

"Okay."

"Did I miss something?" Mallory wondered when Isabel had gone.

"We'll be arresting Hank McBrayer," Rafe told her. "Assault charges filed by his daughter."

Mallory looked blank for a moment, then scowled. "Son of a bitch. I'd heard talk, but Ginny never said anything."

"Most victims of abuse don't," Hollis said. To Rafe, she asked, "Is Isabel going to try to convince her to stay in a hotel tonight?"

"She's going to try to convince her to let you two and a couple of officers go back to her house with a warrant for her father's arrest and get him out of there tonight."

"Can we do that?" Mallory asked.

"Yes. I called the judge from the car. The paperwork's almost ready."

Mallory was still frowning. "Why Isabel and Hollis? I mean, why not just send a couple of our officers? I'll volunteer. Since I hate bullies just on principle, I'd love to accidentally break McBrayer's arm while he's resisting arrest."

"So would I," Rafe said. "But it was Isabel and Hollis who realized what was going on and talked to Ginny about it, and Isabel and I both feel Ginny will be more comfortable if they're along for the arrest." He hesitated, then said, "Plus, I think Isabel has something else in mind."

Hollis looked at him. "Do you, now? Like what?"

"Assuming he's sober enough to listen, I think she intends to take him down a peg or two. Without laying a finger on him."

"If anybody can," Hollis said, "it's Isabel. Guys look at that beautiful face and centerfold body, all that blond hair, big green eyes all wide and innocent, and think they know exactly what she is. Boy, do they get a surprise."

"I certainly did," Rafe murmured.

"Speaking of which," Hollis said. "Are you?"

He didn't have to ask what she meant. "Apparently."

Hollis whistled. "Dunno whether to say congratulations or sorry about that."

"I'll let you know when I figure out how I feel about it."

Mallory said, "Hello? What's going on? Are you what?"

"Psychic."

She blinked. "You're psychic?"

"So I'm told."

"How could you be and not know?"

"The short answer," Hollis said, "is that he always was, but it was an inactive ability, so he wasn't aware of it. I think we talked about latents when we first got here. Rafe, as it turns out, was a latent. Something happened to activate his abilities."

"What?"

Hollis lifted her brows at Rafe.

"Damned if I know. She—I was told it could have been some kind of subconscious shock, which I suppose it had to be since I don't recall any consciously shocking or traumatic events in my life recently. Other than this killer."

"No bump on the head?" Hollis asked. "Concussion?"

"No," he said. "Never, in fact."

Mallory eyed him somewhat warily. "So what can you do?"

"Not a whole hell of a lot. Yet, anyway. The consensus seems to be I am—or will be—clairvoyant."

"Like Isabel? Just knowing stuff?"

"More or less."

"And that doesn't scare the shit out of you?"

"Did you hear me say it didn't?"

"No."

"Well, then."

Mallory leaned back in her chair, tipped her head back, and addressed the ceiling—and whatever lay beyond. "A few weeks ago, I led a perfectly ordinary existence. No killers. No spooky psychic abilities. Nothing on my mind more weighty than which kind of takeout I wanted for my supper. Those were the days. I'm sorry now I didn't appreciate them." She sighed and looked at the others. "I must be paying off karma for a really, really bad decision in a former life."

"*You* must be?" Rafe shook his head.

Isabel returned to the room before the discussion could continue, saying, "We have a slight change of plan. Hollis, we're going to swing by Ginny's on the way back to the inn and pick up her mother; both of them will be staying there tonight."

"Hank's out on the town?" Rafe guessed.

"Yeah. Seems he often spends Sunday afternoons and evenings drinking in an undisclosed location with others of . . . like temperament."

Rafe sighed. "Yeah, we have a few basement bars in the county. Unlicensed, unregulated, and highly mobile. They tend to change location more often than they wash the glasses."

"Well, apparently Mr. McBrayer has a semiregular habit of drinking all evening and passing out somewhere between the bar and home. Or at the bar, sometimes. In any case, he seldom makes it home on Sunday nights. But on the off chance that tonight would be one of those nights, I've persuaded Ginny to get her mother and come stay at the inn."

"I'll have all the patrols keep an eye out for him tonight," Rafe said. "If they don't spot him, we'll catch up with him tomorrow."

"Good, thanks." Isabel frowned slightly.

"I've also arranged to have all single female officers escorted home and their places checked out before they lock up for the night," Rafe said. "And each is under orders to wait for two male officers to meet them tomorrow morning, if they're on duty, to be escorted back here."

"You're reaching through again," Isabel said.

"I am?"

"I was just thinking about Mallory's report that some of the female officers feel they've been watched or followed and wondering what we should do to help protect those most likely to be at risk if it's our killer—the single ones in the right age range. Don't tell me you read that on my face. I may not be subtle, but I'm not a damned billboard."

Mallory looked at Hollis, who shrugged.

"They've got me, too, this time."

Rafe hesitated, then shrugged. "You looked worried; I wondered why; I knew."

Isabel frowned again. "Okay. Now I'm worried about something else."

Peculiarly enough, Rafe found this answer coming as easily as the one before had, just knowledge in his mind. "Sorry. Since neither one of us knows who the killer is, I don't have a solution for your worry."

"It was," Isabel said, "more fun being the clairvoyant one."

"Yeah, I can see how it would have been."

"You're enjoying this."

"Not all of it. Just . . . some of it."

"I know gloating when I see it. I don't need extra senses for that."

"Good thing too. Since yours are all boxed up, I mean."

Straightening her shoulders, Isabel said, "I'm leaving now. We're going to borrow a patrol to go with us just in case Hank McBrayer shows up unexpectedly while Ginny and her mother are packing overnight bags. If that's okay with you, of course."

"Fine," Rafe said, his tone as polite as hers.

"Great. We'll see you guys bright and early in the morning. Hollis?"

Her partner rose obediently and followed her from the room. As she passed Rafe, Hollis murmured, "You're a lot smarter than you look."

"Christ, I hope so," he responded, equally low.

When the two agents had gone, Mallory looked at Rafe. "Do you know what I'm worried about?"

He frowned at her. "No. Not a clue."

"So it only works with Isabel?"

"Apparently. So far, anyway."

"Um, then I'm worried about two things."

"What's the other thing?"

"We've now got an awful lot of people watching an awful lot of women while we try to anticipate this killer's next move; what worries me is that he may have changed the rules."

It was nearly midnight when Emily Brower's bedside phone rang, and she was more than half asleep when she fumbled hastily to answer it before it could wake her parents.

"Yeah. Hello?" She listened for several minutes, then said sleepily, "Okay, but—now? Why now? Yeah, I understand that, but— Right. Right, okay. Give me ten minutes."

She cradled the receiver, then pushed back her covers and sat up, muttering, "Shit, shit, shit."

It didn't take her more than a couple of minutes to exchange her sleep shirt for jeans and a T-shirt and slide her feet into a worn and comfortable pair of clogs.

Her parents slept like the dead, especially these days with the aid of various sedatives, so she didn't hesitate to leave her bedroom and walk down the lamplit hall, down the stairs, and out the front door, snagging her car keys from the foyer table.

She wasn't surprised not to see the customary patrol car parked across the street, since she'd heard it fire up its sirens and speed away sometime before her phone had rung. An accident somewhere, she assumed.

And, anyway, the reporters always left by dark or shortly after, so there was no good reason for the patrol car to stay out there all night. She'd meant to call the police station and ask the chief or one of the agents about it but kept forgetting.

Shrugging off the question, Emily got in her car and backed it out of the driveway. She knew the way, of course, and hadn't thought much about it until she was almost there. But by the time she parked her car off the side of the road and got out, she was beginning to feel more than a little uneasy.

She got a flashlight from the glove box and carried it to light her way, feeling a surge of relief when she reached the clearing and the light turned the shadowy outline of a person into someone she knew.

"I don't understand what I can show you out here," she said immediately. "And this is creepy, in case you hadn't realized it. We might not have been close, but still—this is where my sister was murdered."

"I know, Emily. She was quite a woman. Very intelligent. It's a pity you aren't."

"What?" Emily moved her hand, the flashlight's beam cutting through the hot, humid night. And that was when she saw the knife.

She tried to scream, but only her killer heard the bloody gurgle that emerged as she was nearly decapitated.

**Monday, June 16, 7:00 AM**

When the phone rang, he rolled over in bed and had the cordless receiver in his hand even before his eyes opened.

And even before his eyes opened, he smelled it.

"Yeah?"

"We've got another one, Chief." It was Mallory, her voice bleak.

Still holding the receiver to his ear with his left hand, he held out the right one and stared at it in the early-morning light streaming into his bedroom.

His hand was stained with blood.

"Where?" he asked.

"Isabel was right when she said he'd probably start taunting us. He used the same place. As far as I can tell from the report that came in, the victim is exactly where Jamie Brower died. I'm on my way there now."

"Who is it? Who's the victim?"

"It's Emily. Jamie's sister."

"Goddammit, where was the patrol watching her?" Rafe demanded, sitting up in bed.

"They were pulled away from her house last night at about eleven-thirty and were only away a couple of hours. A traffic accident with fatalities."

Rafe drew a breath and let it out slowly. "Which takes precedence over watchdog duty."

"Yeah. As per standing orders."

He shoved the covers away and got out of bed, heading for the bathroom. "Have you called Isabel?"

"Not yet. I only took the report instead of you because I went into the office a bit earlier than usual. I couldn't sleep past six, so I just came in."

"I thought I ordered you to accept an escort."

"You suggested, just like you suggested it for Stacy, the only other female detective in the department. We both passed. She's a black belt, and I can take care of myself. And neither one of us is a blonde. You want me to call Isabel?"

"Yeah. Have them meet us at the scene. I'm on my way."

"Right."

He turned off the phone and literally dropped it on the bathroom rug, immediately turning on the water and washing his hands in the hottest water he could stand.

Again.

Jesus Christ, again.

The gnawing fear that had been with him for so long was less acute this time, and he understood why. Because this morning he knew something he hadn't known all the other mornings.

This morning, he knew there was something new and unfamiliar going on in his brain, and it wasn't homicidal madness.

It was psychic ability.

*You could be calling me rude names in your head or worrying about some deep dark secret you don't want anybody to know, and I wouldn't necessarily read that either.*

Deep, dark secret. That's what it had been all this time, a secret fear buried so deep he had almost been able to forget about it during the bright, sane light of day. Almost.

He was no killer. He knew that. He *had* known that all along, even with the fear that something inside him might have been capable of such acts.

But if he was no killer, then why had he been waking up with blood on his hands for nearly three weeks?

Yesterday morning, he hadn't had a clue. This morning . . .

Rafe thought he was beginning to understand what was going on—though he only had a hunch as to why. And he thought he understood why his shield was so strong that it not only enclosed Isabel but also blocked her.

Gripping the sides of the sink, he stared into the mirror at his unshaven face and haunted eyes. "I have to be able to control this," he murmured.

Because he couldn't keep blocking Isabel, not even to keep her from knowing his secret fears, his self-doubts and uncertainties, all the demons a man carried inside him if he lived long enough and saw too much. In shutting that away from her, he had both shut her out and imprisoned her.

Imprisoned her abilities, the extra senses that could be all that was standing between her and a killer.

Isabel stood just inside the area blocked off with yellow crime-scene tape, her hands on her hips, grimly studying the clearing.

"Jesus, I don't know where to start," T.J. said as she and Dustin arrived with their crime-scene kits.

"Follow procedure," Isabel advised.

Eyeing the ME, who was examining the body, Dustin said, "Even Doc looks queasy. And he was a state medical examiner, until he got tired of the parade of bodies."

T.J. murmured, "Bet he's sorry he chose Hastings to finish out his professional life."

"I'm having second thoughts myself," Dustin told her.

"I know what you mean. Come on, let's get to work."

Hollis joined Isabel as the two technicians moved away, saying, "Sorry about that."

"Don't be. I lost my breakfast the first three times I was called to an early murder scene."

"I'll remember that. Next time. I thought I could handle something like this, especially after a couple of weeks of classes at the body farm. But, Christ . . ."

"Yeah, he made a real mess this time." Isabel half turned as Mallory joined them. "I'm betting her car's clean, though."

Mallory nodded. "Looks like it. It'll be towed back to the

station so T.J. and Dustin can go over it thoroughly, but the only difference I noticed is that she didn't leave her purse in it."

Isabel said, "If the doctor confirms that she died around midnight, then she'd have had to leave her house just after the patrol was called away for that accident. Maybe she left in a hurry and didn't even bring a purse."

"Had to be to meet someone," Hollis said. "You're a twenty-something blonde in a town where twenty-something blondes are being killed, including your own sister, and you go out alone near midnight? She was either very stupid or really trusted whoever she went to meet. Or both, if you ask me."

Isabel looked at Mallory. "When we were in her home, I didn't get any sense of a steady boyfriend."

"Far as I know, she didn't have one. Dated, but never anybody serious."

Hollis shook her head. "Who could she possibly trust enough to meet, around midnight, at the scene of her sister's murder?"

"And why?" Isabel mused, frowning. "The only reason I can think of is that someone must have told her she could help by coming out here so late. That there was something out here she needed to see, and after dark. If that's true, I can't see any possible answer as to who called her out here except—"

"—a cop," Mallory said. "Has to be."

Hollis looked around at the police technicians and the dozen or so uniformed officers searching the area surrounding the crime scene and in various positions between this clearing and the rest stop at the highway, which had also been roped off, and sighed. "Great. That's just great."

"We still can't rule out some other authority figure," Isabel reminded them. "For that matter, we can't rule out a member of the media. Who's to say some reporter didn't offer Emily a nice big

293

chunk of cash to meet out here where her sister was killed? And being here well after dark was the only real guarantee a passing patrol wouldn't see them, since we've had all these areas under watch. Her car was well off the road and behind that thicket, so either the killer moved it there afterward or told Emily to park there to avoid being seen by a passing patrol."

"But a reporter? For a story?" Hollis said. "That's sick. Would Emily have gone for something like that?"

"To step out of Jamie's shadow? I'm thinking yes."

"That might explain this," Mallory said, "but what about the other victims? Could a reporter have lured them out of their cars and into the woods?"

Hollis said, "You know, maybe we're making a giant assumption that he does it the same way every time. He could be gearing his approach to each woman individually. Isabel, you and Bishop both believe he has to get to know his victims. Maybe this is why. To find the right bait for each catch."

Isabel looked at her for a moment, then said, "If you ever feel useless in an investigation, remember this moment. Damn. Why didn't I see that?"

Hollis was pleased, but nevertheless said, "You've had a lot on your plate."

"Still." Isabel took a step toward the body, then stopped and turned back. The other two women also turned to watch as Rafe approached them from the highway. He looked grim, and on a face as rugged as his, grim was an expression to make even the bravest soul take a step back.

Isabel met him halfway.

"Sorry I'm late," he said. "I got held up at the station."

"What else has happened?" she demanded, reaching out without thinking to touch his hand.

His fingers immediately twined with hers. "The accident that pulled the patrol away from the Brower house," he said. "There were two fatalities."

"I'd heard that much." She waited, knowing there was more.

"Hank McBrayer was one of them," Rafe said flatly. "He was driving too fast, drunk, and apparently crossed over the center line. Hit the oncoming car head-on. The other victim was a sixty-five-year-old grandmother."

"Jesus," Isabel said. "Poor Ginny. This is going to eat her alive."

"I know. I've got the department counselor with her and her mother now." He glanced past her at the taped-off crime-scene area.

"He was incredibly vicious this time," Isabel warned. "He cut her throat, probably first, and with enough force to nearly sever her head. And then he started to enjoy himself."

Without releasing her hand, Rafe continued toward the crime scene. "Has the doc offered his preliminary report yet?"

"No, but I think he's about to."

They ducked under the tape that Mallory and Hollis automatically held up for them.

"If nobody minds," Hollis said, "I think I'll stand right here. I've seen all I want to."

Nobody objected, and as they walked toward the body, Isabel murmured, "Hollis is dealing with her own guilt. She saw Jamie again, last night in the conference room, obviously desperately trying to say something."

"And Hollis couldn't hear her."

"No. At the end, Jamie was so frustrated she apparently focused enough energy to scare the hell out of Hollis by scattering half the paperwork on the table across the room."

Rafe looked at her, frowning. "I seem to remember you telling me something like that would be unusual."

"Oh, yeah. Jamie was a very strong lady. And she was trying very, very hard to communicate. She must have known her sister would be the next victim. Which is another indication to me that Emily knew something dangerous to the killer."

"You don't believe she was killed just because she fit the victim profile?"

"No. She was too young, I think. Not successful enough for his tastes. I also think she would have died no matter what color her hair was. Emily snooped in her sister's life, and it got her killed."

"And we still have a reporter missing."

"Who may also have found out something dangerous to the killer," Isabel said.

They stopped several feet from where Dr. James was still examining the body, and Rafe muttered an oath as he saw her up close for the first time.

Isabel didn't respond to that. Neither did Mallory. There wasn't much they could say.

Emily Brower lay sprawled out almost exactly as her sister had lain and almost exactly three weeks afterward. The slash across her throat was so deep the white vertebra of her neck was visible, and the gaping wound had literally drenched her in blood. Her once-pale T-shirt was soaked with it, and her blond hair lay in a pool of congealing blood and dirt.

"You were right about the escalation," Rafe said, his deep voice raspier than normal. "That son of a bitch. Sick, evil, twisted animal . . ."

The killer hadn't just murdered Emily, hadn't just repeatedly stabbed her breasts and genitals as he had the previous three victims. It looked as if he had stabbed her once in each breast—but had twisted and turned the knife as though trying to bore holes through her body.

And rather than stabbing her genitals through her clothing, he had pulled her jeans and panties down around her ankles, pulled her knees up and pushed them apart, and used the knife to rape her.

"If it helps," Isabel said, holding her voice steady, "she never felt that. Never knew about it."

"For her sake I'm glad," Rafe said. "But it doesn't help."

Dr. James straightened and came to join them, his face very, very tired. "Anything you need me to tell you that you can't see for yourself?" he asked wearily.

"Time of death?" Rafe asked.

"Midnight, give or take a few minutes. She died almost instantly with both the jugular and the windpipe slashed. Blood gushed like a fountain, the last few beats of her heart pumping it out as she fell. He didn't touch her face, but he used something heavy to crush her skull in two places once she was on the ground."

"Why?" Mallory wondered, baffled. "She was already dead, and he had to know it."

"Rage," Isabel and Rafe said in almost the same breath.

She added, "He had to make certain she couldn't see him. Couldn't see his sexual failure."

"He knew before he tried that he'd fail," Rafe said.

Isabel nodded. "He knew. Maybe he's always known."

The doctor looked at them rather curiously but continued with his report in a monotone. "She fell backward, and he didn't move her much. Spread her arms out to the sides, judging by the abrasions I found on the backs of her arms. Fanned her hair out and then pressed it into the pool of blood around her head. God knows why. I don't."

"What else?" Rafe asked.

"What you see. Did his best to gouge out her breasts, then

brutalized her with the knife. It was a big knife, and it did a lot of damage. If I had to guess, I'd say he drove it between her legs at least a dozen times."

"Excuse me," Mallory said in a very polite tone. She walked to the edge of the clearing, lifted the crime-scene tape and ducked underneath it, and took several steps beyond, then bent over and vomited.

"I plan to get drunk," Dr. James announced.

"I wish I could," Rafe said.

The doctor sighed. "I'll write up the preliminary report when I get back to the office, Rafe. You'll have the rest when I get her on the table. It's going to be a long day."

"Yeah. Thanks, Doc."

When the doctor walked away, Rafe said to Isabel, "I'm not getting anything but rage here, and just the vaguest sense of that, not even enough to be sure it isn't my imagination—or the training telling me to draw logical conclusions from what I'm seeing here. I don't know how to reach for anything more. You have to do it."

"I can't. I'm not getting anything either. Silence. Like you, I know he was furious from what I'm looking at, not from anything I hear or feel."

"We need more, Isabel."

"I know that."

"We have to stop him here and now. Before he goes after anybody else. Before he comes after you."

"I know that too."


*You have to do her. The first chance you get, you have to do her.*

He tried to ignore the voice, because it wasn't telling him anything he didn't already know. All it was doing was making his head hurt even more.

*She knows. Or she will soon. And he's helping her know. Look at them. You understand what's happening, don't you?*

"No," he whispered, because he didn't, he really didn't. All he knew was that his head hurt and his gut, and it had been so long since he'd slept that he'd forgotten what it felt like.

*They're changing.*

An icy jolt went through him. "No. I'm changing. You said. You promised. If I did it. If I killed them before they told. You promised."

*Then you'd better do her. Kill her. Before they finish changing. Or it'll be too late. Too late for you. Too late for both of you.*

# 17

IT WAS NEARLY NOON by the time T.J. and Dustin had
done their work and the ME's people had removed Emily's
body from the scene. The search of the area had produced
nothing, not a scrap of anything that looked even remotely like
evidence. There were still officers at the highway keeping the media and the curious away from the scene, but most of the other
cops had returned to regular duties.

Isabel had spent the morning prowling the area, restless,
watchful, making what she knew was a futile effort to reach
through the barrier Rafe had created. To protect her.

She didn't think the irony was lost on either one of them.

"Anything?" Hollis asked as they studied the now empty
crime scene.

"Nada. You?"

"No. And I am trying." Hollis shrugged. "But from what

you've said about her, I doubt Emily's is the sort of spirit we could expect to gather enough energy to come back. As for Jamie . . . I didn't hear her when it mattered."

"Don't beat yourself up about it. I'm not exactly firing on all cylinders myself."

"Is that why the watchdogs?" Hollis asked with a slight sideways movement of her head toward an area between them and the highway.

Isabel sighed. "The taller one is Pablo. The other one is Bobby."

"Pablo? In Hastings?"

"Struck me too. But, hey, melting pot."

"I guess." Hollis studied her partner. "So when Rafe went to break the news to Emily's parents, he left two of his uniforms watching you."

"They're not to let me out of their sight. I heard Rafe tell them so. He made damned sure I heard him tell them so."

"Well . . . you could be next, Isabel."

"I can't work hobbled," she said irritably.

"Then take the hobbles off," Hollis suggested mildly. "And I don't mean the watchdogs."

"Don't start spouting Bishop stuff at me, all right? I'm not in the mood. It's hot, it's humid, there's a storm building, and all I can smell is blood."

Hollis grimaced. "Yeah, I was going to ask—how do we turn the spider senses *off*?"

"We don't. Once you learn to enhance, the increased sensitivity is pretty much always with you. There are a few team members who have to focus and concentrate, but for most of us it's just there. Like raw nerves."

"That might have been mentioned *before* I was taught how to enhance."

"Talk to the boss, not me."

"You really are in a rotten mood, aren't you?"

Isabel pointed to the blood-soaked ground several yards away. "This should not have happened," she said. "I should have seen it coming."

"You did. You warned us Emily was a possible victim, and Rafe did everything he could to protect her. It's not your fault or his that a drunk caused a fatal traffic accident."

"That's not what I mean. I should have been . . . tuned in. I should have been listening. Instead, I did just what you said I did—I let Rafe take control. I let him build this shield around my abilities. I went from needing to have absolute control over everything in my life to just . . . handing it over to him. Why in God's name did I do that?"

"You didn't hand over all control. You just let him shut off your abilities."

"Why?"

"Maybe to find out if he could."

Isabel stared at her, baffled. "Okay, if that's Bishop stuff, it doesn't make sense. I mean even more than his stuff sometimes doesn't make sense."

"You're a strong woman, Isabel. You don't want to be dominated, but you *do* want to be matched, if only subconsciously. I think you felt Rafe reaching through this link you guys have, and I think you needed to know, before you decided whether to commit yourself, before you could take that leap of faith, just how strong he was."

"And now that I do know, O wise one?"

Hollis smiled faintly at what was only a token stab at mockery. "Now you know he matches you. He has as much strength of will as you, possibly as much psychic ability as you, and is certainly as stubborn as you."

"So?"

"So stop fighting him. You haven't said, but I'm willing to bet Paige told you that the two of you would have to work together to control his shield."

"Rookies," Isabel muttered.

"I'm right."

"Yeah."

"Then I'd say there's one last little bit of control you'll have to give up. You'll have to stop trying to control the relationship. To guide, or aim, or shape it—whatever it is you've been trying to do since the moment you met Rafe. If you'll forgive the cliché, we don't master love, it masters us. The more you struggle against it, the tighter those hobbles are going to be."

"This should not be about my relationship with him," Isabel said in a last-ditch effort. "Four women are dead in Hastings, five if you count Hope Tessneer, and more are missing. It can't all hinge on my love life, it just *can't*."

"Human relationships are at the heart of everything, you know that. You said yourself they were at the heart of this case. It's about relationships, you said."

"Maybe I didn't know what I was talking about."

"You knew. You know. Relationships matter, Isabel. History's been changed by them, armies toppled, societies rebuilt."

Isabel was silent, frowning toward the bloody ground.

"They have power. Human relationships have power. Family. Friends. Lovers. The closer and more intimate the relationship, the more power it can and does generate. Use that energy. And use it wisely."

"To break through Rafe's shield?"

"No. To make it your own."

———

"Got it?" Rafe asked, meeting up with Mallory in the bullpen at the station.

"Yeah, not that it's helpful. The call Emily received was from a pay phone in town. One of the few remaining pay phones in use."

"Doesn't miss a trick, our guy."

"No. I've got T.J. checking out the phone, but I'm betting she'll either find a million prints or none at all."

"I'll cover that bet. Come on, let's get back out to the scene."

"Isabel and Hollis still out there?"

He nodded, leading the way from the station. "Pablo and Bobby are keeping an eye on them."

"I'll bet Isabel loves that."

"Frankly, I don't give a shit how she feels about it at this point. She's a target, and I have a strong hunch she's next on his hit list."

Mallory looked at him curiously as they got into his Jeep. "Why?"

"Word's getting out. I've had at least two calls from media and one from the town council today asking if it's true we've got a psychic investigator working the case."

"Lovely."

"And the reporter who replaced Cheryl Bayne was one of those calls; he's looking to make a reputation for himself, and it's obvious. His predecessor missing and a psychic working the case? Sounds like a dandy story to him."

"He's going to broadcast that?"

"On today's six o'clock news, he says."

"Shit."

Rafe shrugged. "At this point, I don't think he'll report anything the killer doesn't already know. That's what worries me. If I were him, the killer, I'd go after Isabel, and I wouldn't wait a week to do it. I'm assuming he's thinking the same way."

Mallory sighed and said, "Safe assumption, probably. Plus, if Isabel's right and he really did kill Emily because she knew something rather than because she was one of *his* blondes, then he could have been—for want of a better word—unsatisfied by the murder."

Rafe muttered a curse under his breath and increased the Jeep's speed. He didn't say anything else until they reached the informal rest area and pulled off the highway. Ignoring the questions called out to him by several members of the media still braving the hot day hoping for a photo or a news bite, he headed toward the clearing, relaxing visibly when he saw Isabel and Hollis.

"The phone call?" Isabel asked as the two cops reached the agents.

"No joy," Mallory reported. "Pay phone."

"And there won't be prints," Isabel said with a sigh. "He's using gloves. Not latex, I think, which is odd."

"What do you mean?" Rafe asked.

"Well, latex gloves leave you with a much more tactile sense of what you're touching, you know that. And since they're form-fitting, they don't get in the way."

"No, I mean how do you know he isn't using latex gloves? We haven't found a sign either way at any of the crime scenes."

"I touched them," Isabel said slowly, surprised that she only now remembered that.

"Excuse me?" Mallory's voice was very polite.

Isabel realized she was being stared at, and shook her head. "Sorry. I forgot none of you had seen it here. Or even knew, I guess. I wonder why I forgot that part?"

"What part?" Rafe asked with visible patience.

"I told you that sometimes, rarely, my abilities manifest themselves physically in a vision. During one of those, I *am* the victim. I feel what he or she feels, and I usually come out of it covered in blood. Blood that fades away completely after a few minutes."

"I'd call that creepy," Mallory said.

"Yeah, it's not much fun." Isabel shrugged. "Anyway, what really brought me to Hastings is that I had a vision while Tricia Kane was being killed. I felt what she felt. And when he drove that knife into her chest for the last time before she died, her hands reached up to touch the knife—and touched his hands. He was wearing gloves. Not latex gloves, but thick leather gloves, like working gloves. His hands were big, or at least that was the sense I got."

"And you're just now telling us this?"

"I'm just now remembering." Isabel frowned. "I guess the voices crowded it out. Maybe that's one in the plus column for your shield."

Thunder rumbled just then, and they all glanced upward at the threatening sky.

Half under her breath, Hollis muttered, "Oh, God, I hate storms."

"We're about to have our crime scene washed away," Rafe noted. "Weather's calling for heavy rain today and tonight, with and without thunderstorms."

Isabel hesitated, looking at him. "I've tried," she said. "I've tried all morning to pick up something, and I can't. I can't break through the shield."

"Stop trying to break through it." He held out a hand to her. "Work with me, not against me."

"Rafe—"

"We don't have the luxury of time, not that we ever did. We can't afford to wait any longer. Like it or not, this is it."

"Should we leave?" Hollis asked, indicating herself and Mallory.

"No," Isabel said, then hesitated, recalling what had happened with Paige, and added, "But you might want to step back a little bit."

Both women did, watching the other two warily.

Slowly, Isabel reached out her own hand and felt the spark, felt his fingers closing around hers.

"I wish we had more time," Rafe told her. "I wish we had the luxury of dinners and movies, and hours of talking to each other about what matters to us. But the truth is, we don't have that time. We need every possible tool we can get our hands on—or our minds wrapped around—and we need it now."

"Yes. I know."

"You're next on his list. You know that too."

Isabel hesitated again, then nodded.

"Paige said we'd have to work together. That it would take both of us to figure out how to use this shield."

"Yes." Isabel looked at their hands for a moment, suddenly realizing something. "You're right-handed; I'm left-handed." Those were the hands clasping.

"Like closing a circuit," Rafe said slowly. "Or maybe . . . opening one. All this started when I held your wrists. Both of them."

"Alan, why on earth would I trust you?" Dana Earley demanded.

"Because you want a good story, you want to find out what happened to Cheryl Bayne, and you don't want to be the next blonde on the menu." He paused. "Probably in that order."

Dana didn't bother to be indignant. "So you found out that I have police sources in Alabama you want me to tap, and in exchange you'll share information you got from your own sources in Florida."

"Yes. Look, you're TV and I'm newspaper; if we work this right we can both be heroes."

"Or one of us could be dead. Like me. Alan, if Cheryl is dead it has to be because she got too close. I'm not so sure I want to get too close to this guy, story or no story."

"Which," Alan said, "is why we have to move fast."

"Jesus. I know I'm going to regret this."

Isabel turned slightly so that they were facing each other, glanced down at the bloody ground where the horribly mutilated body of a young woman she had both liked and felt sorry for had so recently lain, and her mouth firmed. "We should be somewhere else," she said.

"No."

She looked at Rafe.

"We should be here. We need to be here, Isabel."

"Why?"

"Because two women died here. Because evil did what it wanted to do, needed to do, here."

The sound of thunder grew louder, more ominous.

"It's disrespectful. Let the rain wash away her blood."

"That isn't the investigator talking," he said.

Isabel smiled wryly. "No. It isn't. I liked her, you know. She felt isolated and misunderstood—and I could relate. I'm sorry she's dead."

"I know. So am I. But the only thing we can do for her now is stop her killer before he does that to someone else."

*Before he does it to you.*

Isabel could almost hear his words in her head. Or maybe she did hear them. Whichever it was, she knew he was right. "Yes," she said.

"The universe put us *here*. And it put us here, and now, for a reason. Remember what you told me? We leave footprints when we pass. Skin cells, stray hairs. And energy. He left his energy here, and recently. He left his hate, and his anger, and the stamp of his evil."

There was a flash in the distance, and Isabel said, almost to herself and with a touch of fear in her voice, "I can smell it. But it's lightning, not brimstone."

His fingers tightened around hers. "Is it? You said you had to face it this time. Confront it this time. That ugly face evil always hides behind something else. You have to face it. But, Isabel, you won't do it alone. Not this time. Not ever again."

She drew a breath and let it out slowly. "I didn't expect that. I'm not quite sure how to deal with that."

"The same way you deal with everything else," he said, smiling faintly. "Head-on."

"Before the storm gets here."

He nodded. "Before the storm. Before the rain washes away the blood, and the lightning changes the energy here. The energy in this place—his and ours, even anything left of hers—is what we need to help us take the next step. There's nothing disrespectful about that. It's doing our job. It's fighting evil the only way we can."

"How do you know so much?"

"I've been paying attention."

Isabel hesitated only another instant, then held out her right hand. "Okay. Let's see where the next step takes us."

He put his left hand into her right one.

Hollis said, at the time and long afterward, that there should have been something, some outward sign, to indicate what turned out to be a most astonishing event. But, outwardly at least, there was nothing. Just two people facing each other, holding hands, their faces calm but eyes curiously intent.

Mallory took a step closer to Hollis, murmuring, "I get the feeling I've missed something important."

"Beats the hell out of me," Hollis told her. "I mean, I know it has to do with this shield of Rafe's, but I have no idea what they're trying to do about it."

"Get rid of it, maybe?"

"No, from what Isabel told me, that would probably not be such a good idea."

"Why not? I mean, if it's blocking her voices?"

"I don't know. She said something about their combined energy being too strong, especially now when it's new and not under their control. That bad things could happen if they just . . . let go of it."

Mallory sighed. "I long for the days when all we had to deal with was trace evidence, footprints, the occasional half-blind or very stoned eyewitness . . ."

"Yeah, I imagine that was easier. Or simpler, at least."

"I'll say."

After several minutes of silence except for the growing intensity of the thunder rumbling overhead, Hollis ventured a step closer to Isabel and Rafe. "Well?"

"Well, what?" Isabel asked in perfect calm without turning her head.

"What's happening?"

"Good question."

Hollis looked at Mallory, then back at the other two. "Guys, come on. People are beginning to stare. Pablo and Bobby look real nervous. Or real embarrassed, I'm not sure which. What's happening?"

After a moment, Isabel turned her head to look at Hollis. "I don't want to sound like a country song, but I can feel his heart beating."

"I know she didn't eat breakfast," Rafe said, also looking at Hollis.

"And he's uneasy because—" Isabel turned her head abruptly to stare at Rafe. "Jesus, why didn't you tell me?"

"You know damned well why I didn't tell you," he replied, meeting her gaze.

"It was your abilities manifesting themselves physically. Which, remember, is a rare thing but not unheard of. In your case, probably caused by guilt because you believed you should have stopped him after the first murder. The blood of the innocent, literally on your hands."

"I realize that. Now. Before we talked yesterday, the possibilities were a lot more creepy."

"So that's why you were blocking me. That was the part of you I couldn't get at?"

"I'm guessing yes. Isabel, I was waking up with blood on my hands every morning and had no idea where it had come from. Women were dead. Other women were missing. You were offering me theories of a serial killer who could be walking around most of the time not knowing he was a murderer. So I was afraid I was blacking out."

"And killing blondes? I could have told you there wasn't a chance in hell of you doing that."

"Well, I was . . . afraid to ask."

"*Guys,*" Hollis's voice was just this side of strident.

Isabel looked at her partner, frowned slightly, and then let go of Rafe's hands. "Oh. Sorry. We were . . . somewhere else."

"I noticed. Where were you?"

"In a galaxy far, far away," Rafe murmured.

311

"You really are beginning to talk like me," Isabel told him.

"I know. Spooky, isn't it?" He took her arm and guided her toward the yellow crime-scene tape on the highway side of the clearing. "I say we head back to the station before the heavens open up."

Hollis and Mallory went with them, wearing almost identical expressions of baffled interest.

"Blood on your hands?" Mallory said to Rafe. "You were waking up with blood on your hands?"

"Yeah, for the past few weeks."

Hollis muttered, "Man, have you got a great poker face." And waited until they were outside the crime scene to add, "If somebody doesn't tell me, right now, what's going on—"

"I'm not so sure I can." Isabel shook her head. "All I really know is that everything's different."

"Different how?"

"The voices are back. But . . . very, very quiet. Distant."

"What about Rafe's shield?"

"It's still there. Here. I think we punched a couple of holes in it, though. I told you I wasn't sure I could explain."

"And I should have listened," Hollis said.

Addressing his patrolmen, Rafe said, "You two can take your lunch break and then head back to the station; unless you hear otherwise, follow your assignments on the board for the rest of the day."

"Right, Chief."

"Yes, sir."

"No watchdogs?" Isabel asked.

"I'm your watchdog," he replied. "Mallory, if you'll ride back with Hollis?"

"Sure."

By the time they reached the parked vehicles, they saw that the media had vanished, along with any curious passersby.

Isabel said, "Did the weather happen to mention that the storms today and tonight could be mean ones? The sort to keep golfers off courses and reporters with electronic equipment indoors?"

Rafe nodded. "We're not in the Southeast's tornado alley, but close enough."

Isabel didn't say anything else until they were in the Jeep heading back to town, and then her voice was tentative. "Back there at the scene when we . . . did whatever it is we did, I got a flash of something. That box. The box of photographs. We have to find it. The answer is in there, I know it."

"If it's in a bank under an assumed name—"

"I don't think it is. I think we've missed something."

Rafe frowned as thunder boomed again. "We've checked all the properties she owned."

"Have we?" Isabel turned in her seat to look at him. "Jamie had a secret life. A secret self. And she hid her secrets very, very well. What if, once Hope Tessneer died, Jamie decided to bury all the secrets for good?"

"We found her playhouse," Rafe reminded her.

"Yeah, but Jamie didn't count on dying herself. I think if she'd been granted just a little more time, we wouldn't have found anything but an empty storage building there. And nothing at all of her secret life."

"Wouldn't she just have burned everything? I mean, if she had wanted to destroy the evidence of that other life."

"She didn't want to destroy it. Destroy the strongest part of herself? No way. It would have been like cutting off her arm, or worse. She wanted to bury it. To put it where nobody but she would ever find it. Look, when Hope's body turned up missing—and I'm still convinced the killer took it from wherever Jamie had put it—she had to know someone else knew about the death. She had to be afraid that at best the body would turn up and it would be traced back to her, or—possibly worse from her point of view—that someone could be planning blackmail."

"So," Rafe said, "she would have wanted to remove any possible evidence of their relationship."

"Of all her secret relationships. If we found one, we'd find them all; that's what she would have thought. So she started to move, and fast. Listed her properties for sale, maybe started shifting money she wasn't supposed to have, between accounts we weren't supposed to know about."

"We've got people checking area banks today."

"Maybe they'll at least find evidence of those secret accounts. But I don't think they'll find the box. I think Jamie was planning to leave this place, or at least go on a long vacation somewhere until Hope's body turned up and she could determine whether she was going to be suspected of murder."

"And spent the final days of her life trying to erase or hide all the secrets," Rafe said.

"Exactly. I think she found or created a place to bury the Mistress for Hire. The box of photos went there right away, especially since she must have suspected Emily of snooping. The stuff in her playhouse would have followed, but the killer got to her first."

"Okay," Rafe said. "I'll buy the theory. But how do we find out where this hiding place is? We've tapped every source we have, short of going door to door and asking every soul in Hastings. What else can we do?"

Isabel drew a deep breath. "We ask the one soul who knows."

The heavens took their own time in opening up. By three that afternoon, it was twilight, with a hot wind blowing gustily and thunder rolling as though it had miles and miles to go. Flashes of lightning provided eerie strobelike images of very little traffic on Main Street, and clusters of media camped all around the town hall across from the police station. Print media, at any rate; most of those with electronics to consider had, as Isabel predicted, wisely chosen to remain indoors.

"You can feel the nerves," Mallory said, gazing out the window of the conference room. "Even the reporters. I don't have any extra senses, and I can feel it."

"Extra senses make it worse," Hollis told her. She was sitting at the conference table, both elbows propped on it and her hands cupping her face. "My head is throbbing in the weirdest way." She yawned as if to clear her ears. "And I feel like I'm going up in a plane."

"Not the best time to try a séance, I guess."

"God, don't call it that."

"Isn't that what it is? Technically, I mean."

"I don't know, but I can't help feeling a stormy afternoon spent summoning the dead just can't be a good plan."

"We're not doing it in a haunted house."

"Oh, goodie, one for the plus column." Hollis sighed.

Mallory turned her back on the window and half sat on the sill, smiling faintly. "You two are unconventional investigators, I'll give you that much. But, then, this hasn't exactly been a conventional series of murders. If there is such a thing."

Before Hollis could respond, Travis rapped on the open door and said, "Hey, Mallory, Alan Moore is here. He says it's

315

important, and since the chief and Agent Adams are out in the garage with T.J.—"

"Send him in. Thanks, Travis."

Since the bulletin boards were already covered, neither woman had to move, and Mallory remained at the window as Alan came in. She said, "The chief of police has no comment for the media. Didn't you hear him on the front steps a couple of hours ago, Alan?"

"I did," he replied imperturbably. "Which is why I went back to my office. Where I received two bits of news I thought I'd be gracious enough to share with the police."

"I think he rehearsed that," Hollis said to Mallory.

"Probably." Mallory frowned at him. "The news?"

"First, Kate Murphy called a friend who happens to work at the paper. Seems she left town in a hurry—and on a bus—because she got a threatening call from an ex-lover and panicked. Especially with blondes getting killed in Hastings."

Mallory said, "We haven't found a sign of a lover in her past, and we've looked."

"Yeah, but this is about ten years ex. Even she admits the panic was somewhat extreme."

"Sounds like it," Hollis murmured. "Not that I can really blame her."

"Anyway, she's safe," Alan said. "She claims she left a note for her store's assistant manager but hadn't had a chance to call until today. I think she's about four states away, but she refused to say where."

Mallory shook her head. "One less on the list, thank God. And thank you for sharing. What's your other bit of news?"

"This." He produced a folded paper from his pocket and unfolded it on the conference table. "Probably no prints other than mine, since there weren't any on the last one."

"Envelope?" Mallory asked.

He pulled that out of a different pocket. "I figured it'd be worthless for prints, too, considering how many people handled it. The postmark is Hastings. Mailed Saturday."

Hollis leaned a bit sideways to read the note, brows lifting. "Well, well."

Mallory joined them at the table to study the message. Like the previous note to Alan, it was block-printed yet virtually scrawled in a bold, dark hand on the unlined paper.

THEY WERE GOING TO TELL.
HE KNEW THEY WERE GOING TO TELL.
THEY WEREN'T WORTHY OF OUR TRUST.
NEITHER IS SHE.
NEITHER IS ISABEL.

# 18

D USTIN FOUND IT," T.J. reported. "He knows cars better than I do. Since it's a guy thing and all."

Rafe said, "So the cruise control was engaged. McBrayer was drunk; he could have done it accidentally."

"Dustin says he couldn't have. Something about the way the cruise button is on the wheel. Of course, the wheel is mangled as hell right now, but he swears it's a safety issue or something."

Isabel straightened after looking into what was left of Hank McBrayer's car, and said, "Dustin thinks somebody else set the cruise control?"

T.J. shrugged. "I admit I thought it was pretty far out. But we checked the rear end of the car, which is mostly intact, and found signs of a jack. Lift the rear wheels off the ground, put it in gear and push the accelerate button on the wheel, set the cruise control, and, when you're ready, shove the car off the jack. The marks on the car are consistent."

"There would have been tread marks on the road at the point it came off the jack," Rafe said.

"Dustin's out now, backtracking from the scene of the so-called accident. We also found a bit of rope on the front floorboard. I'm thinking it was used to tie off the steering wheel to keep the car going in a straight line. And if that's not enough, I'm pretty sure the headlights were off." She shook her head. "A nice, neat little way to kill somebody. With McBrayer reeking of alcohol and enough in his blood to knock out a squad of marines, who would suspect it was anything but an accident?"

"Good work," Rafe told her. "You and Dustin."

"Thanks. I'll tell him you said so. And I'll send up the report when he gets back and I finish up with the car."

As they left the basement garage of the police station and headed upstairs to the offices, Isabel said, "A diversion. That *accident* happened only a couple of miles from the Brower house; the patrol on watch outside would have been the closest squad car."

"I wonder if he aimed McBrayer's car at one he could see coming or just trusted to luck he'd hit something or someone eventually?"

"I don't think our boy trusts much to luck," she said. "Finds a dark, straight stretch of road in a little-frequented area, sets up the car with McBrayer passed out inside. And waits until he sees headlights. By the time the other driver even saw the car coming at her, it was too late."

"The pay phone he called Emily from was only a few blocks from the scene of the—accident. He probably waited for the patrol car to pass him, then called her."

"I have the feeling that killing two more people just so he

319

KAY HOOPER

could lure Emily out was another of his taunts: *Look at me, look how clever I am.*"

"You don't think it was a personal grudge against McBrayer?"

"No, I think he was convenient. From what I got talking to Ginny last night, her father's Sunday-night binges were hardly a secret around here. The killer found McBrayer, maybe even followed him to one of those basement bars you talked about. Then all he had to do was wait for his mark to pass out or be thrown out."

"And use him as a tool to get what he wanted. Emily." Rafe grasped her arm to stop her as they entered the hallway leading to the conference room. "Tell me something. Truthfully."

"Sure, if I can."

"He'll come after you next."

"Maybe. Probably. Especially if the news breaks that I'm psychic. He'd view that as an increased threat, I think."

"Will he wait a week?"

Isabel hesitated, then shook her head. "I'd be surprised if he did. Emily was damage control; she knew something he didn't want her to tell. Or at least he believed she did. I'm guessing something about that box of photographs."

"But you he wants."

"Even without the psychic nudge, yeah. Me and the last blonde on his list, whoever she is. And he's moving faster, getting sloppy. We shouldn't have found jack marks on that car, far less a bit of rope that didn't belong in it. He's feeling pressure, a lot of it. Whatever is driving him is driving him hard."

Rafe hesitated, but they were alone, and he finally said, "Whatever happened earlier did open up the shield for you, didn't it?"

"A bit. But the voices are still distant." She looked at him steadily. "There's still a part of you I can't get at."

"I trust you," he said.

320

"I know. You just don't trust you."

He shook his head. "I don't get it."

Isabel had to smile. "I'm not surprised. See, I think I figured out something. We both have control issues and we both know it. The difference is, I don't trust someone else to run the show, and you don't trust yourself to."

"That's a control issue?"

"Yes. I have to learn to let go, to trust someone else without giving up who I am. And you have to learn to trust yourself in order to be who you need to be."

Somewhat cautiously, Rafe said, "Are you channeling this Bishop of yours?"

"I know how it sounds, believe me. Why do you think I've been fighting this so hard? But the truth is, neither one of us has enough faith in ourselves."

"Isabel, that sounds to me like something that will take time to get itself resolved. We don't have time."

Isabel began moving down the hallway toward the conference room. "No, we don't. Which is why we'll have to take care of our issues on the fly."

"I was afraid you were going to say that."

"Don't worry. If there's anything I've learned in the last few years it's that we can make giant leaps when we have to."

"That's the part that worries me," Rafe said. "Why we might have to."

"Alan, I don't have time for this," Mallory told him as they stood just inside the foyer of the police department.

"Make time," he insisted. "Look, Mal, I know you don't want us publicly linked, but I've been doing some digging, and there's something you need to know."

321

Warily, she said, "About the case? Then why tell just me?"

"Call it a good-faith gesture. I could have put it in today's paper, but I didn't."

After a moment, she said, "I'm listening."

"I know there were two other sets of murders, one five and one ten years ago, in two other states."

"How did you—"

"I have sources. Never mind that. I also know that the FBI has sent investigators back to those towns to ask more questions."

Mallory hesitated, then said grudgingly, "We don't have the reports yet."

"There hasn't been time, I know. But one of my sources had occasion to talk to an investigator from the second series of murders."

"'Had occasion'? Alan—"

"Just listen. The investigator said there was something about the first murder that bugged him. It was just a little thing, so minor he didn't even put it in any of his reports. It was an earring."

"What?"

"They'd found her body out in the open, of course, the way all the others would be found. But the investigator checked out her apartment. And when he searched her bedroom, he found an earring on her dresser. Never found a match for it."

"So? Women lose earrings all the time, Alan."

"Yeah, I know. But what bugged the investigator was that the victim didn't wear earrings. She didn't have pierced ears."

Mallory shrugged. "Then a friend must have lost it."

"None of her friends claimed it. Not one. A valuable diamond earring, and nobody claimed it. It was an unanswered question, and it bugged him, has ever since."

Patiently, she said, "Okay, he found an earring he could never explain. How do you expect that to help us?"

"It's a hunch, Mal, and I wanted to let you know I was following it up. I've already talked to a friend of the second victim in Florida, and she claims to have found a single earring among her friend's things. I have somebody checking out the Alabama murders too. I think it has something to do with how he got the women to meet him."

"Alan—"

"I'm going to check it out. I'll let you know if I find anything."

Mallory thought he said something else, but a crash of thunder made it impossible to hear whatever it was, and a moment later he was gone.

She stared after him.

**4:00 PM**

"It's no use," Hollis said finally. "I don't know if it's the storm or me, but I just can't concentrate. And the energy of you two is not helping. If anything, it's hurting."

"We were with you the first time you saw Jamie," Isabel reminded her. "Right here in this room."

"Yeah, but it was before you two started seriously sparking," Hollis reminded her.

"Just tell me we don't have to hold hands or light candles," Mallory begged, pulling another folder toward her and looking through it with a frown.

Hollis shook her head. "What I'm telling you is that if Jamie is hovering anywhere around a doorway, it isn't mine. Or I can't open the door. Either way, it's not going to happen today."

Rafe leaned back in his chair, saying, "Look, there has to be another way to do this. Plain, old-fashioned police work. If Jamie had a secret place, there has to be a way for us to find it."

Hollis said, "And we need to do it before the six o'clock news. But no pressure."

Mallory said, "Reports coming in from all area banks have been negative. Nobody has recognized Jamie's photo or her name, and there's no way for us to guess what alias she might have used. If she's been socking away money for years with her little S&M sideline, she's had plenty of time to construct a really solid one we may never find. And I can't find anything about stray or missing jewelry, so I think Alan's off track with that one."

"It's that note I don't like," Rafe said.

"It doesn't change anything," Isabel said. "We knew I was on his list."

She pulled the note toward her and frowned down at it. "Our trust. They weren't worthy of *our* trust."

"Maybe he really is schizophrenic," Mallory said.

"Yeah, but even so, the first note made a clear distinction. *He* wasn't killing them because they were blondes. This note links the one who wrote the note and the killer. They weren't worthy of *our* trust. If he's schizophrenic, then I'd say he's on the edge of a major identity crisis."

"He didn't have one before?" Hollis murmured.

"I don't think he knew he had one. I mean, I think there was a part of him listening to whatever it was urging him to kill, and another part of him that had no idea that was happening."

"A split personality?" Hollis asked.

"Maybe. They're a lot more rare than people realize, but it is possible that's what we have in this case. One part of his mind, the sane part, may have been in control most of the time."

"And now?" Rafe asked.

"Now," Isabel said, "I think the sane part of his mind is getting lost, submerged. I think he's losing control."

"It's all about control."

"No, it's all about relationships. It's still all about relationships. Look at this note. He believes these women have violated—or, in my case, will violate—his trust. There's a secret he's protecting, and he's convinced the women he kills threaten to expose that secret."

"So they know him."

"He thinks they do."

Rafe looked at Isabel steadily. "Then he thinks you know him."

"I think I do too."

The looming storm only fed their sense of urgency, at least in part because it seemed to surround them all day long without actually hitting Hastings. Tree limbs were blown around, power crews were kept busy repairing downed electrical lines, and thunder boomed and rolled while lightning flashed in the weird twilight.

It was as if the whole world was on the verge of something, hesitating, waiting.

By five o'clock that afternoon, they had paperwork scattered across the conference table, pinned to the bulletin boards, and stacked on two of the chairs. Forensics reports, background checks on the victims, statements from everyone involved, and postmortems complete with photographs.

And still they didn't have the answers they needed.

When Travis came in with the last batch of reports from area banks, Mallory groaned. "Christ, not more paper."

"And not even helpful," he told her as he handed the notes to Rafe, then leaned his hands on the back of an unoccupied chair. "Nobody recognized the name or photograph of Jamie Brower— except to say they'd seen her picture in the newspapers and on TV."

Isabel waited out another rumble of thunder, then said, "We need a fresh mind. Travis, if you wanted to bury a secret someplace you could be sure it wouldn't be found, where would you put it?"

"In a grave." He realized he was being stared at, and straightened self-consciously. "Well, I would. Once somebody's buried, they're not often dug back up. So why not? It'd be easy enough to strip the turf off a grave, bury whatever it was I was trying to hide between the surface and the casket—assuming it was the right size—then cover it back up and re-lay the grass. As long as I was careful, nobody'd even notice."

"Son of a bitch," Rafe said.

Isabel was shaking her head. "Why isn't he a detective?"

Travis brightened. "I was right?"

"God knows," Hollis said, "but you're sending us in a new direction, so I say good for you."

"Hey, cool." Then his smile faded. "We got lots of cemeteries in Hastings. Where do we start looking? And what're we looking for, by the way?"

"We're looking for a box of photos," Rafe said, feeling the younger cop had earned the knowledge.

Isabel added, "And it has to be connected with Jamie Brower. We need to know where any deceased family or friends are buried."

"I'll go back to my phone," Travis said with a sigh. "Start calling all the local clergy and asking them. I do *not* want to have to call the Browers directly, not today. Or tomorrow, or next week."

"Yeah, let's avoid that if possible," Rafe told him.

When he'd gone, Isabel said, "You really should promote him."

"He was on my short list," Rafe said. "The only reason I've hesitated is because he's currently sleeping with a reporter who isn't quite what she appears to be."

Hollis asked, "What is she?"

"According to my sources, she works for the governor's office, and is sent in quietly during tricky investigations to keep an eye on local law enforcement. So we don't do anything to embarrass ourselves. Or the state attorney general. They're keeping a very close eye on this investigation."

"That shows a distressing lack of faith," Isabel said, but without surprise.

Mallory was looking at Rafe with lifted brows. "You know that for a fact."

"Yes," he replied with a faint smile. "I keep a fairly close eye on my people."

Mallory stared at him, then said, "Oh, don't tell me."

"You and Isabel have something in common. Neither one of you is as subtle as you think you are."

"I resent that," Isabel said.

"Besides," Hollis said, "Alan Moore is the one who isn't subtle. Even I picked up on it."

Mallory got to her feet with great dignity. "Being outnumbered by psychics is hardly fair. I'm going to use the computer in the other room. Excuse me."

"I think we pissed her off," Hollis said absently as she opened the local phone book to begin making a list of churches and cemeteries.

"She'll get over it." Rafe shook his head. "Although I don't know if Alan will. Never seen him fall so hard before."

Isabel pursed her lips thoughtfully. "Mallory doesn't strike me as the settling-down type."

"I don't think she is. I also don't think Alan has realized that yet."

"It's always about relationships," Hollis murmured, with a sidelong glance at Isabel.

Ignoring the glance, Isabel said, "We need to go back through every piece of paper associated in any way with Jamie's life and death and check out the names of all family and friends."

"Chicken," Hollis said.

"We have more imperative things to think about," Isabel told her. "Like finding that grave."

Rafe said, "You think it's there, don't you? You think Jamie buried that box in somebody's grave?"

"I think it makes sense. She was burying a part of her life, so why not put it in a grave? And I'm betting it won't be a family grave, but the grave of someone else who was important to her. A teacher, a mentor, a friend. Maybe her first lover."

"Male or female?"

"At a guess, female."

"That does help narrow the field."

"Let's hope it narrows it enough."

Of all the family and friends who had died during Jamie's life, Isabel considered three women the most likely candidates for Jamie's burial of her secrets. One was a former teacher that friends reported Jamie had seemed especially close to, one was a close friend from high school who had been killed in a highway accident, and the third was a woman who had worked in Jamie's office, dying young of cancer.

Three women, three cemeteries.

"I think we should check these out before the storm breaks," Isabel told Rafe.

Rafe wanted to argue, but he was reluctant to put off doing anything that could help them catch the killer before he took aim at his next target. Isabel.

And before the press took aim at her.

"It'll be faster if we split up," she was saying. Since she had already told him privately that she wanted to stick close to Hollis because her partner seemed to be so affected by the tension of the storm, Rafe didn't object when she added, "Hollis and I will take Rosemont."

"You'll also take Dean Emery," he added. "There's only one entrance to Rosemont, and it's fenced; he can stand by at the entrance while you two find the grave. Mallory can take Travis along to Sunset."

"And who will you take to Grogan's Creek?" Isabel asked politely.

"I might take the mayor," he answered wryly. "I need to stop and see him before he blows a fuse."

Mallory said, "We're doing all this on the way home, right? Because I'm beat."

Rafe nodded. "Check out the cemeteries, phone in reports— once you're out of the storm, that is—and then head home."

"Got my vote," Isabel said.

Twenty minutes later, Hollis was saying, "You had to pick the largest cemetery, didn't you? The one with all the tall monuments and acres of graves."

"And don't forget the pretty little chapel with the stained-glass windows," Isabel reminded, raising her voice a bit as the wind tended to snatch at it.

"I just wish the place had a caretaker on duty to point out Susan Andrews's grave," Hollis said, pausing to squint at a headstone. "Because unless . . ."

"Unless what?" Isabel asked, half turning to look at her partner.

Hollis would have answered, but she was hardly aware of

Isabel in that moment. The sounds of the wind and the thunder had retreated into that peculiar hollow almost-silence. Her skin was tingling. The fine hairs on her body were stirring. And in the strobe flashes of the lightning, she could see Jamie Brower several yards away, beckoning.

"This way," Hollis said.

Isabel followed her. "How do you know?" she demanded, raising her voice again to be heard over the rising wind.

"It's Jamie." Hollis nearly stopped, then hurried forward. "Dammit, it *was* her. But I don't see her now."

"Where was she?"

"Somewhere in this area." Hollis jumped as thunder crashed, feeling her skin literally crawl. "Have I mentioned how much I hate storms?"

"You might have, yeah. This area? We'll find it." Isabel paused as thunder boomed, and added, "Unless we get struck by lightning, that is. I just think we need to do this now. And if you saw Jamie, that makes it even more imperative, I'd say."

Hollis didn't argue, just began checking the headstones in the area, flinching with every crack of thunder and flash of lightning. "I hate this," she called to her partner. "I really hate—"

"Here." Isabel knelt by a simple headstone with the name *Susan Andrews* engraved on it.

"It doesn't look disturbed," Hollis said, then swore under her breath as Isabel dug her fingernails into the turf and neatly lifted a perfectly square section.

"You'd think it would have rooted by now," Isabel said, folding back the turf. "It's tight, but not that difficult to pull up."

Hollis knelt on the other side of the grave to help. "A very neat section just at the headstone. Now I'm glad we brought the shovel Dean had in the cruiser's trunk."

330

"I'm an optimist," Isabel said, unfolding the small emergency shovel.

Hollis sat back on her heels suddenly. "You knew we'd find it, didn't you?"

"I had a hunch."

"You heard a voice."

"A whisper. Help me dig."

"We should call Dean," Hollis said, but it was only a minute or two before the shovel scraped across something metallic and they were able to drag a small box about twelve inches square and five or six inches deep from its resting place at Susan Andrews's headstone.

"I think we'd better take this back to the station to open it," Isabel said, the reluctance in her tone clear despite the gusty wind and rumbles of thunder.

"You just forgot to bring your lock-pick tools," Hollis said, a little amused. "Need help carrying that?"

"No, I've got it. You get the shovel, will you, please?"

As they started back across the cemetery, Isabel carrying the box and Hollis the shovel, the latter stopped suddenly.

"Shit."

Isabel stopped as well, following her partner's gaze. "What? I don't see anything."

"Jamie. She's—"

At first Isabel thought the rumble of thunder had drowned out whatever Hollis had been saying, but then she felt a sharp tug at the small of her back and whirled, instinctively dropping the metal box, filled with the sudden cold certainty that she had been blindsided again.

A flash of lightning brilliantly lit the scene before her. Hollis falling on the ground with blood blossoming on the back of her pale blouse. Mallory standing hardly more than an arm's length from Isabel, a big, bloodstained knife in one black-gloved hand and Isabel's gun in the other.

"You know," she said, "I'm really surprised you didn't pick up on it. All those vaunted psychic abilities, yours and hers. And Rafe's, I suppose. It was so clear, and none of you saw it. None of you saw me."

Rafe was able to soothe the mayor's worries, but just barely enough to allow his own escape. He headed toward Grogan's Creek church and the cemetery behind it, a name neatly printed on a piece of paper tucked in his pocket.

But when he reached a stop sign, he found himself hesitating, looking not east toward Grogan's Creek, but west toward Rosemont.

There was no reason to worry, of course. She could take care of herself. Besides which, she wasn't alone. Hollis was with her, and Dean.

He started to turn the wheel toward the east, then hesitated again. "She's okay," he heard himself say aloud. "She's fine."

Except that his gut said she wasn't.

His gut—and the blood on his hands.

Rafe stared at the reddish stains, shocked for an instant because it had happened so suddenly.

But then, just as suddenly, he knew the truth. He understood what it meant.

And he knew Isabel was in deadly danger.

He turned the wheel hard, heading west, and reached for his phone to call Dean.

# 19

MALLORY—"

"You still don't get it, do you? Mallory doesn't live here anymore."

Gazing into eyes that looked dead and empty even when the lightning flashed in them, Isabel fought to keep her voice calm. "So who are you?"

With an amused little chuckle, Mallory said, "This isn't some split-personality deal, you know. That's a bunch of bullshit, what you read in the books. I was always the stronger one. Always the one who had to take care of Mallory, clean the messes after she screwed up. Always. We were just twelve when it happened the first time."

"When what happened?" Was Hollis alive? Isabel couldn't tell. And what had happened to Dean?

"When I had to kill them. Those bitches. All six of them."

"You were— Why? Why did you have to kill them?"

"Are you stalling?" Mallory asked, interested. "Because Rafe isn't coming, you know. Nobody is coming."

"Well, then," Isabel said, her mind racing, "it's just you and me. Come on, impress me. Show me all the signs I should have seen along the way."

"The only thing you and that Bishop of yours got right was gender. Male."

"Trapped in a female's body?" Isabel was deliberately flippant. "I think that's been done."

"Oh, no, I was male first. Always. I kept telling Mallory, but in the beginning she wouldn't listen. And when she did listen, she got confused. She thought she was a lesbian."

Recalling the riot of emotions and hormones of adolescence, Isabel said, "When she was twelve?"

"Those girls at camp. In her cabin. There were six of them, all giggly and girly. The one who slept with Mallory started touching her one night. And Mallory liked it. It made me sick, but Mallory liked it."

"So what happened?"

"I heard them the next day. All six of them, giggling and looking at Mallory. They knew. All of them knew. The one who'd touched her had told the others, and they were going to tell too. I knew they would. They'd tell, and everybody would know Mallory wasn't normal."

"What did you do to stop that?"

"I killed them." Her voice was eerily Mallory's and yet . . . not. Deeper, rougher, harder.

Isabel told herself what she smelled was the lightning, not brimstone. But she knew the truth.

Nothing this side of hell smelled quite like brimstone.

Except for evil.

"See, they weren't supposed to take the boats out onto the

lake, not without one of the counselors. But I made Mallory talk them into it. So they took a boat out, way out, and I made sure there were no life jackets. And then I turned the boat over. None of them made it to the shore, but I got Mallory there, of course. So sad, those other girls drowning like that. Mallory was never the same afterward."

Rafe found Dean Emery slumped over the wheel of his cruiser. He knew nothing could be done for him, but he called for backup and an ambulance, then hurried through the gates of the cemetery, gun drawn, reaching out desperately with every sense he possessed, old and new.

To hell with the goddamned shield.

Mallory shrugged. "That was when her parents moved here to Hastings. So nobody would know what had happened and she could get over it."

"But she didn't." Isabel was dimly aware of the voices, whispering louder, but the thunder and her own fixed concentration on Mallory kept them distant.

"No, not really. She was afraid to have girl friends after that, so all her friends were boys. She played sports, got tough, learned to take care of herself. So I didn't have to worry about her."

"When did that change?"

"You know when it changed, Isabel. It changed in Florida. Mallory was in college in Georgia, but she transferred to a college in Florida to take a few courses one semester."

"There was a redhead," Isabel said. "She was attracted to a redhead, wasn't she? A woman. Were they lovers?"

In the eerie twilight, Mallory's mouth tightened. "That bitch.

She got Mallory drunk and slept with her. And in the morning, she acted like it was nothing. But I knew. I knew she'd tell. I knew she'd tell her redheaded friends. So I had to take care of them, of course. All six of them, just like before."

Isabel didn't waste her breath with any reasoned argument. Instead, she said, "We wondered why the women were going with . . . him. Why they didn't feel threatened. It was because Mallory was a woman."

"It's not my fault if people don't look beneath the surface." She—or he—laughed.

"Mallory didn't know what you were doing, did she?"

"Of course not. She wouldn't have been able to hide our secret. I had to do that. And I had to protect her. When she got abnormal that way."

"What about the women in Alabama?" Isabel asked, only vaguely aware that the wind was gusting wildly now. "The brunettes? Mallory got involved with a brunette woman?"

"She was staying with a cousin over there. Just for a couple of weeks. But that was long enough. Long enough to start mooning over that dark-haired bitch. I didn't even wait for that to get started. I just took care of it. I got rid of her. And the rest of them. The other five."

"The ones who would have told?"

"Of course."

"How did you know they would have?"

"Oh, don't be stupid, Isabel. I always knew who'd tell. As soon as I saw you, I knew you would."

"But Jamie was first, wasn't she?" Isabel asked. "Jamie was the one who caught Mallory's eye."

"I thought she was over it," the thing inside Mallory said. "She was involved with Alan, she was—was *normal*. But then she talked to Jamie about buying a house. And she felt . . . that . . .

again. That longing. That desperation to be touched like that. By her."

"They became lovers."

"*Lovers?* What they were doing had nothing to do with love. Mallory thought she deserved to be punished, because she'd lived when the other girls had died. So she let Jamie punish her. And take pictures of it. But I made her stop. I made her go back to Alan."

Realizing, Isabel said, "And you made her forget. Always. You made sure that her attraction to other women was … like a fantasy to her. Didn't you?"

"It was an aberration. She didn't need to remember that."

Isabel nodded slowly. "That's why Mallory never reacted to anything we found out about Jamie. As far as she knew, as far as she could remember, they'd never been involved."

"I protected her. I always have."

"So you sent her back to Alan. Then you watched Jamie for a while, didn't you?"

"So sick. Ugly. And she was mad at Mallory for not wanting to do those things anymore. That's why she got too rough with her next *lover* and killed her."

"Hope Tessneer."

"I decided to scare Jamie before I got rid of her. Besides, I was curious. So I took that one's body and hid it. It was fun to watch Jamie panic. Of course, she was thrilled when Mallory called her. Thrilled to meet her. And, you know, she didn't struggle at all. Isn't that interesting? Supposedly all dominant and powerful, and she died with hardly a whimper."

"But you killed her too quickly," Isabel pointed out, glancing toward the box she had flung aside. "You didn't know where she'd hidden the photos. The proof of what she and Mallory had done together."

"I thought they'd be in her apartment. But they weren't, of course. I didn't know where they were."

Isabel swallowed. "Until Emily?"

"Well, you told me to put her on the list, Isabel, didn't you?"

The sick sensation in Isabel's stomach churned even more. "I did?"

"Sure. You told me she might have seen something. Might know something about her sister's killer. And she'd seen the photographs, of course; I knew that as soon as she handed over the ones with Jamie and that other bitch. I didn't think she'd seen Mallory's, but I couldn't be sure. So I had to get rid of her."

"Blood on my hands," Isabel murmured.

"You and Rafe, both so guilty. I think part of him knew all along. I could feel it, even though Mallory never did. I think that's what made him psychic. You said the trigger had to be a traumatic shock, didn't you?"

"Yes. Yes, I did."

"Poor Rafe. He couldn't consciously believe Mallory could do anything like that. Not his friend and fellow cop Mallory. But I think he noticed something there where Jamie died. I'm not sure what; I'm very good at cleaning up after myself. Whatever it was, it told him Mallory had been there. So he knew. Deep down, he knew."

"And woke up with blood on his hands." Isabel drew a breath. "He'll know for sure now. Both Hollis and me dead, probably Dean, too, and you—Mallory—still alive. He'll know."

"No, see, you still don't get it. The change is finally complete. I got tired of only coming out sometimes, of being asleep inside Mallory so much of the time. So I've been taking over. More and more. Mallory's gone now. She's never coming back. And after I've taken care of you, I'll leave."

It was true, Isabel realized. She looked at the shell that had once held the personality, the soul, of a woman she had liked very much, and knew without doubt that Mallory Beck was gone. She had started going away when six little girls had died on a lake, and over the years more and more of her had fallen away.

Until now. There was only this. This evil thing that had lived deep inside.

Isabel knew.

This was the evil that had killed Julie. The evil Isabel had sworn to destroy. Crouching in the darkness. Waiting to sprint.

Wearing the face of a friend.

He/she glanced down at Hollis, faintly dissatisfied. "She's not blonde. Neither was that stupid, nosy reporter."

"Cheryl Bayne. She's dead?"

"Of course she's dead. Little twit hadn't even realized, but I think she'd seen me slipping into the gas station a couple of days before your partner and I *found* the body. It bugged her enough to send her snooping around the place, but I don't think she even knew what she was looking for. Until she found it, of course."

"What did you do with her body?"

"A cop to the last, aren't you?" The thing inside Mallory laughed. "They'll find her, eventually, at the bottom of a well. I didn't have time to play with her, you see. I had to get busy. Because she wasn't a blonde. But you are, and you'll make five."

Isabel knew she didn't have a hope of getting to her calf holster and second gun. Not without a distraction. But even as she thought of that, her mind was suddenly clear and calm, and she was aware of a strength and utter certainty she had never felt in her life.

She wasn't alone.

She would never be alone again.

"Mallory." Rafe was there, stepping from behind a tall monument at a right angle to the women, his gun extended in two steady hands.

"Didn't you hear me, Chief?" The black-gloved hand cocked Isabel's pistol and held it aimed at her heart. "Mallory's gone. And I'll kill Isabel if you so much as twitch."

"You'll kill her anyway," Rafe said.

"Go away like a good chief and I might let her live."

"Evil," Isabel said, "always deceives. That's what it's best at. That's why it wore the face of a friend this time. And that's why we can't let it walk away alive."

The thing wearing Mallory's skin opened its mouth to say something, but the wind that had been steadily gaining strength abruptly sent a gust of hot air through the cemetery, and the birch tree beside the chapel flung one of its broken branches through a stained-glass window.

The crash was loud and sudden, and Isabel instinctively took advantage of it, throwing herself sideways to the ground even as she reached for the gun strapped to her calf.

The black-gloved hand started to follow Isabel's path, finger tightening on the trigger, but the evil inside was just a split second slower than Rafe's training and instincts.

His shot spun Mallory around so that his/her gun was pointing toward Rafe.

Isabel's shot finished it.

The storm, uncaring of both human living and evil dying in its path, roared louder and louder as it finally made up its mind to hit Hastings.

# EPILOGUE

YOU'RE A HARD WOMAN to kill," Isabel said.

Hollis raised both eyebrows at her.

"I'm not saying it like it's a bad thing."

Looking at Rafe, Hollis said, "You realize what you're letting yourself in for? She can't *not* be flippant."

"I know. It's a character flaw."

"I resent that," Isabel said.

"You shouldn't. It happens to be a flaw I enjoy."

"Oh, well, in that case."

Hollis shifted slightly in the hospital bed to get more comfortable. Or try to. "I'm just lucky you two managed to stop Mallory's evil twin before he could finish me off."

They all found it less painful to refer to the creature they had destroyed there at the end as Mallory's evil twin—a phrase

341

naturally coined by Isabel. Not that it could be anything but painful, especially for Rafe.

Or Alan, who was still bewildered and in shock.

"What I can't figure out," Isabel said, "is what he planned to do once he left Hastings. He really was trapped in a woman's body—and had been since the male personality split off from Mallory when she was twelve."

"A sex-change operation?" Hollis suggested.

Rafe said, "I don't think so. I think *he* saw a male when he saw himself."

"A very confused male," Isabel pointed out. "He wanted Mallory to be involved with men, not women. But I'm willing to bet he would have been angry and insulted to be called homosexual."

"Didn't Bishop offer a theory?" Hollis asked. "I seem to recall a discussion going on over my mostly unconscious self a couple of days ago."

"We had to talk about something," Isabel told her. "The doctors said you were pretty out of it."

"I was. Mostly. But I remember Bishop and Miranda being here. And talking, like I said. What was the theory?"

"That Mallory's evil twin was delusional. We haven't really gotten past that part."

"It's complicated," Hollis agreed.

"She—he—was right about me, anyway," Rafe said. "I had seen something unconsciously when we were at the first murder scene. From the corner of my eye, I suppose. I'd seen Mallory touch Jamie's hair. Something about it, about the way she did it, was like a red flag."

"And a subconscious shock," Isabel said. "The hardest thing to accept about evil is that it can wear a familiar face. He was very good at hiding."

"Until Mallory did something he couldn't accept," Rafe said.

He sighed. "Just . . . thinking of her dying inside all those years, bit by bit. I keep thinking I should have known. Should have been able to help her."

"Nobody could help her," Isabel told him quietly. "Nobody was there when that boat overturned and six little girls drowned. Nobody but him. Mallory was doomed from that moment."

"And too many other women along with her," Hollis said. "Plus Ginny's father, and that poor older lady, and Dean Emery. And God knows how many others would have died if you two hadn't stopped it."

"It doesn't feel very heroic, what we did," Rafe said.

Isabel smiled at him. "It seldom does. Evil leaves so much destruction behind it that it's like a train wreck. You don't think about what was saved ahead on the tracks, just the devastation of the crash."

"And yet you're inviting me to jump on the train with you."

"Well, I'm sort of committed. To the journey, I mean. It's not something where you can just get off at the next station."

"Excuse me," Hollis said, "but are you two still speaking in metaphors?"

"You noticed that?" Isabel said earnestly.

"It amuses her," Rafe said.

Hollis shook her head. "One for the books, you two. I bet Bishop can hardly wait to get you up to Quantico."

"There was an invitation," Rafe admitted. "He didn't mention trains, though."

"So, did you accept?" Hollis asked.

"What do you think?"

"I think . . . that the SCU just took on a whole new dimension."

"How about that?" Isabel said. "And she's not even precognitive."

343